SOCIETY GIRL
BY ROBERT GOMEZ

Dedicated to those who remembered.
Modified for those who care.

SOCIETY GIRL
BY ROBERT GOMEZ

TABLE OF CONTENTS

1

THE STORE THING

My shoes are wet.

A black sedan limousine pulls up alongside the partially flooded curb, and my shoes are wet.

I get in.

"Hey, kid," the driver hollers over his shoulder, "why you waiting out in the rain? I was gonna honk when I pulled up."

"I didn't know."

We drive off. It's not long before the driver, a loud strong-jawed man in a wool cap named Mack, starts pressuring me to tell personal stories about women.

"I don't really have any," I say, placing my hat on the empty seat next to me to dry, then wiping my glasses on my wrinkled shirt.

Unfazed, Mack starts reciting his own personal stories about women. The car smells like stale cigarettes.

I listen to Mack's rather forward tales for a few minutes before I start to tune him out, giving favor to the sharp raindrops pummeling the roof of the car.

It's been pouring like this all day, with the same hearty deluge covering the entire city, the skyscrapers to the shanty towns, as if shining all of Chicago with the same European brand of shoe polish.

I look down and am reminded that my tuxedo shoes could use some polish, too.

The car rumbles along an increasingly busy avenue in the shadows of Downtown's numerous great towers as those who have managed to retain their jobs head home for a warm supper.

Mack turns the limousine toward the Loop, and we move past a dense Hooverville populated by hundreds of hard-time casualties. I see a man in a wet, yellowed shirt and tie wandering among the makeshift streets that better resemble a junkyard than neighborhood.

My seat is comfortable but my shoes are wet; I imagine what it would be like to live like this man.

I eat my supper out of a used can of beans. I'm hungry, so I am aggressive the first time I dig my spoon into the container of ambiguous meat. My first bite includes a scrape of yesterday's meal's crust that had lingered on the side of the can. My famine subsides.

After dinner, I wash my clothes for tomorrow in a stray bucket that I will use for bathing in the morning. My clothes won't really get clean, but the ritual is symbolic, and will remove any overwhelming odor.

2

I retire early to my shack to be met by insomniac encouragement from erratically-passing trains. Accepting cognizance, I sit atop an old milk crate in my "front yard" that has been defined by three rusted metal headboards staked into the loose dirt. A lethargic rendition of "Tiptoe Through the Tulips" whistles through my chapped lips as I grapple to appreciate the spirited beauty of my colony of discarded wood, brick, and sheet metal.

"Check out the bubs on that dish!"

My sentience re-focuses, and I spot an attractive brunette in a white dress who is visibly lacking the proper undergarments. She is walking against our flow of traffic and has momentarily distracted Mack from the light as it turns green.

The car behind us honks—once at Mack, then twice at the woman—and we continue driving.

"I wonder if that was one of Amy's new girls," says Mack. "She's always finding these new dishes—Eric, you wouldn't believe …"

"I bet."

"You don't have a girl, right?"

I don't say anything.

"You give her a few days, Amy can get you anything you want," he nods excitedly to himself. "And I mean *anything*."

I smile politely. "That sounds great."

The woman has such a crippled scowl upon her face— even in these times, I wonder what must happen to someone to get that way ... I clench my jaw and squint my eyes in semi-conscious mimicry.

We stop suddenly, and my hat slides off the seat with a gentle *whisp* against the cream leather. Mack curses the driver in front of him, and my grimace softens.

We drive further into the Loop, and each passing block is more saturated with offices, theaters, stores, and fine dining than the last. Eventually, Mack turns onto Adams Street and pulls to the curb in front of one of several towering buildings. He honks the horn five or six times, smirking and nodding at me as he draws the glare of several nearby pedestrians.

They're staring at me.

The young doorman runs toward us, signaling for Mack to quiet down. Mack rolls down the passenger side window and asks for "Philo Olin." The doorman nods, and scampers into the building.

"We're a little early," says Mack before cursing another driver who doesn't like where he has parked the limo.

The doorman returns a few moments later accompanying an unimposing man with thin-wired glasses and neatly coiffed white hair. I slide over. The doorman opens the door to the limo, and the old man climbs in.

"Afternoon, Mr. Olin!" exclaims Mack into the rearview mirror. "Another prosperous day in the shoveling business?"

"It was fine," says Philo, pausing before adding, "thanks for asking." He is concentrating on adjusting his coat while

4

settling into his seat when the floor sloshes beneath his feet. He stops and scowls. "Why is the floor all wet?"

"Oh, the rain," I say, pointing to my scuffed and sodden shoes. Philo frowns.

I should be embarrassed by such a first impression— they really are the most awful loafers.

"My father's, actually," I add.

Philo turns toward me with widened steely blue eyes. "You're wearing shoes over a year old?" he astonishes. "We'll get you a new pair for the party."

New shoes are nice.

"Mack," says Philo, sitting back, "you know where we're going, right? John told you?"

Mack smirks.

"Yeah," he says, "Boss told me the deal. You sure you want to do this whole store thing, though? I'm telling you, if you talk to my girl, Amy ..."

Philo stares out the window.

"...they may not be the high society type," Mack continues, "but they make up for what they lack with what they lick!"

My co-passenger doesn't immediately respond. Mack grins anyway.

"Let's just stick with John's recommendation," he finally says, "the Marshall Field's on State."

"Alright," shrugs Mack, muttering to himself, "we'll stick to the plan. You like the plan? I like the plan ..."

Though only a few blocks from the store, the cold December rain that has fallen all afternoon has slicked up the roads, and combined with the usual five o'clock Friday traffic, we find our roadside progress greatly impeded. This plays in Mack's favor, though, as it provides ample time to tell us about Amy's newest Russian import. Neither Philo nor I are listening much, but at least Mack fills the silence.

Philo seems too preoccupied for conversation, and I've never been one for small talk. Still, I search for something to say, but I can't get *"Tell me about the wildest bird you got nookie from"* out of my head.

Damn you, Mack.

"Did you phone your mother about us meeting, Eric?" asks Philo as we stop at our third red light.

Mack looks up in case Philo is talking to him, then carries on with his own conversation: "I asked John how could he be mad if he couldn't tell the difference ..."

"Oh, no, I hadn't," I say.

As if I could afford such frivolities.

"She looked well at the funeral—I'm sure your father would have been proud to see her there. Our teammates meant the world to him ...me as well. Of course, I don't blame you for not making the trip home," he says before lowering his voice. "She told me about your job, Eric— terrible what they did to you. Uproot you from Cincinnati, then let you go once you're here ... classless."

I wince for show. If I put any more meaningful thought toward my old employer Bert & Horner's disloyalty I'm likely to *snap*—

"We're here," says Mack, gesturing toward the impressive store entrance adorned with festoons atop its towering granite columns.

"Give us a once around the block," says Philo. "Doing odd jobs and living off an unsteady income is no life for a capable young man, Eric."

I see my mother's told him everything.

"But that's what tonight's about—a new beginning. Don't feel pressure about making friends with everyone, just put yourself out there and have fun."

I nod.

"A lot of irresponsible twits in the Havens Club, to be frank," he grumbles, "but some are good people."

"I'm just thankful for the invite."

"Absolutely," says Philo vigorously as we approach Marshall Field's front entrance for the second time.

"Am I stopping or going around again?" asks Mack, as he swats at another perturbed driver who darts around our slowing limo.

"Keep going," says Philo, glancing from the window back to me.

"You should have called me months ago," he continues. "That's what your father would have advised, I'm sure of it."

"Perhaps," I concede. "He wasn't much for advice, though."

"Nonsense, Eric, your father was a Cincinnati football player—he helped me and I helped him, even after college," Philo asserts. "That's what teammates do. I'm sure he would've done anything to help you out of your predicament ... given our circumstances, that's why I'm here."

I have no idea if my father would have wanted me to call his "friend in Chicago." I had only heard Philo Olin's name a handful of occasions growing up, and the only time since my father passed over a year ago was a few weeks back when my mother wrote to tell me she had spoken to Philo at another teammate's funeral.

"Unfortunately, the board has us in a hiring freeze at the moment," admits Philo, momentarily distracted by the window again. "I'm afraid I may have used the last of my personal hires, but I'll think of something for you."

"Thank you, Mr. Olin, but I don't want to be a burden."

"Stop?" pipes Mack.

"Yes, we can stop now," says Philo.

The limo breaks hard in front of the bustling storefront. A menagerie of men and women of all ages swarm in every direction at the feet of the wreathed entrance to Marshall Field's, bumping into each other and the absurd amount of wrapped parcels they carry.

"It's no burden at all."

Mack grins at me in the rearview mirror and I relent polite reciprocation while I try to figure the cause of elation.

"Now, Eric, would you ask that sales girl what time the store closes?" says Philo, gesturing toward a plain-looking young woman who has just walked out of the store. She is wearing a light green uniform with a white collar and skirt that sags carelessly from her exhausted posture. "It's almost six now."

"Of course," I agree, quickly exiting the car. If Philo can even get me a lead on another job—and with rent due in a week, I certainly could use it—I would kiss the girl if he asked.

Stepping from the car onto the edge of the hectic sidewalk, it takes me a second to re-locate the sales girl who, of course, is now walking away from me. "Excuse me!" I shout pathetically, trying to catch up, but getting held back by an aggressive row of particularly broad-shouldered Christmas shoppers.

Just as I squeeze through the gluttonous blockade, there is a sudden tapping on my shoulder. "Maybe I can help you," says a cool voice from behind.

I swing around and find myself staring into the fluttering brown eyes of a comely strawberry blond woman with perfectly even red lipstick. She wears a similar green uniform as the first girl, though nothing about it sags. I puff out what little chest I have and straighten my glasses.

"Actually," she says, "maybe you can help me."

I don't know what to say. I quickly wipe my face to discretely make sure my mouth isn't gaping.

"Is that your car?" she says, looking past me toward the limo.

I follow her gaze and see Philo and Mack staring back at me with encouragement. I turn back to her and nod.

"You see, the air is damp and chilled, and I fear I will catch a cold if I have to walk to the taxi stand," recites the woman miserably. "Could I bother you for a ride?"

"I ..."

I really don't know what to say. Of course, I want to say "yes" to this beautiful young woman, but it's not my car. It's not even Philo's—it's his friend John's, another stranger. We were just supposed to take it to the party ... but I also need new shoes ... and I'm supposed to be learning store hours.

"What time does the store close?" I blurt gracelessly.

"Pardon?" the woman laughs.

It doesn't matter. Before I can respond, the red-headed sales girl is climbing into the back of the limo—no one objects. I take a quick deep breath and follow her lead.

"Oh! The floor is so wet!" she shrieks.

"Attaboy, kid!" hollers Mack, and I close the door behind me.

2

THE HAVENS

I pour three glasses of whiskey from a crystal decanter and hand one to Philo. He has been ruminating by the window since we arrived at his office at Olin Crane & Shovel, so it takes him a moment to acknowledge the drink. He takes it and turns back toward the downtown skyline, while I catch a quick glimpse of the photo on his desk. From the white hair and wrinkles around his eyes, it seems relatively recent—it's also the first time I've seen his smile, as his arm is wrapped tightly around an older woman with warm eyes.

I start to walk out of Philo's office toward the rows of mahogany desks where our unexpected companion has been poking about, but stop myself just short of the door.

"Is she coming to the party with us?" I ask.

"If you want," grunts Philo.

I might.

"It's just—she was so comfortable getting into a stranger's limo, and she mentioned living in the South Side, it's almost like she's a ..."

And uneasy excitement rushes up my spine, but I catch myself.

I look out of Philo's office and see the sales girl sitting at one of the desks toward the middle of the larger room, sliding open a drawer and examining its contents. She reaches inside, and there is a sound of a container of something like thumbtacks spilling, followed by a muffled "Shit!"

"What did she say her name was again?" I ask coolly.

"...Annabelle, I believe."

It is.

"That's right," I say, taking a nonchalant sip of whiskey, most of which I nearly cough back on my shirt.

Philo's office is modestly decorated with a beautiful oak desk, and a view of downtown's yellow lights. The window probably offers a peek of the lake during the day. The desks in the larger workers' room, organized in rows, are nowhere near as ornate as Philo's, but they have been recently cleaned—the *generous* office Christmas bonus—so they still look nice.

"You seem nervous, Eric," Philo accurately observes. "Speak your mind."

I do a better job with my next sip, allowing the heat to seep down my throat, hoping it has the same relaxing effect on my head as it's having on my legs, but only my lips oblige.

"I don't mean to be forward," I say, "but I think I know why we were at Marshall Field's."

"You do?" challenges Philo, turning toward me.

I immediately wish I had used Mack's line about the birds and the nookie instead, but I press on.

"After Mack picked me up he mentioned something about this streetwalker we saw," I start, "and he made it sound like the Marshall Field's plan was an alternative to that …"

Philo removes his glasses.

"What I mean is … I know she's for you," I finally blurt, thumbing toward Annabelle. "She was just there when I got out of the car, like she was expecting us—like she knew what to do … I know you were my father's friend, and maybe I was wrong, but I thought you were married."

Philo stares intently at me, then calmly moves to his desk.

"Take a seat, Eric. Let's talk about this party."

I sit in the green leather chair opposite Philo. He raises his glass to his mouth, but stops short of his lips.

"I've always admired your father," he explains. "He was always unquestionably devoted to your mother, as I'm sure you saw. Why, I even offered him a job when Marie and I moved to Chicago, but he knew your mother could never leave Cincinnati."

I never heard this story about my parents—and I'm not sure it matters. My father worked himself to death, and there's hardly anything to show for it. At least Philo Olin admires him ...

"Are you enjoying my whiskey, Eric?"

"Yes, it's very strong," I say, eyeing the door. "Thank you."

"I'm glad," chuckles Philo. "It came straight from Scotland, very difficult to find here."

"I appreciate it, thanks again."

"If you like that ..." Philo gets up and shuffles over to his bar, where he pulls out another bottle with a red label, and pours a small glass. He returns to his desk and slides me the new glass. "This is Japanese whiskey, try it."

I swap out glasses and try the new drink—my eyes widen. "Oh, that's good," I say as Philo nods knowingly. "It's ... spicier ... but smooth."

"It's truly a treat. Most people have never tried it, nor could they appreciate it if they did."

I take another drink, and savor it.

This glass could pay my rent.

"Your father used to be a whiskey man, too," he adds.

"He was?"

Philo nods. "Eric, I have a favor I'd like to ask of you. I want you to keep what I'm about to tell you just between us."

Philo's eyes narrow, and I can't help but think that they appear rather accusatory for someone asking a favor. Or maybe he's just nearsighted—his glasses *are* off. At any rate, I nod and hear him out.

"This club I belong to—the Havens—they put a lot of pressure on a man to show up to these parties with beautiful young women," he explains, "especially if you're having trouble at home, which I sadly admit I am."

My eyes drift to the picture on his desk.

"But all marriages go through rough patches," he states, "especially after nearly 35 years!"

"I'm sorry to hear that."

"Still, this is no behavior for a husband, especially during the holidays—I regret the entire affair already! But here we are, and if I show up with Annabelle it will at least get John and the other fellas off my back about bringing someone to this party."

"I suppose, but—"

"I can handle them. For the rest of the Havens," Philo continues, "we'll just tell them that you met Annabelle outside Marshall Field's, and you invited her to the party—which will be essentially true—just to avoid any gossip. Does that make sense?"

"I think so, yes."

"Yes, what?"

Is he really this paranoid?

My shoes are wet.

"We'll tell people I met Annabelle at Marshall Field's and that she's my date to the party," I oblige.

Philo smiles. "Perfect," he says.

I finish the Japanese and switch back to the Scotch. The cool burning down my throat and into my gut eases the essential truth into an absolute.

"Oh, and Eric, I'd appreciate it if you didn't mention any of this to your mother," says Philo gently. "She'd be so disappointed to hear you and I met under these circumstances. Let's just say we met for dinner—Cuban—how does that sound?"

I raise my glass again, but see this one's also empty and place it down.

Philo has me ask Annabelle if she'd like to accompany me to the Havens' Christmas party that night. She accepts, and Philo sends her back downstairs to our driver, Mack, who is going to take her to get a new dress and her hair done.

"Tell him to have you back here by quarter to eight," Philo instructs, then adds with a wink, "and pick up new shoes for Eric."

We arrive to the party twenty minutes past eight, after Annabelle—who is now fancied up in a wine-colored gown with her hair in a tidied finger wave to complement her already-crimson lips—returned to Philo's office late. I can tell Philo isn't pleased with this, but he is putting up a good show. Mack drops us off at the curb, and Philo is escorted by the LaSalle Hotel concierge into the lobby, with Annabelle and I trailing close behind.

We are whisked through a garden of marble planters and golden lanterns, until we reach a set of double doors, guarded by a pair of men close to my age in matching uniforms who have been trained to stare straight forward. The concierge nods at the them and the doors swing open. "Enjoy your evening, sir," says the concierge, excusing himself with a bow.

There is a shock to every sense that is even stronger than Philo's whiskies. The ivory walls, accented by gold trim, command attention to not one, but two glass chandeliers. Dozens of fancy-footed ladies and gentlemen mingle below their grandeur, muffling the seven-piece musical ensemble serenading the partygoers with a swirling rendition of the latest Duke Ellington number. A few couples dance along freely, causing the tuxedoed wait staff to cut around the guests like football halfbacks, equally careful not to spill a drop of liquid from their trays or graze a swinging shoulder. And that aroma ... for the first time since I moved to Chicago my nose is cleansed of lingering wet garbage, as the room is filled with overwhelmingly pleasant scent of pine needles emanating from far back wall, where there sits a 30-foot tall spruce tree neatly decorated with silver tinsel.

"Holy shit," gasps Annabelle. She grabs my hand to lead me to the dance floor, but my instincts resist. She smiles at me and pulls harder. I start to surrender, but we are interrupted.

"Philo!" hollers a sturdy man with a chiseled face and meticulous side part, swooping toward us from the dance floor. He had been dancing with a pretty young woman who doesn't seem too concerned with his abrupt departure.

"Andrew," mumbles Philo.

The man's eyes dart from Annabelle to me, before he flashes an uncomfortable grin.

"And who do we have here?" he asks.

"Not now, Andrew," asserts Philo. "Let's talk in the lobby."

Philo looks beyond Andrew and gestures across the room for a tall man who looks around his early forties with slicked-back hair and a pencil mustache. He catches Philo's eye and walks toward us with a curvy, blond woman draped on his arm like the moon.

"Ed, these are my guests Annabelle and Eric," says Philo quickly. "Introduce them to the fellas while I speak with Andrew."

Annabelle and I begin to follow Ed when Philo grabs my arm and mutters, "It's alright, he knows about her."

Philo similarly grabs Andrew—who is still grinning at us—by the arm and pulls him away. Then, "Ed Carmen," properly introduces himself and his date, "Wendy."

"Don't mind Andrew Coppock," assures Ed. "He's a strange kid, but Philo keeps him in line."

Ed leads Annabelle and I to another pair of couples standing near one of several red velvet couches pushed up to the side of the ballroom walls.

"Everyone, I want you to meet Philo's guests, Eric Mihlfried and his date, Annabelle," says Ed. "Eric, Annabelle—this is Charlie Lords."

A portly man with short, curly hair and round tortoise shell glasses steps forward with an outstretched hand. "Pleasure to meet you," he says hoarsely. "And this fiery red fox with me is Audrey Campbell."

"A pleasure," mutters the flame-haired woman on Charlie's arm.

"Hello," says Annabelle with bridled enthusiasm. "I love your glasses, Charlie, are they French?"

"Oh, I dunno," blushes Charlie.

"And this is John Mattingly," says Ed, turning toward a confident-looking man with salt-and-pepper hair and a thin mustache, puffing on a cigar.

"Annabelle," nods John suavely. "Whose date are you again? Philo's or this kid's?"

I freeze for a second. "Oh, uh, mine," I stammer.

John cocks his eyebrow at me, then grins. "I'm horsing around, I know what's going on—Philo told me when he asked for Mack's services tonight. Nice to meet you, young fella," says John, shaking my hand.

"Right—you're John!" I exclaim, realizing this is whose limo we were in. "Thank you for the ride, sir."

"Sir!" exclaims John, mugging for his audience. "My reputation precedes me."

Ed and Wendy exchange glances.

"Don't mention it, Eric," John continues. "I tell Philo he's always welcome to use Mack—I don't get why he's so resistant."

The thin-faced weasel of a woman in a white fur shawl at John's side faintly squeaks.

"Excuse *me*," amends John, still chuckling to himself. "This is Gigi."

John lowers his cigar to his side, errantly flicking some ashes to the ground, many of which land on my new shoes. No one notices. John leans toward Annabelle, and uses his head to motion to his date.

"If you were impressed by Charlie's specs, doll, you'll love Gigi—*she's actually French*."

"You don't say!" gasps Annabelle. "How exotic!"

Annabelle starts to smirk; Ed and Wendy see this and aren't nearly as good at suppressing their own.

"*'Ello,*" says Gigi coldly.

Annabelle snorts, and proceeds to play with the fake red carnation in Charlie's lapel, making a comment about it looking like a sponge. Everyone laughs. I do, too. Annabelle turns to me, shrugs, and mouths, "Her accent's Russian."

Another couple with a remarkable age difference strolls by. Ed clears his throat to make sure the rest of us are aware—John and Charlie seem impressed.

"So, where'd you two kids meet?" asks John of Annabelle and I, winking at Ed and Charlie.

As I hesitate to answer, Annabelle steps up, then proceeds to be the center of attention for the rest of our introduction. Rendered conversationally obsolete, I am afforded preoccupation with the interactions between the other Havens and their dates. Young girls—all of them—and beautiful, just like Philo said. And there are three rings in our circle, all on the men. I seamlessly fade back into the conversation, where everyone is listening intently to Annabelle's never-ending supply of oath-ridden anecdotes.

"So I said, 'Holy fuck, Claude—pull up your trousers!'" shouts Annabelle, eliciting several head swivels from other parts of the ballroom. "When I told you I wanted you to *get off the squash* I meant for you to stand up or else we'd need to think of a new type of soup!"

Ed, John, and Charlie all roar with laughter, while each of their dates look like they just swallowed a fly (though Wendy lets out a slight snicker).

"Daniel!" shouts John to a passing young man around my age with sharp dimples and short, wavy brown hair. "You have to listen to this bird here, Annabelle—I'm in stitches!"

Annabelle isn't amused.

"This is Daniel Kruger," says Ed. "He's our host for tonight's party."

"Evening fellas … ladies," says Daniel, turning toward Annabelle. "Very nice to meet you. Say, you lot swapping naval stories? We could hear you from the other side of the room!"

"I'm sorry, Daniel, we'll try to keep John under better control," says Annabelle. "This is my date, Eric."

I offer my hand.

"Hi," says Daniel brusquely. "Say, fellas, is this the guy replacing Sid?"

"Maybe," says Ed, motioning for Daniel to say less.

"Philo just kicked Sid out of the Havens," adds Charlie. "Don't look at me like that, Ed, everyone else is talking about it."

"Ooh, a scandal!" says Annabelle. "For what?"

"Eric's father went to college with Philo," says Ed, changing the subject. "He's from Cincinnati like John, Philo, and my dad."

"Another Philo nominee?" says Daniel. "Then we'll be seeing you around … as long as you're not a jackass like Andrew Coppock, I think we'll be okay."

"Daniel, don't you hang around Coppock?" says Wendy.

"Yeah, so I really know," says Daniel. "Say Eric, you don't happen to work on Michigan Avenue, do you?"

"No, I'm between jobs," I say, struggling to wiggle my toes in the new shoes Philo bought me. I catch Wendy staring at me staring at my feet.

"Damn, does Philo know what we lost with Sid?" laments Daniel. "Ah, we'll think of something for Paul's toast—forget it."

"He's still not Coppock," reminds Ed.

"Annabelle," says Daniel, "come with me to meet the others. Herb's telling us about his trip to Bermuda—I'm sure he'd love to hear your thoughts on it."

"Sounds lovely," agrees Annabelle, and a little too easily. She starts to leave me behind to follow Daniel when she says, "Eric, aren't you coming?"

Daniel impatiently peers back at us—he's handsome, rich, and probably bought his own shoes, just like every other man here. And Annabelle is beautiful, just like every other woman here. A waiter walks past carrying a tray filled with small desserts.

"Not right now," I say. "I'll catch up with you later. Nice to meet everyone."

Annabelle goes with Daniel while I stalk the waiter. By the time I finally catch up he has passed out all but one dessert.

"Jesus! I didn't see you following me," says the waiter. "Tart?" He presents the last strawberry tart on his tray, which looks especially appetizing tonight.

I start to reach for the dessert when a squat, sweaty man with a scrunched face waddles up and makes a croaky sound in his throat, grabbing both the waiter's and my attention.

"Are you going to eat that?" wheezes the tubby man. I don't respond right away, which he takes as "no." He grabs the dessert with his pudgy fingers, pushes it into his mouth, and says, "Thanks," crumbs falling over his protruding belly.

"No problem," I mumble.

The waiter walks away.

A few more dessert-wielding waiters pass by, but I never get my tart. Everyone here seems to have no problem dancing, laughing, and getting their dessert while I can't even join a conversation. Even Philo, who appears relatively antisocial here, is constantly surrounded by three or four partygoers telling jokes and tapping their feet.

After an hour-long set, the band shrinks down to a singular piano player while the others take a break. I would probably quite enjoy the simple contrast of the piano ballad were it not for the boisterous chattering overwhelming the solemn ragtime melody.

"The cats keep getting younger and younger," says a tan man with friendly eyes who has pulled up beside me. "You must be new—Felix Castaneda, I play bass."

He pulls out a cigarette and offers another one to me. I decline.

"Eric Mihlfried," I say, shaking Felix's hand instead.

"You came in with Philo Olin, right?" he asks as he lights up.

"That's right. He's my father's friend."

"In with the big wigs!" says Felix through a long drag. "I better get used to the added competition around here."

"I don't know about that."

Felix spots the other musicians finishing their cigarettes and meandering back to their seats, while he continues sucking on his own.

"I'm joshing, pal, I'm just a dirty a musician and you're a Haven—you'll be cool," says Felix.

"I'm not a Haven, just Philo's guest."

"Trust me, if Philo Olin brought you to a party with their girlfriends, you're a Haven. He and John Mattingly founded this club, and no one comes to one of these parties unless they say you're in." Some of the other band members walk past us on their way back to the bandstand. Felix pats one of them on his back, then lowers his voice like Philo had done earlier in the limo. "That's why this is the hottest social club in Chicago—none is more discreet."

Across the ballroom, Annabelle has gained several men's attention. She's talking, and moving her hands, and they're all having a grand time, unfettered by what's going on outside of this ballroom.

"I just don't know if this is for me," I shrug. "I can't even pay my rent—how can I keep up with this lifestyle?"

"Pally, we're all struggling out here. But you've been given a great opportunity," Felix assures. "Philo's going to take care of you—boy, you better believe I'd give anything to be in your shoes right now."

I still can't wiggle my toes.

Surveying the room while Felix continues to comfort me, I spot Philo, Ed, and John locked in a heated discussion.

"I heard Philo kicked someone out recently."

"Sid Reid," sighs Felix. "'Course, we never get the low down, but you'll hear things."

"Like what?"

"No," corrects Felix, "I mean when you hear things, let me know. That's why we smoke." I crack a small smile, and

Felix reciprocates. "You really should try to make the most of this, Eric ... Do it for the rest of us Joes—and report back!"

I look back at my date surrounded by other men, and must agree with Felix's advice. Annabelle's a regular working girl, and she fits right in. She's just being more confident than I am. It's just so hard ...

"Speaking of, I better scram—the boys are warming up."

"It was good talking to you, Felix."

"We'll do this again. Now stop staring at that redhead you came in with and go talk to her," urges Felix, double-checking his cigarette for any residual tobacco. "You need to stay close to a bird like that—once she's out of your sight, the gentleman's code can get blurry at a party like this."

3

THE GIRLFRIEND RULES

Felix tosses his cigarette and heads back to the bandstand, and soon enough the full band fills the auditorium with another bold, jazzy tune.

With the new song, the party reshuffles. Philo, John, and Ed have gone their separate ways, with Ed meeting his date, Wendy, on the dance floor, and Philo taking a seat at a couch at the far end of the ballroom, followed closely by a couple other guys around my age pestering him with more questions. In the middle of the room, I see Annabelle step in between John and his date, Gigi. She grabs John's cigar from his mouth, puffs on it a few times, shakes her head in disapproval and presses it into the ashtray. John's eyebrows raise, but he laughs it off, as Annabelle carries on. Gigi is unimpressed.

"Annabelle!" shouts a voice from the crowd.

Daniel's voice.

I follow it.

"Anna!" shouts another, louder voice as I approach the circle. "I'm ready to try it again."

"Her name's Annabelle, not Anna you drip," says Daniel to Andrew Coppock, the man who Philo talked to when we arrived.

"I was practicing the line, not her name," retorts Coppock, shoving Daniel's shoulder. "Listen to this Anna—*Ee-say-cotta!*"

"NO!" shouts Annabelle, placing a hand on his shoulder. "It's *ee-SVAY-cotta*—you are too damn *drunk* to get it! You make Lithuanians everywhere weep."

Daniel turns to Coppock with in disbelief and the pair exchange a roll of hearty laughs. They don't even notice I'm here.

"Look, Eric's here," says Annabelle blithely. "It's your turn to try a line."

As Daniel and Coppock exchange blatantly incorrect Lithuanian-y sounds, Annabelle whispers a barely comprehensible string of syllables into my ear.

"*Chee-ulp-k bee-bee?*"

"That's perfect!" exclaims Annabelle, much to Daniel's and Coppock's chagrin—and my own surprise. "*Erikas*, you must have some Lithuanian in you!"

Erikas ...

"I'm thirsty," proclaims Coppock. "Anna, come grab another drink with us."

"Actually, Annabelle," I interject, "I was wondering if you wanted to dance. I was talking to the bassist and—"

"Annabelle, you promised!"

"I would love to, Eric, but I did promise them a drink, then I'm going to take care of some personal business," Annabelle pauses so Coppock can make a disgusted face, "but then after that we shall dance."

"Okay."

And now I'm standing alone in the middle of a crowded dance floor. Philo's talking to Ed again, John and Charlie are laughing with their dates, and Daniel and Coppock are pounding drinks by the bar while Annabelle starts flirting with yet another man. I start to wonder again why I am here. I can butt into another conversation, but assume I'll just get left alone again. I should say something (in English) this time …

Birds … nookie … forget it.

"Looks like someone could use a drink," observes Wendy. "I'm getting Eddy another whiskey. Want something, Eric?"

"I'm all set, thanks."

"Well, I wouldn't mind the company then. Join me?"

Wendy wraps her arm around mine— "It's okay, Ed's not the jealous type," she says at my stiff reception, leading me to the bar. Wendy orders two whiskies and a champagne and we take a seat on an empty red couch.

29

"You're not having a good time," she observes. "Your date not working out?"

"Your date," she says.

"Or is she your girlfriend? I assume you're not married," says Wendy, tapping my bare ring finger.

"No, I'm not married," I say, distracted by Annabelle from across the room. She and the current object of her affection have been joined by Coppock, Daniel, and yet another new man. She takes turns touching all of them to various extents, inciting delighted laughter from each.

I slump back into the couch, feeling my dullest.

"She's a pretty girl," Wendy continues, "but she won't make it in this world with that behavior."

Sinking further into my seat, I recall Felix's words about making it as a Haven, even though I know I don't fit in. Annabelle clearly does—everybody loves her ... *but Wendy says she won't?*

"And why's that?" I ask.

"The boys like her, sure, but she's not the society type," says Wendy. "There are ... certain qualities the Havens look for in a girlfriend, and it goes beyond looks—well, not too far."

I scoff.

Wendy points to a tall man with a cherubic face and wavy side part talking to a short, scrawny blond. "Take this girl with Herb Galloway—she's standing in an awkward position, and her hands are on her hips. If you can't present yourself as interested, alert, and never bored, you won't be back."

Indeed, this Herb Galloway seems as disinterested in his date as she does with her posture.

"And this girl with Paul Jaeger—" says Wendy, referring to a stunning, large-bosomed brunette blotting her touched-up lipstick with a handkerchief, "the men hate it when you borrow their belongings—doesn't matter for what—but especially if it's going to leave lipstick marks. She probably won't be back, either."

That, and Paul Jaeger is probably one of the fool's gawking at Annabelle at this very moment.

"Then, of course, there are the obvious avoidances: don't drink too much … don't curse or cry … don't flirt with the other men …"

Sounds familiar …

"Not to say she's a bad person, of course," Wendy clarifies. "I don't know anything about her character, just that she doesn't seem very Haven-like."

Tell that to Andrew Coppock.

"But doesn't it bother you that there are all these rules for the women when the men are …" I trail off, tapping my ring finger.

"Unfaithful?" Wendy completes. "I suppose it does, but I've been coming to these parties for a few years now … Ed doesn't expect that nonsense of me—he respects me. And he knows I behave. But some of these girls are real trouble, Eric."

"Is that what happened to Sid?"

Wendy shakes her head.

"I don't know what Sid Reid did to get kicked out. Everyone's been asking Philo and John about it, but they're not talking. They'll eventually tell Ed and Charlie, I'm sure. It's just surprising with Sid ..."

Wendy picks up on the transparent skepticism on my face.

"Ed really is a good man," insists Wendy. "Of course, I don't like that he's married, but you've got to understand that with him it's different—he's in a bad marriage."

"I'm sure," I say, imagining every adulterous man here's confession would carry some fantastic explanation or another.

"No, really," assures Wendy. "Ed got married young, before he knew what he really wanted. They had a rough first few years, and thought a child might fix things. But everything just got worse between them, and ... they're just not right for each other anymore. He was miserable when he met me, but now I think we're both happier," Wendy shrugs. "It's not a perfect love story, but it's ours."

Wendy smiles, but the sides of her eyes conceal a frown. Maybe I'm not the only one who doesn't belong here ...

"What are you kids talking about?" says Ed coyly, walking up.

"I was just telling Eric about the girlfriend rules, sweetheart," says Wendy, quickly composing herself as she rises from the couch to greet Ed with a kiss.

"Did you tell him women should never speak while dancing?" quips Ed.

"Oh, I didn't—also, she should please and flatter her man by talking only about his interests."

"Those are good ones!"

"You think so?" laughs Wendy, grabbing Ed's arm.

Ed and Wendy return to the party, while I stay seated. I look towards the door and wonder if I stand a better chance of having a meaningful conversation with a stranger on the street than I do in here. Everything about this night has been about rules, and deceit, and hierarchy, and—

"Erikas!"

I recoil. Annabelle is standing inches from my face. She is holding a glass of champagne and her face is slightly pink.

"Eric!" she says again, snapping her fingers at me.

"Annabelle," I gasp, "I didn't see you come over."

"God, this is magnificent," she swoons. "It's more than I could've imagined ... the music ... the decorations ... this damn good champagne!"

I grimace at her curse. I don't know what makes me feel worse: that I agree with Wendy's assessment of Annabelle or that when she's next to me I don't ...

"Sorry, did I interrupt something? You look contemplative."

"No," I say, "it's just ... the longer I'm here the more I'm certain I shouldn't be."

She swats away some indiscernible dirt from my lapel.

"That's bullshit, Erikas," she mutters. "Tell me what you don't like here—better yet, tell me anything about yourself. You're my date tonight and I don't know anything about you."

Me?

I'm not immediately sure what to say. I haven't had to give this speech tonight.

"Well, this world is new to me," I start slowly. "And …"

Annabelle smiles. Her face is warm and understanding.

"…I used to work in finance," I say, words starting to flow more naturally, "but it's a competitive industry even in prosperous times …"

Annabelle takes a deep breath and lightly pats the perspiration from her chest.

"…and it's been difficult because I moved here without knowing anyone …"

She tugs on her bust line and pats lower toward her slightly exposed bosom.

"…and it's been r-really d-difficult f-finding a new job," I stammer, barely hearing my own words.

A smirking waiter strolls by and takes Annabelle's near-empty champagne flute and hands her another.

"Thanks, Alan, dear," she croons to the waiter's satisfaction.

34

"What I'm trying to say is," I continue, "I'm in a lousy place."

Annabelle frowns. "You don't need to be in that place, Erikas," she consoles. "But you're here now! You just need a task."

"What do you mean?"

Annabelle surveys the room and points to a group of men huddled around Philo. They're all badgering Philo with questions.

"Look how grumpy Philo is," she observes. "Doesn't that make you feel better?"

Philo's face looks like one of the waiters just dragged a tray filled with the wet trash from my neighborhood under his nose; his obvious disgust is not slightly dissuading to his young Haven devotees.

"It does," I laugh, "I certainly don't want to look like that!"

We both laugh, and Annabelle gently rubs her hand on my shoulder. "It feels so good to laugh with someone tonight!"

We smile at each other.

"Right," says Annabelle, deliberately breaking our gaze. "But he brought us here tonight so we owe him a favor— let's rescue him!"

"Ah, our task," I nod. "What do you have in mind?"

"Hmm, let us think," ponders Annabelle. I do the same.

"What if we said the maître d' had a phone call for him?" I suggest.

"Oh, I *like* that, Erikas!" she exclaims. "And we could say it was his wife—shit, they'd have to excuse him for that!"

"Exactly!"

"This is perfect!"

"And—"

I am cut off by clanging glasses. The music has stopped and the entire room moves toward the bandstand, where one of the men Annabelle was talking to earlier is trying to get the room's attention.

"Oh, look, Paul's got something to say," notes Annabelle.

"I'd like to propose a toast!" this *Paul* fella calls out as he buttons his jacket. "Sounds like everyone's having a swell time tonight—except for Charlie over here. I don't blame you for looking confused—all this talk about Sid Reid when he'd never even be at this party if he was still a Haven!"

The crowd erupts, and a few men clink their glasses, while Charlie laughs at his own expense.

"But really, I'm loving these wonderful new faces," he continues, staring in our—well, *Annabelle's* direction. "Love and new friends—that's the Christmas spirit, and what," Paul's meter suddenly slows down, "this event," but quickly returns to normal, "is all about. But before we go back and celebrate with our families, Havens, let's show our appreciation for our marvelous host tonight, Daniel Kruger!"

The speaker raises his glass to the crowd.

"Cheers, gentleman."

All the women raise their glasses and respond in a smattering of "cheers"—but none of the men move. For a few seconds, the room is filled with an eerie pause. Finally, the beanpole with a boyish face Wendy pointed out earlier, Herb Galloway, raises his glass with a reluctant "HuzZAH!"

"HUZZAH!" chorus the other men in response.

The crowd disperses, and the band starts up again. In the initial chattering, I hear a few utterances along the lines of *"Thank God for Herb,"* before everyone resumes their previous conversations. I turn to Annabelle to do the same.

"So, our Philo plan—" I begin.

But I am cut off once more.

"Annabelle!" says Daniel, of course.

"Danielius!" she replies.

He is Danielius now …must have finally said his line correctly, too.

Annabelle follows Daniel into the sea of society, leaving me with the scowling waiter, "Alan," who has returned and is waiting expectantly for a tip.

"I don't have any money," I snap, and depart for the path of least resistance through the crowd toward Philo.

"Eric!" shouts Philo upon spotting me. "Find Annabelle. We heard the toast, it's time to go."

"She was just with me," I sigh, wishing I had paid attention to where she and Daniel had gone.

"Then she should be easy to find."

I turn around maneuver my way back through the crowded ballroom floor when I hear Annabelle's voice.

"Go fuck yourself!" she asserts.

I turn, and see Annabelle push away chiseled-face Andrew Coppock. Daniel and Paul chortle in disbelief, and I think Daniel even points at her like a zoo animal. Coppock grabs both of Annabelle's upper-arms.

"C'mon now, baby, you're just a bit blind," snarls Coppock.

My face burns and I take a swift step toward them. But before I can get there, Annabelle screams and casts her glass to the ground. It shatters everywhere. Coppock releases her. Everyone—including the band—stops and stares.

Annabelle sees me and grabs my hand. She pauses, turns back, curses, slaps Coppock, and we run off.

"What the devil?" gasps Philo as we run past.

4

AN UNEXPECTED OFFER

"Is a French omelette a good Christmas breakfast?" asks Charlie.

"No, Charlie," says Ed, "the French don't celebrate Christmas—they're too good for it."

John, Philo, and I snicker.

"Then again, John, maybe Gigi could lend her expertise on the subject," Ed continues. "Where in France is she from? Lyon?"

Philo and I laugh again, with Charlie joining in a hair late.

"Okay, gents, I get it," says John uneasily, "you're jealous because once again I brought the sweetest dish to the ball."

"I'm sorry, did you say, 'Swedish dish?'" chimes in Philo wryly. "I thought she was French."

Everyone but John roars, and Ed shakes Philo's hand.

"I don't know, fellas," grins Charlie, "Audrey is a good-looking girl ... I may have John beat this time!"

"Really, Charlie?" implores John.

"Wasn't she John's girl in the summer?" asks Ed.

Charlie's smile fades.

"It was March, actually," corrects John, "and I told Charlie she was fair game then. What did it take—nine months to get that chick to go out with you?"

"Well, she—"

"Speaking of," says John, cutting off Charlie, "it was nice to finally see Philo getting in on the fun."

Philo buries his face into the menu.

"Oh, come now, Philo, it's nothing to be ashamed of!" says John. "That one is something special. No doubt about it—she's a real looker. But that stuff with Coppock at the end ..."

"I don't wish to talk about it," grumbles Philo. "She's Eric's girl anyway."

All eyes turn on me.

"That's what you said yesterday, too," counters John, "but she didn't seem to spend much time with either of you fellas."

The waiter comes by to take our orders.

"So, you won't be bringing her again?" says Charlie.

"Excuse me?" says the waiter.

"Damn it, Charlie!" groans Ed, carelessly shoving his cousin. "We've moved on. Just order your Christmas omelette so we can get out of here—I've still got presents to buy!"

Ed and Charlie bicker a bit more until the waiter finishes taking our orders, when John changes the subject.

"Speaking of who's coming back," says John, looking around to make sure no one is eavesdropping, "have you told the young fella here about the toasts."

"The toasts?" I repeat.

"Remember Paul Jaeger's little speech on the bandstand last night?" says Ed.

I nod.

"Every Havens event has a toast," explains Philo. "That's where we find out when and where the next party is."

"But I didn't hear Paul say anything about another party," I reply. "He just thanked Daniel for hosting—"

"—and made fun of Charlie," adds Ed.

Charlie shrugs.

"But how he made fun of Charlie is important," continues John. "Every toast contains a little joke or story about a few of the Havens—that's a code."

"Who Paul mentions tells us where the next party is," says Philo. "Last night was Charlie, who works on Oak

Street, and Sid Reid, who works on Michigan Avenue—the next party is at Oak and Michigan which is …"

"*The Drake*," say the others in unison.

"He gives the date, too" says Philo. "At some point he'll work a number into the toast."

"It corresponds to the number of days until the next party, excluding Sundays," says Ed. "Those are for the family. Anyhow, Paul snuck it in pretty well—when he said, 'this event' he said it like 'thi*s event*' …"

"… Oh, seven," I conclude.

"And with one Sunday that puts us at December 31ˢᵗ," says Charlie. "New Year's Eve."

I nod my head.

"The rest of the code is even easier," says John. "If the toastmaster is wearing his jacket the party is for the wives— if not, we get to have some fun."

"And whoever raises their glass to lead the 'Cheers' is giving the next party's toast," concludes Philo. "It's simple, but it works."

Our food arrives, and everyone seems content to move on. I dig my fork into my scrambled eggs, but hesitate to take a bite.

"Is something the matter?" says Philo. "Eric?"

I take a quick bite and shake my head. "It just seems elaborate, that's all."

"It's so none of these gentlemen get in trouble," explains Philo. "With the code we don't have to speak openly about the parties. No one overhears, and no one sees anything they shouldn't."

"Unless you're Sid Reid," says Charlie. Philo drops his fork on his plate and glares at him.

"Subtle," says Ed.

"Sid didn't follow the rules," says Philo bluntly. "The Havens have no room for disobedience, and that's all I have to say about it."

"Come on, Philo," pleads Ed, "Sid hasn't played by the rules for years—what could he have done that made you kick him out now?"

Philo frowns at Ed.

"Philo, let's just tell them," says John. "I don't want this getting out either, but we can tell the fellas ... Founders' inner circle."

"Fine," Philo relents. "No one repeats this—Sid's getting divorced."

Ed gasps, "Evie found out about the hookers?"

"It was fine when he stuck to Amy's girls, but he was acting like a dirty junkie, running all over town looking for his next fix," says Philo. "Cat houses, massage parlors, even street girls. Apparently, one followed him home but Evie answered the door and now they're getting divorced."

"Sid didn't tell me any of this," says Ed, his face much paler than it was just a few seconds earlier. "I didn't know it was that bad."

"Sid never went to a single mistress party, Eric," explains John. "He loved his wife, but she lost a baby a few years back and there were complications … Sid needed to get it somewhere and thought prostitutes were a victimless solution."

Ed stares intently into his *Eggs à la Benedick*.

"That's why we have rules, Eric," says Philo. "We've created a safe space where everything is under control, so no one gets in trouble, and no one gets hurt. I overlooked Sid Reid's deviation over the years because he was generally careful and a friend of the Carmens."

Ed glances sharply at Philo, who continues, unfazed.

"But Sid got arrogant and sloppy, and now he's getting divorced."

"In our world," says John, "divorces bring headlines and attention, and we don't like that."

"Havens don't get divorced," concludes Philo, "and certainly not because of some damn hooker."

Ed laughs to himself. "Philo, weren't you driving around with Mack last night?"

"What are you getting at?" says Philo, adjusting his glasses.

Ed shrugs.

"Wasn't Mack driving Eric anyway?" playfully interjects John. "Philo was just along for the ride."

Philo exhales.

"He did pick me up first ..." I say.

"Eric, you're an animal," says John, "isn't that right, Ed?"

After a quick eye roll and a sip of water, Ed leans forward. "You're not wearing a watch, Eric" he points out. "Did you lose it?"

"No, I—"

"I bet you had a good time last night, too, didn't you?"

"Yes, I suppose, but—"

"Then you can get the hell out of here before you give us all the syph!" he exclaims. "Surgeon Sage says."

The others smile, as I realize I've been turned into an omnipresent poster slogan.

"Eric, you poor boob!" laughs Charlie.

"Damn it, Charlie!" says Ed. "You've taken the joke too far!"

After we finish eating, John picks up the tab—his Christmas present to everyone. As we exit the restaurant and wait for the drivers to arrive, there is a quick rundown of everyone's holiday plans: Ed and Charlie, who have younger children, are going to their in-laws' homes. Philo and John, who have grown children, are having Christmas at their own homes. Finally, I lie about going back to

Cincinnati tonight to visit my mother because that's better than admitting I still don't have the money for simple train fare home.

Philo's actual driver, Sam, is the last to arrive, and he insists on giving me a ride home, too. The fifteen-minute ride is mostly silent—Sam isn't as vivacious a chauffeur as Mack—until we arrive at my apartment. I open the back door to leave, and am about to thank Philo for the invitation, when he finally speaks:

"I know Ed was joking with you earlier, but I do hope you enjoyed the party last night."

"I did."

"And breakfast, too," he says. "The fellas can be a bit chatty at times."

"Yes, I enjoyed breakfast."

There's another silence, but it's short-lived.

"Also, if you change your mind about going to Cincinnati," says Philo, "you're welcome to join my family for Christmas."

"I'll let you know."

Philo nods. I step out of the vehicle, and am about to close the door behind me when Philo interjects again. "Whatever you decide, meet me at my office at eight o'clock Monday morning. I want to talk about your job situation— have a nice Christmas, Eric."

"I—"

"That's right, I'll see you then," he finishes for me. "Let's go, Sam."

Christmas comes, and I don't take up Philo's offer. Instead, I call my mother. She cries over my father. I tell her about meeting Philo, but skip the details. I eat chipped beef and toast, go to bed early, and fall asleep late.

Merry Christmas, Eric.

Monday arrives, and I take the train to the Loop, get off at Adams, and walk to Philo's building. I am greeted by his doorman, who mistakes me for a delivery boy, but then am led up to Philo's office.

I step off the elevator and am greeted by a large green sign that reads "Olin Crane & Shovel." I check in with a receptionist with neat brown hair and stale eyes, who tells me to wait in the lobby until Philo finishes a phone call.

I take a seat on a couch. At first, I can't get comfortable, but soon my ears are mildly occupied by the rhythmic symbiosis of scraping pencils and clinking typewriter keys. I look up at the receptionist and attempt a smile, but I don't think it comes out right, which she doesn't notice anyway. Occasionally, a middle-aged man gets off the elevator, quickly greets the receptionist, then strides into the sea of wooden desks (only a handful of which are occupied), where Annabelle had wandered just a few days prior.

Then, a younger man around my age approaches the receptionist. His steps are quick and his motions are sudden, almost violent.

"I need you to deliver this," says the man, thrusting a piece of paper in the receptionist's face.

"What is this?" she drolls.

"What does it matter?" asserts the man, leaning into her desk. "I just need it at 160 North LaSalle by ten, or else we're both out of a job. Got it now?"

The receptionist begrudgingly rises. "Let me grab my coat," she says.

As the man waits for her to return, he raps his fingers on her desk. He starts to whistle an unharmonious tune while his eyes wander around the waiting area until they land on me.

I blink hard—it's the man Annabelle slapped at the Christmas party, Andrew Coppock. His eyes laugh with recognition but he doesn't utter a word. Still, he won't look away. I start to squirm again—I had just gotten comfortable on the couch, too …

The receptionist returns.

"Alright, I'll have the letter now, Mr. Coppock."

"160 North LaSalle," he repeats. "And go straight there—don't stop off for nothing frilly."

"Of course," she says, biting her tongue.

Coppock retreats back into the main office.

"Eric, right?" says the receptionist while fastening her overcoat.

"Yes, that's me."

"Mr. Olin is ready to see you now."

I thank the receptionist, then walk past several rows of desks, and into Philo's office. Our three used whiskey glasses are still on his desk, and his head is resting on his hand as he reads through a messy stack of papers.

"Hello," I say, clearing my throat.

"Eric," Philo looks up briefly, "sit."

I do.

Philo keeps reading. His office looks a great deal more pleasant in the morning sun than it had in the amalgamation of moon-glow and incandescence, and there is, indeed, a slight view of Lake Michigan. Finally, he organizes the papers into a neat pile and straightens his posture.

"Eric, I was thinking about you all weekend," he says.

"You have?" I say, feeling bad for not even calling to decline his Christmas invitation.

"You're a smart man and practically a long-lost son to me, and I can't stand how your company treated you—who was it again?"

"Bert & Horner."

"That's right—a lot of grifters, anyway," he mumbles. "At any rate, you'll find a job soon enough. In the meantime, there's no reason to pay bills you don't have to."

Philo slides a small golden key across the table.

"What's this?"

"Your mother said you moved here last January, so your lease must be expiring soon. When it does, I want you to move in with me and Marie."

I pull back. "I don't know what to say."

"We have a spare room that's been empty for two years. It was Marie's mother's before she passed, so it even has its own attached bath—you'd have plenty of privacy."

"Wow," I exclaim, still processing, "this is such an unexpected offer—"

"Now, I know you want to be polite," interrupts Philo, "but unlike Christmas, I must insist upon this offer. Times are tough, Eric, and for the moment you need help."

I look down at my new shoes. Already slightly scuffed, they're still a marked improvement over what I was wearing before last week. At the same time, Philo says he and his wife have been having problems—do I really want to get in the middle of that?

"Look," says Philo, "I know your father wasn't a sentimental guy, but I know you miss him. We just met, I get it, but I still feel responsible for your well-being on behalf of your dad because that's what teammates do—for life."

Philo gets up from his chair and steps toward the window.

"You'd also be doing me a great favor. Marie still isn't quite right since her mother died. I've tried everything, but just can't be with her all day while keeping all of this afloat ..." he says, waving his hand in a circle. "With our children grown, I'm worried if she doesn't get more company soon she'll do something she regrets. There have been signs."

I try to imagine the elderly woman in the picture on Philo's desk having an affair, but my thoughts are clouded by an indiscernible intuition. My eyes shift focus to my Japanese whiskey glass from the other night. It transforms into a soiled tin can and a thought emerges: *I cannot afford my rent, and I don't want to eat my supper out of a used can of beans.*

"I suppose …"

Philo's eyes light up.

Off to the side, I notice the fourth whiskey glass, which was poured for our special guest on Friday. "But what about Annabelle?"

Philo adjusts his glasses, and sighs, "I thought that might come up." He rummages through his top desk drawer until he procures a brochure with a drawing of an ivory-covered building on the cover. "As I alluded to John and the other fellas, I'm quite ashamed of that night—the whole affair was a mistake, and she won't be coming around the Havens anymore."

She called me "Erikas."

"In fact," Philo continues, "that whole incident with Andrew before we left made me realize how much help that poor girl needs."

Philo puts his glasses back on.

"But I have a plan for her, too."

The building on the brochure doesn't look like anything I've seen in Chicago, and my stomach suddenly fills with air.

"I found a school in Mount Cary that will turn her into a real society girl. The next semester starts next month, but I was still able to get her in."

"Oh, good," I say quickly.

"She won't be any more trouble to us."

"That sounds ... helpful."

"It better be," Philo mutters, "for the amount of money I'm paying them."

5

UNCLE PHILO

Sam arrives at my apartment at precisely half past seven on a biting cold Saturday morning. As the prudish driver helps me load my belongings into Philo's car, my hat gets momentarily lodged beneath the larger of two suitcases. I manage to extricate it almost as instantly, but not before an offensive crease is pressed into the brim. I put it on anyway and we drive several blocks to Philo's Hyde Park home.

At eight o'clock sharp we arrive at the house, an imposing yellow-brick townhome. A crisp gust of air rushes into the car as Sam unloads my luggage. I stuff my hat under my arm—it's already misshapen—so it doesn't blow away, and carry my share up the front porch. Sam beats me to the door, drops off my trunk, and turns up his nose as passes me heading back to the car.

I'm about to meet Marie.

I drop my bags, and my hat falls, too—right into a puddle. Now it's all wet. I pick it up anyway.

I knock. No one answers. I shake my hat dry, but it still has that nasty crease. I almost toss it over the railing, but don't. I knock again and there is still no answer, but find that it is unlocked so I let myself in. I first slide my overstuffed trunk into the doorway, then my two suitcases before turning around to close the door behind me.

"Eric!"

I wheel around and see a matronly woman with gray, short-bobbed curls and thin-wired glasses like Philo's standing in the doorway at the end of the hall. She's also holding a knife the size of my forearm, its blade coated in a dripping scarlet residue—

"Hello, Eric."

—which she as soon notices.

"Oh, my!" she giggles. "What a misleading sight!"

She wipes the knife on her apron—which is now stained red—places it in her front pocket, and capers toward me.

"Philo is upstairs getting dressed and should be down any moment," she says. "Oh, we are both so excited to have you here!" My arms pin to my side as she wraps hers around me like I am a child's rag doll. "You're so thin and easy to hug!"

The stairs' screeching announces Philo's arrival. "Eric," he says amidst a slow descent. "I see you've met my wife, Marie."

"Yes," I simper, still enduring Marie's embrace.

"And you are more than that," says Marie, finally releasing me. I take a deep breath and straighten my shirt— *and did her fingers just linger against my chest?*

"Have you had breakfast yet, dear?"

"No," I pant, gradually inching away.

"We have coffee, and orange juice from concentrate, and layer cake with a new filling I'm trying!" she proudly points to the front of her apron.

I peer at the apron but am very careful to focus on a church-appropriate zone—so careful that I forget to stop.

"See something that you like?" giggles Marie.

"Let's go, Eric," grumbles Philo, shaking his head then leading me into the kitchen.

We sit at the table and Philo immediately begins reading the newspaper while their maid, a dispassionate woman named Margaret, pours us coffee. Then Marie grabs a four-layered cake with exposed sides from the counter and sets it in the center of the table, where she begins cutting three overzealous portions.

"Philo only likes frosting on the top of his cakes," explains Marie as she hands me the first piece. "It's so he knows he's only getting one layer in each bite—isn't that right?"

"It's because I don't like a lot of frosting," mumbles Philo, still buried in his newspaper.

Marie smiles at me, then frowns at her husband ... then frowns at me.

"Eric, your hat!" she exclaims. "It's all wrinkled."

"Oh, right," I say, playing with the brim. "It just got caught under a bag this morning."

"Did you hear that, Phy? Sam ruined Eric's hat."

"Maybe we should fire him, Marie."

Marie tuts, then refocuses on me. "That's probably your only one, too …"

"It's no problem, really," I say, setting aside my only hat.

"We'll get him a new one," says Philo flatly, taking a single minuscule bite of cake and thoroughly mouthing it before flashing a disgusted face. "Where's the strawberry filling, Marie?"

"It's raspberry," prides Marie. "I decided to try something new."

"On a weekday?" groans Philo, spitting into his napkin. "I need to go."

"Philo has business meetings in California," preens Marie. "He'll be back Thursday, though."

Philo rises from his seat and folds the newspaper under his arm.

"Don't worry, Eric, we'll have a great time without him."

Marie rubs my forearm just as I stick the fork in my mouth, and I nearly choke on my cake.

"Eric," says Philo as he walks toward the door, "I need your help for a few days when I get back. You should be settled in by then, yes?"

"Of course," I say quickly.

"Good. And sorry to leave on your first day here—this just came up."

"No, that's fine."

"They're building a bridge in San Francisco and they want Philo's help before they get too far along," adds Marie.

"Yes, well ... goodbye," says Philo, fastening his coat then mechanically leaning in to give Marie a dry peck on the cheek.

"Oh, my," she gushes.

"Thursday, Eric," he reiterates as he rushes out the door.

"Thursday," I nod to myself through another bite of cake. The door closes and Marie's still smiling after Philo. I turn to her. She's really beaming. "The cake is good," I say.

The rest of the morning is spent unpacking my new room. It's a good size—only a little smaller than the entirety of my old apartment—but it is rather dusty, likely seeing little attention since Marie's mother died. The walls are also covered in flowery wallpaper, which will serve as a constant reminder of who last slept here and where she is now ... Conveniently for Marie on this day, the room is located on the first floor just off the kitchen, so she can easily pop in to say whatever is on her mind while she continues to bake the entire day. Eventually, I relent to keeping her company and join her in the kitchen.

"Our oldest, Philo Jr., was just starting high school when we moved to Chicago and he wanted his privacy so he got the first-floor room ... then he went off to college but still stayed here during breaks ... then Cal—our youngest—

wanted it after Philo Jr. got his own apartment, but Cal only had it a few months before Mother moved in after my father died—she couldn't handle the stairs—so Cal went back to his old room ..."

For the rest of the afternoon, Marie repeatedly proves her love of talking about her children. However, no one lights up her eyes more than Philo Jr. After Marie sends Margaret to the store to buy meat for dinner to "sturdy" me up, I learn that Philo Jr. and his wife have recently written a book but that they won't say what it's about until it's printed.

"Philo Jr.'s always made us wait, though" says Marie. "He made us wait to give away his room ... he made us wait about Edie ... he's making us wait on this book title ... and he's still making me wait for more grandchildren ... Of course, his brothers have always had the opposite problem ..."

While helping Marie with her third cake of the day—this one with frosted sides to send to Philo Jr. and his wife Edie for completing their book—Marie divulges that in two weeks Margaret will have been working for the Olins for five years. She offers to bake any type of cake she wants, but Margaret says she'd rather have an evening off.

"I'll make her one anyway," says Marie behind her hand.

Later, we peruse the picture album of Philo Jr. and Edie's trip to the Olins' vacation home in Florida last March. "It's a shame there are only two bedrooms," says Marie longingly, "so we can never be there at the same time." When I silently challenge her math, Marie clarifies that she inherited her mother's bad back and must sleep in a separate bed from Philo, who now sleeps in middle son Raymond's old room.

"Doctor Anderson says sleeping alone allows the body to move more freely and comfort itself," says Marie, bouncing her elbows toward each other behind her back, "and it seems to be working!"

Then, at dinner Marie brings up Annabelle.

"Philo told me about your date to the Christmas party, and it just breaks my heart …"

I nearly choke on a chunk of meat.

"…Doesn't talk to her family anymore and stuck working a horrible department store job—they work those poor girls to death, you know."

I nod vehemently and gulp down water to clear my throat.

"When Philo told me about her, I said, 'You have to help that girl'—I think sending her to school is the best thing for her. Philo says we have the money …"

There were a lot of empty desks at Philo's office.

"…and young women today can get a lot from education, especially at a school like Shiner, I'm sure. In fact, Philo Jr.'s Edie went to college and she is just full of conversation."

After dinner and an evening cocktail at Marie's urging, I finally settle into bed. I have mixed emotions about Philo's openness about Annabelle with Marie, but a full day of listening to every pent-up thought in Marie's head has sapped any attentive capacity for internal dialogue—and there are five days to go before Philo returns.

After overcoming the anxiety of my first day as the Olins' houseguest, the next few are easier than expected, even with Marie's clear need for constant companionship. Save for her Wednesday night bridge game with John's and Charlie's wives and Ed's mother, there is hardly a moment when Marie is not recounting a story or gossiping. I learn family histories, theories on Philo Jr.'s book, and the latest rumors about what really happened with Sid Reid—which I add nothing to. We also bake cakes at a daily rate—and on Tuesday, I was even allowed to frost, a privilege that has yet to be re-extended.

When Thursday arrives, Philo does not. His flight from San Francisco was delayed, and everyone is fast asleep by the time he finally arrives at the house early Friday morning. That's when I wake to a soft knock on my door.

"Eric," hisses Philo, cracking open the door just enough to hear him add, "get up, get dressed, and pack an overnight bag—we're leaving in fifteen minutes."

All I want to do is sleep all morning, but then I cruelly remember I'm Philo's houseguest, and he did ask for this favor in advance. I summon myself out of bed and get ready for whatever he has planned for me. I arrive at the car in exactly fifteen minutes, and Philo arrives shortly after. After a concise greeting, Sam loads our suitcases, and we drive off.

"Where are we going?"

"Bronzeville to start," says Philo. "We're picking up Annabelle and driving her to school."

We head a few blocks north into a visibly more vicious than virtuous neighborhood versus Hyde Park. The few souls walking the sidewalks at this hour look frozen and frail, and they stop and stare at the car as we pass them. We stop in front of a maimed brownstone with a crumbling stoop and a freshened bright green door. Annabelle is waiting out front, sitting atop a single black trunk, and wearing a cerulean tweed suit and matching hat. She smiles at us like a blue jay in a coal mine, ready to fly free.

"Thank you, Sam," says Annabelle as the driver fastens her heavy trunk to the back of the car. Then, she turns to Philo and I. "Good morning, boys."

At Philo's urging, I get out of the vehicle so that Annabelle can sit in the middle.

"Hi, Annabelle," I say, sliding back in next to her, "you sure look nice today."

"Hold the niceties, Eric" says Philo. "We haven't much time and I have a lot to go over before we get to Mount Cary."

"Obviously," says Annabelle, before tilting her head toward me and whispering, "Thank you, Erikas."

Philo pulls out a small handbook and begins flipping through pages until he stops somewhere in the middle.

"Now, the school has sent me their record for the year and we need to pick your courses," says Philo, his eyes fixed on the little book. "It says girls are required to attend Sunday mass ... I'll talk to the dean and get you out of that."

"Why would we do that?" asks Annabelle.

Philo looks up from the record.

"Are you religious?"

"I am," says Annabelle boldly. "Catholic."

"Fine, you can go to church," mumbles Philo, adjusting his glasses, and turning the page. "Ah! Here's what I wanted to read to you. Listen—"

As Philo clears his phlegmy throat, Annabelle flashes me a sly smile.

"Every Shiner lady is expected to practice and mature whatever social gifts she may possess for the general benefit. Appropriate dress, a pleasing disposition, poise, politeness, pleasurable conversation, and the ability to appear at ease before an audience are as much a part of the Shiner School ideal as are academic achievements. With the assistance of class instructors, the students give class parties, lunches, dances, bazaars, teas, lawn fetes, concerts, and plays—this place sounds wonderful!"

"What about tennis?"

"Yes, they have that, too," scowls Philo.

Annabelle squeals.

Philo flips through a few more pages.

"And they have several clubs you can join. Let's see ... Bible discussion ... Athletics ... Ah! Books ... and Poetry! Those would both be fine choices ... The Splash Club? I don't even know what that is ... Glee Club could be good, though. What do you say, Annabelle?"

"Isn't there any club where they teach you how to do something fun, like cutting jigsaw puzzles?"

Philo frowns again, and flips another page.

"Actually, they mention that in Arts and Crafts," Philo admits.

Annabelle smirks again. I look at her curiously.

"Alright, classes," says Philo. "Second semester starts on Tuesday, but you have to register on Monday."

"Is Eric still my date?" Annabelle asks dreamily, sliding up next to me, and pulling my arm around her.

"Eric, stop that," orders Philo, and I do (though maybe with a grin). "Now, it says here you must pick four courses per semester on top of weekly exercising ... well, we definitely need a speech course, and something cultural ..."

"How about a finance course?"

"Hm?" grunts Philo. "Oh, Eric could probably teach you that better in an hour than those old bags could in a year."

I nod assuredly. Annabelle gushes and leans her head against my shoulder, but then Philo grunts and she bitterly returns erect—then we both snicker.

"Now, here's something—*Survey of English Literature: Overview of Classic Novels from Past to Present*—that's one to mark for sure. And look at this—French! Wouldn't that get to John if we got you speaking French better than that phony girlfriend he's been bringing around lately—you could really show her up!"

"I can speak Lithuanian," says Annabelle, but Philo doesn't hear as he folds the corner of the page.

"Well, here's something," continues Philo. "They offer a physical education course in the lower school that meets four times a week, counts as a class and the exercise requirement, and offers weekly dance instruction—I like that, it's very efficient."

Annabelle thrusts her hands into her lap and pouts.

"So that's it—my semester is decided, just like that."

Philo glances at her then back down at the record, and flips another page.

"Well, let's see ... they have secretarial studies—forget that nonsense ... and that's it," he says, closing the register. "Yes, just like that."

"And I don't get any say at all?"

"I pay the tuition, so I get final say."

"And suppose I don't agree to go anymore?"

Philo works his jaw back and forth, throws me a miffed look, and re-opens the record.

"I suppose we do have options for culture," he sighs. "I thought *Survey of English Literature* would be a nice start, but they also have *Survey of European Art*, *Survey of Music*, and *Survey of Hygiene* if you'd prefer one of those."

"I'll have to think about it," says Annabelle, catching my eye before looking away entirely.

The car falls uncomfortably silent, and we have 150 miles to go. The next two hours pass with little spoken ...

"Look, cows—or *karvés.*"

...except for Annabelle's occasional Lithuanian lessons ...

"Lena Rice was the first Irish woman to win at Wimbledon," notes Annabelle as we pass the small town of Lena, Illinois.

...and then tennis facts.

Truthfully, this enlivens the ride, as Annabelle and I silently giggle together at Philo's ire. Of course, neither of us dare let him see this—his slouched posture allows us to do so covertly behind his back— but it's still a fun inside joke.

We arrive in Mount Cary just a little before noon. Northwestern Illinois is much hillier than Chicago, and Sam almost got lost on one of the twisting roads. Still, we arrive at the black steel front gates of the Shiner School for Girls with only modest steam leaking from Philo's ears.

The campus is a collection of several one- and two-story, Georgian-style red brick buildings, connected via winding paved paths lined by mature frost-tipped hemlocks and maples. In the center is a large snow-covered mall decorated with a pair of gazebos and a small center fountain that has frozen over. Then, at the end of the paved road is a small parking lot beside a comparatively plain building named Myrtle Hall.

"This is your dormitory," Philo reads from Annabelle's acceptance letter. "Christ, they sleep you in the worst building," he scowls at the architecturally-incongruent dormitory.

Sam is unloading Annabelle's trunk when a plump woman scuttles toward us, her short gray curls bouncing excitedly.

"Hello! Hello!" shouts the woman vigorously. "You must be Annabelle!"

Annabelle demurely offers her hand.

"And you must be Uncle Philo," she says.

Uncle Philo?

I look to Philo, but he avoids my eyes.

"A pleasure," he says, still frowning at the dormitory.

"I'm Miss Beulah, one of the deans here at the Shiner School for Girls," she beams. "What are we doing out in this cold? Let's get you inside so you can get settled."

Miss Beulah leads us to the second floor of the dormitory, and unlocks the door to one of the far corner rooms. It is a decent-sized room—not quite as large as Marie's mother's, but with plenty of space to move around even with the errantly arranged bed, armoire, and small table. The furniture is all clean, but looks and smells old.

"Here we are," announces Miss Beulah, "our nicest vacant room, as you requested, Uncle Philo."

"Is it?" he says.

"Just a bit musty, that's all," says Annabelle breezily.

"It's not the *Drake*, but it's our last single," says Miss Beulah, "and I think Annabelle will find it quite suitable to her studies."

Philo looks around the room again, then steps out into the hallway. "Rather quiet for a girls' dormitory, don't you think?"

Annabelle jostles the window, struggling with it until she forces open a crack, and a sharp coldness whisks through.

"The girls are taking their first semester exams," explains Miss Beulah, casting a concerned glance in Annabelle's direction. "But they should be finished in a few hours."

"Exams, you say?" says Philo, trying the door across the hall from Annabelle—it opens.

"Yes, but they're no bother if the student is engaged in class," says Miss Beulah, somewhat distracted by Philo's snooping. "I'd really rather you not—"

"Eric, tell me what you think of this room," says Philo.

I hesitantly poke my head into the room across the hall. It is the same size as Annabelle's, but with two sets of the same furniture, and with books and pictures strewn across.

"It looks the same," I say, "except there are two beds and it has a view of the parking lot."

"Very well, we'll take the first one," concedes Philo. "Close the door behind you, Eric—leave the poor girls their privacy."

Miss Beulah rushes to lock the neighboring door and mutters, "Oh, Martha …"

"Is there any sort of welcome reception before the semester starts?" says Philo.

"Well, since we made an exception for Annabelle to start in the middle of the term, we don't typically have an orientation this time of year," admits Miss Beulah.

"However, there will be a nice luncheon tomorrow afternoon you and your companions are welcome to stay for."

Miss Beulah turns to me.

"And who are you, young man—her brother?" she asks optimistically.

"Eric's her *friend*," says Philo quickly. As if on cue, Annabelle affectionately grabs my left arm.

"Well, you know overnight guests are strictly forbidden."

"Eric and I will be staying the night at a hotel in town— no need to worry about him."

Annabelle caresses my shoulder with a longing sigh.

"Wonderful," says Miss Beulah shakily. "I'll let you get settled then. We're so excited to have you, Annabelle— you're going to adore the girls in your hall ... all so lovely."

"I can't wait to meet them," says Annabelle.

"Don't worry, Uncle Philo," Miss Beulah continues. "We will make sure your niece gets a moral and disciplined education while she's at Shiner. With that, I must be off— these exams aren't going to proctor themselves! Welcome again, Annabelle, our newest Shiner girl."

Miss Beulah scurries out and Sam starts unpacking Annabelle's trunk. After we set up her room, Annabelle convinces Philo to stroll around campus as "it's not particularly cold with the sun out." With exams, all the school buildings are closed to visitors, but we are able to take a quick look at the gymnasium and playhouse. After that, Sam drives us into town where we head into the first tavern for a quick lunch of rice soup and bread. Since we're in town, we check into our hotel—which Philo suggests Annabelle stay at tonight—before driving back to campus, as there seems to be nothing else to do in Mount Cary.

Back at Myrtle Hall, we are let in by a petite girl with an innocent face framed by shoulder-length raven black locks. I thank her for holding the door for us, but she ignores me.

"So lovely," comments Philo. "She must get top marks."

We head to Annabelle's new room, and as we approach hear voluminous laughter filling the end of the hall.

"Louise, you must *jeté entrelacé*, not *slip and fall on your face!*"

"Martha, stop!" whines a second voice. "I just don't have grace … I wish I was a tiny girl like Betty so I could just do lifts for my exam."

"Speaking of, where is that cherry?" asks a third voice, a little deeper than the others.

"She should be right behind us," says the first voice. "I'll check."

A sable-headed girl with honey brown eyes like saucers emerges from the back-corner room opposite Annabelle's that we intruded upon earlier. She greets the quiet black-haired girl before noticing the three of us staring at her.

At first, she glares, then smiles and calls out, "You must be the new girl! I'm Martha Honeysuckle."

"Hi, I'm Annabelle."

"Well, this is Shiner," laughs Martha. "You're just across the hall from me and Betty," she says, pointing to the room behind her. "Who are your friends?"

"This is Uncle Philo, and this is Eric," says Annabelle. "He's my secret overnight visitor."

With a nervous twitch, I extend my hand to the unamused girl, but Philo brushes it back as he walks between us.

"My feet are sore," he says, entering Annabelle's room.

"Charming," jokes Martha. "Annabelle, do you want to meet some of the girls? We're just chatting in my room."

"Sure," says Annabelle. "Can Eric come?"

Martha nods, and we file into her room. The quiet girl Betty is placing ballet slippers in a bottom dresser drawer, while two other girls are strewn across one of the beds.

"Ladies, meet Annabelle," says Martha. "This is Louise Haney."

A gangly copper-headed girl with bad posture sits up and says, "Hi!"

"And her roommate, Ethel Morgan," says Martha, gesturing to a prurient girl with long caramel waves, scarlet lipstick, and heavy mascara.

"Hello," murmurs Ethel.

"And this is my roommate, Betty Rice," says Martha, patting the cowering girl on her shoulder to get her attention.

"She and Eric already met," says Annabelle.

Betty simpers and sits on the other, unoccupied bed.

"Good one, Annabelle," I say, turning red.

"Where you from, Annabelle?" asks Martha.

"Chicago—Uncle Philo decided it was time I got a proper education."

"Good luck finding that here," scoffs Martha. "I've been trying to take chemical biology for three semesters and they're still not offering it for 'lack of interest.' We had better courses in high school!"

"Martha wants to be a doctor!" adds Louise.

"They told me I can take *Survey of Foods* instead, as that will 'quench my recreational interest in human health,'" she seethes. "Please."

"Damn," says Annabelle.

Martha draws back with a smirk-like wince.

"And what do you want to be?" Annabelle asks Louise.

"Oh, I don't know," says Louise. "I just want to get married."

"I'm glad you've come to terms with your potential," says Ethel flatly.

"And I'm glad we finally have a new hallmate who won't steal the emerald brooch Daddy gave me for Christmas!" shrieks Louise.

Ethel pantomimes a yawn.

Soon, Philo returns to the room so he and I can head back to the hotel, as he wants to read the newspaper and the dormitory is too loud. The next morning, Philo and I grab a light breakfast in Mount Cary before Sam drives us back to Shiner for the luncheon. We park the car and are instructed to walk to the gymnasium. There, we are greeted by two students wearing badges who direct us to our seats at a big round table. On one side, there are three name tags set up in a row: "Uncle Philo," "Annabelle," and "Male Guest."

Only a quarter of the seats in the gymnasium are occupied when Philo and I take our seats, but after a couple minutes pass, nearly all have bodies in them. Though a few other family members are in attendance, the room is predominantly populated with young women, some who look as young as fourteen. I continue to scan the room until I realize something: "Where's Annabelle?"

Miss Beulah stands on a small podium at the front of the room, thanks everyone for attending, and requests a warm reception for Shiner's president.

A man with a bushy mustache (and his jacket on) talks about the "special" past semester, then how "proud" he is of the students, before concluding with some general optimism. Partway through his speech, Annabelle her three new hallmates tiptoe into the gymnasium and sit at the empty seats next to the quiet girl, Betty. They are clearly trying to avoid causing a commotion but they are a seat short, and after several chair screeches and muffled howls Louise ends up sitting on Betty's lap. Fortunately, the president is extremely focused on his speech, for he doesn't bat an eyelash at their folly. Miss Beulah's eyes, on the other hand, are glued on the four giggling girls.

After the president's speech concludes, we are served lunch, which begins with sandwiches, and then cake. During the dessert, we are treated to a disorderly performance from the school's choral ensemble, before the luncheon concludes with Miss Beulah thanking everyone's attendance and extending an open invitation for afternoon tea. After Miss Beulah's dismissal, people start milling about, while Philo asks me to summon Annabelle to our table. He wants to say goodbye, and then leave, so I walk across the room to where she and her new friends are still working on their cake.

"Excuse me, girls" I say, clearing my throat, "But can I steal Annabelle for a minute? Uncle Philo wants to see you."

"What are you, his goddam page?" slurs Ethel.

I don't have a snappy comeback so I don't say anything.

"Ethel!" hisses Louise. "Don't talk like Annabelle!"

"Erikas is just being a good friend …" Annabelle smiles.

I smile back.

"…and we have been drinking champagne," she adds with a hiccup.

Ethel snorts.

"I think we're leaving now, Annabelle," I say. "He just wants to say goodbye."

"He can't wait until we're done eating?" snaps Martha.

"It's okay," says Annabelle, rolling her eyes to me as she props herself against the table to stand up. "I'll only be a moment."

Martha rolls her eyes, as well, and Annabelle subtly gestures toward her and mouths to me, "She's like this all the time ..."

"Nooo! Don't go, Anna-belly," whines Louise. "I know—let's go to the boys' dorm while the instructors are all in here!"

"Louise, this is an all-girls school," reminds Martha.

Ethel snorts again.

"Thanks for the input, girls, but Eric and I have a date with my uncle," says Annabelle, clutching my arm to help her walk straight to where Philo is sitting.

"Found her," I say.

"Eric and I are leaving," says Philo. "Do you remember which classes you're registering for?"

"I do so believe."

"And the clubs?"

"I do so believe."

"And you'll remember to write Eric if you need anything?"

"I do so b—"

"Answer me seriously, Annabelle," barks Philo.

She practically falls into me laughing. "Everything will be fine," she slurs as I hold her up.

"I sure hope so," says Philo skeptically. "Have a good semester—Eric, stop touching her and let's go."

6

CRASHERS & KEYS

On the drive back to Chicago, I ask Philo if he thinks having Annabelle at Shiner will erase what happened with the Christmas party, but he hushes me until we stop for gas and Sam is out of the car.

"The fellas won't tell anyone, the school thinks she's my niece, and Marie thinks she was your date to the party."

"But isn't the point of having the code and these rules that your wives don't find out?"

"John, Ed's father, and I made the rules to help idiots like Charlie Lords and Sid Reid from getting caught and bringing scandal to the club," says Philo firmly. "I'm not so recklessly in need of such discipline."

"Does John's wife know about these parties, too?"

"No, she doesn't."

"Well, doesn't Marie wonder why she wasn't invited to the party?"

"Marie's not my mistress and she knows I never bring anyone to one of the girlfriend parties," he explains. "And she wouldn't want to go, anyway, and find out who does."

"But why would *you* want to go?"

"Because someone needs to make sure the others follow the rules so we don't get another Sid Reid," says Philo irritably.

"But why would you *want* to go?"

Philo pauses. "… It's nice to look."

After a few weeks, I settle into life in the Olin household. When Philo's around, I spend far less time alone with Marie (though I am still every member of her audience while Philo is at work). I tag along with Philo a few times a week to grab dinner or drinks with the others in the founders' circle, usually at a stylish European restaurant or the Havens' Clubhouse in the Loop.

I also occupy a few hours a week earning pocket cash helping the Havens' mistresses with their tax forms. The idea came to John over "near-beer" at The Berghoff, and he initially offers up the clubhouse as a makeshift office.

"Meet them in a café," amends Philo. "We can't have those girls going in and out of the clubhouse, the wives might see. From you of all people, John—this is why I go to the parties, Eric."

On a Saturday in mid-February, Philo and Marie have invited me to the Havens' annual Valentine's Day party— one the wives always attend. While they are upstairs in their house getting ready, I hear Margaret answer an unexpected knock on the door.

"Is Uncle Philo in?" says a cool familiar voice.

I dart to the door and ask Margaret to fetch Philo.

"Just because you said please," quips the maid before heading upstairs.

"Annabelle, what are you doing here?" I say softly, mostly closing the door behind me.

"Hello, Erikas," she says, flanked by Martha, Ethel, and Louise. Martha holds up a suitcase.

"We were bored in Mount Cary, so Annabelle says, 'We should go to Chicago,'" says Louise, peering in, "so we did."

"We hitchhiked," says Martha with a disingenuous grin, stepping inside the entranceway and setting down the suitcase.

"You what!? How are you getting back?" I ask.

The three girls on the porch shrug with Annabelle adding an airy smile.

The steps creak as Philo and Margaret start to descend.

"Excuse me," I say to the girls. I rush past Margaret to meet Philo halfway up the stairs and hiss, "the girls are here."

Philo sees Martha in the doorway and his face drains to be as white as his hair. "Out," he says, pushing me and Martha outside to the porch and closing the door behind him.

"What are you doing here?" he growls.

"Uncle, are you upset with me?" mocks Annabelle.

"Yes, I'm upset with you! Why did you come here?"

"We were bored."

"Is that it?" says Philo, checking over his shoulder into the house.

"Yes."

Philo sighs. "Look, I'm happy to bring you to the City, but I need more notice than this. My wife—your *aunt*—is up there."

"We're not close," remarks Annabelle to her friends' furrowed expressions.

"I need to get ready for tonight."

"Are you going to a party?"

"Eric will entertain you and your friends," says Philo firmly. "I'll give him money."

"Can't we go with you?"

"No, you can't go."

"How will we get back to school?"

"We hitchhiked here," proudly adds Louise.

"You're taking the train back. I need my driver," says Philo, handing me a small stack of cash. "Eric—dinner, a show, and a room at the Congress."

"Very well," pouts Annabelle. "Erikas, are you ready?"

"Yes, I just need to shave."

"You're ready, Eric" corrects Philo. "Show these girls a good time, and then get them back to the hotel and on that train."

"He will—let's go," says Annabelle. "Goodbye, Uncle!"

The girls step off the porch and I start to follow, but Philo grabs me. "Keep them away from the Palmer House," he huffs. I nod.

We flag down a cab, cram in, and drive downtown. For dinner, I take us to the Atlantic, one of the few restaurants the fellas have taken me to whose entire menu I can pronounce. Ethel and Louise seem underwhelmed by my choice …

"I think it's humble and refreshing."

…but Annabelle seems to appreciate it.

When we get to our table, one of the waiters takes our jackets and we sit. Suddenly, Louise shrieks.

"I knew it! My emerald brooch, you thief!"

"Oh, this?" says Ethel casually. "I found it."

"That's a lie and you know it!"

"Now, ladies, loud voices have no place at the dinner table," says Annabelle wryly.

Louise harrumphs while Ethel folds her hands proudly.

"Is that something they taught you at school?" I ask.

The girls exchange knowing glances with each other.

"Oh, yes," says Annabelle, "Shiner Girls are known for their fine table etiquette."

"For example, one must refrain from fidgeting while waiting for their food," says Martha as Louise starts poking her napkin with her knife, causing her to blush.

"Gee, that reminds me of another one!" says Louise. She thinks for a moment, then recites, "Constantly dab your lips with the corner of your napkin, even if there isn't any lingering food."

"It's *demure*," adds Ethel.

"Oh, and you cock your eyebrow and tap your face if your dining partner has a speck of food on it!" says Louise.

Louise turns to Ethel, cocks her eyebrow, and taps the side of her mouth. Ethel, in response, picks up her napkin, dabs the side of her mouth, turns to Annabelle, cocks her eyebrow, and taps the middle of her chin. Annabelle then picks up her napkin, dabs the middle of her chin, turns to Martha, cocks her eyebrow, and taps her chest, just above her bosom. Martha smiles and shakes her head.

"That seems ... useful," I say, as Annabelle and Martha exchange absurd faces and unbridled giggling.

"Don't be fooled, Eric," scoffs Ethel. "Shiner is a laugh. They don't care how we act as long as they can keep up appearances."

"So don't show up hitchhiking," adds Annabelle.

"It's just an old ladies camp to please the man in charge," says Martha. "They don't bother preparing us for anything other than finding a husband."

"That's too bad," I frown.

"Don't sit there looking so dramatic," says Martha. "That's just how it is—and that's why we're here tonight."

"So let's get drunk and act wild!" exclaims Louise, playfully rocking into my side.

"Okay," I chuckle, "but I don't know how wild it will be—we're just going to a show."

"We will," assures Martha, draping her arm around my shoulder, "eventually."

Annabelle procures champagne from the headwaiter, who meets us behind the restaurant to hand over the bagged bottle, and we each take pulls from it in turn as we walk down bustling, shimmering State Street. Louise finishes it off just as we walk into the Chicago Theatre for a showing of *She Done Him Wrong* with the salacious Mae West and a newcomer named Cary Grant. Sufficiently corked, we almost get kicked out while still in the lobby after Ethel "accidentally" bumps into a ladder that causes the painter touching up the ceiling mural to streak an unbecoming red mustache over Apollo.

Unfortunately, the movie doesn't do much better to calm the girls, who grow increasingly comfortable with shouting their best Mae West-ian double-entendres at the screen.

"Haven't you ever met a lady that could ... tell your fortune?" drawls Annabelle as Grant's character tries to reform West's. She finishes her line by tickling my side, causing me to jump, then Louise to snort.

An usher finally asks us to leave when Louise won't stop jeering during a particularly dull musical number performed by a tenor with dreadfully curtained hair and a handlebar mustache.

Outside the theater, Ethel proposes we find more champagne, but Annabelle chimes in with another suggestion: "Let's be crashers at Uncle Philo's party!"

"Yeah, Eric," says Louise, "let's go to the party. You're supposed to be there anyway!"

"I'm sorry, girls," I say. "Philo didn't want you there—maybe we should just go to the hotel."

"So early?" blushes Annabelle, grabbing my arm. "My, my, Erikas …"

"We can't go to the hotel yet," protests Martha. "We don't have our belongings."

"What?" I say, distracted by Annabelle blowing kisses at me, which incites more giggling from Louise.

"I left our suitcase at Philo's," Martha explains.

"Fine," I sigh, reaching for my keys in my inner jacket pocket, "we'll stop by the house." I pause—my pocket's empty.

"Something the matter?" asks Ethel.

"M-my house keys—" I stammer, "they're missing!"

I can't get inside the house.

"Oh, damn," says Annabelle.

Philo let me into his home, trusted me with a key and his secrets ...

"We'll have to get a key from Uncle Philo then, won't we?" she adds, kicking a littered tin can into the street.

I barely know him—why would he put up with me when I can't even get these girls to their hotel?

I look around frantically, as if somewhere on the various glittering marquees surrounding us was plastered another solution.

"It's sure getting cold out here, isn't it girls?" says Annabelle, rubbing her arms. Four pairs of eyes are pouting dependently at me.

I'll beg him to let me stay—what pride do I have left anyway?

"Let's go to the party," I relent.

The girls all cheer and throw their arms around me— this part's not so bad, I must admit.

"Alright, let's go then," says Annabelle rather seriously. "I really am getting cold—can I borrow your jacket, Erikas?"

"Wait up!" I shout to the other girls who have already scampered ahead (and whom I have no faith in to know where they're going). "Of course," I say to Annabelle, handing her my jacket. "I should have offered."

Annabelle puts it on and inhales. "Smells good," she says.

I'm glad I gave her my jacket—I'm not cold at all.

Though the Palmer House is only three blocks away, the girls still manage to finish another bottle of champagne. Annabelle coaxed it out of a valet that we came across on his smoke break, which didn't seem to sit as well with Martha as it did the others.

After carrying Louise the last block so she doesn't fall on her face, stopping Ethel from tearing down every handbill she sees posted to the side of a building, and keeping Annabelle from greeting (and Martha from berating) every man that whistles as we pass by, we finally make it to the Palmer House—and the doorman won't let us in.

"But I'm actually supposed to be here," I explain. "I'm just late—you have to let us in!"

"What about your lady friends here, pal?"

"I'm his date," states Louise, still clinging to my side.

"Louise," hisses Martha, pointing to the rest of the girls.

"*We're* his dates," revises Louise.

"Aren't we a lucky lothario?" says the doorman dryly. "I can't let the five of you in at once—plus, you reek of booze. I'll lose my job."

The doorman retreats, the girls start to wander, and all I can think about is the disappointment on Philo's face.

He put me in his son's room and I let him down within a month ... Where will I live?

"Eric, where was your *date* before we got here?" inquires Louise.

I'm either a nearly-thirty-year-old dip moving back with his mother, or I'm eating my supper out of a used can of beans.

"Eric? What are you doing here?"

I turn around to find Ed Carmen walking toward us.

"Ed, I need your help."

"Well, can it wait?" he asks. "I'm about to give my toast."

"Eddy!" exclaims Annabelle.

"Eric," hisses Ed, leaning in, "the wives are here!"

The doorman returns and the girls swarm, teasing him and mocking his ire (and stifled temptation to flirt back).

"They showed up at Philo's house earlier and I was supposed to be entertaining them, but I lost my keys and they left their suitcase at the house—"

"It's alright," reassures Ed, "This isn't a disaster—yet— I may have a plan. I need one of the girls, though."

"Why?"

"Credibility. John asked where you were tonight, and Philo mentioned you were out with someone. Now let's see our options ..."

Ed takes a good look at the four girls, who we've managed to get in a somewhat orderly row. He starts with Louise, who raises her hand a bit too eagerly ... then Ethel, whose heavy makeup is starting to run … then Annabelle, who's sporting a knowing grin—

"Definitely not you," says Ed, clearly recalling Christmas.

… then Martha.

"You'll do," says Ed, grabbing Martha's hand, who mutters an oath under her breathe then grabs mine. "Just follow my lead—you three, stay."

The ballroom at the Palmer House is more proper than the Christmas party at the LaSalle. Music is still playing—I spot Felix concentrating on a solo—and people are still mingling, but there is an air of formality that was missing with the mistresses. There are also dozens of glowing plaster cherubs floating from the ceiling that utterly captivate Martha—or at least to provide a cover to point out that she's "only going along with this for Annabelle."

"There he is," says Ed, spotting Philo and company.

"… but he shot Cermak instead? I completely missed that part of the story," concludes John. "Ed, you're here! Aren't you toasting soon?"

"I am," says Ed carefully, "but I was practicing in the lobby and I ran into these two kids."

"Eric!" squeals Marie—Philo scowls at me. "What a nice surprise!"

"Hmm, yes," grumbles Philo, "a surprise, indeed."

"The new fella was on a date and decided to show her off," says Ed, ruffling my shoulder. "Isn't that right, Eric?"

"Yes, that's right," I say, looking sorrily at Martha, but she plays along nicely.

"Eric!" says Marie exasperatedly. "I didn't know you were seeing someone new! What's her name?"

I open my mouth hoping something clever will come out, but Martha saves me.

"It's Martha, and tonight is our first date. It's a pleasure to meet you, Mrs. ..."

"Please, dear, call me Marie."

Martha politely gushes.

"And this is my husband, Philo—I'm sure Eric has told you all about him, though."

"Oh, yes," replies Martha. "We were just at the show after dinner, and Eric mentioned he was missing a party tonight and I told him I wanted to come and ... well, Eric is such a gentleman ..."

"I just knew he would be!" beams Marie. "Just like his father. And here I was thinking Eric was too busy meeting up with a college friend."

"That's what he told me," says Philo through gritted teeth.

"Well, he didn't lie," says Martha. "I go to Shiner College in Mount Cary. Eric and I met a few weeks back when he was helping a friend move in and here we are today!"

"Was that Annabelle?" Marie asks Philo concernedly.

Philo nods.

"Oh, Eric, they probably know each other" tuts Marie sternly. "At any rate, dear, I'm still pleased to meet you. Oh! Tell me—is there a particular type of cake you're fond of?"

"Marie, let the young lady breathe," says John. "They haven't even met everyone yet. Here, I'd like you to meet my wife, Helen."

"Nice to meet you both," says a petite woman with a tight face framing two expressive sapphire eyes. Her sleek dark brown hair makes her look like she could be a magazine model—surprisingly, she is effortlessly more attractive than John's date from December.

"Philo," I start, noticing Philo's increasingly agitated fidgeting, "I have bad news—I lost my house keys and Martha's suitcase is there. I was wondering if you had a spare I could use to grab it so we could get her settled into her hotel for the night?"

"Eric," says Marie, impressed again. "Quite the gentleman—going to the house but taking her to a hotel …"

I smile.

"You know," Marie continues, "Eric is such a good house guest, he's never brought anyone around late … never once."

John raises his eyebrows at me and chuckles to himself.

"Lucky me," says Martha.

I can feel my ears turning red.

"I have an extra key somewhere," says Philo, rummaging through his pockets.

"We better get the locks changed tomorrow, Philo," says Marie, "just in case someone picks up Eric's key. Remember to call the locksmith."

Philo grunts as he hands me the key. As I grab it I spot Ethel and Louise wandering about the opposite end of the ballroom. Philo notes my widened eyes, cocks his eyebrow, and jerks his head in their direction as if to say, "get them out of here!"

"Well," I say tensely, "it was great seeing everyone, but we should get going."

I pull Martha away as she manages to get out a quick "Bye!" We're off, but I still faintly hear Marie mutter, "I can't believe he's dating her classmate ..."

"Eric, don't pull me," says Martha firmly, as we weave around conversations to snatch hold of Ethel and Louise. "Now what's going on?"

"Your friends are loose!"

I lose sight of Ethel and Louise for a moment, but Martha spots them almost as instantaneously. "Over there!" she says. "Getting hors d'oeuvres!" With a final dart past Paul Jaeger, Daniel Kruger, and their wives, we catch the snacking schoolgirls.

"What are you doing in here?" I snap.

Distracted by deviled eggs, it takes them a moment to notice us, but Louise eventually looks up and says, "Oh, hi, Eric."

"Girls, I think we should go," says Martha.

"Martha, you have to try these," says Ethel through a full mouth. Her scarlet lipstick is now smeared across her cheeks from sloppy egg-eating. "They're really good!"

"I'm sure they are," says Martha patiently. "Where's Annabelle?"

"She was talking to a man outside," says Louise, taking another bite. "Seemed rather crude, but he was driving a limo ... she got in and they left."

Martha and I both shout *"What!?"*

"I know, I can't believe none of these men are paying attention to us," pouts Louise. "Are we forgetting a rule?"

"It shouldn't matter, we're so much younger and prettier than these women," Ethel adds.

"I can't believe she took off like that," says Martha as I shake my head in agreement.

7

REGULAR LETTERS

I climb into bed prepared to stare at the ceiling until Philo decides to barge in and kick me out. He's fed me and clothed me for weeks, and all he's asked of me in return is to keep four girls entertained for an evening—and he even paid for that—but I let him down and then some.

What if Annabelle never made it to the hotel? What if she really did stay out all night with another man—what if it was Coppock?

I shudder.

There's a gentle rapping on my window. I'm alert. It happens again, and louder. I get up. I peer around the curtains but hear a sharp, sudden creak and recoil before I see what's outside. I hear a door close on the second floor above me.

"It's only Philo," I say to myself.

I pull back the curtains more this time and see two big brown eyes staring up at me.

"Annabelle!"

"What?" she mouths silently on the other side of the glass.

I thrust open the heavy window. "What are you doing here?"

Annabelle holds up my suit jacket, her teeth chattering as she says, "I needed to return something."

"Get in here," I say, taking my jacket then helping Annabelle into my bedroom, "you must be frozen out there."

"Oh, thank God, a bed," says Annabelle, stripping down to her brassiere and knickers, then jumping under the covers. I lay down my jacket and start to put on a pair of trousers to cover my flannel drawers. "Don't bother," she says, "just come here and warm me up."

I let my trousers fall back to the floor.

"Wait!" she hisses. "Lock the door—Philo can't know I'm here."

I lock the door then join Annabelle in bed. She smells so distinct … like smoky, spicy vanilla.

"Warm me up," she says, rolling into my side and placing a hand on my chest. I struggle to move my left arm around her but eventually get it comfortably beneath her shoulder.

"We were all so worried about you, not knowing where you were."

"I'm here," she says with her eyes closed. Her eyelashes rest beautifully against her smooth cheeks.

"Well, earlier," I clarify. "Louise said you went with some man."

"It's so cold outside," she shivers, sliding closer to me. "The girls made it back to the hotel?"

Her breathing slows and grows heavy, and I can feel her gaining comfort by the moment—*She's safe now* ...

"Yes, and we grabbed Martha's suitcase before dropping them at the Congress. I'm going to pick them up from the lobby in the morning then take them to the train station."

Her head nuzzles my chest, coming to rest in the perfect spot, and my eyes weaken.

"You're so caring," she murmurs, practically asleep, "Good night, Erikas."

The floor above me creaks again, and I wait until another door closes.

"Good night, Annabelle."

Smoky, spicy vanilla ...

The next morning, I wake to Annabelle shaking my side.

"Eric, get up," she says as I wipe my eyes. "I just heard Philo in the kitchen. We need to get out of here before he finds us."

We throw on our clothes and Annabelle waits in the room as I tiptoe out. The kitchen is clear so I creep into the empty parlor, beckoning Annabelle to follow. I continue to shuffle out toward the dark front porch and carefully open the door, with Annabelle not far behind.

"Good morning, Eric," says Philo plainly, seated on a wicker chair with his face buried in the newspaper. I hear the remnants of a shuffled retreat as I pull the door shut.

"Good morning," I say, squeezing the new hat he bought me. "You're up early on a weekend. Aren't you cold out here?"

"My body wanted to sleep in," he says, "and cold air wakes it up. Where are you headed?"

I glance back in the house to see where Annabelle went, but don't see her.

"I was on my way to take Annabelle and her friends to the train station," I say. I pause to reconsider my next words. "Don't you want to read upstairs in your room? You seem awake now and heat rises you know."

"I know heat rises, Eric ... and who reads in their room?"

Just then, I see Annabelle's head pop out from behind the side of the house, and she gives me a tiny wave.

"I read in my room," I continue.

"That's because you're not comfortable enough in my house yet to read on the porch."

"I'm not uncomfortable ..."

Annabelle scurries down the sidewalk, then turns and waves again when she's safely a few houses away.

"... but I am getting cold, and don't want to be late."

"Go—and get them back safe, Eric."

I jog to catch up with Annabelle and we take the 'L' into the Loop, from where we must walk a few more blocks to get to the Congress Hotel.

Annabelle takes a deep breath of the crisp morning air, and sighs, "That was so great last night …"

And waking up next to her was even more divine—until the panic of being discovered by Philo set in.

I hope my sheets still smell of vanilla.

"… I miss being around people at night. It's too quiet and rural at school—gives me the creeps."

"Oh, right," I say. "I suppose you're just a city girl at heart."

"Must be why I moved here in the first place," she admits. "Ah, that was the best sleep I've had in weeks …"

We walk up to the hotel where Martha, Ethel, and Louise are waiting for us with bags under their eyes.

"Why the tired faces, ladies?" chirps Annabelle.

"I hate this hotel," crabs Ethel.

"We didn't sleep a wink, Anna-belly," adds Louise.

"Oh, that is a shame," laments Annabelle.

"Can we just grab a cab and go?" says Martha, slugging her suitcase toward the door.

"It's too bad I missed staying here," comments Annabelle, peering around the lobby as her friends trudge ahead like zombies, "this place looks really nice."

We arrive at Union Station appropriately early for the girls' train back to Mount Cary. Annabelle, still the only one with any energy, is the first to board.

"Goodbye, Erikas," says Annabelle, politely kissing me on the cheek. "I had a lovely evening—I won't tell Philo if you won't," she winks.

I smirk.

The other girls follow her in a disoriented row, each humming "Bye" as I help Louise and (offer to help) Martha into the car. I offer my hand to Ethel last when a cold, hard object plops in my hand. I look down and see my house keys. I look up—Ethel simpers and apologizes …

"Sorry, but I'm too tired to make a smart comment."

… in a way.

The train departs and I take the "L" back to Hyde Park. Back in the house, Philo is seated alone at the table. Margaret has arrived for the day and he is finishing a cup of coffee while still nestled into the newspaper. I sit down across from him and Margaret places a plate of eggs and sausage in front of me.

"The girls are on their way back to Mount Cary," I say.

Philo turns the page, and without looking up, says, "Margaret, go upstairs and draw Mrs. Olin a bath."

"With pleasure, Mr. Olin."

When Margaret is out of the room Philo finally puts down his newspaper. "Did you have fun last night, Eric?"

The door to my room just off the kitchen is open and I peer into it. My sheets are still ruffled.

Vanilla ...

"Yes, I did."

"Because I didn't. I cannot believe they showed up to the Palmer House ... drunk, no less! I bet Annabelle was most gone of all, wasn't she?"

"Oh no," I say quickly, "she was definitely all there."

"That so?" questions Philo. "Because, a blessing and a curse, I don't remember seeing her."

"She was there," I lie, "she was just waiting in the lobby ... she knew you wouldn't want her there. But her friends—"

"Eric, I told you to keep those girls away from the party last night and you let me down."

"I know, sir," I say. "I'm sorry."

Here it comes.

"I couldn't have been clearer, Eric—after all I've given you, I thought I could trust you with this one simple task."

I'm gone.

"It's best that I move out," I say.

At least I have new shoes and a hat to last me through winter ...

"Eric, what are you talking about?"

"I let you down, and don't deserve your hospitality."

"Eric, cut the dramatic nonsense," says Philo, picking up his paper again. "You let me down, but I don't want you out of here. I just wish you understood the importance of what I asked of you last night."

"To keep Annabelle away?"

"To keep Annabelle in Mount Cary until she's properly socialized. She should know better than to drop in unannounced—it doesn't look good."

"In her defense, I think she's bored there. You saw the town ..."

"You have a point," he says, adjusting his glasses. "The occasional weekend in Chicago could be arranged ... and you could take her and her friends around, of course."

There can be more nights like the last ...

"But until then, I'd like you to write to her regularly," Philo continues. "Ask her about school and how she's spending her time—get her invested in her life there."

"...Sure."

"Once a week, Eric, and keep me updated on what she says. If all goes well, we can bring her to Chicago sometime. Can you do that?"

I nod, but then almost immediately feel reason to pause—what if I don't want to report back what she writes? It feels like a betrayal of her trust to share what she believes is a private conversation between us.

I could write her twice a week and only share one with Philo.

I decide to table that decision until we come to that bridge. For now, I need to get started on my first letter: *"Dear Annabelle ..."*

Over the next few months I meticulously follow Philo's orders, writing to Annabelle at least once a week, and getting prompt replies like—

"French class is going wonderfully. This week we learned how to do le breaststroke kick, and next week, Martha and I are taking the train into Davenport to practice speaking with a guy who makes his own moonshine. Bon appétit!"

As with most of my life, my letters center around the Havens, especially when there's a party. Annabelle is particularly keen on the one Ed hosted at the Allerton Hotel in March. While the St. Patrick's Day theme (Wendy's part-Irish) was initially mocked by some of the fellas for being "lower-class," Ed impressed everybody with the incredible bagpipers and dancers he hired.

"I hope you were watching the dancers closely, Erikas," Annabelle writes back, *"Irish I could come up with a better punch line, though."*

"Looking for a better punch line, you say?" I write back. *"Don't ask Andrew Coppock, because he already threw his best one starting a fight when the bartender refused to overserve him!"*

"He doesn't scare me. I took him once I can take him again."

I also tell her about Herb Galloway's April garden party that was unfortunately rained out. Once everyone moved indoors, the party itself was rather forgettable. I only bring it up because at one point John referred to himself as "The Mattress," a detail I decide needs to be shared with

Annabelle the next time we meet in-person—whenever Philo decides that will be.

With the Havens, the buzzy topic of late has been the upcoming World's Fair, which is opening in late May. Beyond the enticement of the theme, "A Century of Progress," many of the Havens' have a professional stake in the fair. Herb Galloway is the primary cultural consultant for one of the historical exhibits; Charlie's and Ed's companies are involved in the home-building and automobile exhibits, respectively; and Olin Crane & Shovel is involved in the fairgrounds construction, where Philo has placed Andrew Coppock in a superficial field manager role to "get him out of the office and away from me for a few weeks."

"If you can only get one extra ticket, Erikas, know that I can keep a secret!"

I also chronicle Marie's unflappable infatuation with my faux relationship with Martha. While we bake cakes, after Philo Jr.'s book, Marie's favorite topic of conversation is "that spirited girl, Martha." Whenever Marie asks when I'm going to bring her around again, I say, "She's studying French."

"Oh, Eric, you're so funny!"

What I don't tell Annabelle about, however, is the Olins' relationship. My days with Marie are friendly and cordial, and my nights with Philo are pleasant, too—but they'd be so much better if Marie ever joined.

Since the day I met Philo and he first told me of his marital problems, I had been waiting for Marie's "true colors" to shine, but she's been nothing but lovely to me and devoted to her husband. Then Valentine's Day came, and ever since she's been coming up with excuses for every one of his invitations. She bakes cakes with me, goes to bridge on Wednesdays, and leaves the room when Philo enters.

I wonder what she tells her bridge friends about her marriage ...

"I don't know what I did," exclaims Philo one morning after Marie silently shoves a piece of cake in front of him and walks away.

I shake my head in support, but privately wonder if Marie learned the truth about Annabelle. She's talked about her in the past, and seemed fine with Philo paying tuition for my "Christmas date"—though, I can't help but wonder if she caught a glimpse of Annabelle at the Palmer House, or heard her with me in her mother's room ... that certainly would muddy our explanation of her, and I couldn't blame Marie for being mad.

She finally agrees to come to the Havens' annual Mother's Day luncheon at Helen Mattingly's urging, but cancels the night before because of "Not wanting to go anymore." I can see Philo's fury in his eyes, and the entire Olin household goes to bed early. These are the nights I feel most foreign in this house. Then, as I'm getting ready to turn off the light for the night, Philo wants to talk.

"I'm sorry we keep putting you at the middle of this," he says from the doorway. "It isn't fair that you're here at our worst."

"It's fine."

"It isn't," urges Philo, shaking his head then running his hand over the flowery wallpaper. "It's been two years since Marie's mother died, and she still hasn't forgiven me."

Philo removes his glasses and rubs his eyes.

"Forgive you for what?" I ask slowly.

Philo sighs, then says, "It's funny how different our reactions to death can be."

I try not to think about my father.

"I remember being angry with your mother for having a closed funeral for your dad," Philo continues, staring at the floor, then cracks a smile. "As if I had a say!"

I wonder if he knows that was actually my request …

"Well, I didn't shed a tear at her mother's funeral," he admits. "I suppose I put more value on being a father to my children who had just lost their grandmother, or husband to my grieving wife, but I could not cry. … She never forgave me for that."

The last conversation with my father was an argument about me moving to Chicago …

"To Marie, her mother's funeral was yesterday," says Philo, moving from the doorway to sitting beside me on the bed. "I've tried to help her cope, but she refuses to let me. Our children are grown and living on their own, and I thought bringing you here would give her the distraction she's been needing—"

"She seems happy to me," I interject woefully.

"She compartmentalizes her time with you," he explains. "With me, well, that funeral never ended, and I'm still dry-eyed.

"As a husband, it's hard to accept that you don't have the same emotional impact on your wife as her mother, but I'm not ready to give up. Let's go to that luncheon tomorrow, Eric, just you and I—and if anyone asks about Marie we'll tell them she's in Florida. What do you say?"

...I miss you.

I don't put any of that in the letters, either.

Philo and I are among the first to arrive the next day at the luncheon. After we are greeted by the day's party hosts, John and Helen Mattingly, they immediately inquire on Marie.

"She's in Florida," I say.

"That's a shame she had to go again this weekend," laments Helen. "I suppose the warm air is good for her back."

Philo and I exchange glances.

Dozens of other Havens with their wives and mothers trickle in throughout the morning. We mingle until the lunch bell rings and we take our seats. I am placed between Philo and Winnie Carmen, Ed's plump wife, whose blond hair, blue eyes, and the general idea of her figure are reasonably attractive—even somewhat reminiscent of Wendy, but with far less confidence.

"Winnie, how is Little Ed these days?" asks Helen.

"He's fine," sighs Winnie, covering her belly with folded hands. "My sister is watching him this afternoon."

"I hope she can handle that boy!" says Ed excitedly. "Every day he's getting into something new. I already got him throwing the baseball around—nearly took my ear off the other day!"

Ed jerks, pantomiming getting hit with a fastball, eliciting laughter from table, especially his mother, Patsy Carmen. Winnie even snorts, then immediately covers her mouth with her napkin.

"What's everyone laughing at? Not my Pearl, I hope," says Charlie, taking the last empty seat at the table. "She's not even here to defend herself."

"Making your wife watch your daughters on Mother's Day," glares Ed. "You're a class act, Charlie, you know that?"

"Hey, mother's duties never take a break, do they?" Charlie playfully nudges Winnie, who winces.

"Are you sure he's related to us?" says Ed to his mother, who rolls her eyes at her nephew.

"I'm glad you made it, Charlie," says John. "I wanted to talk to you about the World's Fair."

"Aunt Patsy, my company put me on their exhibit committee for the fair," explains Charlie proudly.

"I think it's that time girls," says Helen to Winnie and Patsy. "We can let the boys discuss business—I saw them cutting the cake, anyway. Let's grab a piece before they're all gone. Philo, we'll save a piece to take home for Marie, okay?"

Philo smiles and nods.

"That's nice, sweat pea," says John warmly as the women leave. "Alright fellas, let's get a group together."

"I can get opening night passes from work," says Charlie.

"Perfect," says John. "Now, Helen doesn't like the opening night crowds, so what do you say we bring some girls along? Just imagine how excited they'll be with all the lights and sounds—the possibilities are endless."

"I don't know," says Charlie. "Audrey has been really busy lately—why don't we just have a guys' night?"

"Are you homosexual, Charlie?" scowls John. "Guys' night on opening night? Hey, young fella, you still talking to those college girls?"

I look to Philo for approval. He nods. So do I.

"Yeah, that brunette you were with and Philo's redhead … they sure are something," grins John. "Why don't you see if they have a few friends for the rest of us."

I struggle to read Philo's reaction, so I say, "I can see if they're up for it."

"Why wouldn't they be?" implores John. "The pale moonlight, sweet music, the dishes love that stuff! Tell him, Philo."

Philo said he'd bring Annabelle to Chicago, but it's been nearly three months since our night together …

Philo thinks for a second then grumbles, "Alright, they can come. The end of their semester is coming up, this can be their treat. But I can't go—Eric will take care of them."

"Can't go?" implores John.

"Dinner with Philo Jr.," boasts Philo. "He and Edie just signed with a publisher."

"That's great for Philo Jr., but it's your loss, my friend," shrugs John, then turning to me. "Back to that brunette—you still seeing her?"

"Well, no, not really," I say.

"Great! Then, she's mine. I know Charlie's in—Ed?"

"Sorry gentlemen, but I already made plans to go with …" starts Ed, looking around before mouthing, "*Wendy.*"

"Unbelievable," spouts John. "It's like you're married to the broad."

"John!" snaps Philo.

"Calm yourself, people," says John. "The wives are on the other side of the room. Either way, we'll see you there, Ed—Eric, we're counting on you for these girls."

The next day, after reaffirming Philo's permission, I write Annabelle, inviting her to the opening night.

"We'd love to, Eric! The girls and I are tickled about the World's Fair! Count all five of us in, including Betty!"

8

CENTURY OF PROGRESS

"**S**he was afraid to come?"

"Yes, Eric," says Martha patiently. "Betty isn't fond of crowds, and she read in the paper that they're expecting thirty-thousand tonight, so she stayed back at Shiner."

"That's Betty for you," says Ethel to Louise.

"Bug-eyed Betty!" adds Louise.

"Lay off," scolds Martha.

"Where are the other gentlemen?" asks Annabelle.

"Maybe Eric's played a trick to get four girls to himself again," says Louise.

"Eric, you hound," purrs Ethel.

"He's not your date, girls," scolds Annabelle. "Please don't be familiar with Eric without Martha's permission."

"Are you going to be this way the entire night?" Ethel scoffs.

Annabelle proudly nods.

"She's been using 'Shiner speak' since we boarded the train," explains Martha. "It drives Ethel nuts."

I chuckle, "You'll be pleased to hear the other fellas will be joining us at the fairgrounds' gate," I say in my best radio voice, responding to Annabelle's original question.

"How lovely," she replies with a petite clap.

"Isn't it?" mocks Ethel. "Now, can we go? We still need to stop at the hotel, and I want to get to the Fair before dark."

Despite some protest about Philo booking the Congress Hotel for them to stay the night— "Not that place again," complains Louise, "it's drafty and reeks of rotten eggs."— we drop the girls' belongings at the hotel and they freshen up. From there, we walk to the Burnham Park fairgrounds near the lakefront, where John and Charlie are waiting for us just outside the north entrance.

"Tell me, what's your name again, darling?" says John to Martha, blowing past my outstretched hand and wrapping his arm around her shoulder. "I know I've seen those pretty brown eyes before."

"It's Martha, thanks," she says tersely, nudging John's arm away. She turns to Annabelle, "I thought Eric was my date."

"You've been upgraded, my dear," boasts John, coaxing his elbow around Martha's arm—Martha glares at Annabelle as Charlie pairs up with Ethel.

"Gee, Anna-belly, I guess we'll have to fight over who gets Eric," says Louise.

"Why fight?" replies Annabelle. "I say we embrace it—Erikas, have you ever had a *ménage à trois?"*

There's no vanilla tonight.

"Can we go inside already?" pleads Ethel, already fed up with her date.

"Oh, you've got a live one, Charlie," says John. "Although, I must agree—let's go to the Fair!"

We step into the fairgrounds, and are as soon greeted by a stunning structure of blue and yellow, boldly assembled around a bright silver entrance. Entranced, our feet guide us down a long, crowded boulevard lined with hundreds of billowing red banners the size of boats. Amidst our gasps and awe, I see why John considered this the perfect place to bring a date—and here we are: John with Martha ... Charlie with Ethel ... me with Annabelle—and Louise.

To our immediate right so looms the Illinois Building, a noble seven-story tower of silver and gold that Philo's company helped construct. To our left is a large lagoon, where eager fairgoers dressed in their finest clothes return to their cheerful, problem-free adolescence while they marvel across the water at the impressive, tri-fluted towers glowing over a tangerine dome.

"It really is a Rainbow City," swoons Louise.

After the initial impression subsides, Martha suggests we check out the Hall of Science. Alas, we end up on the "Sky Ride"—an aerial gondola that transports us to the other end of the lagoon, offering a thrilling view of the fairgrounds hundreds of feet above the water.

Once we return to the ground, we head south along a second lagoon until we reach the colorful, multi-exhibit *Midway*. Here, we walk past areas called *The Belgian Village*, which features medieval milkmaids driving real dog-pulled milk carts, and *The Streets of Paris*, where Annabelle and I share a culpable glance.

"Shall we?" I suggest.

"*Non merci,*" she says, causing us both to snort and grin.

"Huh?" says Louise.

In *The Oriental Village* we are greeted by several exotic beauties shaking their bare torsos to a mesmerizing rhythm. The girls convince Charlie to pay for camel rides, but after only a few trots around the dusty compound, Annabelle's the only one who seems at all comfortable bouncing atop the humped creatures.

"This is such a lovely evening, wouldn't you say?" taunts Annabelle, sitting with perfect posture and both legs to one side of the saddle. She is directly facing Ethel, who huffs at Annabelle, while clinging for dear life to her camel's neck.

"Those are some nice gloves," remarks John as he helps Martha down from her camel. "What's embroidered on them? A chick?" he says, brazenly nudging Charlie and me.

"A mockingbird," says Martha bluntly.

Next, we visit *The Midget Village*. The girls want to see the Lilliputians, like the ones in *Gulliver's Travels*, which they heard about in their *Survey of English Literature* class.

"I wonder if they're going to ask us to make the Paris exhibit a province of *The Midget Village*," jokes Martha as one of the Lilliputians offers her a plastic tulip.

"I sure hope not," says a new voice from behind us. "There's no way the French could afford the Lilliputian tax structure."

"Ed!" exclaims Charlie to his cousin as he saunters up to our group, looking especially satisfied to have Wendy by his side.

"How's everyone doing tonight?" says Ed, looking over our couplings.

"Marvelous, how about you, Ed?" says John.

"Oh, I'm dancing in the street."

"Well, I'm not," says Wendy. "These little people give me the heebie-jeebies."

"That's Wendy," I say to the girls. "Ed's girlfriend."

"Girlfriend?" mouths Martha, alternating pointing at her ring finger and Ed.

"I know they do, sweetheart, says Ed, "we'll get out of here soon. It's almost nine, and we should probably get going for the opening ceremony, anyhow. I hear the Hall of Science is the place to be."

"See, doll? We're going to go to your science building after all," says John.

"Gee, thanks," mutters Martha, once again shaking away John's wandering arm.

We pack ourselves into the Hall of Science courtyard like canned sardines and listen to the opening remarks over the loudspeakers. Among the bustling crowd, however, we can barely discern what's happening when a sudden blast ignites the lakefront—the crowd roars as the fairgrounds are entirely illuminated beyond our imaginations. After a punctuating fireworks display to close formal ceremony, our group heads back to *The Midway* to take in the late night showing of Sally Rand's "fan dance" at *The Streets of Paris*.

"*Non merci,*" I say to Annabelle as we approach the club, but she doesn't hear me.

The passes Charlie has procured for us allow us to skip the line so we can take our seats before the general public. While waiting for the show to start, John asks Martha to switch seats with Louise, but Martha refuses, so John and I switch seats so that John is sitting between Annabelle and Louise, and I'm between Charlie and Martha.

"Oh! Are we switching?" blurts Ethel, motioning to Martha.

Martha shakes her head.

"Please!" Ethel pleads while Charlie pretends not to notice.

Martha relents and switches with Ethel so that now Ethel is between me and Ed, and Martha is between Charlie and Annabelle.

"It's like a carousel," says Annabelle pleasantly.

When the show is about the start, the house lights dim, and the crowd falls silent until the orchestra strikes its first note. Then, a shapely blond woman takes the stage wielding a pair of white, man-sized ostrich feathers, which sway in every direction while she glides across the stage like a fairy. At one point, she strides behind a backlit screen curtain where she appears to disrobe, before coming back to the stage and twirling the feathers in front of her more womanly features. With every male hoot at her teasing, Martha's scowl tightens until she finally stands up and leaves—I slide into Martha's vacated seat to be next to Annabelle for the remainder of the show.

"I definitely saw her bubs up there," delights John with a stupid grin on his face as we're walking from the theater.

"Not a chance," says Ed. "She was wearing a leotard; they wouldn't let her go nude—not that I'm complaining either way!"

"I thought the whole show was offensive," injects Martha, as she joins back up with us.

"Aren't you a cute little suffragette?" says John to Martha as he rubs Louise on the small of her back.

Martha's eyes burn.

"I'm with you," says Charlie, hesitating to follow John's lead by placing his hand on Martha. "She shouldn't have to do a sexy dance for her money."

"I was talking about you and every other man in there!" snaps Martha, slapping away Charlie's hand with a sharp glare. "Sally Rand has every right to do what she pleases without every man and his ego whistling at her like a dog."

"It's okay, honey," soothes Wendy, "It's only Charlie. There's no need to get riled."

Ethel and Louise exchange nervous glances.

"No, we should get riled," urges Martha. "Why did we decide to stop talking about these things?"

Annabelle elbows my side and whispers, "Like I said—she's like this *all* the time."

"Hey, now," Ed steps in. "Where's that calm, cool girl from the Valentine's party?"

"I don't know," says Martha, wagging her ring finger at Ed. "Maybe she's with your wife."

Ed's smile vanishes.

"Don't do that," says Wendy firmly. "You're all worked up about a woman you know nothing about—don't you attack a man you know nothing about, either."

The rest of us march swiftly ahead to avoid getting sucked into what has as quickly become a shouting match. While John continues to get close to Louise, and Ethel sulks about being stuck with Charlie again, I try to talk to Annabelle—

"Shh, I want to listen."

—but am unable to draw her attention away from Martha and Ed's debate a few steps behind us.

"... You're right, I don't know how she ended up on that stage," says Martha, "but I refuse to support all the men in there who left their wives at home to watch their kids so they can slobber over Sally Rand like a free steak."

This second dig on Ed's extramarital activities is too much for Wendy, who storms ahead of her date and

Martha, closer to the rest of us—the argument doesn't skip a beat.

"Like Wendy said, you don't know anything about anybody in there!" counters Ed. "Now you're just gossiping."

"Because women's issues are gossip? We're in an economic depression and you think I'm here to gossip—I speak from daily experience, Ed."

Wendy saddles up next to Annabelle and me as we approach the fairgrounds' exit. "How's your night going?" she asks shakily. "Better than mine, I hope …"

But it's hard to concentrate on anything else, as Martha is really going off now, her growing volume now making her impossible to ignore.

"… Women have been completely forgotten in all this," Martha continues. "It's impossible for us to have real careers because everything's about creating more jobs for men."

"You're right, women shouldn't be forgotten," says Ed, clearly trying to deescalate. "Women are incredible, and America needs such a civilizing force more than ever these days."

Martha throws her hands straight up into the air. "You're missing the point entirely!"

"I'm trying to agree with you, but you just want to argue!"

"Hey, Lincoln! Douglas!" shouts John as the rest of us stop at the exit. "You going to put down your spears and say goodbye, or should we see if NBC wants to broadcast you?"

"No, we're done," says Ed, breaking eye contact with Martha, then catching up to Wendy.

"Just in time, Ed," teases John. "Your first date was starting to get jealous."

"You're a big help, John."

"Well, everyone, it was a great evening, but Lou and I are headed off now," says John, pulling giggling Louise to his side. "Charlie, do you want to ride with us?"

Charlie turns to Martha. "I know we didn't get a chance to talk much, but—"

"Not a chance," says Martha coldly.

"Charlie?" repeats John.

"Yes, I'm coming."

After the fellas and their remaining dates depart in John's limousine, I walk the girls back to the Congress. Despite Ethel's and Martha's sour presence, I try once more to talk to Annabelle before she goes up to her state room.

"So, what did you think of tonight?" I ask.

"It was a nice evening," says Annabelle. "Though I was disappointed they didn't have a *Lithuanian Village*."

I laugh. "Yeah, that—"

"It was some evening, alright," says Ethel caustically. "At least the only thing we lost this time was Louise's dignity, isn't that right, Eric?"

I harrumph—*I have nothing more to say to her.*

"I do hope Louise remembers to act like a lady with Mr. Mattingly," says Annabelle properly, getting under Ethel's skin as if she knew that's what I needed. "Then again, love is a sneaky devil. One never knows where she's lurking ..."

"And here we are at the Congress," sighs Martha as we arrive at the hotel. "There couldn't be a more fitting end to the night. Wish us luck, Eric. Oh, and next time you and your dirty friends want to invite us to Chicago—"

"Yes?"

"Don't."

"Okay," I say sheepishly. "Good night."

After a deep breath, Martha enters the hotel, followed by Ethel—who again drops my house keys in my hand. Annabelle has stayed back, however, and is staring up at the sky.

"It really was a nice evening, don't you think?" she says breezily. "It's always good to be back in Chicago."

"I really enjoyed seeing you," I say. "Too bad I had to share you most of the night. I suppose that's better than what Martha and Ethel had to go through ..."

Annabelle looks me straight in the eyes. "You were a lovely date, Eric."

Then the world moves at half-speed as her warm, crimson lips softly press against mine.

9

PARLOR GAMES

"All that for a Chick," groans John, then stuffing a sausage in his mouth.

"I don't think the Reds gave that much up to get Chick Hafey," grumbles Philo, "but he's still a bum."

"That bum's still the only Cincinnati Red we'll see," points out Ed, "if we ever finish eating and go to this game."

Through work, Ed got us tickets for a special "All-Star" baseball game at Comiskey Park, held alongside the World's Fair, and featuring the best baseball players from across the country. Ed's been trying to hurry us along throughout breakfast, but John and Philo have been stalling, probably to avoid having to go outside in this scorching July sun.

"Speaking of chicks, how about that Romanian broad with me at the party last weekend?" says John.

"She was great, John," says Philo.

"I was going to invite Gigi again, but when I was with Helen at the *Old Mexico* exhibit last Saturday I caught her making eyes at me," continues John. "Slipped her Mack's number and we met at the party that night."

"Come on, John, have a little discretion," urges Ed. "We're in public, you know the rules."

"When have we ever followed the rules, Ed?" inquires John. "It's just the fellas, it's okay."

"I think you ought to take it easy, that's all."

"I'm not Sid Reid over here, screwing up and getting caught, I'm a pro—hell, I'm an All-Star!"

"John's our Chick Hafey, Ed," adds Charlie. "He's 'The Mattress!'"

"More like Babe Ruth," continues John. "Man wasn't meant to be monogamous. You should know that better than anybody, Eddy."

Ed bites his tongue.

"You know you've had a real stick up your ass ever since this Fair started, Ed," says John.

"Yeah, well," starts Ed sharply, "I've just been thinking."

"What kind of thinking?" says Philo, adjusting his glasses.

All eyes turn on Ed.

"Nothing like that, fellas," clarifies Ed. "You know I've been a Haven since I was a kid. I've just been thinking about Winnie lately—how she used to be so different before Little Ed came along … she's such a great mother, I just wish she could be a great wife again, too."

"It's alright, Ed," consoles Charlie, "it took Pearl awhile to come back around after she had our kids. That's why you have Wendy."

"I just wish she'd do something about it—join an athletic club, or go for a walk," continues Ed, "but I can't get her motivated to do anything. It's like I took that from her …"

"Well, Ed," says Philo, tossing his napkin over his plate, "I think you've convinced me to go to the game."

"I'll get the check," agrees John.

Ed wipes some sweat from his forehead with his napkin, then tosses it on the table. Avoiding all eye contact, he's the first to rise.

"So, what did you fellas think of that girl I brought last week?" says Charlie proudly.

"Shut up, Charlie," says Ed.

At the game, even John is thoughtful enough to steer all conversation away from Ed's personal life and focused on the game. Still, I question my inclination to pity Ed, even with his earlier outburst.

The Havens' lifestyles are nothing like I've ever seen before—then again, so is the current economic landscape, and I am certainly benefitting from the revolving door of clients their mistresses provide for my advisory services. After eight months with the Havens, I have nearly daily appointments their girlfriends, leaving hardly any time to help Marie with her cakes anymore. Even better, since tax season has passed, my sessions have moved from tax preparation into the daunting frontier of wealth management.

"Sorry, but what is the difference between preferred and common stock again?" asks Wendy.

"Basically, preferred stockholders have an earlier claim on their shares than those with common stock."

"So, I will get more of Ed's money?"

"Typically, yes," I respond slowly, "but not necessarily."

"I'm joking, Eric!" she grins. "Ed takes good care of me already—I just want to impress him."

I even offer to help Annabelle. In one of my letters I suggest she comes to Chicago for an in-person session; unfortunately, since she started Shiner in the middle of the academic year she is stuck in Mount Cary in summer school … *"But I'd love a private session once I get a break from all these makeup classes!"*

Since Valentine's Day, even though the only time Philo brought Annabelle to Chicago was for the World's Fair opening, we have both kept up with our weekly letter to each other. Her letters always suggested relative indifference toward Shiner, but when her friends started making plans to head home after final exams, her tone shifted to outright disdain for her summer schedule. Then, Martha also decided to stay in Mount Cary through the summer to *"work in the administration building and avoid her father,"* and suddenly her summer didn't seem so intolerable.

With Annabelle's busy schedule, I try to save some money for train fare to Mount Cary. Unfortunately, when there isn't a Havens event to attend, Philo has an out-of-town work trip, which necessitates me to stay home to keep Marie company. When late-September rolls around, however, I finally get a free weekend when both Philo and Marie are set to head to New York together to celebrate Philo Jr. and Edie's book launch. I was going to take advantage of the opportunity on the 6am train to Mount Cary to surprise Annabelle, until I receive her latest letter:

"I am very excited for this weekend! Going to Martha's parents' home in Milwaukee for her birthday, and looking forward to finding out if her father is as awful as she says he is."

I think both of her parents are awful.

"He's going to think both of his parents are awful," laments Marie after she and Philo cancel their trip. "but it's just too much. We'd have to go all the way to New York ... and they'll be busy with their publisher ... and we don't know anything about books anyway."

Marie's excuses are the last I hear about Philo Jr.'s book. Then, the two of them unpack their suitcases, and carry on like nothing happened. The sudden disinterest in the topic is curious—this was *the* occasion I wouldn't expect Marie to miss—but I realize it isn't my place to pry. Also, I am still frustrated about my own cancelled trip, especially when I find out my ticket is not transferable to the Milwaukee line ...

Then, just as it feels like the week will never end, Philo surprises everyone when he invites the Mattinglys, Lords, and Carmens for dinner and a night of parlor games. Initially I wonder what excuse Marie will come up with to miss a party at her own house, but then Sid Reid's divorce is very publicly settled on Friday, and suddenly she is tickled to gossip about it with the other wives and Ed's mother.

"I can't believe Sid would do that to poor Evie, and for so many years," laments Helen. "It's bad enough that she lost her baby—but her husband, too?"

"I heard from Paul Jaeger's wife that she was never herself again after the miscarriage," says Marie.

Winnie Carmen, who's barely said a word all evening, somehow grows even more silent. Ed dutifully grabs her hand, but it doesn't have any effect.

"Having a healthy baby can be hard," says Patsy Carmen. "Why, David and I lost one baby before we had Ed, and another before his sister, and it was devastating. But you have to find a way to pick yourself up—you can't seriously expect a man to be celibate the rest of his life."

Ed hisses at his mother, then tries to rub Winnie's shoulder but she recoils.

"Aunt Patsy has a point," says Pearl, ignoring Charlie's stupid grin. "But Evie did ask for a lot of money, and Sid didn't fight it."

"Well, he's a broken man," counters Helen. "He's embarrassed, ashamed, and probably humbled—but he's not a bad person, he just did a bad thing."

Philo, John, and Charlie all rise from their seats to sneak away ... then, after another failed attempt to comfort his wife, Ed does, too.

"What do you gentlemen think?" blurts Patsy.

"Ahem, yes, very bad"— *"So embarrassing"*— *"Not good at all"*—

"Oh, just go," murmurs Patsy. The fellas scamper off into the kitchen. Realizing I'm the only man left in the room, I try to follow but it's too late.

"What about you, Eric?" says Marie.

I sit back down. "I never met the man," I shrug, displeasing the eager eyes on me, "…but, he sounds bad."

Marie smiles. "You're such a good boy, Eric. I'm always telling these ladies how nice it is to have you around."

"Well, it's no wonder," says Helen, tossing back her long, brown hair to reach for an unopened bottle of champagne, "hanging around our husbands all day—great minds learn from great men."

My lips tighten.

Winnie pulls on her own blond locks, then folds her hands over her belly.

"You know, Philo kicked Sid Reid out of the Havens as soon as he found out what he did," says Marie. "He was so angry at Sid, but at the same time I think he was hurt even more—after all, he is his best friend's son!"

"My husband and Joe Reid let Ed and Sid hang around the Havens when they were still boys because they followed the rules," says Patsy. "If either of them was here, I don't think they'd have a problem with how Philo handled Sid."

"He's a good man," adds Helen, topping off everyone's drinks, including a drop into Winnie's untouched glass.

Winnie's head jerks up.

"I think I'm going to get a hard drink," I say.

After joining the fellas for a round of whiskey in the kitchen, Ed brings out an assortment of beverages to the living room and soon enough the party's mood lightens—Winnie even speaks at one point—and we're ready to play some games. We start with charades ...

"You're Charlie!" shouts Pearl during Ed's impersonation of a comedian.

"I was Oliver Hardy, but I'll count it."

... followed by Messenger ...

"I'll begin!" says John, before whispering a message into Helen's ear.

Everyone takes a turn quietly passing on the message to the person next to them until I deliver the final recitation.

"Oh, Eric!" squeals Marie. "Such scandalous words!"

I blush as everyone roars.

"I-I was just repeating what I was told," I explain.

... and then Twenty Questions ...

"It's in Chicago, isn't and never was alive, doesn't have anything to do with the World's Fair, but is something we've all heard of ..." says Helen carefully. "Is it an event?"

"Yes!" says John.

"An event?" ponders Philo, struggling to suppress a cough. "Are any of us—going to it?"

John pauses. "No," he smirks.

"It's an event, but none of us are going," recites Marie. "Then it can't be a Havens party."

John doesn't say a word.

"Wait," I say. "It is! Coppock's party at the end of the month!"

"And we have a winner!" cries John. "Nice job, Marie! Eric, you spoke out of turn."

"How lovely!" exclaims Marie. "Thank you, Eric."

"Good one, John!" says Charlie.

"Say, Philo, why are we letting that bonehead host this party, anyway?" says John. "We've still got to pay off that bartender he tried to fight back in March."

"We have to let Andrew host occasionally—ahem, otherwise people will wonder—ahem, why he's even in the club," Philo explains.

"I wonder that every day," mutters Ed.

"I've always liked Andrew," says Marie, instigating a small coughing fit from Philo. "So friendly and spirited!"

"Philo, you know it's going to be awful," says John. "I get that Halloween's supposed to be a little strange, but the Stockyards? How did he even find this place?"

"I'm just happy there's finally going to be a Halloween party," says Pearl. "I can't remember the Havens ever having one before."

The fellas all look to the ground.

"First one," says John finally. "All the more reason why Coppock should not be hosting it."

"Oh, I didn't know it was the first," says Marie. "What a pity Phy and I won't be in town!"

"Hold on," says John. "Philo, you're not even going to be here?"

"Marie and I—are going to be in—Florida for October," rasps Philo. "Won't be back—until—November 1st."

Florida? Together?

"Convenient," says John. "Well, I'm sure you'll have a grand time being anywhere but here."

Philo doesn't look the least bit apologetic, making no effort to conceal a cough in John's direction.

I can accept setting aside their problems for an evening with friends ... but now they're willingly going away for a month together?

"Well, I still want to go," says Helen. "A Halloween costume party sounds like fun!"

"That's swell, sweat pea," says John. "Hey, Philo, you okay, old boy?"

Philo's coughing has become unmanageable, and he gets up from his seat, nodding to John—

"Philo!" shrieks Winnie.

His glasses slide across the hardwood floor, coming to rest at Winnie's feet. John and I rush to his side to help him up, while he mutters, "I'm fine, I just stood up too fast ..."

"Oh, dear me, we should call a doctor," blubbers Marie, frantically waving her hands over her husband like fans.

"Everyone just leave me alone——" growls Philo through another hack.

As Marie's eyes well a little more with each subsequent cough, I get a devilish feeling that this is all a convenient show for sympathy——*Every weekend he travels or goes to a party in perfect health, but when he finally gets his wife in front of his friends ...*

"Your face is white as a ghost," notices Helen. "Maybe we should call the doctor."

A rocky marriage and "sick" husband——what does he have planned in Florida?

"That's a good idea, dear," says John as the front door slams. "Hey, Ed, where do you think you're going?"

Ed slows up, and already halfway out the door says, "I have to go after Winnie, I'm sorry——I'll call later, Marie!"

Then, I notice that Winnie has already left and nobody, except for Ed, saw it happen. Thereon, their exit is similarly ignored.

What's going on with the Olins?

After the excitement of Philo's fall subsides, and he convinces John and Marie that he will call his doctor in the

morning, everyone decides it is time to hea‹
Lords leave with the Mattinglys, while I
Carmen—who originally came with her son aı
in-law—hail a cab.

"I appreciate you standing out here on a cold night with
an old widow," says Patsy as a half dozen non-yellow
vehicles speed by. "I imagine you'd rather be out with
people your own age about now."

"No, I had fun tonight."

"I suppose there's always excitement when the Haven
boys get together. That certainly was a memorable ending—
you'll make sure he calls that doctor of his, won't you?"

"Of course," I reply, considering a thoughtful way to
brooch the Olins' marriage and this vacation. "Mrs.
Carmen, I was wondering what you thought of Philo and
Marie's vacation."

"Well, it's about time they used their house in Florida."

She's not getting it.

"What I mean is, do you think it's a good idea?"

Patsy squints at me, then sighs. "Oh, you must be
worried about Philo's health," she deduces. "That little
cough of his normally wouldn't have concerned me," she
explains. "He's an old man, and they tend to cough. But
Winnie's reaction made me wonder if it wasn't something
more serious."

"Yeah, what was that all about?"

"Didn't you know? Winnie was almost a nurse, but she dropped out to marry Ed," says Patsy casually. "Medicine has been a touchy subject for her since.

"Not Philo's fault, of course. Still, to this day she blames my son that she gave up on her dreams. But they've both wanted to have a family, so what did she expect?"

I shrug.

Patsy harrumphs. A taxi running the opposite side of the street spots us and quickly U-turns to pull up alongside the curb. She gets in.

"Eric, I was serious about Philo. Make sure he calls the doctor—he likes to do things his own way, but he shouldn't risk anything with his health."

"I will. Good night, Mrs. Carmen."

After the taxi drives off, I go back inside the Olins' house. On my way to bed I pass by Philo pouring a glass of water in the kitchen.

"Eric—"

I ignore him. My head hurts. There is so much happening around me and I need time to process it all.

"Eric—"

I enter the bedroom and collapse on the bed … I hate that my instincts are telling me one thing about Philo when the facts say another: *He's given me a home.*

Why am I like this?

"Eric, do you hear me?" growls Philo.

I sit up.

"Why didn't you tell me about Florida?"

"We own a second home there," says Philo. "I don't even think twice about going."

"Even with everything between you and Marie? Or is that all better now that you're throwing parties together again."

In no rush, Philo takes a long gulp of water. He then wipes his mouth, and adjusts his glasses. "Are you done?"

I look away.

"Maybe I should have told you about Florida sooner," he starts, "but I need to make sure you're going to be okay here by yourself."

I shrug.

"I'm serious, Eric. I've given Margaret the time off, and of course I'll leave plenty of food money for you, but I want to know you won't burn the place down while we're gone."

"I'll be fine," I say. "I'm a grown man. Thank you for the money, though."

"Also, you'll remember to keep writing to Annabelle while we're away?"

New York was only a weekend ...

It's as if a gust of wind has swept all the tension in the room away. Sitting on my bed I suddenly smell it—*vanilla.*

"I'll remember."

"Good," smiles Philo. "And check the postmark to make sure she's actually sending them from Mount Cary."

"Of course," I say.

Philo starts to head to his room.

"And what if she wants to come to Chicago?

He pauses.

"Absolutely not," says Philo, walking away. "Keep her at Shiner, Eric."

10

WIGS & DRESSES

My first few days alone in the Olins' house pass noiselessly. Amidst a slow period for my appointments, I struggle to occupy my time. With Margaret also gone and the kitchen to myself, I muster the nerve to try my hand at making Marie's cakes, and manage to bake flawlessly-frosted sawdust.

By day four I am bored to sloth. Three days later, when I realize I haven't tasted fresh air in as many, I force myself to go for a walk, which turns into a daily pleasure. Once I feel I have conquered Hyde Park, I start venturing further until I'm comfortable exploring all over the city. Some days I go down Michigan Avenue, others to Union Station, and even sometimes past Annabelle's old apartment in Bronzeville.

Then there are the days when, utterly unplanned, I find myself on the outskirts of the shanties. I avoid eye contact with the ragged casualties, but I can feel their bitter stares on my European shoes—*Can they tell I didn't buy them?* ... Occasionally, I venture to one of the North Side parks, wearing Philo's blue trilby hat so I can try to blend in with the other dandies without the crutch of having the other Havens around. I always end up in another shanty after.

One day, I am walking down the porch steps when I see John Mattingly's black limo parked in front of the house.

"Hey, kid," hollers his driver, puffing on a cigarette, "get in!"

"Mack, what are you doing here?"

"Good to see you again, too. You're not busy, are you?"

"I was just going for a walk."

"On a weekday? Must be nice!"

I get in the back seat, Mack tosses his cigarette, and we drive off.

"Boss told me you'd be home, but looks like I just caught you," explains Mack. "Where were you headed, anyway?"

"Nowhere," I lie. "I'm sorry, was I expecting you?"

"Whoa! Check out the vines on that tomato!" howls Mack. "You were saying?"

"Where are we going?"

Mack lays on his horn as a couple of kids run in front of him as he's making a right turn onto Lake Shore Drive. "Boss has a favor to ask you," he says distantly, constantly gazing into his mirrors at the woman we just passed.

"What kind of favor?"

"He'll tell you," says Mack, now whistling to himself. "Say, have I told you about this new broad Amy's got? Let me tell you about the whiskers on this kitten …"

Soon enough we stop in front of a small, seedy office building in the Loop on Monroe. Half of the windows are blacked out and I'm starting to question the legitimacy of John's lifestyle. Mack lays on his horn again and John trots out.

"Look who I found, boss!" shouts Mack as John rushes into the back seat next to me.

"Mack, weren't you supposed to honk and wait around the corner?"

"That's my fault, boss. Won't happen again."

John catches me staring at his building.

"Temporary office space, Eric. Say, how are you, young fella?" says John, sporting an unsettlingly wide grin.

"I'm doing well, thanks."

"Mack, just drive around the block while we talk, will you?"

"You got it, boss," says Mack. "I don't have to be anywhere for an hour and circles are my specialty."

John wipes his hands on his trousers then picks up the empty bottle that was left on the floor of the limo, checking it for any residual champagne.

"Are you okay, John?"

"Pardon? Oh, yes, I'm fine. Thank you, Eric."

John's hand won't stop shaking and I try to ask him again if everything's okay but he cuts me off.

"I have a favor to ask. Are you still chummy with those schoolgirls?"

"Sure, I write to Annabelle every week."

"What about Lou?"

"Louise? I suppose through Annabelle, yes."

I look up and see Mack talking to himself about yet another vaguely promiscuous woman.

"You see, we had a good time at the Fair in May, and I've been thinking that I'd like to see her again."

It's been nearly five months since we saw the Shiner girls, so I'm skeptical as to why John is pining over Louise now.

"I thought you could get those girls out here again, Annabelle and Lou … the others can come, too, and we all could hit the town. What do you say?"

"I don't know, John. Philo made it clear to keep Annabelle at school while he was away."

"Come on, Eric. She's been calling the house ever since she's returned to school this fall—I can't have her doing that with Helen home all day!"

I've never seen John desperate. I'm waiting for him to whip out a cigar, crack an arrogant smile, and brag about the new girl he's bringing to the next party. Instead, he's panting, sweating, and pleading for help.

"Eric, you were at Philo's the other day," says John. "I can't be Sid Reid—my scandal would be a hundred times worse. I know Philo wouldn't like this, but he'd hate the alternative so much more. Look, he's gone for another few weeks still and this could solve a lot of problems. What do you say, Eric?"

"But Philo—"

We pass the Palmer House, the first place Philo ordered me to keep Annabelle away. I didn't, and later that night ... *smoky, spicy vanilla.*

It's been five months since I've seen her ...

Annabelle softly presses her lips against my cheek.

"It was a magical night, wasn't it?" says Annabelle. "Why does it have to end?"

"It doesn't," I say, "and Uncle Philo isn't home."

But then ...

"Seriously, Eric—John?" fumes Martha.

Annabelle looks down at her feet.

"This was a favor for him?"

"He was going to get in trouble," I say.

"What are you, his page?" sneers Ethel.

And, finally ...

"Unbelievable, Eric," says Philo. "Your father and I were teammates—he'd be so ashamed of you."

"I'm sorry," I say, *looking down as Annabelle had just done.*

"You're pathetic," growls Philo. *"No job ... spineless ... untrustworthy ..."*

But then again ...

"Erikas ..."

"Let's do it," I say.

"Oh, you're a prince," sighs John. "I've got the perfect place in mind ..."

After Mack drops me off in Hyde Park, I draft my letter to Annabelle inviting the girls to Chicago. I decide to be honest with Annabelle and tell her that John really wants to spend time with Louise, but that the rest of the girls were invited, too.

"But we can't tell Philo," I remind her several times.

I do feel guilty over betraying Philo, even though the temptation to see Annabelle again has won out. I question my level-headedness on the situation because the urge to see her is so strong, and even consider changing my signature on the letter in case it ever gets back to Philo, but that seems overcomplicating so I sign it like any other one: *"Always, Erikas."*

Next Friday arrives, and Mack and I pick up Annabelle and her friends from Union Station. From there we head to the Silversmith Hotel, where John has booked a room for us. Though seated next to Annabelle in the limo, it's difficult to catch up while Martha and Ethel argue over Betty's absence.

"There's no point in studying all weekend if she's never going to show it off," contends Ethel. "If she's the top of our class she should have been married twice by now."

"It's not her fault she's shy," snaps Martha. "Even so, I don't blame her for avoiding these heels. I certainly could learn something from her …"

We arrive at the Silversmith, get the key John left for us at the front desk, and head up to the room.

"I must admit you chose a nice place, Eric," says Martha brightly as we enter the room. "Wait—what's he doing here?"

"Hi, girls," says John stiffly.

"Annabelle, I thought you said we were meeting Ed."

"Did I?" ponders Annabelle. "I must have confused them."

"Hi, Johnny," says Louise, twirling her hair.

"The rest of you knew all along!" exclaims Martha.

"Lou!" says John. "You smell wonderful."

"Really?" says Louise, initially taken aback, but she suppresses that reaction and is soon enough caressing John's arm. "I bet you say that to all the girls …"

"Thanks, Eric," whispers John.

We each have a drink, and everyone but Martha is having a good time, laughing and singing. When we finish our second round, Annabelle, Ethel, and Martha are eager to move to a nightclub …

"Let's go," whines Ethel, wiping the excess lipstick smudges from her glass. "We didn't come all this way to sit in the hotel."

...but John insists we have another drink. We do, and the girls continue to laugh and sing, and Martha smiles a little, but eventually even Louise wants to get going ...

"I just really would like to have another drink first," says John, slightly slurring. Louise vehemently agrees.

...So, we have another drink. Then one more. Then John pours yet another round, but when Louise starts nibbling on his ear Martha stops him.

"Alright, what's going on here?" she demands. "Why are you trying to get us all liquored up?"

"I'm going to liquor you up," giggles Louise, straddling John and rubbing her fingers down his chest.

"Eric, are you in on this?" accuses Martha.

"Erikas wouldn't harm a flea," says Annabelle.

"Fly," corrects Ethel.

"Oh, your fly!" squeals Louise, reaching for John's trousers, but Martha pulls her off him prior to any exposure.

"I don't want to hurt you girls," says John, wobbling in his seat and generally looking a mess. "I just wanted some company."

"Well, I don't trust you," says Martha. "You're a selfish, misogynist pig, and I never would have come here tonight if I knew we'd be seeing you."

John frowns.

"Why don't we go to a club," I suggest. "That way we can see other people."

"Eric's right," says Annabelle warmly, causing a similar sensation in my chest. I can do no wrong today. *Now I just need to get her alone ...*

"John, didn't you have a place in mind?" I say boldly.

John lifts his head. "Diamond Lil's," he mumbles.

"Let's go to Diamond Lil's," I conclude.

After persuading Martha a little more, we head to a part of town none of us has spent much time in. It's not terribly far from Downtown, though, and it's home to this new club John says he heard was fun. Mack drops us off at the door, and after receiving a few confused looks from some peculiar characters wandering by we will our way through Diamond Lil's entrance—the place is packed. Wall to wall, the small, smoky club is filled with the most colorful crowd I've ever seen—a carnival of gaudy dresses, makeup, and lots of hair.

"Isn't this something?" comments John, grinning ear to ear. "Everything we thought we knew is out the window!"

"Is that a man?" asks Ethel, pointing to a rouge-lipped individual in a black sheer dress with solid velvet stars covering their chest and groin.

"Hard to say," I ponder. "That's definitely a man," I say, pointing to stringy fellow in bawdy makeup carrying a wand and wearing a tiara atop a long, frizzy mane.

"Look at this pretty one," adds Annabelle.

"This is where you wanted to go, Johnny?" asks Louise.

A man in a blond wig and deep purple gown with a beautiful diamond necklace and crafted eyebrows blows a kiss at John. He starts sweating again.

"What are we doing here?" inquires Louise again. "John?"

John looks at Louise, then to me, then toward the door. Martha steps up and suggests, "We should dance."

"Dance with these pansies?" chuckles John. "That would be a real laugh."

"Yes, let's dance," agrees Annabelle. "*They* are."

"They're freaks," says John boldly. "We saw it. Let's just go."

Martha frowns.

"Fine, let's dance," I say, grabbing Annabelle's hand and charging full steam into the crowded dance floor.

Who am I?

I'm not a very good dancer, but I let the music guide me as I lead Annabelle around the dance floor. Fortunately, none of the drags mind when I clumsily bump into them.

Martha jumps in next, sliding in with the man in the purple gown, who curiously obliges her ridiculous shimmying. Ethel joins next, and starts toddling beside Martha.

Despite the rest of us letting loose, Louise is still terror-stricken, but not as much as John. She clutches his arm tighter, and he closes his eyes and says, "That's it, we're going in."

Suddenly, John and Louise are bumping into the men in dresses even more than Annabelle and me, and still no one cares.

"It's intoxicating!" cries John.

At the end of the night, we drop John off at his apartment first. Before stepping out of his limo, he gives Louise a kiss on the cheek and says, "I had a great time, Lou." He turns to me and says, "Best if neither of us mentions this to Philo, I should think." Then he leaves, so it is just the Shiner girls, Mack, and I in his limo. Martha is smirking at me.

"What?" I grin back.

"I had fun," she says. "You were great tonight, Eric."

"I'm a lucky girl," says Annabelle.

Mack's raising his eyebrows at me in the rearview mirror.

"I'll say," agrees Louise.

Mack does it again.

"I can't believe the nerve of those people," Ethel fumes. "You don't think I dress like a drag queen, do you?"

Mack drops the girls off back at the Silversmith before he will take me to the Olins'. I lean into Annabelle for another goodnight kiss, and we politely peck each other's cheeks (so as not to make the others jealous). We drive off and I can't stop smiling.

"Feels good to have a little freedom from the bossman, doesn't it, kid?"

I wanted to see Annabelle and I made it happen—without Philo. This freedom *is* intoxicating. Mack drops me off at the house, and I strut down the sidewalk and hop up the first two steps to the front door. Then my heart stops—a light is on inside.

It can't be.

I instinctively check my inner jacket pocket to see if my keys are gone again, but they're still there; I've never been so disappointed in Ethel. I take a deep breath—*maybe it's just an intruder*—and quietly shuffle the last two steps. Standing at the front door, I can hear someone scuffling around inside. I grab hold of the knob, my sweaty palms struggling to get a firm grip, and push.

"Eric," says Philo, "nice of you to join me."

11

THE BAD FRIEND

Philo is rummaging through the kitchen, looking for something to eat. He is completely lost without Margaret or Marie around, and has gathered a loaf of sliced Wonder Bread, a jar of peanuts, and a box of corn flakes on the kitchen table.

"What are you doing back?" I ask. "I thought you were in Florida for three more weeks."

"Plans changed," says Philo, feebly pulling on the jar of peanuts. "Work came up."

"But it's Friday night," I say, trying to guide the conversation.

Philo manages to pop open the lid, but the unbridled force causes a dozen peanuts to scatter across the table. He curses. "Eric, I'm trying to run a company in a depression," he snaps. "Sometimes you work weekends."

It's working.

"Where were you tonight?"

It's not.

"Out," I say coolly.

"I see that," says Philo, adjusting his glasses and assembling his sandwich. "I noticed Mack dropped you off."

He knows, and I've been caught.

"Just be careful with those girls," he continues. "I don't know how well Amy has them tested."

I almost correct him on my actual whereabouts, but think better of it, and just nod.

"And I don't want any of that around here. Always go to them—I'm sure you figured as much."

"Well, I'm pretty tired," I say quickly, heading toward my room. "Going to bed now."

"Hold on, Eric," says Philo, looking up. "You're not doing that again this weekend, are you?"

"No."

"Good, we're going to Mount Cary to visit Annabelle—I want to see how she's doing."

"She's doing fine—" I wince, hoping I haven't said too much. "That's what I've gathered from her letters."

Philo struggles to pick up his sandwich without its contents overflowing. "I think it's time we see it with our own eyes," he concludes. "I'd really like you to be there, too."

Now everybody needs me.

"I'd love to go, Philo."

"Great, we leave first thing in the morning."

I turn in for the night, but spend the next hour staring at the ceiling, wondering how I am going to stall Philo long enough so we don't beat the girls' train home ...

The next morning, since I told the girls I would take them to the train station, I wake up especially early in a futile effort to get out of the house before Philo sees me. Of course, that doesn't happen— "Here I am waiting for sleeping beauty again," says Philo from his wicker porch chair—and I am left praying they make it to their train on time without me. Even if they do, Sam already has the car ready for us, so I do my best to delay our departure.

"I'm sorry, I tripped!"

"I told you not to bring any cake!" growls Philo, wiping a mix of crumbs and frosting from the front of his gray pants.

"I know, but I was hungry and it was all we had in the house," I explain. "I'll go unlock the door so you can change."

Philo mutters something, then finger scoops a bit into his mouth. "That's awful," he blurts instinctively. "Hm, got the strawberry right, though ..."

Philo has changed into a fresh pair of blue trousers, just like the ones I'm wearing. I offer to change so we don't match, but Philo turns it down, and we end up departing at exactly the same time as the girls' train. Like a cruel joke,

Sam's chosen route to Mount Cary runs alongside the train tracks. Good or bad, no locomotive is in sight during any part of our three-hour drive to Shiner. That doesn't stop me from keeping a constant eye for it, though, a good distraction from thinking about what Philo will say if we get to the school and Annabelle isn't there ...

We pull onto Shiner's campus shortly after ten, again matching the train's schedule. Sam parks the car, and we get out—the curtains on Annabelle's window are not drawn. Suddenly, there's a sharp cry echoing from across the campus.

"Oh, Uncle Philo!" squeals Miss Beulah, scurrying towards us.

Maybe they just got in.

I stare harder at Annabelle's window for any sign of movement inside, but its dark and still.

"What's the matter with you, Eric?" says Philo as Miss Beulah approaches. "Stop acting weird."

"Oh dear," sputters Miss Beulah, "you're here, too."

"We're here to see Annabelle," says Philo. "The girls aren't at breakfast, or basket weaving or anything, are they?"

Concern streaks across Miss Beulah's face—she knows the girls aren't there. "I'm not sure she's up yet."

"We'll check her dorm then," concludes Philo.

"We c-could," stammers Miss Beulah, "but no boys until ..."

Four messy mounds of hair slowly bounce behind Philo's head, then halt upon recognizing the three figures standing before them. Miss Beulah purposely looks away. The girls each turn in a different direction, bumping into each other. Then I catch Martha's eye and mouth "Breakfast." She nods and the girls hurry off.

"What are you doing, Eric?" says Philo.

"Breakfast," I repeat. "I didn't have my cake, obviously—maybe we could check there first and grab something to eat?"

Miss Beulah fiercely nods.

She leads us on a meandering route to the dining hall, pointing out how beautiful the campus looks with the leaves changing to vibrant oranges and reds ...

"Yes, we have leaves in Chicago, too," says Philo.

... until Miss Beulah has no choice but to take us to the dining hall. Our nerves are calmed as we see Annabelle, Martha, Ethel, and Louise (again on Betty's lap with one chair short) seated at a table in the far corner, looking implausibly innocent.

"Thanks, Beulah," says Philo. "Eric, let's go."

"Eric!" squeals Louise from across the dining hall, eliciting hushing from Martha and Ethel. Annabelle rises to meet us. Louise quickly jumps into her vacant seat.

I pick up my pace to get ahead of Philo and whisper to Annabelle, *"He doesn't know!"*

"Hello, Uncle," she says. "What a pleasant surprise to see you here."

"Indeed," says Philo, examining her unkempt appearance. "Late night?"

The girls all try to wipe the running makeup from their faces, but it looks woefully obvious they went out.

"We had a slumber party, and did girly things to each other," says Annabelle, twirling her hair and batting her eyelashes. "Do you like?"

I nod and grin. Philo gives me the side eye. "You finished eating? I want to talk," he says. "Eric, entertain yourself with Annabelle's friends and you can meet us at her dorm later."

"Right away, Uncle," says Annabelle, escorting Philo out of the dining hall. "Goodbye, Erikas!"

Louise moves back on top of Betty's lap so I can sit. "I'm so glad you made it back," I say once Philo's out of earshot.

"What happened, Eric?" says Martha. "We waited for you, but you never came."

"He was supposed to be in Florida still, but he was at the house when I got back last night, and I couldn't get away. I didn't know we were coming here at the crack of dawn until it was too late."

"We almost missed our train," chides Ethel.

"I'm glad you're here now, Eric," says Louise. "Do you want some of my muffin? I'll let you butter it if you'd like."

Ethel scoffs into her plate of eggs. Louise transfers to my lap with a giggle and picks up her butter knife.

"That's one dedicated Uncle," says Martha.

"*Friend!* What are you doing with Ms. Haney?" scolds a passing Miss Beulah as Betty's eyes widen. "Louise, you be more respectful with that maple syrup!"

After the girls and I finish breakfast—Louise made eye-opening use of just about every condiment—we head back to their dorm to meet Annabelle and Philo.

"Everything okay?" I ask, genuinely curious what Philo came all this way to talk to her about.

"Annabelle's going to give me a tour of her classes," says Philo.

"Do you want to come?" says Annabelle

"Sure."

"I'm coming, too, Anna-belly!" exclaims Louise, still hanging by my side.

We start the tour at a building just a few paces from their dorm, where the girls are taking *Greek Dance* and *Descriptive Astronomy*. Annabelle and Louise each give us a quick demonstrative twirl, then they take turns pointing to the sky and reciting a quick fact. Philo is pleased.

Next, we enter the building next to the dining hall where Annabelle is taking *Survey of Foods*. Philo is less satisfied with this course selection.

"Do you want to see me serve?" she asks, placing a few pieces of fake fruit on a stray tray.

"Annabelle, cut the act," says Philo sharply. "I'm not sending you here to be a waitress."

"I wanted to take a class with Martha," Annabelle points out, "and this is the only one where they let you use a knife."

"Martha wants to be a surgeon," points out Louise, "but her parents want her to be a wife."

"You're not here to chase some fool's dream, Annabelle," says Philo. "You're here to learn some class."

"Oh, but I am," says Annabelle, picking up the tray with her right hand and facing away. She raises her chest, relaxes her shoulders, and takes a few steps forward. Her strides are even, and her left elbow stays in as her arm gracefully sways at her side. She pivots and heads back toward us in the same subtly poised manner. "See?"

"You do seem to be walking better," grumbles Philo. "How's your French coming along?"

"Oui," says Annabelle, casting a subtle wink at me.

"Is that all then?" he says.

"Just tennis left," says Annabelle. Philo's face turns red. "You'll like the courts, though, there are plenty of benches."

"I don't have tennis this semester, Eric" says Louise, rubbing my arm. "Do you want to see my last classroom instead?"

"I should probably stay with Philo and Annabelle," I say.

The two of them exchange glances.

"Go with Louise, Eric," says Annabelle, hesitating. "I'll keep Uncle Philo company until you get back."

She's not trying to get rid of me, is she?

As Louise leads me away from Annabelle, I periodically peer back, waiting for her to change her mind and run after me—but she doesn't. We head up a small hill until the tennis courts are out of sight and we're standing at the rear of the gymnasium.

"I have a surprise for you," says Louise, tapping her hand on an old rusted door. "The pool is supposed to be closed today, but Ethel lifted the key from one of the groundskeepers." She unlocks the door, and unbuttons the top of her blouse. "We'll be alone—"

"Ms. Haney!" bellows Miss Beulah, causing both of us to jump back. "And *friend!* First breakfast, now this? Annabelle would be so hurt if she saw the two of you like this."

Would she?

"You're coming with me."

From what I gather, Louise's punishment has something to do with reading, while I spend the next few hours sitting in the chapel under the watchful eye of the Shiner's chaplain. I plead to Miss Beulah that it was all a misunderstanding, but she refuses to hear it until she finds Uncle Philo. I don't sense much haste in her search, and the sobering stare from the Virgin Mary statue and the dark chapel puts me in the mood for a nap ...

"Eric's right" ... *"Go with Louise"* ... *"I'm a lucky girl"* ... *"Go with Louise"* ... *"I want to be with you Eric"* ... *"Go with—"*

"There you are!" sings Annabelle. I lift my head up from the pew. "Philo's ready to leave, and we've been looking for you. So is—"

"Louise, I know."

The sun is starting to set on Shiner's campus as Annabelle walks me from the chapel to the parking lot, where we pass Louise standing in the middle of the lawn with a book atop her head. She sees me and gives me a little wave. "I got in trouble again," she says, nearly causing the book to fall.

"Ms. Haney, shoulders back!" scolds Miss Beulah as she trots after us. "Not that far back! Oh, dear lord ..."

Philo is already in the car when we walk up. "I've been waiting for you, Eric. Get in," he says. "Remember what we talked about, Annabelle."

I look at Annabelle and am completely unsatisfied. Yesterday was amazing, and we dodged the bullet of getting her back to Shiner without Philo finding out about her Chicago visit, but a day later and we've gone from goodnight kisses to utter indifference. I physically hurt.

"Goodbye, Eric," she says, stiffly pecking my cheek.

This isn't the same kiss.

Not a word is spoken on our drive back to Chicago. I stare out the window and meaninglessly count cows, while Philo stares forward with a satisfied grin plastered on his wrinkled face. The tortuous silence is only broken for a few seconds when Philo whistles "Tiptoe Through the Tulips" at tempo.

Back at the house, Philo gathers the ingredients for another sandwich and says, "I think it's time we brought the girls to Chicago more often."

12

THE OTHER HOUSEGUEST

The rest of October flies by with the Shiner girls now a constant weekend presence—especially Louise for me. It's nice to have someone who always looks forward to seeing you, and who can warm up long cab rides on these increasingly cold autumn nights. Even though it's nice to wrap my arm around her, I can't keep my eyes from wandering to Annabelle.

Even though she and Philo aren't spending an inordinate amount together, I still question what they spoke about during our recent Mount Cary visit ... and the timing of Philo's premature arrival from Florida ... and what I'm even doing with him. Then I fall sleep under his roof and let it go.

With the Shiner girls, we dine at French restaurants, dance at Mexican cantinas, and Philo, Ed, and I even play hooky from Andrew Coppock's Halloween Party to go to the World's Fair one last time before it closes. Today's Fair atmosphere carries a less jovial mood than opening night in May, as this day marks the last steady paycheck for most workers. We're unhindered, though, until a drunkard at the rhythm and blues show catcalls Martha, sparking an argument between her and Ed about why she's not surprised he didn't do anything about it.

"What did you want me to do—fight him?" says Ed. "He wouldn't have felt anything if I did."

"So, you won't hurt another man, but he can do anything he wants to a woman?"

"He only whistled because he thinks you look good!"

"That's not why," scoffs Martha. "He whistled because he knew none of you would stop him. Heaven forbid you men lose your free life pass!"

"Now I'm responsible for all men!"

We end the night with fireworks.

The next Friday afternoon, Marie returns from Florida. I'm reading the newspaper in the parlor when she drops her bags at the front door and gives me a paralyzing bear hug. "Oh, Eric, I missed you so!"

With Philo at work late, I sit through Marie recounting her trip in meticulous detail, and with the accompaniment of pictures for most of it. It doesn't take long for me to recognize familiar faces in her pictures, for nearly each features the same smiling couple.

"They were so in love with each other, it hurt," gushes Marie. "I just love this swimsuit on Linda." Marie points to the wrinkled woman baring more skin than I was comfortable with. "Whenever she wore it her husband Schuyler couldn't keep his eyes off her. Oh, I miss the Hendriks ..."

If only to do anything else, I'm tempted to ask Marie about Philo coming home early, but I know he wouldn't like that. Plus, Marie doesn't seem too upset—in fact, it seems like this was the trip of her lifetime.

Then, Philo comes home from work. I look up to greet him, but his back is turned to us as he takes off his overcoat. Marie doesn't miss a beat in recounting the time Schuyler bought a souvenir beanie in Fort Lauderdale and she and Linda said that he looked like a small, lost child. Marie guffaws at the memory while Philo walks straight into the kitchen and sits at the table until Margaret serves him dinner.

"We were joking, of course," clarifies Maria. "Linda would always address him as 'Handsome,' and he would cut her meat for her. They were just the sweetest!"

There's a slam in the kitchen, and Philo stomps into the parlor. "Now that's enough about Schuyler Hendriks," he barks. "I don't want to hear another word about that schmuck."

"He's staying here, Philo, get over it," says Marie, her hands clenched on the picture album.

"You offered our spare room without asking."

"They were on their honeymoon and don't know where to live in Chicago," counters Marie.

"They used to live in Chicago, Marie—he worked for me for five years!"

"Please don't shout in front of Eric!"

Philo looks down at me, like he just now realized I was here. "She's bringing another man into my house, Eric," he says. "You heard her admit it."

I turn to Marie. Tears are welling in her eyes, but she tries not to let me see.

Philo storms out of the house.

"Where are you going?" I call after him—no response.

Marie gets up and goes to the kitchen. "What kind of filling would you like, Eric?"

"It doesn't matter."

Philo doesn't come back that night, and we don't hear from him the next morning, either. Marie and I avoid discussing their argument, focusing on the Florida trip, which sounds a lot lonelier than it had last night.

After lunch, John's limo pulls up to the house. Mack and Philo come in and head straight upstairs without acknowledging Marie's presence in the parlor. When they come down carrying a load of suitcases, Philo sarcastically grumbles, "Thanks for the help, Eric."

"Don't worry, kid," says Mack as brightly as ever. "We have more than enough hands as it is."

"Thanks, Mack," I say.

"Eric, if you need me, I'll be staying at the Stevens Hotel," says Philo, placing the one bag he was carrying on top of the mountain in Mack's arms. "Stop by this week."

"Okay."

The week goes by, and Marie is still steeped in her blue funk. I feel guilty not following through with meeting Philo at the Stevens, but I'd feel worse about leaving Marie in her fragile state—she hasn't baked a cake in three days!

Only when Schuyler Hendriks finally arrives does Marie seem to perk up. Save for his insomnia which results in nightly creaking of the floorboards above me, Schuyler Hendriks is generally a low-key guest, and rarely at the house. Even so, finding myself caught between enemy trenches, I cannot bring myself to leave my room whenever I hear Schuyler milling about. It may seem unlikely, as we are technically housemates, but I have yet to see him in-person and prefer to keep it that way. As such, I start revisiting my long walks from the previous month. Then, one glistening mid-November morning—

HONK!

"Hey, kid!"

I need to be less predictable.

"What are you doing here, Mack?" I say, getting in the back of John's limo. We drive off.

"The bossman wants to see you."

"About what?"

"Whoa!" exclaims Mack, nearly ramming into the back of a stopped car. "Check out this twist—I'd like to peel a bit of that lemon! What did you say, kid?"

"What does John want now?"

Mack laughs to himself, "Not my bossman—Philo!"

We drive to the Stevens where we pick up Philo and continue driving around Downtown.

"Is he there yet?" Philo asks. "Schuyler?"

"Yes."

"I knew he would be from the day they arrived at the resort," Philo grimaces. "He looked at Marie with eyes no woman her age can resist—I'm sure that's how he nabbed that 'wife' of his."

"I know the look well," adds Mack into the rearview mirror.

"She does seem happy that he's there," I say, "but I really don't think anything is going on between them."

"Open your eyes, Eric," says Philo. "You're living in a very adult world—married women don't simply live with other married men."

"I don't think Marie is like that."

Philo removes his glasses and rubs his eyes.

"Remember when I first brought you in, Eric? I told you I was worried Marie was going to find alternative solutions for her mother's death."

"Yes, I remember."

"It looks like she found it, doesn't it?" he says. "And it makes perfect sense. Schuyler was working for me when the market crashed, and I had to let several employees go. He was one of them. I hired a few back once business got a little better, but by then he was back with his parents in Michigan so he was never in position to regain his job."

"So, you think it's about revenge," I say. "But why Marie?"

"You saw Marie's pictures; Schuyler's wife is an old widow! What young man wants to be with someone so worn and wrinkled when they can have someone young and firm?"

"Schuyler's just a gold digger," I humor.

"And I'll be damned if he uses Marie to get to my money!"

But he's never at the house and Marie hardly leaves …

"Their wedding was in July," continues Philo, "but they waited until October to go on their honeymoon? He knew I had the house in Florida from when he worked for me, and probably called my secretary until she told him 'Mr. Olin's on vacation', all so he could work my wife. It all adds up, Eric!"

"That's so elaborate."

Mack smacks just below the partition between the front and back seats and points at a blond prostitute on the sidewalk. "That's Amy's newest girl!"

We gape at Mack grinning into the rearview mirror.

"Thank you for that," says Philo gruffly. "Anyway, Eric, I'm telling you this because I need a favor."

"Sure."

"I want you to see if anything of Schuyler's is in Marie's room," he says. "If there is, we'll know Marie is cheating on me."

Philo is paranoid.

"But what do I say if Marie asks why I'm snooping around her room?"

"Tell her I asked you to retrieve my father's old cufflinks. I keep them in the top dresser drawer," says Philo, handing me a key. "Try this. If it doesn't get you in, Marie's changed the locks."

"On the bedroom door?"

"Yes, Eric," says Philo, who is confused why I'm confused. "Mack, do you keep a crowbar in the trunk, just to be safe?"

"Sure thing, Mr. Olin," says Mack. "I've got a crowbar, cat's paw, cow hammer, gooseneck ..."

"Perfect," says Philo as we pull back up to the house. "Got it, Eric?"

"Yes, I've got it," I say. "Looking for your father's cufflinks ... but really looking for men's underwear."

"Don't be funny, Eric," grunts Philo, pushing me out of the car, "just stick to the plan."

We always stick to the plan.

I walk up the front steps and carefully open the door. I pull out the key to Marie's bedroom that Philo has given me and look back at the limo. Philo's gives me an assuring thumbs-up while Mack enthusiastically shakes the crowbar. I close the door behind me and start my ascent.

The creaky stairs feel foreign beneath my feet—in the year I've lived with the Olins this is the first time I've gone to the second story.

"Hello," I announce. "Marie?"

No one answers.

"Hello," I declare again, feeling silly announcing myself in the same house I sleep—still no answer.

I walk the rest of the flight. Raymond's room—where Philo had been staying—is to my left, and Marie's is to my right. I peek into Raymond's first, but it's completely empty. There's a bed, and sheets, and a dresser, but there are no signs of a visitor: no luggage, no stray clothes, no leather shaving kit, nothing. I softly close Raymond's door, and stare across the hall.

"This is silly," I mutter.

Still, I approach Marie's room and try the handle, but it's locked. I pull out the key again and slide it into the doorknob and—*CLICK*—it works. I push the door open and that's when I see it: Sitting at the foot of the bed are two leather suitcases. I crouch down to get a better look, the floor creaking beneath me. I turn over one of the luggage tags and it reads:

SCHUYLER HENDRIKS – NILES, MI

I run out of the house as fast as I can, not bothering to cover my latest tracks, the world a blur in my peripherals.

How could Marie do this?

"What is it, Eric?" says Philo.

"He's in there," I pant. "In her room. He's staying in her room. His luggage—his name—*everything*."

"Whoa," mutters Mack.

"Damn," Philo curses. "I was hoping I was wrong."

"I'm sorry," I say. "And I'm sorry I doubted you, Philo."

"It's not your fault, Eric," says Philo. "Marie doesn't seem the type … Now where are my cufflinks?"

"W-what?"

"My cufflinks, where are they?"

"Oh, I didn't think you actually wanted them. I thought that was just—"

"*Damn*," Philo curses again. "Dammit, Marie."

13

UNUSUAL RHYTHMS

"**S**hould we celebrate?" I ask, reading the December 5th headline of the *Tribune*.

Philo turns his newspaper around to re-read the headline while I reach for a muffin among the smorgasbord strewn across his new Moderne dinette table.

"Ah, they repealed prohibition," reads Philo. "After dinner let's open that bottle of sorghum wine John gave us at the housewarming."

After breakfast, I make my couch and, before Philo heads to work, start writing my weekly letter to Annabelle. I had skipped a few letters following our Mount Cary trip in early October, but have gotten back to on schedule since moving into Philo's new apartment at the Stevens Hotel. Though its outfitted with beautiful furniture and paintings and has a view of the lake, it is significantly smaller than the Hyde Park house, putting me closely under his watchful eye.

"Dear Annabelle," I write, knowing Philo is staring over my shoulder on his way to the door.

I put my pen down.

How can she act like nothing's changed?

Lately, my letters have concentrated on my courtship with Louise, but it's like I'm writing in invisible ink, because she continues to write sweet nothings like *"I had so much fun seeing you last weekend, Eric, and can't wait to see you again on Friday!"* and *"Bring that cute nose of yours because I'm wearing a new perfume and want your opinion of it!"*

Why can't she just tell me it's over between us?

"Keep writing, Eric," grumbles Philo, fastening his overcoat.

I pick up my pen and Philo leaves for work.

"Going to Cincinnati for the holidays," I write, *"see you at New Year's."*

For Christmas, to thank me for "helping me through these dark times," Philo buys my train fare to Cincinnati to see my mother. It's a nice visit for both of us, until I return to Chicago on New Year's Eve.

My train pulls into Union Station just a little before the girls are scheduled to arrive from Mount Cary, so I wait for them so we can share a taxi to the Havens party at the Drake Hotel. As we arrive, we pass Andrew Coppock, who is leaning against the side of the building smoking a cigarette.

"Looks like you've got a few extra dates there, Eric," says Coppock, tossing the butt and following us in. "I can help you out."

"Sorry," says Annabelle, locking arms with Martha and throwing me a wink, "but we're lesbians now."

"What a shame," scowls Coppock, "I was hoping you'd get rough with me again!" He turns to Ethel, now the only one of us without an escort. "What about you, doll?"

Martha locks her other arm with Ethel's and the three of them march into the lobby.

"This is why we need to make Betty come with us," Ethel mutters to Martha.

"Andrew," calls Philo, "remember what we talked about?"

Coppock rolls his eyes, then presses another cigarette between his lips and retreats back outside.

"That's over, and now we're here," says Louise. "Let's get into that ballroom and have a swell time!"

The ballroom is nothing short of enchanting. It has been brightly festooned with silver garland, silver evergreens, and a dozen glass chandeliers dangling ornate crystal teardrops above the dancing partygoers' heads. I nod at Felix across the room as he plucks away to the snappy jazz tune the band is playing, and he throws a quick nod back. Ethel runs off to grab a drink, but Martha and Annabelle are still with interlocked arms, and playing into the extra attention they are getting with coy waves and hair whips.

"Don't worry about those two, Eric," giggles Louise. "We'll give 'em something to really look at later."

I gulp.

Near the door we greet John, tonight's host for this New Year's romp, and his date, a pretty brunette whom he proudly introduces as "Hazel."

"It's very nice to meet you, Hazel," says Martha. "She's gorgeous, John."

"That's how I like them!"

John leads Philo and Charlie to a large table he has reserved for the founders' circle. I start to follow, too, but Louise pulls me to the dance floor with the other girls.

Coppock reemerges on the opposite end of the dance floor and, as one of the few Havens who has showed up stag, is scanning for a doe.

"Annabelle quick, dance with me," says Martha, averting her eyes.

"Always," says Annabelle, grabbing Martha's hand and putting her hand on her waist. "I don't want that bad boy talking to you, either."

"Eric, dance with me," whines Louise, positioning my hands on her like Annabelle's on Martha.

"But what about Ethel?" I say.

Ethel is scanning the dance floor like Coppock. "That's okay, Eric," says Ethel, pinching the buttocks of a tall man facing the bandstand. "Hey, pants!"

"Hey, what's the big idea?" protests Herb Galloway, his innocent face scrunched in a harmless scowl. "Oh, hello."

"Ah, you're a pushover," says Ethel. "Where are the real men hiding?"

A group of younger Havens walk by and capture Ethel's gaze. Daniel Kruger brushes by last, waving his arm toward the bar, yelling, "Paulie, wait up!"

"Yeah, Paulie, wait for me ..." purrs Ethel in close pursuit.

We dance another two songs before the band takes a break. "There's my buddy," says Felix, laying down his bass. "I saw you walk in with all those girls—seems like you're finally embracing the Haven lifestyle!"

"I don't know about that," I blush. "Just having a good time."

"Gee, you know the band, Eric?" says Louise.

"Only Felix here," I reply.

"Who's this angel?" he says smoothly.

"My apologies. Felix, this is Louise Haney."

"Pleasure," says Felix, lighting a cigarette. "How'd you cats like the set?"

"It was steaming hot," gushes Louise. "You play really well!"

"Appreciate that," Felix chuckles to himself.

"I didn't recognize any of those songs, Felix," I comment. "Are they new?"

"Trying new things tonight, Eric," says Felix in-between drags. "New Year's Eve, you dig?"

Across the ballroom, Annabelle and Martha join Philo, Charlie, and John his date Hazel at the table.

"Keen!" exclaims Louise.

Annabelle sits next to Philo, but they don't interact, or do much of anything for that matter. John and Charlie laugh, and Hazel rubs John's arm, but Annabelle and Philo just sit. While idleness is Philo's preferred activity at most Havens events, Annabelle already appears bored and is glancing longingly at the rest of the party.

Why isn't she out there flirting with … everybody?

"Felix!" shouts one of the trumpeters from the bar.

"Uh-oh, looks like I need to fade," says Felix. "Good to see you getting out there, Eric. Louise, be sure to tune your ears for the next set …"

Felix struts off to meet his bandmates and I suggest to Louise that we join Annabelle at the table.

"I need to find Ethel," she counters, and we part.

I slide into the empty seat next to Annabelle just as she gets up and announces, "I'm going to get champagne. Would anyone like anything?"

Annabelle notes Martha's and John's hands.

"I'll go with you," I say, rising.

"You just sat down," grunts Philo.

I lower myself. Annabelle turns and leaves.

She is avoiding me.

"Eric!" Martha repeats. "Where's Louise?"

"Oh, what does she want?" mutters Philo to himself.

"She's with Ethel, I think," I say, but Martha isn't listening.

Wendy is barreling toward the table, her chest and forehead slightly pink. "You all need to come to the hallway right away," she blurts. "I think Ed's going to fight Coppock."

"What?" gasps Martha.

"We just walked in and Daniel Kruger was yelling at Andrew Coppock for bothering his date," pants Wendy, "and Ed got involved—it's escalating so quickly!"

"*Andrew*," grumbles Philo as the men rise from their seats and follow Wendy to the hallway.

"I'm going with them," says Martha.

I'm left at the table all alone with John's date. The band is starting to set back up on stage, and I can no longer spot Annabelle at the bar.

"Hazel, is it?" I say freely. "Some party, right?"

"Ze pleasure is mine," she recites in a thick eastern European accent.

I wish I had a drink right about now.

"She doesn't speak much English," says Annabelle, handing me a champagne flute and taking a large sip from her own. She takes a seat, but the distance between us is uncomfortably noticeable. We each take a large sip.

"The others are in the hallway," I say stiffly. "Ed's going to fight Andrew Coppock."

"I heard something about that."

We sip again. Hazel is staring at us. Annabelle furrows her brow at her.

"I think she's upset you didn't get her champagne."

Annabelle throws her hand over her eyes and snorts.

"She didn't know you were offering earlier," I add, "because she doesn't even speak English!" Annabelle's laughter grows, then subsides.

"What am I going to do?" she sighs. "This is all so weird, Eric … you're with Louise!"

Everyone but Philo and Coppock returns to the ballroom. John is consoling Wendy, while Martha and Charlie try to talk down Ed.

"I don't think you need to worry about Louise," I say.

"Of course, I do," says Annabelle. "You're both my friend, but if anything goes wrong at least one of you won't be—I don't want that to be you."

"I don't want that, either. I treasure our relationship, and really believe that whatever *this* is with Louise won't change that."

The band finishes tuning and Felix takes a new spot in the center of the stage. Louise and Ethel have found space in front of the bandstand, which has not gone unnoticed by the new singer—or Annabelle.

"Eric, she's a child. You deserve so much better."

We both watch Louise flutter her fingers at Felix, whose dangerous eyes twinkle back at her. I lean across the empty seat between Annabelle and I, so close that I can feel her breathing accelerate, and whisper, "I've missed you."

She's smiling at me.

Felix clears his throat then shouts, "Everybody, let's R-R-RUMBA!"

The music strikes up and Felix starts wiggling his hips to the pulsing drumbeat. Louise slowly creeps closer to the stage until she is practically drooling on Felix's shoes. Our concentration lapses as Annabelle and I catch each other noticing this.

"Are you okay with that?" Annabelle asks, concernedly placing her hand on my arm. I look at her dully. "I'm kidding!" she says. "Come on, let's dance while they sort out this 'fight.'"

"So, you and I are good?"

With another grin, Annabelle takes my hand and leads me to the dance floor.

"Do you know how to dance to this?" I shout over the crying trumpets.

"Haven't a clue!" she hollers back.

We do our best to move our bodies to the unusual rhythm, but mostly step on each other's feet, bumping into the other equally-struggling dance couples—they are not nearly as forgiving as Diamond Lil's patrons. Occasionally we move our feet in sync, which leads to so much surprised laughter that we end up stepping on each other again.

After a few songs, we show no signs of improvement, but are also past the point of caring. Then, in the middle of a nearly-disastrous dip, the music stops. Charlie, who cheered the toast at the last party, gets up on stage and the other Havens and their guests congregate around him. Martha is back with Ethel and Louise, Ed is with Wendy, John is with his date, and Philo is with his scowl—it looks like this crazy year is going to end with a refreshing state of normalcy.

"1933 is in the bag!" exclaims Charlie. "I'd like to thank all of you for making this such a special year. With so many great events, the Havens really do keep me young—I feel *sixteen* again! I'd especially like to thank *Daniel Kruger* for poking the lion tonight and giving this evening a little more excitement. I'd also like to thank *Herb Galloway* for once again hosting every party that no one else wanted to—cheers to you my friend."

There are a few muted chuckles from the room as Charlie holds his glass up to the crowd and says, "Cheers …"

The men all stare at Herb. "Cheers," he relents.

"CHEERS!"

"Now, before I go, I'd like to welcome your favorite—" Charlie stops himself, "—*one* of your favorite founders to the stage … 'The Mattress,' himself, John Mattingly!"

The ballroom roars as John swaggers to the microphone with Hazel at his side. Martha rolls her eyes at John, but laughs a bit, too.

"This thing is telling me we're just a few seconds to midnight," says John, holding up his pocket watch. "I'd like all of you to help me count down. Ten ..."

Everyone joins in with, *"Nine ... Eight ..."*

Louise runs up to the band shell and Felix helps her on stage.

"Seven ... Six ... Five ..."

Ethel finds Herb, who sweats and squirms as his actual date pulls him back to her.

"Four ... Three ... Two ..."

Ed whispers something to Wendy and wipes a tear from her eye. They embrace.

"One ..."

Just as the rooms shouts *"Happy New Year!"* Annabelle pulls me in by my shirt and gives me a firm, passionate kiss on the lips unlike any that have come before. "Happy New Year, Erikas," she says, patting me on the cheek then walking away.

I take my time staggering back to our table, trying to recall anything that happened this evening before midnight ...

What good is the past anyway?

"What a wonderful party," I observe, sitting down next to Annabelle. "Wouldn't you agree?"

"Eric," scowls Philo, "we're talking here."

I wonder if any of the fellas saw our kiss …

"Do you think the band knows any Lithuanian songs?"

Annabelle shakes her head at me.

"I can ask my friend, Felix, if you'd like."

"What's the matter with you?" says Philo. "Annabelle and I are having a conversation!"

"Now's not the time, Eric," says Annabelle softly. "Maybe later."

"Go find Ed or someone," snaps Philo. "Make sure he doesn't start any more trouble."

Annabelle is taking Philo's side again. I linger, but neither is paying me any more attention. I get up to grab more champagne.

Am I that bad of a kisser?

"I'll go with you, Eric," says Martha.

We cross the dance floor on our way to the bar where we find Ed and Wendy, who are draped over each other while the bartender hands them their drinks.

"This is definitely your whiskey, Eddy," says Wendy with a bitter expression, handing Ed a glass when she spots Martha. "Oh, it's Martha."

"Hello, Wendy."

"Happy New Year," says Ed carefully.

"Feeling better, *Eddy*?" says Martha curtly.

"Since Philo sent that jackass home, yeah."

"I'm glad you spoke up to him."

Wendy takes a big drink from her glass.

"I'm trying," says Ed.

Something happens between Ed and Martha that Wendy doesn't like. She looks over Martha with a stiff jaw, but Martha won't lock eyes. Wendy starts to put her hands on her hips, but knows better than to stand in an awkward position, and stops herself. I can tell she wants to say something, but knows better than to do that, too. Just the same, she's said everything.

14

THE BLACK BLIZZARD

After the holidays, Annabelle returns to Shiner to begin her second year of school. Since our talk at New Year's Eve, her letters to me have become much more engaged again—this may also have something to do with and Louise and my subsequent decision to break up. But as with our puzzling departure, whenever Annabelle is in town and in Philo's presence her behavior toward me is far less affectionate. We're still cordial, exchanging pleasantries and the like, but more akin to how I am with Martha than our letters would suggest—*it's maddening.*

May, on the other hand, is sobering. The black blizzard hits Chicago, with its hollow, stinging whistles monopolizing our ears for two full days as the storm dumps thousands of tons of prairie soil on the city. The temperature drops, and it's nearly impossible to see anything outside, discouraging even the heartiest fools from venturing to the street. Sensibly, Philo and I have not left the Stevens since it started.

With communications hindered, our inability to check on others' well-being during the storm increases tensions within the apartment. When the dust finally clears, we call those we can and send a wire to rest, including Shiner. To our relief everyone seems to be okay.

Conveniently, the storm has subsided just in time for this year's Havens' Mother's Day luncheon. This turns out to be the perfect medicine for everyone's nerves to see their friends safe and healthy. Marie even shows up, though she and Philo share nothing more than an acknowledging glance. She gives me a hug, however, and even more forceful than those given to Helen Mattingly and Pearl Lords.

"I'm so glad you're safe!" she wails. "I was stuck all alone with Margaret and kept wishing you were with us, Eric."

"I'm happy to see you were safe, too," I say, prying myself away.

"Have you heard from Martha? I heard that side of the state got struck even worse."

I had forgotten about my "relationship" with Martha, at least from Marie's point of view. Between Martha, Annabelle, and Louise, it's hard to keep all my liaisons in order ...

"She's well," I say simply. "Nice to see you again, Marie."

I rejoin Philo, who is seated with John and Charlie while they discuss the damages endured by their work sites.

"Everyone in New York got better warning than we did," says John, "but our Cleveland operation got hit pretty bad."

"The Gary project was blanketed," adds Philo. "I hope Ed's plant wasn't too dinged."

"I haven't heard," bemoans Charlie. "Haven't gotten through to Ed yet."

Most conversations around us hold a similar tone: morose, yet thankful. But after lunch is served and Ed and Winnie still haven't shown up, a bad feeling starts to set in. Then, Patsy Carmen shows up in a fluster.

"Philo, thank God you're here," she pants. "Where's Marie? I need to see Marie."

"She's with the other ladies over there," points out John.

"Little Ed's in the hospital," she sobs, hurrying towards her friend.

The eight of us pack into the crowded waiting room in Children's Memorial Hospital. There are only seats for Philo, John, and Marie, so the rest of us stand, while Pearl Lords paces nervously while we wait for news on her nephew.

"Go be with the kids," says Charlie to his wife. "Send the babysitter home, and I'll stay here with Ed."

After a little more convincing Pearl agrees, but just as she's about to leave Ed and Patsy emerge.

"The doctor said they have most of the dust cleared from his lungs," says Ed, lighting a cigarette, heavy bags dragging down his eyes. "He's still having trouble breathing, though."

John gives Ed his seat and Pearl hugs Charlie.

"They expect a full recovery," adds Patsy, "but he needs to rest so the pneumonia doesn't get worse."

"Winnie's still in there with him," says Ed, his knee chattering like teeth. "She hasn't left his side for a second. But here I keep going in and out—what's wrong with me?"

"Ed, you're doing everything right," comforts Helen.

"It was the scariest thing," says Ed distantly. "Little Ed wanted to throw the ball, but I told him he couldn't play outside with the storm. I turn my back on him to take a phone call and then he was gone ..."

"He's five, Ed," says John. "Kids get in trouble."

"You mustn't blame yourself," urges Marie. "You and Winnie being here for him now means everything."

"You're absolutely right," says Ed, fighting back tears. "I'll tell you, this has given me some real perspective. Everything else ... all the bullshit we do ... none of it matters."

Philo and John exchange glances. "Take a deep breath, Ed," says Philo.

Ed wags his finger at Philo. "No," he says. "I've got to make some changes—I can be a better man."

Patsy gives her son a hug as he continues to stare into space.

A nurse comes through the door. "Mr. Carmen, the doctor is asking for you."

Ed bolts upright, pats me on the arm, and rushes back to his wife and son. Not long after, we all return home.

Little Ed's scare seems to have struck a chord with the Havens—maybe less so with Philo. The next weekend, for the first time all year none of the fellas go out with their mistresses, opting to spend time with their families. Philo and I, on the other hand, still have nothing to do with Marie. Philo uses his free weekend to work straight through Sunday night, while I volunteer in the neighborhood cleanup effort.

Even more surprising is that the next weekend identically passes ... as does the weekend after that. Then, on a Friday in early June, John has snagged a reservation at the newest club in Uptown. Mack and I pick the girls up from Union Station before getting the fellas from the Stevens.

"Where are we going again?" asks Louise as everyone gets situated in John's limo.

"The French Casino," says John proudly. "The show's gotten nothing but rave reviews—it's called '*Revue Folies Bergere.*'"

"A review full of *what!?*"

"Annabelle, translate the French," says Philo.

"It means 'man-bears frolicking with other man-bears,'" she says coolly.

"Really?" exclaims Louise.

"We'll ask Betty when we get back," mutters Ethel.

"You're a riot, Annabelle," chuckles John nervously. "Don't worry, fellas, this show's got women—lots of beautiful women!"

"I can't wait, John," smirks Martha.

The show opens with a thirty-five-piece orchestra providing a lively accompaniment to an elaborate introduction to the city of Paris, including mannequins representing the Eiffel Tower, Moulin Rouge, and Montmartre.

"I love Paris," sighs Martha.

But the dutiful march of the first act takes a quick turn when a baggy, white-faced clown enters the stage. The act ends with the clown being undressed by a troupe of ballerinas, revealing that *she* is actually a *he*.

"John, what the hell is this?" hisses Ed, before being shushed.

Then the disrobed clown is dragged to hell and the curtains close for intermission. The stunned audience is invited to dance as the orchestra switches to some snappy jazz tunes. Predictably, the girls want to hit the dance floor and, perhaps due to their month-long absence (or to forget that first act) the fellas actively want to join in.

"Hey, watch where you're going, you blimp," snarls a man with wild hair and a cocky grin.

Charlie cowers as the stranger looks him up and down with his chest puffed out. Everyone stares at Ed, waiting for him to step in but he stays back. "Sorry," says Charlie finally, after it's clear his cousin isn't going to intervene.

"That's what I thought," says the man rubbing his sleek, shiny chin.

"Hey Jimmy," shouts a voluptuous woman in a red dress. "Leave tubby alone and come dance with me."

"Watch your step—*all* of you," says the man sternly, "or the next could be your last ..."

The man struts away and everyone exhales. Martha slaps Ed's chest.

"What's the matter with you?" she implores. "Why didn't you do anything?"

"I thought you didn't like me fighting!" exclaims Ed. "You were so mad at me for getting into it with Coppock at New Year's, I thought I was being good tonight."

"Here we go," mumbles Philo.

"I wasn't mad about the fighting," explains Martha, "I was mad about Wendy!"

"That's not what you told me!"

"I was upset," she says. "So much was happening at once and you should have seen the way she was looking at me."

"Lucky for you, there's nothing to worry about there anymore."

Ethel and Louise run off with the first two well-dressed young men who look their way, with Ethel instructing them, "Dance with us—now."

"You broke up?" says Martha.

"How are you upset about this? I thought this was what you wanted."

"That was before I saw how happy you were together."

"I'm happy with Winnie."

"But what about Wendy?"

"Winnie's the mother of my child—there's nothing more important than that."

"Is that all she is to you?"

Ed blasts a sigh off exasperation.

John ushers Annabelle and I away. "They'll be at it the rest of the night."

We find an opening on the dance floor in front of a young couple performing a lively jitterbug. Opposite us, I see that Ethel's already lost her date while Louise is embracing hers. The other fellas (minus Ed) have also joined us in the crowd, clapping along to the dancers as they swing, flip, and crawl their way around the circle. Annabelle, however, is sporting an especially satisfied grin as she stares at the hostile stranger from earlier, who is frantically searching his coat pockets.

"What is it?" I ask.

"I got a present," she says, flashing a pair of Cubs baseball tickets to tomorrow's game at Wrigley Field, "courtesy of our pal, Jimmy."

Ethel will be so proud.

"Who are they playing?" asks Philo, snatching for the tickets.

"Someone named 'Red,'" she reads, clutching her prize away from Philo. "I wonder if Martha would like to go …"

"The Cincinnati Reds?" he gasps. "I pay your tuition, give them to me."

"Give me this … give me that …" Annabelle mocks as she hands over the tickets. "I'm starting to feel taken advantage of, Eric."

15

THE DEVIL IN THE KNICKERBOCKER

Betty Rice is a doe.

With a porcelain face and green eyes framed by long, black curls, Martha's seldom-seen soft-spoken roommate stands out as a beacon of innocence among her friends' conspicuous personalities. Despite previously resisting every prior invitation to join the other Shiner girls on their Haven-sponsored Chicago trips, Betty has finally agreed to attend this year's Halloween Party, hosted by Paul Jaeger.

"I didn't convince her," insists Martha. "Betty thought it sounded like fun, didn't you?"

"I did," pips the waifish girl. "I love costumes."

"Boy, someone's going to have some fun tonight!" grins Mack into the rearview mirror.

Paul has used his connection at the Oriental Theater to secure dozens of costumes from past vaudeville shows for the Havens and their guests to wear to tonight's party. For our fittings, Paul also rented out one of the smaller dining rooms at the Knickerbocker Hotel. There a professional wardrobe director will set up shop to make sure every couple is dressed to impress.

"The other parties clearly weren't up to Betty's standards," says Annabelle. "I admire a girl who holds out for the best."

Ed has paid for a stateroom at the Knickerbocker for our group to congregate in beforehand. By the time the Shiner girls and I arrive, the fellas are already a few drinks deep.

"Girls! Come on in!" shouts Ed.

Ethel and Louise head for the wet bar where Charlie is eager to make them a cocktail. Annabelle stops briefly in front of the couch to say hello to Philo, then joins her friends for a drink.

"Boys, this is my roommate, Betty—make her feel welcome," announces Martha. The fellas all wave and slur general greetings in Betty's direction. "That wasn't so bad … Do you want a drink, Betty?"

Betty shakes her head.

"Okay, but come with me anyway," says Martha, "I do."

Following Martha and Betty, I finally make it out of the doorway just before it swings open again.

"The party has finally arrived!" proclaims John, gliding into the suite accompanied by his new date, a busty auburn-haired woman with a smile like a balloon. "Everyone, feast your eyes on Ruby."

A half-dozen half-hearted waves greet John's new mistress while Charlie's jaw hits the floor.

"Where are all the other kittens?" asks John. "Don't tell me I'm the only one with a belle for the ball."

"They're downstairs getting their costumes," explains Philo.

"Ooh, can we do that, too?" squeals Louise.

"Sure, Lou, you girls grab your drinks and get down there," says John, ambling to the wet bar.

The Shiner girls gather their drinks and head down to their costume fittings.

"Why are you so late, John?" says Ed conversationally.

"That's what I asked him!" blurts Ruby.

"Girls, take Ruby with you," adds John; Ruby begrudgingly follows them out of the suite.

Ed's still waiting for an answer.

"Ah, well ... you know ..." mumbles John. "Say, what's this gloomy shit hanging here?" he says, pointing to the large painting above the mantle depicting a bell tower set under a full moon.

"Looks almost medieval," supposes Charlie. "See those spires ..."

Charlie's date is the first to return in her costume. She is wearing a short red dress with a small pointed tail in back and matching opera gloves. There are also two black horns protruding from her head, drooping much like her frown.

"I ask forrr something cute and zey give me zis," pouts Hazel.

"Yeah, Ed, it does look familiar," says John, doing a double-take. "Really, Charlie?" implores John, getting his first look of Hazel since she was his New Year's date. "This is who you brought?"

"You said it was okay!" pleads Charlie.

"Ten months," says Ed. "Once you think you can't get any more pathetic …"

"Hazel's had a busy schedule," remarks Charlie, putting an unwelcome arm around his devilish date. "And I don't see how your date's any better, Ed!"

"Not at all the same thing," says Ed intensely, grabbing Charlie by his collar.

The door swings open again. It's Wendy, and she's wearing a frilly pink dress that exposes even more leg than Hazel's costume—Ed releases.

"Excuse me," says Wendy suggestively. "But can any of you boys tell me where I can find my … *sheep*?"

"Wow, look at you!" says Ed, his eyes wandering madly.

"Oh, there he is," she says, hooking Ed's neck with her bowed staff, and pulling until they are close enough to kiss.

"Fellas, can you believe how good Hazel looks?" says Charlie excitedly.

"Not now, Charlie," shushes Ed, falling into the couch with Wendy on his lap. "We're getting close on this painting, and must concentrate. What do you think it is, darling?"

The door opens again: It's John's date, Ruby. She is wearing a crimson leotard with pale gold trim, and a tall red feather in her hair.

"How do I look?" giggles Ruby like a goat, kicking one leg in the air.

"It looks almost Flemish," says Ed, still examining the painting.

"What are you supposed to be?" says Philo gruffly.

"I don't know," replies Ruby. "But I told them I was John's date and they gave me this."

"Ah, I think you're right, Ed," squints John. "That's not Brussels, is it?"

"Johnny, don't you think I look good?" whines Ruby.

"Oh yeah, I want you so bad … You know, it could be St. Michael and Gudula."

Ruby crosses her arms and stomps toward Hazel. "He's been like this since he picked me up," she pouts. Hazel looks at Charlie. They both pout.

"No, that's not the church," says Philo.

There is a soft tapping at the door.

"Oh, boys," says a soft voice. "Can we come in?"

The door opens for the fourth time in minutes, and in strut the Shiner girls: Annabelle is dressed like a gypsy in a multi-colored, layered dress with a sparkling blue scarf covering the top of her strawberry blond hair; Martha is wearing a brown German barmaid girdle with a green skirt and white stockings; Louise is dressed similarly to Annabelle, but in all black with a three-cornered pirate's hat; Betty walks in with her eyes firmly fixed on the ground, as she is dressed like Cleopatra and clearly embarrassed by her heavily-sequined sheer floor-length skirt and immodest costume bra.

Hazel and Ruby whistle at Betty's entrance, cruelly taunting her discomfort.

"You like nice, Betty," assures Martha, "like you walked right off a movie screen."

"It's not Brussels, it's Bruges," I state. *The Belfry of Bruges!*"

"Ah, that's it!" exclaims Ed as Wendy hands him his whiskey. "Well done, Eric."

"Say, what happened to Ethel?" says Louise, looking around.

That was enough praise anyway—don't want it going to my head.

"I'm here," mopes Ethel, dressed like Alice in Wonderland, down to the big blue bow in her hair. "I look like everyday Betty."

At this point, Betty is staring past the floor, through the lobby, and down into the Knickerbocker's foundation. Then Hazel and Ruby start adjusting their cleavage, and Betty catches enough of a glimpse for her eyes to bug out.

"Fellas, look at Hazel now!" blurts Charlie.

Hazel tugs her dress up.

"It's getting late," says Philo, rising from the couch.

"He's right, we better get fitted too, gents," says Ed, finishing his drink and struggling to get up. "*The Belfry of Bruges* ... How did I miss that?"

The fellas and I head downstairs to receive our costumes for the night. Philo brashly cuts the line and brings the rest of us with him, so we are dressed and headed back up to the room in no time. Charlie needs to stay behind a little longer, however, because the wardrobe director assumed he had come stag and wouldn't re-fit him to match Hazel until Ed finally confirmed Charlie did, indeed, have a date.

Back in the room, the girls smile and laugh at Ed's Little Lord Fauntleroy outfit, but he is drunk and plays it up. Philo is not nearly as sprightly as Napoleon, especially when Ed playfully knocks on his bicorne hat. "Can he give us a smile? Corsican!"

John is dressed like a ringleader of a circus, with red coattails and a black top hat, which prompts crimson leotard-ed Ruby into guessing her costume's meaning.

"So, am I a ... ballerina?" guesses Ruby.

"No, I'm a ringleader of a *circus*," repeats John. "The big top ..."

"Are you staring at my chest, Johnny?"

"No," sighs John. "Actually, yes, I am," he amends.

I am fitted in a white shirt with dark green lederhosen and a brown Bavarian hat. "Looks like they matched us," I say as I walk up beside Martha.

"Oh, I'm so relieved!" exhales Martha. "The costume director said I'd have a pair—I'm so happy it's you."

"Well, we finally got it on," boasts Charlie, waltzing into the room wearing a one-piece red suit, swollen to its seams. There is also a pointed tail that hangs an inch off the ground, and black horns that match Hazel's. Charlie stops in front of the mantle and his head pokes up just high enough to be framed by the painting. "Why are you looking at me like that, Ed?"

"The devil," gasps Ed, glancing at Charlie, then at the painting, then back at Charlie, "and the belfry … The Devil in the Belfry!"

"Poe!" exclaims Annabelle.

"Precisely!" replies Ed. He turns to Wendy, who has returned to his lap. *"Vondervotteimittis?"*

"Von!" cries Wendy.

"Doo!" cries Ed.

Ed and Wendy jump to their feet and slowly approach Charlie, who squirms uncomfortably.

"Ed, w-what are you doing?"

"Dree! Vour! Fibe!

Betty and Martha look at each other excitedly.

Sax! Seben! Aight!

Hazel and Ruby look at each other confused.

Noin! Den! Eleben!

John and Philo revel in Charlie's fright.

Dvelf!... Dirteen!"

Ed grabs hold of Charlie's shoulders, Wendy wails, and Ed starts shaking him madly. *"Mein Gott, it is Dirteen o'clock!"*

"Please, just make it stop!" whimpers Charlie.

"Calm down, Charlie," says Ed frigidly, releasing the driveling devil.

"Really," adds Wendy, "it's only satire."

We head down to the party as a group, eliciting a few intrigued stares from the non-Haven guests of the hotel. Once in the ballroom, we are greeted by a collage of cowboys, masqueraders, and animals of all types. For those who have come to the party without a date they are flittering about trying to find their costume's match. Before our group starts mingling we file behind Philo and John for the night's special drink: *Blood Punch*.

"Alice?" wheezes the sweaty fat man with the smashed face who once stole my strawberry tart. He's dressed in a fluffy white bunny suit, and Ethel tries to ignore him while pouring a glass of punch. "I'm the white rabbit."

"I hate this costume," mutters Ethel to Louise as she tops off her drink, as the man is still staring … just waiting.

"Francis, leave her alone," says Ed, swooping in and leading the pudgy bunny away from Ethel. "I see you've gotten into the carrot cake patch again …"

"What was that?" implores Ethel.

"Francis Papp," says Philo. "Old money, and follows the rules."

"Honestly," mumbles John to me, "I think Philo only let him in because we needed someone that worked on Congress for the toasts."

"Let's grab a table," suggests Ethel as Louise finishes pouring her drink. "Hurry up before the rabbit returns!"

"Alright, almost done," says Louise. "Let's find a table close to the band!" Louise wheels around but crashes into a brown-haired pole, spilling her entire glass of red liquid on his bright white sailor suit.

"I'm so sorry!" shrieks Louise, scrambling for napkins, not finding any, then using her pirate's hat to pat Herb Galloway's chest dry. Suddenly, her patting slows. "Oh dear, I've ruined your costume."

Ethel shakes her head and leaves.

"That's alright, really," smiles Herb, as Louise unapologetically caresses his chest. "But you can keep drying me if you'd like."

Louise giggles.

"Your friend who just walked away—the one with the bow—she grabbed my butt at New Year's," says Herb.

"Oh, I see," frowns Louise, ceasing her fondling.

"It kind of hurt, but this—," he says, lifting Louise's chin, "feels much nicer."

Louise beams a mile wide. Herb does the same, and the two of them hop off toward the dance floor.

"Eric," says Annabelle as we near the front of the punch line, "think you and Louise will ever get back together?"

"It's hard to tell," I grin.

Martha mocks Louise by pantomiming drying Betty's chest, but Betty pushes her hands away. "I'm sorry, Betty," says Martha with a small laugh, "let me pour you a drink." Betty looks at the punch, then walk away before being cut off by a man in a dirty blue jumpsuit, red neckerchief, and floppy black cap.

Andrew Coppock, dressed as a train engineer, leers at the frozen Cleopatra. "Well, aren't you a broad to admire?"

"Martha!" Betty softly quivers.

"Don't worry, dollface," presses Coppock, wrapping his arm around her bare shoulder, "I ain't going to bite you—I love me a nice, gentle doe like you."

"Coppock, leave her alone," I say, tactfully preparing a fist, and doing everything I can to keep my voice steady.

"Why are you talking?" snaps Coppock. He laughs, "Look, it's Philo's stooge ... well, *stooge*, you want to keep bumping gums? Know that I'm not like these other fellas—I'm plenty rugged." Coppock flashes a much less subtle fist.

Martha!

"Who is this?" says Martha sharply. She pushes his arm off Betty and leads her away. "Doesn't matter. Keep walking."

Coppock glowers at Martha, but Paul Jaeger soon passes by, which causes Coppock to turn around and stomp away empty-handed.

"Why do you come to these things?" Betty asks Martha, still trembling.

"That's a great question," replies Martha, their voices trailing off as they leave Annabelle and I in line. "I guess when you think about it, these guys are still more progressive than Ma Beulah ..."

"That was very brave of you, Erikas," says Annabelle as we finally make it to the punch bowl. "I don't think I've ever seen you so combative."

Still live, I down an entire glass of punch in a single gulp. "He's always bothering us," I say, re-filling my glass and downing it again.

"Eric, you're shaking—come sit down with us."

"I'll be there in a minute."

I start to pour one more glass when a shadow emerges over the punch bowl. I look up and there is a short, disheveled young man staring at me. His shirt is torn from the top down to his navel, and his eyes are unsteady and dilated ... this is no costume and he is no Haven. The intruder shakes his head, sniffs loudly, and screeches, "Where's John?"

"What?"

His eyes widen and he places his hands on the tablecloth for traction, propelling himself forward as he darts around the table to a nearby group of people screaming *"John!"*

I try to grab him, but am too slow. My pursuit is equally as hapless, for he's already jumped on John Mattingly's back, knocking off his top hat. Daniel Kruger, dressed as a silver-armored knight, and his date, dressed as a medieval lady, stand agape, awaiting John's reaction.

John tenses then removes the young man—who lets out another loud sniff—from his back. "Wes," says John as the young man slithers in front of him.

"You thought that you could leave me," says Wes, wagging his finger, "but I found you, John."

"Johnny, who is this freak?"

The knight, lady, Ruby, and I eagerly await John's explanation. Other nearby couples are starting to look, too. Daniel clears his throat.

"You mean, *Uncle* John," says John. "Everybody, this is my nephew, Wes."

The disheveled intruder glances around the room, as confounded as we are. "Ah, this is a costume party!"

"Yes, and you haven't got a costume yet, Wes" remarks John, pushing his "nephew" toward the door. "You should take care of that ... down the hall, first double-doors on your left."

Wes halts and turns to John. "I can have anything I'd like?"

202

"You can have any *costume* you'd like," clarifies John.

Wes' face distorts into a frenzied smile. With another sniff, he wraps his arms tightly around John's torso. "I'm going to make you most pleased, *Uncle*."

"Out the door and to the left," says John reluctantly, and the impish man lopes off. "My nephew," titters John. "Strange kid, but very spirited."

Daniel Kruger and his date excuse themselves, and John says he needs another drink. I do, too, and start to follow he and Ruby, but am cut off.

"Eric," grunts Philo, pulling me out of John's earshot. "Who was that with John?"

"His nephew, apparently."

Philo stares at John swallowing his drink. "I want you to keep an eye on that kid," he says. "He's not on the guest list—if this were anyone but John we'd have already thrown him out."

"Sorry," huffs Ethel as she cuts between us, followed closely by Francis Papp.

"Francis," growls Philo, causing the round man to halt, "play nice." He nods and continues after Ethel.

Philo turns back to me. "I'm going to sit. I'm trusting you with this, Eric—I don't want any trouble tonight," he says. I nod, and he shuffles off.

I continue back to the punch line—

"It's only apple-bobbing, Betty," explains Martha as she and her timid roommate rush by. "I'm just trying to help."

"It's too much, Martha!"

Betty doesn't belong here.

"Let me at least get a drink, and then we can decide from there," proposes Martha. Betty agrees and the two girls get in the back of the line, where I file behind them. Martha briefly acknowledges me, which is followed by a restless silence.

Whether she is trying to entice Betty to do the same or not, Martha keeps glancing at the apple-bobbing happening on the other side of the ballroom. In her defense, it does seem like everyone there is having a riot. Ed has his head buried in the water, and Wendy keeps trying to pull him back to the surface but he's swatting her hand away …

"He's been under there awhile," observes Martha.

As the line slowly moves forward, I spot Wes re-enter the ballroom. He's partially wearing a black-and-white striped prisoner's jumpsuit with the top half of his buttons still undone. He scans the party and starts to wander in when John and Ruby head him off.

John is saying something to Ruby, then tries to help the fidgety young man with his buttons, but Wes jerks away from John's hand like it is electrically charged. John tries fastening Wes' shirt again and Ruby stomps away. Then Wes throws his arms around John's neck. He tries to back away but Wes' grip is so tight that his feet drag across the floor like two screeching garden hoes. "Dance with me John, dance with me!" he screams.

John is handling this beautifully.

Across the room, Ed finally emerges with a shiny red apple in his mouth, and a face to match.

Martha laughs and claps at Ed's feat. "He got one, Betty!"

Betty weakly nods. Martha sighs.

"Eric!" exclaims Martha, just now fully appreciating my presence. "Wouldn't it be fun if we went apple-bobbing?"

"I—"

Martha nods for me.

"Yes, it would," I agree.

Betty is unconvinced.

Just then, the music pauses, and Felix shouts, "Everybody, let's *R-R-RUMBA!*"

The voice inside my head guffaws. Then I do it out loud—Louise is so busy flirting with Herb Galloway that she didn't even flinch at the thirsty bassist's overture.

"You know what?" I say, piquing the girls' interest. "Forget this drink, let's bob."

Betty thinks for a second. The line moves again and we're almost next.

"We should do something," I continue. "These people aren't so intimidating once you get to know them."

A small crowd has gathered around the apple tub, where Annabelle is entertaining them in a noticeably more refined manner than that first Christmas party nearly two years ago.

"You're a Shiner girl, Betty, you belong here," I say.

We're next. Betty steps forward and picks up the ladle.

"You're the best in our class," Martha confirms.

Betty stares into the red liquid, her big green eyes staring back at her. The revealing Cleopatra top is also somewhat visible in the reflection. She notices this and frowns, swirling the punch until her image disappears.

Betty thinks she doesn't belong here.

I lean in. "And what's the point of looking so good in that costume if you're going to hide it behind a punch bowl all night?"

The punch liquid settles and Betty stares at herself again, contemplating.

"You look so good, Betty," adds Martha.

She drops the ladle into the bowl, causing a small red splash—

"Alright, let's go," says Betty.

—that just misses my shoes.

Martha praises a deity, then mouths "thank you" to me. We head across the dance floor to where the rest of the group is cheering on Charlie, while Ed forces his head in the tub. Then I hear an unwelcome voice shouting at me from behind.

"Hey, hold up!" Coppock shouts again, running to keep me back from Martha and Betty. "Hey, I want to talk to you about your friend—the one in the bra."

Martha and Betty go back to not noticing me (including that I'm no longer with them), only this time they are smiling and laughing with each other.

I clench my fist, turn to Coppock, and say, "Leave her alone."

"Don't get tough with me, Eric," says Coppock, "I don't want to fight you over a broad. Just tell me, she here with anyone?"

"Leave Betty alone," I repeat.

"Come on, Eric, don't be a pill. You and I've got a bond—we should be able to talk to each other about broads."

"I don't want to talk to you about anything."

My eyes dart after John as he chases after Wes who is racing toward the apple-bobbing tub.

"Hold on," says Coppock in a softer tone; I sense a morsel of desperation in his eyes. "Which one are you laying with? I promise I won't go after that one."

"Aren't we supposed to be a little more discrete than that?"

"Please, Philo and them don't even follow their own goddam rules—why do you think Sid Reid got caught?"

He has a point.

"Just tell me, Eric, which one's yours?"

I glance over at the apple tub and see Annabelle laughing as Wes kicks his legs in the air to get over half of his body in the water, splashing everywhere.

"Well, if I had to pick," I say casually, "let the redhead be."

Coppock bursts out laughing. "I knew it! The first time he brought you around I told Philo you would."

Does Coppock know?

"Listen, we both get how this works. But he's not going to do nothing with her here, so if you want her, take her. We're talking men and mistresses—no one's innocent."

Coppock knows.

I look to the other side of the ballroom where Philo is glaring at either John and Wes, or Ruby complaining to him.

"At this point I think we're better off as friends."

"Eric—if you want her, take her. Don't let Philo control you."

Philo spots us, and is now ignoring John's dilemma and is glaring at Coppock and I.

"He's not your dad, Eric. Be a man."

Coppock leaves, and I continue walking.

You can talk to her. She's not with anyone.

Water flies everywhere as Wes whips his head up from the tub with an apple stuffed in his mouth. He hops up and down with his arms in the air until John holds him still.

"Settle down, Wes," urges John. "It's just an apple."

"That's quite the talented nephew you have," says Ed, his hair still dripping as he munches on his own prize.

"Erikas," says Annabelle brightly.

"Annabelle," I begin, "do you want to—"

"It's your turn."

Suddenly, my head is surrounded by water, with dozens of large lumps smacking my face from every direction. A stinging liquid enters my nose, so I chomp down, and come to the surface with my teeth buried in a remarkably bland apple—actually, there's a piece of cloth wrapped around it.

"You found the magic apple!" says Annabelle, removing the cloth—her garter—and kissing my cheek.

"Darn it," laments Charlie. "Put it on another, it's my turn again!"

"You should be so lucky," says Annabelle, demurely stuffing the garter down her dress. "But, alas, Eric's our winner."

"Good job, Eric," says Betty.

"Martha," says John, still struggling to restrain Wes, "you going to let some Lithuanian gypsy kiss a fine German boy in front of you like that?"

"Watch it, he's my German boy," snarls Martha.

"Yeah? What are you going to do about it you bitch?" says Annabelle, poking Martha.

Okay, perhaps she's not so refined after all.

"Maybe I'll kiss him, too," offers Martha, until she starts poking back, "or maybe I'll sic Betty on you!"

"Maybe you two should kiss each other!" suggests John.

"It's Halloween—let's go bananas!" says Wes, pulling away from John. "Girls kissing girls ... and *boys* kissing *boys!*" He turns to John and plants a gigantic kiss on his lips. John simpers but everyone else roars with laughter. Ed nearly chokes on his apple.

Martha turns to Betty and says, "This is why I come to these things!"

But Betty's no longer there. In the distraction of Wes and John, Andrew Coppock has swooped in, put his arm around Betty's shoulder, and is leading her away—Martha quickly spots them halfway across the room.

"Betty!" Martha calls after them.

Betty looks back with a desperate doe-like expression as Coppock continues leading her away; then mouths *"Help!"*

Martha starts after them, which draws Ed's attention. From her haste, he swiftly realizes what's happening.

"Andrew!" bellows Ed, drawing Coppock's attention.

Betty pushes Coppock's arm off and runs, but Coppock chases after her.

"Eric, come on," says Ed, pulling me by my suspenders.

Ed and I run after Coppock as Betty leads us out of the ballroom and into the lobby.

"Andrew!" shouts Ed again, pulling a few steps ahead of me.

A deafening scream echoes throughout the Knickerbocker. Then a muffled thud.

I round the corner and find Ed, his damp hair dripping over Coppock, whose hands are covering a bloody nose. Betty is cowering a few steps to their right, in the doorway to the women's washroom. Martha hurries to Betty's side.

"Andrew!" barks a gruff voice from the back of the crowd that has swelled behind us.

"Philo," says Ed after Philo pushes his way to the front, "it's time. Either you get rid of this goon or I'm calling the police."

Annabelle and Ethel have joined Martha at Betty's side.

Betty is a doe.

"Now, Ed, let's think about this for minute," says Philo.

"What's there to think about?" says Ed sharply, soberly. Ed and I lift Coppock to his feet so that we each detain an arm. "You dropped Sid from the club for less. Coppock's been bothering this poor girl since we got here, and he just tried to force his hand up her dress. He's done."

"I'm done?" says Coppock. "I've got nothing to lose."

Charlie looks at Hazel. John looks at Ruby. Daniel and Paul and the other Havens look at their dates—and Ed locks eyes with Wendy for a powerful moment.

"Come on, Philo," urges Ed. "No one will believe a word he says—even the wives hate him!"

"Try me, Olin," sneers Coppock. "I know all of your dirty secrets, and I have a beautiful singing voice!"

"Philo!" Ed barks. "What are you going to do?"

"Drop me, and it all comes out," Coppock cackles. "You, too, *Eddy.*"

The desperation I saw in Coppock's eyes earlier has turned maniacal. Every heated incident with Coppock, from Annabelle's slap at that first Christmas party, to his near-fight with Ed at New Year's, to tonight with Betty, all boils down to this:

I can't believe I listened to this monster ...

"Make the call, Philo, or I will," says Ed intensely.

...that I let him into my mind ...

"And I'll tell you everything," says Coppock, looking up at me with a crooked smile. "I bet you'd like to know what you really are."

...but why does he know Philo's secrets?

Philo casts piercing eyes at me and, instinctively, I glare back.

"You're done, Andrew," growls Philo.

Coppock laughs, and Ed knocks him out cold.

16

AL KOHLER

My shoes are wet.

A black sedan limousine pulls up alongside the curb, and my feet slush when I walk away from *bobbing for apples*.

"Hey, kid," the driver hollers over his shoulder, "nice lederhosen—you sure you want to walk around at night like that?"

"He's lying to me," I say, my eyes fixed straight ahead as John's limo crawls beside me.

"Maybe, but his house his rules. Now get in, everybody's been looking for you."

I look askance at Mack.

"Alright, two or three people told me to look for you ... but that doesn't mean they're not worried, especially after you walk out like that. Now get in, you don't want to sleep on the street, do you?"

I pause. *I really don't.* I get in.

"I'm not going back to Philo's, though," I say firmly. "Not tonight."

"That's fine, you can stay with me."

Mack takes off his cap and drives off. He opens his mouth to say something frivolous but I cut him off.

"It's maddening," I growl, "this control he has over me, and I just let him!"

"Listen, kid, the boss does things to me I don't like all the time," explains Mack, "but for guys like you and me, without the Johns and Philos of this town we're just a couple of bindle stiffs."

As if he drove this way on purpose, we rumble past a shanty, the same one we passed the first time I rode in this car. Even so, Mack's words are of no comfort, for a life in someone else's control has none. At the same time, what makes Coppock right? I knew listening to him would be foolish, but I walked away from Philo anyway …

"I think what you need is a little independence," says Mack. "John's got me driving Amy's girls around town for their calls, so I bring in some extra bread. Now I can afford my own place—it's not much, but when I'm there I'm the boss."

"I get it, Mack," I say, "but I don't have a steady job, so how can I afford my own place?"

"Why not? You've been working with those girls for months."

"That's true, but—Philo controls my hours," I realize. "I only ever have appointments with Havens' mistresses, and Philo has the final say over who can come to events—once a girl is no longer welcome, I never see them again ...

"I have one means of independence, and even there he has influence," I say. "If he wanted to, he could completely cut off my supply."

What am I saying? If ... Could ... But would he?

"I won't say nothing bad about Mr. Olin," clarifies Mack, "but I think you found your problem."

I feel just like I did last year when he came back from Florida early, and I was completely wrong about that. But then again, things have been strange with him and Annabelle, and then add in what Coppock was saying back there ...

If only Ed had punched him out ten seconds earlier.

I realize I've sweated through the costume leather.

"Don't worry, kid, we're almost there," says Mack. "You just need to sleep it off, and start over tomorrow."

"You're right," I say. "I just need to clear my head."

"Now you're talking," he says with a sneaky grin, "So tell me, what happened to that tasty dish in the fancy brassiere?"

Betty is a doe.

I spend the night bunking with Mack in a bed that is too small for him alone. Despite his relentless snoring, I do manage to get a few hours of much-needed sleep. The next morning, before leaving to pick up John for breakfast, Mack lends me some clothes (as I left my street clothes in the hotel last night) that are one size too wide, and two short.

We stop in front of the Knickerbocker Hotel, and as we're waiting for John to come outside, Mack turns around and looks me square in the eyes. "Eric, about our conversation last night, like I said, I won't speak poorly of Philo or John. But my advice to you is keep your head down, mouth shut, and recognize what you can get from them."

There's no wink, no smile, and nothing wavering in his eyes. Just then John saunters to his limo and Mack cheerily greets him, as he always does. John mumbles "Morning," and climbs in. He looks like he hasn't slept at all.

We drive to meet the other fellas for breakfast. As John and I sit down, Philo greets us with a warm, "Christ, Eric, how did they let you in dressed like that?"

"Good morning," I say, heeding Mack's advice.

"I suppose John still brings some credibility with him after all," Philo continues. John barely flinches, which seems fine to Philo. "I assume amidst your tantrum last night you have no idea if the girls made their train or not, am I correct?"

"The girls—I forgot!"

Philo sits up tall, and rightfully so. I was so concerned with myself and Philo that I neglected my responsibility to the girls. I can feel Annabelle slipping further away ...

"It's okay," appeases Ed. "Herb said he'd take them to the station this morning."

"That's right," exclaims Charlie. "Herb was all over John's old fuss last night!"

John shrugs. Philo straightens his posture even more. Charlie's delight subsides and Ed shakes his head.

"How is Betty?" I ask.

"Now he cares," grunts Philo.

"Very shaken," states Ed, "but Martha and them were taking care of her so I'll think she'll be alright—how are you?"

"Better," I say. "I just needed some fresh air."

"You can't just leave like that, Eric," says Philo, trying to force my attention. "Unless you really are that selfish."

"I bet you'd like to know what you really are."

I clench my jaw so hard that my head hurts.

Coppock, get out of my head!

"About that, Philo" says Charlie, "have you decided what's next for Coppock?"

"I'll let him keep his job," says Philo, still keeping an eye on me, "but he's done with the Havens. There's no other work for him out there so his job will be enough to keep his mouth shut."

Betty is a doe.

The waiter comes and starts to take our orders.

"I just hope that girl doesn't press charges," says John, starting to perk up. "People are still gossiping about Sid Reid, and the last thing we need is another scandal."

Betty is a doe.

"I doubt we'll see Betty anymore," supposes Ed.

Betty is a doe.

"I don't think we ought to see any of them anymore," says Philo firmly.

"Why?" challenges Ed. "They didn't do anything wrong—it was all Coppock!"

"Every time they come around, something like this happens. They attract trouble."

"Maybe the Havens are the problem! I don't see us bailing those girls out of Mount Cary prison every other weekend."

"You sound just like Martha," grins Charlie.

"Shut up, Charlie," says Ed quickly through Philo's glare. "Martha thinks I'm 'a pig' anyhow. I stick up for her friend and she still gives me heat about Wendy."

John rolls his eyes and Philo picks up his newspaper, burying his face in an article titled, *"Employees Wish Fair Lives On To Keep Jobs."*

"She gets mad when I break up with Wendy," Ed rants. "But when we get back together she hounds me anyway."

"It's the hormones," says Charlie.

"Can you not get into this today?" says Philo from behind his newspaper.

Ed's about to say something harsh, but John silently urges him to back off.

"Yeah, I suppose," sighs Ed, playing with his food.

"Good," Philo says, putting down the newspaper. "Because now I'm in the mood for a hamburger. Who wants to go to the Fair?"

The rest of the fellas head to the World's Fairgrounds, while I opt to walk back to Philo's apartment and write Annabelle about the fallout from Betty's assault. Mostly, I want to beg for forgiveness about the train station, but she doesn't even address that part in her response—in fact, she's as warm with me as ever.

The next week in the apartment, however, is particularly tense. Despite my best efforts to act like things are good between us, Philo barely interacts with me. And when he does he its staring over my shoulder as I read Annabelle's letter ...

"She's visiting her mother for Thanksgiving," he mutters.

...or continuously nagging me about abruptly leaving the Halloween party ...

"How do you think that makes me look, Eric?"

...so that when he goes to San Francisco for an extended business trip the next week, I heed the second part of Mack's advice and start to explore options for getting my own apartment. After a quick, depressing comparison between my bank account and the apartment listings, I switch over to the classifieds to look for a real job. Fortunately, I find a bank that is hiring and schedule an interview.

"You'll do great, Erikas," writes Annabelle. *"If you start to feel nervous just smile and show them how smart you are."*

"They didn't like me," I write back.

"Then it was just very good practice. Next time you will charm them, I believe in you!"

But the next interview doesn't end well, either.

"Keep pushing, Erikas!" she writes. *"I know you are tempted to, but don't shut yourself in. If the next interview does not work out, then you find another one and go after it with all of your heart."*

I don't get that job, either.

Even so, when Philo returns from California, I give him my big news:

"I'm moving out."

"Are you? And where are you going to go?"

"I'm moving in with Mack for now," I say. "I'll help with the bills as best I can until I find a job, then I'm going to get my own place again."

"Interesting life choice, Eric."

"I'll still help out with Annabelle and the other girls when they're in town, of course," I say. "I just need a little space, that's all."

"I understand."

But I'm not sure he does, for we don't talk until the next Havens party, a sort of pre-Thanksgiving dinner at the Shoreland Hotel with the wives, which is a little disappointing having to sit through what I'm assuming will be an awkward meal without Annabelle's company. I arrive late—I called for a taxi at the last-minute when I couldn't bring myself to take a ride from my "landlord" to a party he wasn't invited to—and the maître d' leads me to the fellas' table where the others are already seated. There are two open chairs left, and I boldly take the one between Philo and Helen Mattingly.

"Sorry, Eric," says Philo. "This one's taken."

"Taken?"

"Yes, that's what I said. You may sit between Pearl and Ed if you'd like."

I take the seat and join the rest in listening to Helen Mattingly talk about her opera days when she met John.

"He was in the first row, alone, every night that week," recounts Helen. "Finally, one of the tenors invited him to one of our receptions. Halfway through the night he bought me a drink and the rest is history!"

Nearly everyone swoons at Helen's happy memory. Philo, however, keeps fidgeting in his seat and scanning the dining room entrance.

Who is he expecting?

"Ed," I hiss. "Who's Philo saving that seat for?"

"No idea," says Ed, "but he's been squirming since I got here—saving it for Marie maybe?"

Definitely not Marie.

The waiters serve our first course, and as we get ready for our second, a tall man approaches the table. He has short brown hair fashioned into a disastrous attempt at a side part, and is wearing a brown checkered suit that's about two sizes too large.

"Say, uh, do you mind if I join you?" asks the man in a low voice as loud as a trumpet.

"Al!" beams Philo, looking up at the stranger. "I'm so glad you made it!"

Al? Who's Al?

"Don't mention it," says Al politely, sitting down. "Hi, folks."

"Everyone, this is Al Kohler," introduces Philo.

"How do you know Philo, Al?" asks Helen earnestly.

"I don't really, ma'am," says the newcomer, stuffing his napkin into his collar. "I just met him the other day at the Fair. He came by my stand and we got to talking, and next thing I know ... well, here I am."

"What a funny story," smiles Helen. "What kind of a stand did you work?"

"Hamburgers, ma'am," replies Al frankly. "I flipped hamburgers at both last year's and this year's Fairs. It wasn't glamorous but it was steady work, and I got all the free hamburgers I could eat—"

No one says anything. The looks of shock on the fellas' faces tells me no one expected Philo to bring a *hamburger flipper* to Havens Thanksgiving.

I'm starting to fit like a glove with the Havens next to this goon.

"—which is a lot," adds Al, if only to break the silence.

Ed snorts. John's ears perk up, he looks at Ed, and struggles to suppress a smirk until he also snorts. Then, a peculiar thing happens: The table erupts.

"Oh my!" Helen guffaws. "He eats all the hamburgers!"

"Sometimes, I'd even take some buns," says Al proudly.

"Sometimes he takes the buns!" cries John. "He doesn't even need 'em half the time!"

"Once I even took extra onions!" boasts Al, starting to show off his boisterous bellows.

"Stop it, Al! Stop it!" howls Pearl Lords. "Charlie, I can't breathe!"

"Who needs a degree when you've got burgers!?" continues Al.

Everyone is in tears. Winnie Carmen even has to grab Ed's shoulder to keep from falling off her chair. I look around the table in utter disbelief that these people are amused by this schmuck.

"I knew you'd love him," says Philo proudly. "There's just something special about Al Kohler!"

Once the roaring laughter dies down, we're afforded the pleasure to learn even more about Philo's latest find, and none of it is very impressive.

"Let's see," Al begins after John asks him about his life before the World's Fair, "I studied at Northwestern for a year, but dropped out when I couldn't find part-time work that paid enough to cover rent *and* tuition. And lord knows there's no guarantee in this economy that I would've gotten anything good after graduating anyhow!"

"You're absolutely right," agrees John, much to my surprise. "A degree isn't worth anything if you can't find a job."

"Very sensible, Al," adds Charlie.

"That's what I told my old man," explains Al, "but he still had a few words for me when I dropped out to work at a hamburger stand. You know what I say, though? And pardon my French—*Fuck him!*"

"Oh my," gasps Pearl, more thrilled than offended.

"Al was telling me he's been looking for work ever since the Fair closed," says Philo, patting Al on the back.

"I'm still hoping to get a permanent gig at one of the packing houses, but there's a lot of food service guys going after not so many jobs," says Al soberly.

"That sounds awful," remarks Ed. "You don't always think about how many people lost their jobs after the Fair closed."

What about after the market crashed?

"It's a real problem," admits Al. "There was an article in the *Tribune* a while back about it—maybe you saw. The reporter actually used a few quotes from me."

Philo nods, impressed.

"You were in the papers?" says Helen, delighted. "How fun! An awful reason, but it's still nice to see your name in print."

"Thank you, ma'am," says Al. "That's exactly how I feel about it."

"I was telling Al that he has the kind of drive and work ethic that could really take him places," says Philo warmly. "He just needs an opportunity."

"I know I don't have a lot of managerial experience," says Al, "but not only was I very committed to proper handling of the meats, I also honed my skills in customer service."

"You've convinced me!" blurts John.

"You know who he should talk to?" says Charlie, "Herb Galloway."

"Good thinking, Charlie," says Ed. "Herb just closed a bunch of new advertising accounts—he probably could use another salesman."

"For once, I agree with all of you," says Philo, rising from his chair. "We should talk to Herb. Come on, Al, let's meet your future employer."

Where was this for me?!

"Get out!" exclaims Al, jumping to his feet. "Really? I should've bought a nicer suit—I thought I was just here for dames. Gosh, wish me luck folks!"

"There's no point in getting up, Al," says Ed. "Here comes Herb now."

"Happy Thanksgiving, everyone," says Herb Galloway, walking up to our table. "I want everyone to meet my girlfriend, Louise."

The fellas all look at each other.

"Hi, Eric," squeaks Louise excitedly, with her arm linked around Herb's.

"Philo, did you know Herb had a new girlfriend?" asks Ed gingerly.

"We spoke about it on the phone yesterday," assures Philo. "He really wanted to bring Louise, and who am I to deny the heart's desire?"

"It's nice to meet you, dear," says Helen, reaching her hand to Louise. "I can see it in Herb's eyes that you make him very happy."

"You both look happy," observes Ed.

"Herb, can Al here have a job?" asks Philo bluntly.

Herb looks at Al, who licks his hand, fixes his hair, and smiles.

"Sure," agrees Herb. "Can you start on Monday?"

"He sure can!" grins Philo.

"Great," says Herb. "Let's talk after the party, Al."

"Bye, everyone!" squeaks Louise as she and Herb meander to the next table.

"I got the job!" says Al enthusiastically to vociferous applause.

As the fellas and their wives congratulate this practical stranger on his new job, I can't help but feel overlooked. In the two years I've known Philo never once did he try to get me a full-time job—but ten minutes with Al and he's gotten him a career. Of course, I'm taking for granted my lucrative financial planning for the Havens' paramours …

"It's just like what I told Al when I had him re-make my hamburger: 'You get what you want—'" starts Philo.

"'—when you talk to the right people!'" finishes Al.

Now they're completing each other's sentences?

Since Thanksgiving, Al Kohler is everywhere. At Christmas, Al is there. At New Year's, Al is there. The Winter Ball … Valentine's Day … St. Patrick's Day … Al. Is. There.

He's even there when the Shiner girls come to town. With Louise now spending every weekend with Herb, Ethel usually elects to stay back in Mount Cary to be "an old maid with Betty"; as such, usually leaving just Annabelle and Martha on these outings.

"Who's that?" asks Annabelle after Al shows up almost an hour late to the jazz club we're at.

"That's Al," Philo and I say simultaneously, though with rather contrasting tones.

"Sorry I'm late, fellas," says Al. "Long day at work, but I'm not complaining!"

"That's fine, Al," assures Philo. "Say, would you like the rest of my steak? I can't finish it."

"Would I ever!"

And the more Al Kohler becomes a part of our group, the more difficult it becomes to talk to Philo about even serious matters.

"Philo," I say quietly during Paul Jaeger's New Year's toast, "I stopped by the house the other day to check on Marie and she's changed the locks."

"Eric, I don't want to talk about this," he says sternly.

And the more I try ...

"For the final time, I'm not here to talk about Marie!"

"I'm talking to Annabelle, Eric, get out of here!"

"Can you let me sit for a minute, Eric?"

... the more Coppock's words creep back in:

"I know all of your dirty secrets"

What dirty secrets?

"It all comes out."

What would happen if it does?

"I bet you'd like to know what you really are!"

He's right.

With every "Hey, Al!" or "Al, listen to this" from a Haven who has largely ignored me over the past two years, I grow increasingly serious about finding out what Andrew Coppock has to say.

"Hey, Eric!"

But then there's Annabelle.

"Erikas, why haven't you written me lately?" she asks one weekend as I pick her and Martha up from Union Station.

Ever since Al started joining our Haven outings I've been so preoccupied with worrying about being replaced in the founders' circle that I've inadvertently isolated myself from Annabelle. Only now do I realize how I've neglected our private written world lately—and when I'm finally able to enjoy it without Philo reading over my shoulder.

This is my chance.

"There's no excuse," I say. "I'll do better."

"I sure hope so," she says. "Your letters are all that keep me sane when I'm at school!"

Still, once we're in the company of Philo—and Al—I have a hard time getting a moment alone with her. And when I try to talk to her with others around it's just different between us, like something has changed, even though our letters suggest otherwise.

On paper, I am honest and open ...

"I miss you, Annabelle."

… and she makes me feel special …

"You're the only man who appreciates me."

… but in-person we have become strangers. I start to question which persona is true, but this type of thinking doesn't help the reality.

In May, the fellas and I head to Lincoln Park where we check out Al's new apartment overlooking the well-groomed North Pond. He explains how he has been saving up since he started working for Herb, and is finally able to afford the move to the affluent neighborhood he "grew up admiring."

Heartwarming.

"This sure is a snazzy neighborhood you've got here, Al," says John, admiring the gushing greenery and bright flowers as the six of us stroll through the park.

"Thanks, John," says Al. "I really like it here. Everywhere you look there's a new surprise—like this!"

Al bends forward and picks up a rusted horseshoe. He glances around at both sides of the walking path and spots an old, abandoned court on a patch of worn lawn. "How 'bout we play a round?" he proposes.

"I don't want to play," croaks Philo, shuffling toward a nearby bench. "You fellas go right ahead."

"Alrighty," says Al, looking over the rest of us. "You all in?"

We all nod and follow Al to the court.

"Sorry, Eric, but we only need four," explains Al. "Maybe the next game, bud."

I glare at Al, but he's already focused on the game. I take a seat next to Philo on the bench.

"I'm with Al!" shouts John, taking his place behind one of the stakes and shaking the dirt off one of the horseshoes.

"Hey, John-o! Good call!" shouts Al wearing his typical cheeky grin.

"Alright, Charlie," laments Ed, taking his place next to Al, opposite John and Charlie, "let's just do what we can."

The game starts with, somehow, Charlie landing both of his horseshoes closer than John's, scoring two points for his team.

"Nice work, Charlie," marvels Ed. "Maybe you weren't adopted after all!"

"Don't worry about it, Al—" encourages Philo before succumbing to a string of coughs. "—show these—old guys—how it's done!"

Al smirks at Philo, then intensifies his focus on his stake like he's performing heart surgery.

It's horseshoes.

Two strident clanks and a roar of approval from both sides and Philo.

Of course, he's good at horseshoes.

"Do we want to keep playing or just call it now?" says John with steadfast approval.

Philo starts to say something, too, but is cut off by another hacking fit.

"Lucky throws," simpers Al. "Show us what you can do, Ed!"

Ed nails a ringer with his first throw, but his second lands wide left. The score is three-to-two in favor of Al's team, but that's as close as the game will be, as Al continues to rattle off ringer after near-ringer after ringer. And while everyone continues to goggle at Al's horseshoe prowess, I take the opportunity to restore my place on Philo's mantle.

"I don't understand the excitement over a silly lawn game," I pose. "Why not play a real sport, like football?"

Philo shakes his head and hacks again. "Football, Eric? Seriously? —I can't even play—horseshoes."

"But you played in college," I say, determined to bond. "Do you have any football stories about you and my father?"

"Four in a row!" proclaims Al, his arms stretched upward.

"That was years ago, Eric," says Philo. "I can't remember much—that far back."

"But—"

"Wait your turn, they'll—let you play next," he says feebly.

A pit forms in my stomach.

Charlie, who has become progressively antagonized over his inability to repeat his early success, rubs a horseshoe between his plump hands and takes two deliberate strides forward when, suddenly, the horseshoe slips and falls straight down.

"My toe! My toe!" wails Charlie. "It's broken, I know it!"

"For Christ's sake, Charlie," mutters Ed as his cousin keels over.

"Charlie, stop being so dramatic!" say Philo with another hack. "Eric, get in there for him."

Charlie stumbles off the court, and I take his place next to John.

"Here comes big game Whit Wyatt," says Al with terribly phony impressment in his tone.

"Who's that?" I scoff.

"A White Sox pitcher," says Philo with a half-laugh, half-choke.

"The Sox bring in Wyatt late in games, but he always loses," explains John.

"I see," I say bluntly.

Al thinks he's so funny.

"Alright, it's sixteen to five," says Al, "so don't get too comfortable up there, Eric."

"Just do your best!" shouts Philo hoarsely.

"I intend to," I mutter.

I pick up Charlie's second horseshoe and take a deep breath. I rotate my wrist so it's facing directly toward the stake at Al's feet, swing the horseshoe back, and let it fly.

CLANK!

There's a silence. For just a second, and probably not even that long, Al shudders—he tries to play it cool but with Philo watching we both know it's on.

"Aces!" shouts Ed. "We may have a game after all."

Despite the determination to prove myself, I'm not quite sure what has come over me. I haven't played horseshoes since my childhood, and I have never been so unstoppable. Every throw twirls around the stake, with my success fueling *flawless* Al Kohler's demise. For every ringer, Al has two that don't get anywhere close. Even Ed's playing his part to stave off any feeble charges from Al, which is more than I need because I still can't miss.

Suddenly, the score has narrowed to eighteen-to-seventeen, and my smug rival has mutated into a shaking bag of bones. There are no more jokes, just a palpable pressure, and a spectator who appears keen to pass judgment following these next two throws. Al picks up his first horseshoe, takes a deep breath, and heaves it with all his might—it lands with a deep thud short of the stake, and slightly to the right.

"Too short," I say. "No point."

John sighs.

"Are you sure?" says Al desperately. "That looks less than six inches to me."

John examines the horseshoe. "I'm afraid Eric's right," he frowns. "That's too far to score."

One more miss and he's done.

Al picks up his second horseshoe, mutters angrily to himself, and tosses it.

It's over.

The horseshoe lands at the stake with a sharp *CLANG*. Al hops up and down, screaming "I won! I won!" John joins the celebration, Ed and Charlie congratulate him, and even Philo ignores his incessant hacking to applaud.

"Good game, Eric," says Al, extending his hand. "I was nervous at the end."

I stare at Al's hand for a second, probably long enough to warrant hostility, but any reaction is cast aside by a commotion from the bench.

"Philo!" Charlie yelps.

Charlie's got his arm around Philo, who has dropped to his knees and can't stop coughing.

"We need to get him to a doctor!" bellows Ed.

"There's a hospital just around the corner," says Al, sprinting off and shouting for an ambulance.

17

THE GOLD ROOM

It took some convincing from Mack, but I finally push myself to visit Philo in the hospital. Of course, had the doctors not have quickly ruled a fully recovery from his lung ailment I would have gone without hesitation. As it stands, I'm still bitter toward him.

I sit in the front of the limo with Mack until he drops me off at the hospital on his way to Edgewater, where the thin brunette in the back seat has an appointment. After some lingering in the hospital lobby I go up to Philo's floor where I cross paths with Al. He stops and greets me as if we are going to have a conversation, but I ignore him.

We're not here to be friends.

Inside the room—which Philo has managed to get to himself—I see him sitting upright in bed, eating a small piece of layer cake.

Perhaps Marie has a heart after all.

I imagine Philo refused to eat it in her company, but she is gone now so he is free to enjoy.

Philo's bedside is littered with flowers and presents, including a bottle of schnapps from Ed. But despite the sympathetic benevolence surrounding him, the most beautiful gift is the strawberry blond woman sitting at his side.

"Annabelle," I say, forgoing all concern for Philo's health. "How did you get here?"

I just can't let go.

Philo takes a deliberately large bite of cake.

"The train," says Annabelle. "Al picked me up."

"Why would Al pick her up?" I say to Philo, bemused. "That's my job."

"You say that as if it's a prize, Eric," says Philo through his mouthful.

"That's not what I meant," I snap.

"I'm not a prize?" asks Annabelle.

"That's not what I meant, either—"

I can't help but smile a little. For a second, I'm reminded of all the funny little things Annabelle would say that the two of us would laugh at behind Philo's back. Even as friends, I miss her—I wish we could say aloud the things that we write to each other, but it's hard when we're never alone.

"Who's taking her back, Philo? I saw Al leave."

"He had to return to work," says Annabelle simply.

"Because he has a job, Eric," adds Philo. "Herb gave him a long lunch to visit me."

"I'll take you back, Annabelle."

Annabelle and Philo hesitate.

"I'm not sure that's a great idea," she says. "What would the porters say if I am picked up by one man then returned by another that same day? Either way, I promised Uncle Philo I'd stay with him until the doctor sends him home."

"You don't have to call him Uncle Philo when it's just me."

"I'm sorry, Eric," she corrects, "*Mr. Olin.*"

Annabelle's flippancy is uncajoling.

"Annabelle," says Philo slowly, and putting down his fork. "Give us a minute. I want to talk to Eric alone."

That's not what I want.

Annabelle obliges, excusing herself under the pretense of needing fresh air.

"Eric, these past few days in the hospital got me thinking," he starts. "Annabelle is graduating at the end of the month, and I'd like to throw her class a proper celebration."

Should we be celebrating two and a half years at a school that hasn't taught her the difference between preservatives and les préservatifs?

"As you know," Philo continues, "I was stuck here during yesterday's Mother's Day luncheon so I wasn't able to give everyone the details about this graduation party. I need your help spreading the word—can you do that for me?"

Why don't you have perfect Al Kohler help you?

"Why do you need *my* help?"

"Don't ask stupid questions, Eric."

He's in the hospital.

"Can't you get somebody else to help you?"

"Eric, I'm asking you," reminds Philo. "It's a celebration for Annabelle, and I need your help."

... For Annabelle.

"Who else knows about this?"

"It's not really a surprise, but so far just you and I."

Al Kohler may be Philo's flavor-of-the-month, but when it comes to truly important matters, he knows who to turn to.

"Okay, I'll help," I say. "Just tell me when and where and I'll make it happen."

In the evening of the first Saturday in June, four black limousines are parked across the street from Union Station, waiting for a group of nineteen giddy Shiner graduates who have chosen to skip a school-sponsored end-of-year movie to attend "An unforgettable night in the *Paris on the Prairie*." Each limo has been assigned an escort from one of the younger (formally) single Havens: Herb and Paul—who have been criticizing Philo's venue choice ever since we pulled up to the station—are in the first two limos, I'm in the third, and Al, with his trendy new slicked back hairdo, is in the last with Mack.

Mack's going to eat that poor sap up.

At once, a herd of young, chattering girls tramp through the pillared exits of Union Station—leading the pack, predictably, is Annabelle. She is a goddess in her flattering white dress, flanked by her three loyal friends. I exit my limo to wave to the girls.

"Hi, Eric!" exclaims Martha, which is followed by Annabelle's warm wave.

I put out my hand to help them in my limo, but they walk past me all the way to the front limo with Herb. Louise runs into his gangly arms, they twirl and kiss, and then he holds the back door for them to climb into his car. Annabelle casts another wave my way before the door closes behind her. Empty-handed, five girls whom I don't recognize get into my limo, marveling at the fine, leather interior and bottles of chilled champagne waiting for them.

"It's only a rental," I remind them.

I don't ask their names, and let them drink what's left of the champagne on our short drive to the Congress Hotel—I feel bad for Herb having to deal with the girls once he tells them where Philo's booked this thing ...

When we arrive, the nineteen girls who erratically piled into the four limos pour out in equal disorder.

So much for molding your society princesses, Beulah.

Herb and Louise enter the massive hotel together, while Paul is happily surrounded by the five girls from his limo. My girls don't wait a second for me to crawl out of ours, and I feel a little bad for not being a more attentive escort until I notice Al Kohler is nowhere near his companions, either.

Shy around the ladies, Al?

In fact, he's just talking to Mack. When he finally walks away Mack shouts, "I'm still picking you up after, right?"

"Not if tonight goes as planned," replies Al rather presumptuously. "Hey, let's catch up soon, you wet smack!"

"Sure thing, Al—still can't believe I was chauffeuring the biggest schmuck in Chicago!"

Inside the Congress' modest white-paneled lobby, the Shiner girls eagerly await my arrival. As I predicted, they do not look happy with our surroundings—I'll have to bring up the mood.

"Finally, Eric," says Martha, rubbing her arms. "Can you tell us the rules so they'll let us inside—it's freezing out here."

"And hurry up, this lobby gives me the creeps," adds Ethel.

Philo asked me to say a few words about etiquette and such—things they should have learned at Shiner—before letting them into the party. It's Philo's foolproof way of avoiding another Coppock incident.

"Hey, Eric," says Al, sniffing my collar like some bipedal bloodhound, "you sure you're okay to give this speech?"

"I'm sure," I say matter-of-factly. "Go into the ballroom and tell Philo we're here."

"Whatever you say," says Al, patting me most unwelcomingly on my back, then going through the closed ballroom doors like my *goddam page.*

"Hey!" I shout a few times, grabbing the girls' attention. I'm not really fond of the nineteen pairs of eyes all staring at me. "I'm going to keep this quick. Before we go into The Gold Room, I want to remind you to be on your best behavior, just like the society girls you've become. Uncle Philo wants you to have a good time, but please respect the facility. We'll mingle, have dinner, dance, and then—who knows?"

"May we go in now?" says Annabelle sweetly.

"Just for you," I say with a point. "Let 'em in, boys!"

Herb and Paul swing the doors open to reveal ...

"Gold!"

Blasted with twittering conversation, laughter, and an upbeat brassy tune, my eyes flutter as they struggle to adjust to the endlessly gilded décor. Annabelle's classmates gasp excitedly at the gold ceiling, and gold walls, with the gold chandeliers hanging over the gold balcony. Behind the gold stage hangs a gold curtain where, in front of, the band is playing dressed in—white, for contrast.

"Where's Felix?" I mutter. "Maybe he got a better gig."

I imagine Felix leading a twenty-piece band in a hot Miami nightclub, while dozens of beautiful couples—none with gray hair—shake their bodies to his rhythms. I've also never been to Miami, so I start to imagine what that's like ...

"There you are, Eric. Oh, your collar's just sticking up a bit," says Ed, adjusting my jacket. He sniffs me, too, then quickly pulls back. "How much have you had to drink?"

"Nothing," I say, shaking my head. "The girls finished the champagne."

"Come on, dinner's about to be served."

Everyone else—even the new Shiner girls—has found their seat incredibly fast.

Probably was a week's worth of lessons at Shiner.

"You're sitting with the usual crew," says Ed as I follow him to the table. I take the empty seat between Martha and Annabelle.

"Erikas!" says Annabelle warmly, before Al—seated to her right—continues to talk her ear off.

After dinner is served, Philo comes around the table and whispers something to Annabelle like, "Let's do it now." She agrees and he escorts her up to the stage where they say something to the bandleader.

After they depart, Ed leans into Martha and says, "Have you thought about my proposition?"

"No," says Martha in a low, stern voice.

"Why not?" presses Ed carefully. "You're done with Shiner; the timing is perfect."

They probably don't think I can hear them through Louise and Herb's obnoxious giggling from feeding each other from their identical plates.

"Out of principle, my answer is no," says Martha. "What would your wife say?"

"I want to do this because of my wife," says Ed. "Don't let your pride stand in the way of your heart."

Annabelle and Philo return. "I'm done talking about this," she says, stuffing a piece of broccoli in her mouth.

"You're making a mistake," finishes Ed.

Martha puts down her fork rather harshly, takes a deep breath, and then turns to me politely. "Eric," she says, "please switch seats with me."

Al compliments Annabelle's makeup as she sits back down next to me. I quickly stuff a huge helping of mashed potatoes into my mouth, and pantomime to Martha being unable to speak as just cause to stay put.

"Oh, for heaven's sake, Eric."

After the rest of the table has finished dinner, and I am halfway through my fifth bread roll, Philo stands up and clinks his fork against his glass to get everyone's attention. The music dies down, and with the help of Al's and my thunderous shouting, we get the raucous school girls to quiet down.

Philo clears his throat. "Your attention, please! I thank each of you for joining us tonight against the wishes of your professors. I speak for all the Havens when I say we greatly appreciate your company tonight.

"Now, I may not have formally met many of you before, but for those of you I have——" Philo pauses and eyes Annabelle, "——I would like to say how much I've enjoyed watching you grow from silly, careless girls into confident, sophisticated women."

Ed looks at Martha like Philo did to Annabelle. I try to follow Philo's speech, but out of the corner of my eye I see Al sliding his hand behind her back as he whispers something *hilarious.*

If you want her, take her.

"With that, I'd like to propose a toast!" announces Philo, raising his glass high into the air.

"To Philo!" shouts Al heartily, jumping to his feet.

Annabelle immediately elbows him in the ribs. "*Uncle* Philo," she reminds him in a low voice.

"To Uncle Philo!" amends Al.

There is a clamoring of clinking glasses and *"Cheers"* as Philo smiles approvingly at his bold, new apprentice.

Philo sits down and the band starts playing a more danceable repertoire, coaxing the young ladies and, in turn, the libidinous Havens to the dance floor. None reach there faster than Herb and Louise, who are fully intertwined before the band finishes their pickup measure.

By now it is evident that this Havens event carries a different dynamic than the typical mistress parties. While those tend to be more of a show-and-tell affair, tonight seems to be a proper mixer, with several additional younger gentlemen—some even younger than I—in attendance than usual.

"Who are all these new guys?" I ask the fellas.

"Philo's idea," frowns Ed, "and John couldn't say no."

"He calls them 'prospectives,'" shrugs John.

"They don't know the rules and wouldn't care if they did," says Ed. "But who am I to say?"

As I wander through the party, I keep bumping into these 'prospectives,' who are not lacking for confidence or words.

"Norman Brown," says a young man with brown hair who bears a striking resemblance to John's wife, Helen. "Northwestern, Class of 1934. My uncle is one of the founders, John Mattingly."

I wonder if he has a brother named Wes.

"Very interesting, Norman," mocks Ethel. "So, you're not a real Haven then, right?"

"You've got me," says John's nephew with an unflappable laugh. "I will be once Uncle John thinks I'm old enough to officially join."

"I see," says Ethel pointedly. "Sorry, junior—have an older brother?"

Other future and bachelor Havens have more success, whether it be attributed to their more elegant conversational skills ...

"Luke Jaeger," says a handsome young man with thick eyebrows. "How about we take a twirl around this dance floor, hun, so I can tell my cousin how I got dizzy with a dame."

Or due to finding a "riper tomato" ...

"Hi, my name is—"

"Yes!" swoons a short, blond girl whose mannerisms remind me of Louise, pre-Herb.

"But I haven't asked you anything yet," says the naïve young man with sharp blue eyes.

I look around the dance floor, trying to locate Annabelle to ask her to dance, but am coming up empty. I'm about to give up, but I notice Daniel Kruger, Paul Jaeger, and Al looking and laughing in my general direction—really chumming it up—from the edge of the dance floor. Everyone accepts Al so easily, and he's not even doing anything special.

I'll show them.

"Hi, Eric Mihlfried," I say to a thin girl with a pretty face and bushy light brown hair. "Xavier, class of 1927—"

The girl before me cringes at the year.

"Why don't you dance with me," I try again, cocking an eyebrow, "and I'll ... tell your fortune?"

"Huh? Are you drunk?"

"Do you want to dance?" I say bluntly.

"Who are you?"

"I'm a friend of Uncle Philo."

"Oh!" exclaims the girl, the sudden understanding on her face (and hand on my arm) putting me at ease. *"You're Al."*

"Just go."

More Herb-and-Louise's find each other with every passing tune, while I can feel a growing number of Haven eyes firmly fixed on my courting contretemps. I search the room for a familiar or even pitying face, but Ed and Martha are arguing, Felix is partying in South Beach, and I still can't find Annabelle.

Why didn't I talk to the girls in my limo? I don't even remember what they look like.

Then, I see her—standing near the doorway like a soft angel illuminated by the golden backdrop. She's all alone while Al chats with his pals. She looks lost, like a doe, like she doesn't feel like she belongs.

If you want her, take her.

She smiles as I approach.

"Annabelle, would you like to dance?" I say, gently grabbing her hand.

"Hmm," ponders Annabelle, glancing around the room. "Not right now, I don't think."

"Why not? Did Al say something to you?"

"No," she says, straightening my tie. "I just don't think now's a good time for us to dance."

Al probably told her I was drunk. Why does everybody think that?

"I don't even remember having a drink today."

"I'm sorry, Eric," Annabelle grimaces, "but I really must go."

"Oh," I say glumly, then mustering a smile. "I'll see you around!"

Annabelle smiles back before carrying on toward the stage. I take a moment to repress my rejection, then make my way back across the dance floor.

"Look, Herb!" squeals Louise. "Anna-belly's on stage!"

I wheel my head around and freeze as the lights dim and a warm amber glow frames her angelic face, and softly glimmers off her unblemished white dress.

"Good evening," says Annabelle precisely as the music stops, drawing the rest of the room's attention. "I'd like to sing a song I prepared for the spring recital," she says, casting the faintest smirk in my direction—she confided in her letters to me that she had never joined the Glee Club at Shiner, despite Philo's belief otherwise.

Several members of the band set down their instruments and fall to the back of the stage. One of the musicians steps forward with a Spanish guitar so all that remains in the stage's saffron glow are a guitar, piano, and Annabelle.

"From my favorite poem by Edgar Allan Poe …"

Martha smiles at Ed, who acknowledges her back, then transitions her smile toward her friend on stage.

The pianist starts with swirling arpeggios in a slow, brooding, minor key waltz. The guitar gradually eases in, creating an air of harmonious melancholy.

There's a log cabin—worn and overwrought with recollection—presiding over the misted body of water below. Inside, there's a fire burning, but the cabin is drafty, and the stories on the shelf are as misleading as the ornamental deer lamp with broken bulb.

The music crescendos, but before it reaches any discernable apex, it softens, and Annabelle begins to sing:

"It was many and many a year ago,

In a kingdom by the sea,

That a maiden there lived whom you may know

By the name of Anna-belly;

And this maiden she lived with no other thought

Than to love and be loved by me."

Annabelle's voice is beautiful. It is mostly flat, and rather breathy, but nonetheless perfect.

I close my eyes, and when I open them, I am in the cabin, and Annabelle is standing before me, beckoning me to join her. She reaches for my hand as if to lead me down to the beach. She runs ahead …

"I was a child and she was a child,

In this kingdom by the sea:

But we loved with a love that was more than love—

I and my Anna-belly;

With a love that the winged seraphs of heaven

Coveted her and me."

... *We're at the first Havens' Christmas party, and I am terribly, uncomfortably out of place. Then Annabelle comes up to me, and actually wants to talk about* me—*she actually wants to help* me ...

"And this was the reason that long ago,

In this kingdom by the sea,

A wind blew out of a cloud, chilling

My beautiful Anna-belly;"

"Annabel Lee— Anna-*belly*," giggles Louise in revelation.

"It's very clever," admiringly hushes Herb.

"So that her highborn kinsmen came

And bore her away from me,

To shut her up in a sepulchre

In this kingdom by the sea."

... *Philo and I are driving to Mount Cary for the first time, and the fields alongside the road are growing progressively barren and gray.*

Annabelle proudly holds up her tennis racket, but it morphs into a snake, and then into a French baguette ...

"The angels, not half so happy in heaven,

Went envying her and me—

Yes! —that was the reason (as all men know,

In this kingdom by the sea)

That the wind came out of the cloud by night,

Chilling and killing my Anna-belly."

... I am standing alone in an empty ballroom. Except it is not empty, it is filled with eager eyes of Marie Olin, John Mattingly, and Andrew Coppock. And I am not alone—I am dancing with Martha—and Annabelle is watching—and Martha is Louise—and Louise is Annabelle—and Philo is watching—and I am Al Kohler ...

"But our love it was stronger by far than the love

Of those who were older than we—

Of many far wiser than we—

And neither the angels in heaven above,

Nor the demons down under the sea,

Can ever dissever my soul from the soul

Of the beautiful Anna-belly."

... Philo slowly walks up to my side, and asks me if I think Annabelle is beautiful ...

"The most beautiful," I say serenely, tears welling up in my eyes.

"Yes," chuckles Philo, "I thought so."

"For the moon never beams without bringing me dreams

Of the beautiful Anna-belly;

And the stars never rise but I see the bright eyes

Of the beautiful Anna-belly;

And so, all the night-tide, I lie down by the side

Of my darling, my darling, my life and my bride,

In her sepulchre there by the sea—

In her tomb by the side of the sea."

Annabelle completes her last note and lowers her head so that it is veiled by fluttering shadows—but the musicians keep playing the minimalist waltz. Philo walks just below the center of the stage, where Annabelle meets him, and the two begin to dance. They dance for a minute. Maybe two. Then other couples join them—Herb and Louise ... and some others.

Why does Philo dance with her? This dance I should have gotten
...

Philo catches my longing stare, and shoots back a potent glare.

... If we don't dance tonight, I may be forgotten.

I march back across the dance floor, carelessly barreling through multiple fledgling couples, on my way to where Philo and Annabelle dance.

May I cut in? I'm cutting in. There's no use for your snarling. If you don't mind, I am inclined to dance with my darling.

"Get in here, Al," beckons Philo, presenting Annabelle like a piece of fine silk.

Al, grinning, twirls Annabelle, and she giggles. And he giggles. And Philo giggles. And they dance. And the song keeps going—and they dance.

"Sir?"

I open my eyes, and a chill runs up my spine as I take in the empty Congress Hotel ballroom. It's still every bit as gold, but with the lights up it looks tired and worn.

"Sir," says the waiter again. "I'm going to have to ask you to leave so we can finish cleaning."

"But the party—"

"Finished an hour ago," he asserts, quite demeaning. "Now scram, unless you want to sleep in here with the ghosts tonight."

The waiter walks away, and continues clearing used plates and glasses from the dozens of soiled, empty tables. I can barely remember the party, as if my mind has been disabled. I *know* what happened, but the details are missing. Or unimportant. Or they're gone. It's time to go. I must go on.

I stand and swivel toward the exit, but in my disoriented haste, I bump into the waiter, spilling old drinks about the place. I look down: a half dozen unemptied glasses of indiscernible liquid masses, much quicker than molasses, are leaking on the ground. And what's more?

My shoes are wet.

18

NOISELESS NIGHTS

A vacant calm upon the street

The coveted sage I cannot greet,

From whom I might suppress conceit;

Oh, silent street, may I inject?

Was I wrong to expect

Our penned exchange to blossom hence?

Would that not fit common sense?

Perhaps my oracle was a cipher,

For if it wasn't, she'd be my wife, or

At least a speck I could protect—

But, alas, my trek is indirect.

My muffled cries, they are observed;

The rise that follows is undeserved;

They spurred her stroll? Imaginary—

Nevertheless spoiling my sanctuary;

Who are you to mock my pity?

Oh, callous girl, smiling pretty

In my city—oh, heartless city!

You know not what I've endured,

A fruitless love left uninsured,

Yet I intrude upon your gait—

Did I intrude when she made me wait?

The few loving pecks I still protect,

They guide my trek, though indirect.

Day is night as night is day;

I see a line—I won't obey

For loaves and fish of Hoover's pigeons—

But here I am, a double-victim!

For some, a friend offers quick assistance,

And fools affected put up no resistance;

With no friend in sight, or thought to commotion

I push ahead in self-promotion;

My scheme's defect leads to neglect—

One I deflect; next hits my neck;

Sore, off my trek, I redirect.

My actions have become austere,

But where it crumbled is still not clear;

Was it her? I should think not;

I can't be sure, but explore the thought

If it wasn't her then it was surely him—

Why did I shine bright to suddenly dim?

Our conversations she coveted most

Led to missed glares of our salty host?

What brought me close made me a ghost ...

Which brings me to her newfound beau:

A misfit stooge found on skid row;

Host's wish taken from respect,

Making my trek more indirect.

But what connection do we really hold?

Only emerging once my father's cold—

Are there even stories? Justly untold?

Oh mother—answer—as I'd like to hear:

Will my rosy hopes ever reappear?

Your thorny thoughts are based on nothing;

I don't need approval—I was bluffing!

So far away, distance keeps you safe,

While insecurities make me a waif—

I am correct—I *am* correct!

If I am wrecked it's from neglect!

Oh, solo trek, do I resurrect?

Feel the free, suppressing heat—

Sudden heat!

The dust storm's come again, a homecoming to

mistreat;

How it looms, looms, looms,

As I resume my solo trek;

I assume that it will doom

My resurrection, then exhume

Defeated demons my fool has kept at call and beck;

And, oh, they sneer, sneer, sneer

'Til my eyes, they burn and sear,

Imploring, "Greet, greet, greet,

"Greet thy cold, compelling heat!"

I ignore this proclamation; they're insistent to repeat,

Continue walking, perhaps mocking all the heat.

Endure the cruel, most certain heat—

Constant heat!

Rolling down in staggered waves, hellbent to defeat,

And they reach my memories, which now I must

inspect,

Alas, I find the proof I need—I am correct;

Through my words, I gave my soul—

I saw hers, too;

I'll press on our weekly scrolls,

Coaxing riffs within her marriage, poking holes

'Til I break through;

I will not accept defeat

In this world, I've discovered even victims still will

cheat,

That's how I'll eat,

While on the street,

It is most pleasing to the heat,

And it will get me off the street;

Can I be garish, to make him perish?

That former man in the street:

With his perish, I'm elite—

But I could perish, then he'll eat!

Oh, which thine street man better tolerates the heat?

The heat subsides, but hope—it strays,

Floats over the edge, it riskily stays,

It's growing old; we can keep it fresh,

Though my bowed switch only taps its flesh;

Slight contact's made, but it swivels as such,

About-face, crooked, effectively blind,

Lowering slowly, requiring crutch—

"Jump out and grab it!" (Subconscious mind);

Tumbling, tumbling, many miles it seems,

Hope clutched in my arms, fulfilling my dreams.

"I'm sorry, I'm sorry!" I plead to the orb,

But hope's fallen deaf, my pleas are absorbed;

I *could* help her feel that I'm willing to change,

A challenge considering my free-falling range—

Instead I attach to the frail orb a chute,

Though velocity slows, fails to alter our route;

"I promise to fix you once we strike the ground"

But that hope-filled orb makes nary a sound.

Plummeting, plummeting, the closer we come

To the stiff ground below, I refuse to succumb

To what seems our fate, for there must be something

I can do for you to amend the affronting.

An affront I endured when you were given away

To a man so below you—oh, unholy day!

Below us both is the earth, crippling and near,

But then I see it right there; my only option is clear:

I heave you above, put a distance between,

Take the brunt of the crash and hope you trampoline.

Feeling bland,

She doesn't land—

Soon I see the poisoned sight:

Hand-held walking,

Gaily talking—

Leads to a noiseless night.

No mistaking,

Done with aching,

I must create my joyous sight—

I will display

Once he's away,

Suggests the noiseless night.

A stalking fox,

While she shops,

Until I find my chosen sight—

A Rothschild's sale,

Here I'll unveil,

And end my noiseless nights.

"You are barred!"

Shouts the guard,

Poisoning my sight;

I get uneasy,

She doesn't see me,

And I resume my noiseless nights.

Why should I endure pain?

I'm not nearly as broken;

I have so much more—

Only my words are spoken!

If my speech causes danger

Still my words are spoken.

I head south to a block

I've heard much about,

Where those beat blow their wigs,

And the junkies are out—

Sweet dough buys a quiff,

And the coppers keep out.

Sweet Hamilton's come along,

I say, "Buy me a dame"—

There's not even a mattress,

And she can't say her name;

If 'The Mattress' was here

He'd be chanting my name.

Low, angry barking

Not far off is heard,

And the madness within me

Is instantly stirred—

She can now say her name,

But her words are all slurred;

When the barking endures

The foul potion is stirred.

I bumble back out to

The street, dodging all light,

But that dull, hazy red

Permeates on this night;

Were they barking at me?

And am I out of sight?

If they're barking at me

Then I may have to fight!

But the culprit is me—

Do I have the right?

I won't have to fight—

I *might have to fight!*

My knuckles are white,

And I'm cursing the night,

After night, after night,

After night, after night!

A nephew crosses my path—

A suit follows his lead;

The nephew throws me a wink

While caressing his steed;

Broken glass reflects, and

I see emotions bleed,

And I'm boxing on my mug

Until my nose starts to bleed.

Why do I cause this pain?

Am I really that far broken?

I need so much more

Than my words to be spoken;

If my speech causes danger

Perhaps different words need be spoken.

With love and war, the hardest fights,

          victors seldom come into sight,

And even in your best condition

          you finish completely frail;

And I find these ruminations turning into declarations,

Watching Hollywood's plantations

          turn into a dancing gale.

Pleading to their rigid master

          to turn from their dancing gale—

          A little girl can prevail.

While a cute, curly-topped rebel

          can freely shoot off a pebble,

A likewise scheme from me

          would certainly mean a stint in jail;

But should I even get the chance

          to pass for curly at first glance,

SOCIETY GIRL

I am most certain song and dance

        would do far less in my tale,

For I know my rigid master would stay rigid in my tale,

        Even with a charming veil.

Thus, we find my aggravation, closed to fancy imitation,

Only merciless damnation drives my sordid, lifeless tale.

Though the sentence came unfairly,

        and my rival knew her barely,

My actions, they far less scare me

        than they did when I was frail,

For I've wrestled with my demons

        that so surely made me frail—

        Acceptance is my prevail.

Though the movie's ending's stronger,

        my story *is* somewhat longer,

Longer than an hour plus ten,

so my outcome fits its scale.

Blame swings to scripted delusion,

and the silver screen illusion,

That infected my conclusion

with its thin and heartless veil—

That I'd ever be the one

who'd get to lift my sweetheart's veil.

I must insist I didn't fail.

Thus, the lesson seems so simple:

Do not worship in false Temples,

For their momentary color

thereon makes you gaunt and pale.

Henceforth I will keep on fighting,

but not for my tale's rewriting,

Though it's rather unexciting, I yearn a permanent

detail;

And I'm not concerned with slighting

with this permanent detail.

This I say: "I will prevail."

So I can digest what they play

upon the screen without dismay,

Because reality is lost in that little rebel's tale.

And I'll put to death my dreaming,

but while desperately not seeming

Like my mind's fixed on and teeming

with adversity to fail;

Why, then, do I have conniptions for adversaries to fail?

It never dies—it draws a veil.

Hope is heroin for desperation.

19

AL'S INVITATION

"**W**hy don't you stay another half hour, baby?"

"I can't," I say, pulling up my trousers and carelessly buckling my belt. "If I stay any longer, I'll go broke."

I pull a wad of cash from my back pocket and toss it on the lopsided side table by the bed. The room reeks of cheap perfume and sweat, but I'm numb to shame.

"Let's get out of here," I say to Mack, running down the steps of the crestfallen brownstone and into the front of John's limo.

"She was good, right?" asks Mack with a stupid grin.

"She was," I say, rubbing out the stray lipstick smudges on my chest, "but a bit lit … Amy's sent better."

"Yeah, but those tits are straight out of a magazine, aren't they?"

"Those were good, you're right."

"I knew you'd love her," says Mack proudly. "Now, I hope you don't mind swinging downtown, but I need to pick up John and I'm running late."

"No problem ... Actually, take me to Hyde Park. It's on your way."

"What's in Hyde Park?" says Mack just before realization hits. "No, Eric, you're not—"

"I want to see how Marie's doing."

Mack shakes his head. "Don't think the bossman would like this."

"The bossman doesn't control me anymore—you helped with that, remember?"

"Sure, but there's a difference between freedom and disobedience ..."

Mack reluctantly alters his route so we drive me to the Olins' house. It's been two years since I've been inside, and it's time I found out where Philo's cufflinks have been hiding.

"Should I pick you up later? I'll be done with John in an hour."

"No, thanks. I'll just see you back at the apartment."

Mack pulls on his wool driving cap and drives off and I walk to the front door and knock. Margaret lets me in— "Did you forget something, Eric?"—and I take a seat in the parlor. Two and a half years seems even longer now that I'm back here. It's staggering to think this is the same room the fellas and their wives mocked Andrew Coppock's

Halloween party and gossiped about Sid Reid's divorce over parlor games.

"Eric," gasps Marie. Her face is tired, and she is wearing an old floury apron. "I wasn't expecting this."

"How are you, Marie?"

"I'm okay. Do you want some cake, dear?"

"No, thank you. I'm here for a pair of cufflinks," I say impassively. "I believe they belonged to Philo's father."

"Haven't you spoken to Philo?"

I shake my head.

"I'm afraid he's already gotten them, Eric—came by just last week. I'm surprised he didn't tell you," says Marie. "Did he send you here?"

"No," I say again. "It was going to be a surprise."

"For the wedding?" Marie simpers.

I nod.

"You know, Eric, he thinks I don't remember who Annabelle is, but I do."

"She was my girl."

"She was the girl whose schooling he paid for out of our retirement fund. He never even introduced us, you know, and now he's paying for her wedding, too. I don't approve of this, Eric—and who's this Al Kohler fellow?"

"Just some grease ball."

"Yeah, well … are you going?"

"I haven't decided yet."

"Well, I'm not," states Marie. "It would be a slap in the face. Really, look at me, Eric—" Marie tugs on her apron, "—I can't even afford a new apron let alone pay for another wedding."

"Ma'am," says Margaret from the kitchen, "I think this cake is done."

"Oh, dear! I forgot all about that!" says Marie, scurrying into the kitchen.

"Marie," I say, following close behind, "there's something else I wanted to ask you."

"What is it, Eric?" she says, scrambling to pull the layer cake out of the oven.

"It's about Schuyler Hendriks."

Margaret's ears perk up.

"Oh," says Marie casually, turning her back to Margaret. "Schuyler is an old family friend who stayed here a while back until he found an apartment—he moved out a few weeks after you did, I believe. As I'm sure you recall, Philo wasn't too fond of that arrangement."

"I do recall. I also came back here shortly after I moved out to check on a few things and found Schuyler's bags in your room."

Margaret tuts as she promptly finds something to tend to in the parlor.

"What are you implying, Eric?" says Marie.

"I'm not implying anything. I just want to know what happened—I've only heard Philo's side since."

Marie pauses. "It's a simple explanation, really— Schuyler was to stay in Raymond's room, where Philo was sleeping, but it only had a single bed. We decided to move Schuyler into my room where there was a queen, so two could fit more comfortably."

"Schuyler did stay in your room then?

"Every night he was here."

This visit was a mistake.

"Three years later and I'm still sleeping in Raymond's room," Marie continues.

"Raymond's room?"

"Yes, that's what I said. Turns out it gets much better light in the morning—I just adore being awoken by sunrise."

"You're telling me that you slept in Raymond's room," I snicker, "and Schuyler Hendriks slept in yours."

"That's right," smiles Marie. "We switched so he and his wife would be more comfortable."

I wipe a few tears from the corner of my eyes.

"I must add that my back has been just fine in the smaller bed—I don't know why Doctor Anderson told me I needed the queen bed all to my own."

Now I can't stop laughing, and Marie can't, either.

"Eric, I must say, this has turned out to be a most pleasant visit. It's so nice to have some laughter around here again!"

"Marie, this has been great to see you, and I'm just sorry that I have to get going so soon."

"Oh, pooh—you haven't even stayed long enough for cake!"

"Is it strawberry?"

She holds it up for me to see. "Fig!"

"Even better," I grin, taking a seat at the table.

"Now tell me what's happening with you and Martha …"

It is dark by the time I arrive back at the apartment. Mack still isn't back so I decide to shuffle through my stack of mail I've been ignoring. I pass over a birthday card from my mother … a month-old letter from a bank offering me a temporary contract for May 1936 … and a letter I had written to Annabelle with a big red "Return to Sender" stamp on the front—then I find it.

"What a day," announces Mack, walking in and taking off his jacket.

I open the letter and my eyes are drawn to the large *"Annabelle's request"* that has been scribbled in jagged, barely discernable handwriting at the top.

"You should've seen the feathers on this last canary," says Mack. "But, boy, she chirped like one, too."

I hold up the letter so he can see. "Can you still give me a ride to the wedding?"

"You mean it, kid? What made you change your mind?"

"I think it's time I showed my face again, and see what I've been missing this past year."

The rehearsal dinner the night before the wedding is in a roped off corner of Henrici's, an upscale Viennese restaurant with an expansive oak-trimmed dining hall. Mack drops off John and Helen before parking the car. He cheerfully tosses off his cap and the two of us walk in together.

"I finally made it to the other side, Eric!" squeals Mack, firmly straightening his khaki sport coat. "Do I look like a Haven or what?"

There is a single long table, with Philo, Annabelle, and Al seated at the head. Moving down we have Annabelle's family, then the Mattinglys and Lords, Al's guests, and finally Annabelle's Shiner friends. Mack takes his seat with Al's party while I take my seat between Ed and Martha ("Where's Winnie?" I whisper to Martha, but she just shakes her head), and across from the two gushing newlyweds:

"Herb bought it for me in Cuba," boasts Louise, showing off a glimmering diamond ring. "He snuck into a jeweler while I was looking at scarves, and the next day we were married in the back of an authentic Cuban *iglesia*—ain't he the swellest?"

"That's good work, Herb," comments Martha as she examines Louise's hand. "I'm impressed."

"He always impresses me," says Louise, and she and Herb share a tender kiss.

"You're a lucky guy, Herb," says Ed.

"Not having a real wedding, Louise?" quips Ethel.

"We're waiting until October," snaps Louise.

"It's going to be in St. Cloud for her family," adds Herb. "It's very pretty in the fall."

"We're going to get some ideas from Anna-belly's wedding," continues Louise. "Gee, with Uncle Philo paying the bill it's bound to be as fabulous as we want ours to be, isn't that right, Herbie?"

Ethel and Louise exchange sneers.

"Say, how's your job, Martha?" says Herb quickly.

"It's a job," says Martha slowly, "at my father's company."

"Doing what?" asks Ed gingerly.

Ethel has completely tuned out anything not glaring on Louise's hand.

"I'm a secretary. But I'm trying to make the most of it."

"That's good," encourages Ed. "What line of work is your father in?"

"You know, it really doesn't matter ... I just make appointments—"

"Tell them about your presentation to the board!" chimes in Louise. "Martha's a real trailblazer in her office."

Ed leans in. Martha blinks deliberately at Louise.

"My father let me propose a 'Women in the Workplace' initiative," says Martha modestly.

"That's great!" smiles Ed.

"Yeah, I thought so, too," assures Martha. "I stood up in front of the board and gave my most compelling pitch … then Father came up with the idea to hire recent mothers part-time to fill some of the vacancies."

"You increased women's jobs," says Ed. "That's good … and part-time, so it probably saves the company money, too."

"Yes, everyone wins," says Martha. "This is what I wanted."

Martha's ensuing silence dampens Ed's elation.

"I'm going to see if there are any rolls left over there," I say, pointing to the opposite end of the table.

"I'll get them," says Martha, but Ed intercepts her.

"You know," he says, "my offer from graduation didn't expire. If you need help—"

"I'm fine," insists Martha. "Stop pretending to be a hero."

Martha walks away from Ed and retrieves the bread basket while ignoring the calls thrown at her by a group of vivacious men in their early twenties. The passive bystander sitting with the young men is an older woman who I presume to be their mother. Ed looks on carefully.

"That's Annabelle's family," says Ethel. "Bunch of farm boys from Michigan. Philo hates how unrefined they are—I think the young one's kind of cute."

Indeed, Annabelle's brothers seem rather comfortable with Henrici's grandeur.

"Oh, waiter," calls out the oldest-looking brother, as the youngest stuffs his silk napkin into his trousers and the middle slides a fork up his sleeve. "The ice in my water is too coarse—can you have them grind it up a bit?"

"And bring more silverware!" adds the object of Ethel's affection.

Philo, himself, is a pair of Melpomene and Thalia masks, wavering between witnessing the horror of Annabelle's family and experiencing the joy of his choreographed love story. To stroke the second fire, Philo parades Annabelle and Al around the table, presenting the pair to each group along the way. Because we've been seated at the far end of the table, the girls, Ed, and I are the last stop.

"I'm glad everyone could make it," finally exclaims Philo. "I can't believe the big day is tomorrow!"

"Hello," says Annabelle warmly, allowing her eyes to land firmly on each of us for a second or two so that we all feel important. "Thank you for coming."

Philo glowers at the groom. "Yes, thanks for coming!" Al suddenly remembers.

"Eric, I'm glad you made dinner tonight," adds Philo, not forgetting his usual dash of disappointment in my name. "Took you long enough to RSVP. Then again, you never did have much initiative when it came to the Postal Service."

"Thank you for having me, Philo," I say politely. "And congratulations, you two."

Martha starts to complement Annabelle on her sleek, red dress, but is interrupted by Philo hastening the couple back to their seats.

"That was satisfying," says Ed, rising. "Now excuse me—I have to make a call before the entrée."

I wait until Ed is clearly out of earshot, then Martha and I lean in at the same time. "Who do you think he's calling?" she says.

"I don't know," I quickly dismiss. "But what was all that about? Philo seems happier about this wedding than they are."

In my head, I replay last year's Halloween party and the vague accusations Andrew Coppock shouted while Ed and I had him restrained.

"It's his niece's wedding tomorrow, Eric, of course he's excited."

Martha's not seeing the bigger picture. I glance around the table to make sure no one else is listening. Ethel's making eyes at Annabelle's youngest brother as he fills his face with roasted pork loin, while Herb and Louise are feeding each other bites of vegetables and calling each other by the same: "You're my little pea!" — "Well, you're my mushy carrot!"

"You know he's not Annabelle's real uncle," I say.

"Really?" gasps Martha. "Yes, we all know that, Eric. She told us Uncle Philo brought her to a party a few years back, regretted it, then sent her to Shiner to make things right."

"Hold up—"

I gape at Annabelle—her posture's so refined, like she's expecting her picture to be snapped at any moment—*how could she tell Philo's secret like that?* We've never even spoken about it …

"—you knew the entire time?"

"Not the entire time," clarifies Martha, thinking. "It was around Halloween of my second year."

"That's two and a half years ago!"

"I wouldn't have done it, but I haven't lived her life," explains Martha. "She's a survivor, there's no denying that."

Does Philo know she told?

"But you don't think it's strange for a married 62-year-old man to pay for his former mistress' wedding?"

"Don't embellish the situation, Eric," warns Martha. "I'm sure this wedding is tough for you, but it's not your decision."

"I'm not jealous," I clarify, leaning back, "I'm just trying to get everything straight."

"Eric, lay off it," she asserts. I'm inclined to snap back, but remember how Ed never got anywhere arguing with Martha so I let it go. "The timing wasn't there for you two, but you obviously mean enough to her to get invited so just be supportive."

"Yes, well—What do you mean the timing wasn't there?"

Martha cocks her head at me and is about to say something when Ed returns. He's now sporting a noticeable grin, which is even more interesting to Martha than my double take. I inch my chair away from Martha, and we don't revisit the conversation the rest of the evening.

After dessert (a strawberry layer cake that doesn't hold a candle to Marie's) I look to Mack to leave, but he's enjoying every moment dining at the same table as his boss, so I take a cab home. I've lost my desire to attend the wedding tomorrow—this isn't my life anymore—but I've already shown my face to Philo, and I won't give him the satisfaction of thinking I am too hurt to see Annabelle say, "I do."

The next day, I sneak into one of the last pews just as the organist plays the first note of the ceremony. The priest walks in, then Al, who looks ridiculous in his top hat and tuxedo with a white flower pinned to the lapel. His parents follow and take a seat in one of the front pews. Martha walks in next, wearing a light, sage-colored dress with loose sleeves, and carrying a bouquet of white hydrangeas. She escorts Annabelle's mother to the other front pew before taking her place just left of the altar.

The music pauses for a second, then the organist switches to the traditional wedding march. Every head turns as Annabelle strolls through the church aisle, escorted by

Philo—and he's beaming. Annabelle is beautiful in her white silk dress with lush deep waves of her soft red hair pressed stylishly beneath a short flowery veil. Philo kisses Annabelle's cheek before they take their places flanking Al.

Everyone listens intently as the priest says a few words about love, adventure, and obedience. Once they exchange vows, many of the women are sobbing, including Helen and Pearl, while Herb and Louise share a kiss. Soon, the congregation is clapping and cheering, and filing out of their rows, following the newlyweds out of the church and into John's limo as Mack—wearing his cap again until Al knocks it off—drives them to the reception at the Congress.

Here, the damage done by my year away from the Havens is much more obvious. Shortly after we arrive, the fellas go up to a state room to smoke cigars, but even after they return to the ballroom, I'm equally excluded. Fortunately, I've palled up with Herb Galloway, who has been equally forgotten while Louise is off with the other Shiner girls in Annabelle's room.

"So are you still working at—"

"I'm unemployed, Herb."

"Oh … You know, I think that's the same stage Benny Goodman played on just last month," remarks Herb of the bandstand. "Louise and I saw him a few times when he was here—he was good."

This space isn't quite as ornate as the Congress' other ballroom, where Philo hosted the Shiner graduation last May, but the dining area is surround by stylish glass walls and there is no shortage of garland and white flowers, creating a falsely intimate vibe.

"Of course, there's this guy, Big Bill, who plays the South Side who's much better," continues Herb, "but I can't get Louise down there for the life of me."

But then Philo, of all people, saves us.

"Eric, just the one I was looking for," he says, dismissing Herb. "I was surprised you showed today after leaving dinner early last night."

"Annabelle wanted me to come, so I came."

"Yes, well, I think we can all agree that today finally puts an end to all the drama these past few years, don't you agree?"

"I—sure, yes, I suppose it does."

"I'm just so pleased that I was able to find Annabelle a man who could take care of her, and do things the right way."

The glare on his glasses cannot hide the cavalier twinkling of his eyes. He loves that he knows that I don't even know.

"How can anyone not like Al?" I shrug.

"Precisely, Eric—I'm glad you're taking this so well."

Philo walks back to his friends, smug as hell. Even when he no longer owns me he still manages to get his way …

"What is she doing here, Ed?"

… but maybe his fortunes are turning.

Philo dashes to the ballroom entrance, where Ed and Wendy have arrived. Philo causes a small scene as he confronts Ed, who stands his ground, wrapping his arm around Wendy.

"Look at Ed," says Martha, walking up alongside me sipping a glass of champagne.

"Philo looks furious," I remark. "That's bold of Ed to bring Wendy to a wives' event."

"You've really been gone that long, haven't you? Ed and Winnie got a divorce."

"No kidding! He really did it?"

"They both did, it was amicable," she continues, "which is why Philo let Ed stay in the club. But he's been giving him a hard time about bringing Wendy around the wives too soon … but now she's here, and at Philo's event."

While Ed and Philo continue to argue, Wendy slips away. Spotting my familiar face, she struts over before realizing Martha's with me.

"This is going well," she says flustered, fluffing her blond hair through a sniffle. "I guess tonight was too soon after all. Where are my manners? It's been a while Eric … *Martha.*"

I spot a big welt on Wendy's thigh. She catches me staring, however, and pulls down her striped dress to cover it.

"Hey Wendy—" starts Martha.

"Sweetie, tonight was a big deal for Eddy and me," says Wendy. "I'd really appreciate if you kept your judgments to yourself right now."

"Wendy," Martha repeats, "I'm happy for you."

"Rub it in," says Wendy, carefully wiping the corner of her eye. "You like seeing me get rejected by Ed's friends? They've known me for years."

"Wendy ..."

"I guess I was always just another whore to them!"

"Wendy," asserts Martha, grabbing her hand. "He brought you tonight."

Something happens between Wendy and Martha that's making their eyes well up, at least until Ed interrupts.

"He's not going to change his mind," sighs Ed, walking up. "I don't want to be more of a distraction, Wendy, we should just go. The Berghoff?"

Wendy simpers at Martha. Then she spots Philo snarling by himself in the corner, shifts her focus back to Ed and gives him two quick sparkly nods.

"We'll try again at the next party, sweetheart ... They'll have to accept you eventually."

"I'm sorry, Ed," laments Martha.

Ed nods. "Yeah, well, I didn't want to stick around another one of Philo's crummy Congress parties anyway." He pecks Wendy on the cheek, and they walk off arm in arm.

With a heavy sigh, Martha suggests we get another drink, but we are intercepted by Helen Mattingly, who is sporting a rather distressed expression.

"That woman Ed was with," says Helen, "that's Wendy, isn't it?"

"Yes," I say. "Ed's new girlfriend."

"Do you know how long he's been seeing her? Winnie never talks about the divorce and it seems soon for him to be dating. I wonder if she—"

"It's been a few months," chimes in Martha.

"I see. And do you know anything about their relationship? I noticed some bruising on her legs—"

"She started watching Little Ed," explains Martha. "Ed said he's been having a little trouble accepting 'Daddy's new girlfriend,' and Uncle Charlie had just given him a pirate sword for his birthday ..."

"Oh, my!" shrieks Helen, throwing her hands over her mouth. "I'm so embarrassed. I really thought ... This whole divorce has put the most terrible thoughts in my head!"

Ed comes barging back into the ballroom.

"I'm just getting Wendy's purse," he barks.

"Ed," says Martha, "can we talk?"

"Wendy and I have already left, Martha."

"It's about your offer."

"Really!" he exclaims, completely changing his disposition. "Of course. Let's talk outside."

Ed and Martha depart.

Helen has also returned to her husband's side at the Havens' table, but with only four of them after Ed's exit, they don't seem to be on quite their usual pedestal. Still, that was my world not that long ago. It's not a jealousy that I feel, staring at them as a true outsider, but more of an anxiety.

"Eric," says Louise, as she and Herb approach. "Where did Martha go with Ed? Uncle Philo wants to do speeches now and we need the maid of honor."

"Out? I don't know where they went, though."

"Sweetheart, they're probably in the lobby," says Herb.

"You don't think they went to the Blackstone, do you?" worries Louise. "It would take forever to go there and back and Uncle Philo's already grumpy."

"The Blackstone Hotel? Why would they go there?"

"That's where she's staying tonight, Eric," says Louise. "We're all staying there."

"Why are you staying there if the reception is here?"

"Uncle Philo isn't paying for our rooms anymore, so there's no way we're staying at the Congress again," says Louise. "Never had a good night sleep here, but we don't have to worry about that anymore—thank God for my Herbie!"

"Is it really that bad here?"

Louise shrugs then nods.

"At any rate, we should check the Blackstone," says Herb. "I'll see if I can get the room key from Ethel, provided I can get her away from Annabelle's brothers."

"Perfect," says Louise. "Eric, will you help me look around here?"

"I don't know," I hesitate. "I don't really want to be more involved than I already am."

"This is important, Eric," pleads Louise. "Do it for Anna-belly!"

Annabelle is sitting patiently at the head table while Al pounds drinks with Mack and some of his other rowdy friends. Even though this is her wedding day to another man, I can't help but feel like *there's a chance*.

I agree to help Louise look for Martha, and we take off in separate directions within the Congress. I wander the corridors frantically but aimlessly. Luckily, I bump into a peg-legged porter, who points me toward a smaller dining room where Wendy, Ed, and Martha are taking shots at an egg-shaped bar.

"It's Eric!" bellows Ed. "One more round, 'keep!"

"We need to go, Martha!"

Martha shakes her head. "I still can't believe this," she says. "Can I tell him, Ed?"

"Yes, tell me, but later," I reiterate the urgency, though sensing I'm being ignored. "Annabelle needs you now."

"Of course! Tell him, dear," urges Wendy.

"I'm going to law school!" blurts Martha, biting her lip.

"Law school?"

Ed puts his arm around Wendy, who hugs his side as they down another shot of whiskey.

"We all know I'm going nowhere at my father's company—just like he wants—so Ed's going to help me go to law school so I can have an actual career."

"But I thought you wanted to be a doctor? Also, we really need to go."

"I did want to be a doctor, but Ed makes a good point," admits Martha. "I haven't taken a real science course since high school, so medical school is probably unrealistic."

"But her debate skills are as sharp as ever," adds Ed slyly. Martha coyly rolls her eyes. "After law school maybe she can use them for her own good!"

This is ridiculous. I don't need to be running around for Philo anymore. I stopped being his page when he chose Al. I should be living my own life now, too.

"Well, then let's take another shot!" I say.

"Yes, Eric!" gushes Martha as Ed passes out four more whiskies.

"What do you think your father's going to say?" says Ed.

"Whatever he pleases," says Martha bluntly.

"Good for you, honey," encourages Wendy.

"It feels good just to have a chance," beams Martha. "I haven't been this excited since before Shiner. I'm embarrassed about how stubborn I was toward your help, Ed."

"Don't be. I'm embarrassed about how I treated my wife—really embarrassed. But between you and Wendy here, it's like I'm getting another chance to do this right."

Wendy grabs Ed's face and gives him a firm kiss, while Martha gushes.

I raise my glass, drawing the others to do the same. "To second chances."

"I like that, Eric," says Martha, and then we drink.

"Gee, I think I need to slow down," winces Martha. "Oh, Eric, I'm sorry, I got caught up. You were saying something?"

"Right," I recall. "Louise said Philo needed you—"

"My speech! Right, I should probably get back there," she explains to Ed and Wendy. "I hate to leave this moment, but ... Thank you, both of you—this means everything to me."

"Don't mention it, just do your thing," says Ed.

Martha bundles the bottom of her dress and scurries off.

"One more round?" I propose. "Philo needed Martha, not me."

"Yes, Eric!" says Wendy, gesturing toward the bartender.

"I wonder what changed that girl's mind," wonders Ed, tightening his grip around Wendy's waist.

Wendy drapes her hands around Ed's neck. "Sometimes it takes a strong woman to level with another."

We're each handed a drink.

"Are you implying you're a strong woman?" asks Ed suspiciously.

"Are you implying that I'm not?"

Ed tenderly rubs Wendy's arm. "I suppose I can feel that bicep now. I better start lifting weights again so I can defend myself."

"Don't you worry your pretty little face," sasses Wendy, "I promise not to hurt you, doll."

I take my shot and walk away as Ed and Wendy stop bantering in the wettest way possible.

Back in the ballroom, I take a seat between Herb and Mack. Martha has just stood up on stage, and the ballroom flurries in quieting whispers.

"If I could have your attention," she announces. "For those who don't know me, I'm Martha Honeysuckle, Annabelle's maid of honor. We've been best friends for nearly four years, ever since Annabelle moved in across the hall from me at Shiner College. We immediately welcomed her into our group, at first because it's tough to be the new girl, but really because she was hysterical! After Uncle Philo dropped her off, our dormitory was littered with the most shocking oaths we'd ever heard—I'm not sure any of us knew what to make of the 'crude country girl across the hall' after that first day!

"But then we started to see the other parts of Annabelle. Her generosity, and cleverness, and she was so brave that I often gave myself an ulcer trying to make sure she didn't get us into trouble. But part of her charm is that things always turned out okay, just like it will with Al."

Helen Mattingly lays her head on John's shoulder and Mack starts to sniffle.

"When she told me she was getting married to a man whom I'd only met a handful of times, I naturally challenged her, as best friends do. But it didn't take much for her to convince me that this was something she really wanted, and now I couldn't be happier for you both."

Annabelle smiles serenely as Philo pushes Al to kiss her cheek.

"And with that I propose a toast—to her new husband and chaperone, I wish you luck. Good luck to the both of you. To the newlyweds!"

Martha raises her glass, and a collection of "*Cheers*" rings throughout the ballroom. She and Annabelle share a hug, and Philo rises.

"Today is special for me," starts Philo slowly. "Not only did I get to witness a remarkable young lady complete her transformation into a true woman of society, but I get to do it with the great privilege of being best man to a good friend."

I let out an audible puff that echoes around the ballroom. From Philo's miffed pause, I know he heard me.

"Seeing Annabelle and Al together gives me much joy," he continues stiffly, "and I look forward to the joy they will continue to give me as they embark on the wonders of marriage."

Philo sits and there is an awkward silence as the wedding guests await another call to toast.

"To Anne and Al!" shouts Mack suddenly, earning another "*Cheers*" while he and Al point and mug at each other.

Al gets another sharp glance from Philo and his posture stiffens like a board. Then, the light goes on in his head, and he jumps to his feet and waves his hands at everyone like they aren't already staring at him.

"I've got something I'd like to say," says Al with an easy boisterousness. "Philo mentioned it was a privilege to be my best man, but really he gave me no choice."

Philo has removed his glasses and is rubbing his temples.

"What I mean is, Philo's done so much for me," Al explains. "A year ago, I was just a college dropout who lost his job flipping burgers—"

Al's dad grimaces, and his son notices.

"But at my lowest, *Philo* helped me get a great job—with this guy!" says Al, pointing at Herb, which gets him another kiss from Louise. "And then he introduces me to Annabelle, and now I've got this perfect life, and I don't know what I did to deserve this. Really, I don't know."

The elder Kohler's face scrunches further. This seems to further antagonize Al, as he is shaking his head feverishly at his father, and mouthing words that align with Annabelle's initial vocabulary at Shiner.

"And if I wasn't already the luckiest crumb alive," continues Al, calming himself, "the good fortune keeps rolling. Just a few minutes ago Philo told me he was sending us on a Caribbean cruise for our honeymoon. Words can't—"

Al is speaking directly at his father now, but the room still eats his words up as a roar starts to slowly build.

"Words can't describe how great this man is!" he prevails. "In fact—Philo, I want you to join us on our honeymoon!"

Philo blushes, and waves his hand reluctantly. The ballroom quiets.

"No, really," presses Al, "we want you to come. Say, if anyone deserves a vacation it's Philo Olin, am I right?!"

And the guests roar again, encouraging Philo until he bobs his head up and down, mouthing, "Okay, I'll do it." And then the room grows even louder, because inviting a 62-year-old man on your honeymoon is a just cause to celebrate.

Annabelle, who continues to sit quietly with her hands in her lap and a pleasant smile on her face, just as she's done all evening, finally rises. The ballroom doesn't immediately fall silent, but Annabelle waits until it does.

"Thank you all for coming to my wedding," says Annabelle simply. "It means a lot to have you here, and I'd like to propose a final toast—in Lithuanian."

Philo's smile fades.

"I believe there's somebody here who knows how it goes. Erikas?"

My eyes burst open like Betty's, and I can feel the ballroom's attention bear down on me.

"Would you lead a Lithuanian toast at my wedding?"

I gulp. I am the unexpected center of attention, and everyone is waiting, expecting. Annabelle looks eager; Philo is peeved but still smug; Al is confused about the word "Lithuanian." A sharp scraping echoes throughout the ballroom as I slide my chair back. Shaking, I stand and raise my glass. I look up, as if reaching into the deepest depths of my memory for the words, but I never forgot them:

"*Ee-svay-cotta*," I say slowly, reigniting eye contact with Annabelle.

Annabelle proudly nods, then repeats an accented, "*Ee-svay-cotta!*"

"*Ee-svay-cotta!*" reiterates the crowd.

Annabelle sits back down, completely content.

20

THE MISSING YEAR

Annabelle's wedding is the last time I will voluntarily see any of the Havens. I thought I had regained control of my life from Philo and his rules, but the taunting that ensued was the kick I needed to sever all ties. Unfortunately, that includes moving out of Mack's apartment. He tries to convince me to stay— "It don't matter to me if you're not one of them anymore!"—but I know the only way I'll ever get out of that world is if I stay as far away as possible. It also helps that shortly after Thanksgiving I am offered a permanent position as a security salesman with a financial firm in the Loop.

Through Spring 1937, I'm still holding steady on my vow to avoid contact with the Havens. That is, until I receive a letter *"From the desk of Philo Orton"* written in sloppily jagged handwriting, informing me to pay $1,000 in yearly dues if I want to remain in good standing with the club. I laugh at the thought then burn it.

I generally enjoy my new life, though I get lonely often. After a few months, I accept that my new job is just a job, below responsibility level at Bert & Horner, but steady work that pays the bills. Unfortunately, it also affords my mind a dangerous level of under-occupation; I must fight urges to revisit what-if's like if I had taken Marie's side during Schuyler's stay, or if I simply listened to what Andrew Coppock had to say before he assaulted Betty—or if he would have at all. I also often find myself wandering in front of the Knickerbocker, the Congress, and a number of other hotels on weekend nights, only regaining sense when I feel the coldness of their door handles.

"Eric?" I hear a voice yell behind me, either John's or Philo's. I dart around the corner before realizing it's two in the morning and the streets are deserted.

"You need to stop this," I tell myself. "You're going to get caught."

Curiosity gets the best of me on a particularly warm Wednesday afternoon in late May, the day before the Golden Gate Bridge, the one Philo has been working on in San Francisco, is set to open. It's an event I am certain Philo will attend, but to be sure I call his office.

"I'm sorry, but Mr. Olin is out of town the rest of the week," says his secretary.

"Gee, what a shame."

"But if you leave your name I can have him call you on Monday."

"I'd appreciate that," I say. "Tell him Schuyler Hendriks called."

With Philo out of the way, I walk to his office during lunch. I slip the doorman a dollar and he lets me in the building.

"I'm here for Andrew Coppock," I tell the secretary.

Incredulous, she looks at me and says, "He doesn't work here anymore."

"Since when?"

"I don't know—it's been a few months."

"Do you know where he went?"

"I certainly do not," she says defiantly. "Who are you? What is this about?"

I'm a little deflated. "Just tell Philo to call Sid Reid," I say, then leave.

Another plan failed. I quickly stride away from Philo's building, lest anyone recognize me, and take a different route back to my office.

"Eric?" shouts a voice as I pass a group of important-looking people. It's broad daylight and doesn't sound like John or Philo. "Eric!" they call again.

I look back—it's Martha. She scurries away from her group and greets me with a hug.

"What are you doing here?" I say with a smile.

"We have so much to catch up on, Eric."

Since Martha is out to lunch with her co-workers we agree to meet for lunch over the weekend. She picks a small French café in the Gold Coast neighborhood, and we order sandwiches.

"I'm working for the Cook County judge this summer," explains Martha of her internship.

"The judge," I exclaim. "That sounds important—I bet you'll be able to have an impact working there."

"Not this summer," admits Martha. "It's a great experience, though, and I think I may even want to be a judge someday. It'll be a fight, though."

"I'm sure you'll make it happen," I say. "So, are you in Chicago for good?"

"Hard to say. I've got two years left of law school, but I like it here—it's just far enough away from my father."

"You need your independence, I completely understand."

"I'm still working on that," sighs Martha. "Ed's paying for my apartment this summer, too. The judge doesn't pay his interns very well ..." Martha purses her lips. "I told Ed it's only a loan. I'm going to pay him back every cent."

Martha's very insistent of this last point.

"You still talk to Ed," I say. "How is he?"

"He's great. He and Wendy are on their honeymoon right now. As we both know, a lot can happen on honeymoons ..."

What is she insinuating?

"Oh, they actually got married."

"That's right, last month," says Martha. "It was just a small ceremony—Little Ed, the fellas, Wendy's parents … Ed's mother didn't even go."

"Because of what happened with Winnie?"

"No one's given Ed any breaks since the divorce, except maybe Winnie, funnily enough. They seem to be on good terms; they even threw a birthday party together for Little Ed a few weeks back. Wendy gave him a book."

"That's tough, but he did cheat on Winnie."

"True," admits Martha, "and I had a hard time with that, myself. But given all that happened between them I think he's done pretty well—I truly believe he's devoted to Wendy."

"It's not just the cheating, though," I push back. "Ed's mother told me Winnie wanted to be a nurse but gave that up to marry him. He ruined her life, Martha—he's just like the rest of them."

"But, Eric, he knows that. Ed's offered to send her back to school, but she just couldn't after having Little Ed. Even so, that boy's her world now, and she's a really good mother."

"Are you his Wendy for that?"

"I don't know," frowns Martha. "Listen, this isn't my ideal arrangement, either, but it's the best I've got."

Martha takes a big bite out of her sandwich, and I catch a glimmer of vulnerability in her eyes until she looks away.

"I'm sorry, Martha," I say. "I'm not a Havens apologist these days, that's all."

"It's fine, Eric, I get it," she nods. "Besides Ed, I don't have anything to do with them, either. It's just that talking about it with someone else who knows is opening some old wounds, that's all ... But enough about them, what's going on with you? Still living with Mack?"

"No," I say. "I moved out after the wedding."

"That long ago? Then you must not know."

I shake my head. "Know what?"

"Eric," says Martha, lowering her voice, "Annabelle and Al split."

In a flash, my posture vanishes, and I fall a few inches forward. "What happened?"

"I don't know. They were fine after the wedding, but then they went on that honeymoon cruise, and when they got back, they moved into separate apartments."

"How could she afford an apartment?"

"How do you think, Eric?"

Philo was on that cruise.

"Ed heard Al lost his job shortly after the divorce and hasn't been heard from since, and Annabelle isn't talking to anybody—" Martha stops to swallow a rather large bite from her sandwich, "not even me."

"I'm sorry to hear that ..."

Something happened on that cruise, and now Annabelle's living in her own apartment. Annabelle doesn't have any money for an apartment, unless Al's supporting her, but he lost his job and likely can't even support himself ...

Philo was on that cruise.

"And it's been difficult, Eric," gripes Martha. "She was my best friend, you know? There is so much is happening in our lives right now but she won't talk to me."

I shrug. Too much to get into over lunch. I pick up my sandwich—

"No, Eric," scolds Martha. "Don't shut me out. I know you like to do this, but I need somebody to talk to. If I do this at work, they call me emotional—I *hate* that."

"I'm sorry," I say, setting the sandwich down. "It's not fair."

"You're right, it's not," says Martha hotly. "I'm getting the opportunity of a lifetime here—I should be happy—but I have no one to be happy with. My parents don't support me, I haven't seen Ethel or Louise in months, and my best friend is no longer my best friend!"

"What about Betty?"

"Please, Eric," Martha scoffs, "I couldn't get close to Betty before the Coppock incident ... But Annabelle told me everything. She told me the truth about Uncle Philo, and about you."

I shouldn't ask.

"What did she say about me?"

"I'm not sure I'm supposed to say, but about how you met at Christmas and she thought you were sweet," says Martha, "but the timing wasn't right for her."

There's a lurch deep in my stomach, but I conscientiously shake it off. "It's fine, I'm over it," I say.

"I think she did care for you, Eric," assures Martha. "She always said you'd be her friend forever—hey, you almost made it five years!"

"Yeah. Try not even four," I correct. "Remember, we haven't spoken since the wedding."

"I know, Eric, I included that," Martha cuts me off. "You met her at the end of 1931 and you haven't spoken since her wedding last year—that's five years. Or four and a half if you want to be precise."

I don't. And I don't want to argue, and I don't want to keep talking about Annabelle. I should let her be right about this because it really doesn't matter—but I work with numbers all day, and God is in the details, so I say it:

"Except we met Christmas of 1932 ..."

"Eric, she told me the story a dozen times: You and Philo picked her up outside of Marshall Field's at Christmastime. It was snowing like a blizzard, and she couldn't catch a cab," she recites dully, "but then you pulled up to the curb like her 'knight in shining car-mor' and offered her a ride."

My shoes are wet.

"I'm almost positive that it was raining," I say.

"Perhaps," continues Martha, "but then she said you and Philo invited her to a Havens party that night. You fought over who was going to be her date, and ultimately Philo felt guilty because he was married so you took her."

"Yes, that's all true, but it was a year later."

"No, because it was right after Jane Addams won the Nobel Prize, which I'm certain was in 1931."

"Jane Addams?"

"Annabelle said you suggested grabbing a hotel room, but because Jane Addams had just won the Nobel Prize— the first American woman to do so, mind you—she was feeling especially feministic. She appreciated the ride but wanted to take things at her own pace so she rejected your overtures that night."

I pause.

"And it was snowing that Christmas?"

"That's right—she said Philo wouldn't get out of the car until someone shoveled him a path to the door."

That does sound like Philo, but—

My shoes are wet.

—it was raining that day.

"I'm sure this is hard to hear," says Martha gingerly. "I do think if she had met you even a few months earlier it may have worked out differently."

These are deliberate lies that Annabelle fed Martha—but were they her own? I was also fed lies about the night Philo and I met her. It was confusing, and misleading, and meant to shield the scandalous truth. Is it possible that our differing memories of our introduction are related?

Is it possible that they're not?

"I've got to go," I say, throwing money on the table. "Let's do this again."

"Eric, where are you going?"

I dart out of the café, my head flying in all directions—*Why did Annabelle lie about the year? Who did she get into that limo with?* —and scan the street for a telephone. I dash into the corner drug store, and head for the phone booth. I give hardly any time for the elderly woman who has just finished her call to exit before I slide in and dial.

What happened in that missing year?

"Hello, Marie? It's Eric."

"Eric! How are you dear?"

"I'm good. Listen, I was just at lunch with Martha—do you remember her?"

I yank the receiver from my ear to keep it from bleeding, as distorted squeals continue to blare from the other end.

"Was that a yes?" I shout into the mouthpiece.

"Yes, of course I remember Martha!"

"She told me something interesting about Annabelle."

Marie's end falls silent.

"Did you hear that? It's about Annabelle—Philo's schoolgirl."

Still nothing.

"I want to talk to you about it," I say.

"Come tonight for dessert, Eric" says Marie steadily.

"But—"

"We're having cake."

"Cake?"

"At eight."

"Great."

"I'll see you for cake at eight."

"Can't wait!"

There's a pause.

"Was that a joke, Eric?"

"No—Sorry, I'll see you then."

And the phone call is over.

Later that night I hail a cab to Hyde Park. The sun has not fully set when I arrive at the house, but the streetlights have come on. With the katydids' buzzing and the harmonious contrast between the graying sky and the streetlights' orange glow, an eager serenity scampers up my spine.

I walk up the creaky steps, clearly under-maintained but synergizing with the wild, unkempt garden growing below the front bay window, and knock. A small light inside shines—probably from the kitchen—and another brighter light flicks on. I hear footsteps approaching, but they're harsher than Marie's shuffling gait. The door swings open.

"Hello, Eric," sneers Andrew Coppock. "Marie," he shouts crassly, "he's here!"

There are butterflies in my stomach—I've never been so happy to see someone I hate.

"I know all of your dirty secrets"

"What am I, really?"

Coppock grins, "I've been waiting for this day for four and a half years."

"You sure?"

Coppock nods.

Marie waddles down the hallway from the kitchen wearing her old baking apron, her smile as bubbly as ever.

"I'm glad you called, Eric," says Marie cheerfully. "Here's what's going to happen—you're going to tell us what you know, then we're going to tell you what we know."

"And we know a lot," smirks Coppock.

"Yes, we certainly do," giggles Marie. "And we have cake if you're hungry!"

21

DECISIVE CLEARANCE

Listening to Andrew Coppock brazenly recount the clandestine details of his previous association with Philo is as enlightening as it is aggravating. At the same time, Marie—who is hearing Coppock's revelations for the second time—is the calming presence I need to get through this marathon knowledge transfer.

In embarrassingly similar fashion, Philo had recruited Coppock to act as his adulterous proxy with a young woman, Julia, whom Philo started dating around Christmas 1927, five years before we first rode in John's limo.

"Philo plucked me from a construction site around August that year," recalls Coppock. "He offered me a cushy desk job, talking on the phone to guys who used to cut my paychecks. A few months go by, then he asks me to do him a favor. That's when I met Julia. It was obvious they had met before, and Philo made it very clear she was his girl, but that I would have an important part in her life."

From there, Philo played his founder card to get Coppock into The Havens Club, where the three of them would spend many nights and weekends over the next three years.

"I went where Julia went," says Coppock.

"Didn't anyone ask why the three of you were always together? John or Ed?"

Coppock shakes his head. "The Havens Club is Philo's kingdom—no one ever questions him. Sometimes he and John would disagree on something, but only when it came to one of the others' behavior. Even if someone asked about Julia he always called her 'Andrew's girl.'"

But Philo's scam was built on the stilts of Coppock's cooperation—once that started shaking it all came tumbling down.

"We spent so much time together, eventually a fire had grown between me and Jules."

Coppock and Julia went behind Philo's back for almost a year before they were caught, speaking in code to coordinate their rendezvous.

"She'd call me at work and we'd set up dates right under Philo's nose using his own code. I'd act like I was getting a new job site address, and then I'd head out like I was following up," boasts Coppock. "Funny thing is, we only got caught when we got lazy. It was a Havens Halloween party and we slipped in a broom closet when he was busy yelling at one of John's broads. But he saw us leave the party together, so he followed us to the hall, and caught us mid-embrace. It was the one time we didn't use the code ... you got to admit the damn thing works."

After Julia had become soiled in Philo's eyes, he tried cutting ties with both her and Coppock. For Julia, he paid for her to go off to an exclusive equestrian academy a few hours north of Chicago—this became the paper trail between her and Philo. There was no paper trail tying Julia to Coppock—because they used the code.

"Philo didn't trust us," says Coppock. "To him, we were both traitors ... either one of us could turn on him and go to Marie."

"Why didn't you?"

"You serious? I had more to gain in blackmail than a divorce," Coppock crassly replies. "The evidence against him was circumstantial at best, and he still had money then—if it went to court, he'd win. But he was paranoid, I could tell."

Marie purses her lips. I imagine she's also struggling to remember that Philo is our ultimate villain.

"The first time he tried to get rid of me was after that Christmas party he brought you and Annabelle to," continues Coppock. "I told him I'd be keeping my job or I'd tell you, Marie, and his company's board about Julia. Of course, he fought back, but he eventually gave in. I kept my mouth shut and he kept paying me money, and in the Havens."

"What happened to Julia?"

"Seemed like he got his way there," he admits. "In the end, I think he felt more betrayed by her than me. Told me to stay away from Julia, and I never heard from her again."

"What about the 'fire' between you?"

"Please, Eric, there are other logs to burn," sneers Coppock, "and I had just been granted unlimited access to all of the sweet Haven dishes." He leans back in his chair with his hands folded behind his head and flashes a greedy smirk. "I was like a fat kid in a soda shop."

"Until you assaulted Betty," I say firmly.

Marie's ears perk up. I'll tell her that story when we're done with Coppock.

"Even so," Coppock leans forward with a snarl, "here I am—I kept my word until he didn't keep his."

"What do you mean?"

"He fired me," says Coppock. "I kept my job for a few years after he sent Julia away, even after he dropped me from the Havens. But I guess some people at the office don't appreciate my straightforward nature ..."

"You don't think it was the secretary, do you?"

"I don't know, did she say something?" he asks. I shrug and he continues, unfazed. "Anyway, he let me go a few months back. Before I packed up my desk I got in touch with Marie, but she wasn't ready to do nothing then."

Marie shakes her head. "I needed time to process it all."

"So, we waited—then you called today."

Should I feel more conflicted about this exchange? This is the same monster who grabbed Annabelle at that first Christmas party ... and who assaulted Betty ... and who harassed the secretary at Olin Crane & Shovel for years, probably.

318

But he corroborates Philo's pattern of exploitation.

"Right after Philo got rid of you, he started bringing this other guy, Al Kohler, around," I say.

"He's the one who married Annabelle," adds Marie.

"Really?" says Coppock.

"I could never put my finger on why," I continue, "but when Al was with us I felt like we were in a sort of competition for Philo's attention. That has to be part of this."

Coppock scratches his head.

"Remember at that Halloween party when you and Ed were struggling to hold me back?" he says (his bravado is astounding).

"Yes," I say plainly.

"I almost blabbed in front of everybody that night," says Coppock, snapping his fingers. "I think that made him nervous. Philo probably thought you were compromised. He couldn't trust you anymore, so he replaced you."

"Just like what he did with you and Julia," concludes Marie.

"But while I didn't know about the master scheme, Annabelle must have always been in on it," I say. "When I was talking to Martha earlier, she told me things that prove Annabelle and Philo had known each other a year before he started bringing me around, maybe even longer."

"Longer?" gasps Marie. "Poor Julia …"

"It didn't matter for Annabelle's part if I found out," I continue. "That's why he only replaced me this time."

"Huh?" says Coppock.

"Philo was nervous about me after the Betty incident, right? His elaborate plan was about to fail twice, so he needed a new, stronger alibi for Annabelle."

"And what's stronger than marrying someone else?"

"No one assumes adultery," says Marie.

"Philo choreographed the marriage," I say, "that's why he was so involved in the wedding. It fits, and would mean he's used the same plan three times: He finds someone he thinks he can trust, then uses them as a diversion for his infidelity."

"But why did he think he could trust us in the first place? He didn't know either of us before."

"Because we were desperate," I explain, then ignore Coppock's attempt to protest, "and he could help us."

"That's right," says Marie. "He knew from your mother that you hadn't worked in months."

"Right," I say, "and he read in the newspaper that Al had just lost his job flipping burgers."

"And I had just gotten fired from a construction site," Coppock admits. "The Crane & Shovel was excavating that job, and he was there the day I beat the shit out of this guy for talking about my sister—my supervisor fired me on the spot."

"Oh, Andrew, I'm sorry," laments Marie.

"It's okay, Marie," says Coppock, "I don't even have a sister."

"Anyway," I redirect, "the point is that it all fits a pattern: Starting with you, then me, and then Al, he found us at a low point and offered us a job or housing in exchange for loyalty."

"I think you're on to something, Eric," says Coppock strongly. "Even with Julia, she hated her old job—they work those department store girls to death."

"I'm sure it was the same way for Annabelle when he first met her," I add.

Way back in 1931.

"My father was a brewer!" blurts Marie. "He earned a modest wage, and Philo knew that when he proposed."

"See, Eric," mocks Coppock, "Marie's a victim, too."

Philo's the one we hate.

"We should call a lawyer," I suggest. "We might have real case."

"Not yet," asserts Coppock. "We've talked a lot about trust tonight—how can we all trust each other?"

"We want to get back at Philo for using us," I say. "Why else would we all be here?"

"Money," says Coppock.

"It's money for me, too," says Marie.

My excitement suddenly wanes. For the first time all evening I feel as though I am sitting on one side of the round kitchen table while Coppock and Marie are on the other.

"At first the Christian woman in me didn't want a divorce," explains Marie, "but Philo's simply not giving me enough to live off anymore. If he keeps spreading his money between God knows how many girls, what will be left for me? I'm an old woman, and I can't stay in this cold eight months a year, but flying back and forth to Florida is expensive."

"How much money are we talking, Marie?" inquires Coppock.

"Well, let's see," she ponders. "I get $100 a month ..."

My jaw drops.

"...but after paying Margaret's and Sam's salaries, and other silly nothing's that come up, it's hard to afford much more than one trip a month."

Coppock completely understands this dilemma.

"Oh!" Marie squeaks. "And there's this new machine called the 'Miracle Mixer'—it has this handsome young spokesman who says it will revolutionize eating, but it's $30."

"We'll ask for $700," Coppock interjects.

"$700!" I exclaim. "A month?"

"Oh, Andrew—*thank you*," gushes Marie.

"Where do you get a number like that?"

"Calm down, Eric," says Coppock. "Marie, does $300 for you work?"

"Certainly, it would," she says.

"$300 for Marie, and $200 each for us," explains Coppock, "...for our trouble."

"I'm not here for money," I say. "I just want to get Philo—"

"Eric, don't be an idiot," says Coppock. "Everything's about money or sex, and I don't think I'm getting laid out of this."

Marie squeaks. I shake my head.

"Believe me, no one acts for free," he continues. "If they say they are, they're lying—a favor is just a delayed request."

"Eric," soothes Marie, sensing my growing unrest with this partnership, "I want you boys to get some money. You deserve to be taken care of."

"Thanks, Marie," says Coppock warmly.

I want to gag. If I go through with this, I will be counting down the days until it's all over so I can tell Marie about the real Andrew Coppock at the Halloween party with Betty.

"But Marie," I continue, "I don't want you to think that I only called you for money."

"It's fine, Eric, really" says Marie. "Andrew, can we call my lawyer now? Before I change my mind again ..."

"First let's just make sure we're all on the same page," says Coppock. "We're asking for $700 a month—$300 for Marie, $200 for Eric, and $200 for me—agreed?"

"Agreed," nods Marie.

Both of their eyes press on me.

"Eric?" urges Coppock.

If I do this I'll be just like him ... Philo made me.

"Agreed."

On Monday morning I call in sick to work so Coppock and I can meet Marie at her lawyer's office. Rudolph Hees is a wrinkled man with a thin comb-over and an impatient face. Still, he greets us warmly, then firmly asks Coppock and me to wait outside so that he can speak alone with Marie. We sit in the lobby for an hour, most of which Coppock snores through, until we are beckoned to join the conversation.

Hees sits in a modest office with a spectacular view of the Chicago River. After we take our seats next to Marie, the lawyer thanks us for joining them then asks us to take turns elaborating on our involvement with Philo's two known affairs. At this point, I can only relay a more polished version of what I recounted Saturday at Marie's house.

"As you can see, Philo exhibits a clear pattern of manipulation from Andrew, to me, to Al Kohler," I conclude.

"It's a start, but we'll need to corroborate your stories." explains Hees. "We don't know Mr. Kohler's whereabouts, but what about the young ladies—will they cooperate?"

Coppock and I turn to each other.

"No," states Coppock. "It's been six years since I've seen Julia. I don't know where she is and couldn't begin to guess."

"What about the paper trail tying Philo to the equestrian school?" I ask.

"I wouldn't count on it," dismisses Hees. "A smart man like Mr. Olin would think to make such records disappear after this many years, and no judge would accept the shoddy historic books from an amateur riding academy. Of course, if Andrew had anything—"

"I don't," confirms Coppock.

"What about you, Eric?" says Hees. "Can you get Annabelle's statement?"

"I can try, but she answers to herself and Philo."

"Eric, this is nearly essential," stresses Hees. "We need a betrayal. How can we get her to turn on him?"

"I-I don't know."

"Without Annabelle's cooperation, if we file on misconduct this case will go to court, and I don't love our chances there."

"Eric?" whimpers Marie.

I really don't understand why the pressure of this case—before we've even filed a petition—is falling on my shoulders. Why is Coppock so easily let off the hook? I don't think I can promise this ...

"We'll file on desertion then, from when he moved out in October 1933," concludes Hees. "It's weaker grounds for the money you're seeking, but is less likely to elicit pushback from Mr. Olin's attorney."

"See, Eric? We have other options," assures Marie, patting my shoulder. "It'll all work out."

Hees' comb-over falls over his eyes as he leans over his desk to sweep Marie's paperwork into a leather-bound case folder. Marie and I start to rise to leave the meeting but Coppock pulls me back into my seat.

"Hold it," he snarls at Hees. "'Weaker grounds for the money?' You saying we're not getting paid?"

"What I'm saying," says Hees slowly, "is that Mr. Olin is likely to contest the amount given desertion is generally a weaker charge than adultery. We build a strong case, though, and you'll get your money."

Hees' explanation does little to comfort Coppock and Marie as the motivation drains from their faces. They are thinking like jurors, and are less impressed by "Philo moved out" than they would be by "He cheated." I imagine Philo's smug indifference toward this lesser charge, and force my mind to race toward a stronger solution. Then it strikes me—

"I can get Annabelle," I declare. "She and Al got divorced. If the marriage was Philo's idea, then the divorce was not. Something made them deviate from the arrangement.

"My money's on Annabelle," states Coppock.

"Mine, too," I say. "And if that's the case, I think she'd turn on Philo again."

"That's brilliant, Eric!" lauds Marie.

"I like the way you're thinking," says Hees steadily, "but those are a lot of assumptions. It's certainly an option—if we can get her. For now, we'll file with desertion."

Coppock starts to object again but Hees heads him off.

"It's just a starting point; we'll make our next move based on theirs," says Hees, showing us to the door. "There's no use getting stressed until we hear from Mr. Olin's counsel. If you do want to help, though, start talking to Annabelle now."

I put this pressure on myself.

"You really think she'll turn on Philo?" asks Coppock as we exit the building and wait for Sam to pick us up. "You heard Hees, without Annabelle we've got nothing."

"It'll be fine," I say, noting Marie's reticence. "While Philo's building his defense, we'll have plenty of time to convince her to testify against him."

"Only if you find her," Coppock sneers.

"Oh, I'll find her—more than you can say for Julia."

"Hey, I'm not going to apologize that I moved on!"

"This is really it, boys," distantly pivots Marie. "I'm getting divorced."

She bows her head allowing Coppock and I to exchange our final jeers. Then Marie breaks down into tears, blubbering into her white-gloved hands.

Officially, Marie files suit to get $700 for separate maintenance on the grounds that Philo had deserted her when he left their house in October 1933. After spending months gathering what documents we could and filing the divorce petition, Hees finally relays word that Philo received his summons as he entered his office on an icy morning at the end of December 1937.

"Now we wait," says Hees. "Mr. Olin's team has three weeks to respond."

"Then we get our $700?" asks Coppock.

"If they agree to settle," says Hees flatly. "Mr. Olin has three weeks."

But by five o'clock that same day a cross-bill is filed by Philo's team asserting Marie's misconduct with a "Mr. S" and "Mr. X"—the latter whom Marie describes as simply her longtime personal banker.

"What does that mean?" Marie asks Hees.

"It means to get your money we'll have to fight," replies Hees. "Your husband's going to play rough, Marie, and is trying to pin this on you—he's claiming you had relationships with two other men, and that's what compromised your marriage and pushed him to leave."

"The nerve," huffs Marie. "How dare he suggest such a thing of me—I'm a 61-year-old grandmother, for heaven's sake!"

"It's his word against yours, Marie," warns Hees, "and it's a cold move. They don't want to give you a dime."

"He can't get away with this, can he?" implores Marie— Coppock practically faints in his chair. "How am I to support myself?"

"These days, a rich man gets sued for divorce and everyone sees it as a shakedown," explains Hees. "Maybe if you lowered the amount to, say, $200 we could settle without a trial."

Coppock comes to just in time for the blood in his face to re-drain at the realization that $200 a month for Marie likely meant little to nothing left over for us.

"Then we'll fight!" hollers Coppock, pumping his fist and nodding encouragingly to Marie.

Easy for him to say, but fighting means asserting adultery by Philo, which requires Annabelle's cooperation. Unfortunately, I haven't managed to track her down yet. She's not listed in the phone book, and none of the Shiner girls have spoken to her since the wedding, either:

First, I speak to Louise who says, "If you find Anna-belly, tell her to give me a call—tell Ethel, too!"

Then Ethel tells me, "I haven't heard from Annabelle in years, and I'm not holding my breath. Neither should Louise."

I even start to look for Betty, but ultimately decide my partnership with Andrew Coppock would make it unfair to ask for her help (which she probably wouldn't be able to anyway).

Finally, Martha comes through with something productive: "I'll see what I can do," she says. "Ed still talks to the Havens, so maybe one of them knows where she lives."

"Thank you, Martha. And please don't tell Ed what this is for—we don't want our strategy leaking to Philo."

"Of course. I'll let you know if I find anything. Good luck, and give my best to Marie!"

Even so, I still don't have an address or phone number for our critical witness, which is starting to arouse some anxiety within the team.

"Are we sure we want to fight?" questions Hees. "We still need Annabelle. Do we have her, Eric?"

"Not yet," I shake my head.

"Can you actually get her?"

"He'll get her," interjects Coppock.

"Please get her, Eric" pleads Marie.

Whereas I am the one true connection to Annabelle, I am forced to bite my tongue about the mounting pressure I am feeling to find her.

Frankly, without eyes on every nook and cranny of Chicago, I don't have many ideas of how to track down Annabelle. I walk past restaurants or hotels in the Loop that we used to go to with the Havens in hopes that I might bump into her. But that doesn't feel persistent enough so, foolishly, I try going to Philo's office.

"Get him out of here!" barks Philo as he catches me getting past his secretary.

Since I'm in the area, I try the Havens' clubhouse next. However, Philo must have tipped them off about me snooping around as I can't even make it inside the building.

Then I try Al's old apartment in Lincoln Park. I figure that if Marie got the house when Philo left, maybe Annabelle got Al's apartment when they split.

"What is the last name again?" asks the withered doorman.

"Well, it would have been Kohler, I assume."

"There was an Albert Kohler here once, but he hasn't lived here for a few years. I don't remember him bringing back any proper ladies, either—not like the one you describe."

It is through this fruitless search that I start to appreciate how trivial my conversations with Annabelle were. The letters we'd write to each other were always focused on the present, (with maybe a taste of the near-future if there was a Havens party coming up), but we never really learned about each other. Perhaps if either of us had any willingness to open up she would have told me about the extra year she spent with Philo ... as it is, the only person whom Annabelle might have ever opened up to was—

"Martha," I say, phoning her from my apartment one evening. "Did you find Annabelle?"

"No," she says, "and Ed doesn't want to talk, either."

"I see …"

"But, Eric," adds Martha, "Wendy called me after I spoke with Ed—she wants to meet."

"Does she know where Annabelle is?"

"She wouldn't say over the phone, only that she can help you, and Ed doesn't know. Can you meet her Sunday at noon?"

I tell Marie, Coppock, and Hees about my lunch with Wendy Carmen, but they are far more concerned with who I'm not meeting than giving me credit for who I am.

"You need to get your priorities straight," Hees asserts.

"And people gave *me* grief over talking to their women," gripes Coppock.

"Wendy wants to meet me about Annabelle," I clarify.

"How do you know?" asks Hees. "Did she say that?"

"No, but she probably didn't want to say it outright if Ed was standing over her shoulder," I explain.

"The judge just ordered the depositions, Eric, and we are running out of time," says Hees. "We can't amend our bill to assert Mr. Olin's misconduct until we can prove our case."

"Just find her, Eric," says Coppock.

"Just do your best, Eric" says Marie.

"Just make sure you ask her about Annabelle," says Hees.

On Sunday, I find myself submerged in a bustling market on Maxwell Street on the Near West Side—an unusual area to find a Haven wife. My new overcoat draws the attention of every cap and scarf peddler in the neighborhood. After I reluctantly agree to purchase a pair of red knitted mittens to get a particularly persistent vendor off my back, I manage to push through the remaining sea of merchants to the Jewish delicatessen where I am meeting Wendy for lunch.

"This place must be good," I say, squeezing between two seated patrons as I join Wendy at a small table near the door.

"I appreciate you meeting me here, Eric—I hope it wasn't too hard to find."

"Not at all," I say, stuffing the mittens in my coat pocket.

"Eddy and Herb come here when they don't want to see any of the other Havens," Wendy explains. "I figure it will work for us just as well."

"Ed and Herb?"

Wendy nods ... then exhales. "I'm sorry, it just feels a little wrong to go behind Ed's back like this," she says. "Okay, here it goes—a few months back Ed and Herb were thinking about leaving the Havens, but then Philo's divorce showed up in the papers, and they didn't want to make things worse."

"Hold it—they were thinking of leaving *before* the divorce made it in the newspaper?"

"Before *Philo's* divorce," Wendy emphasizes. "Things have been bad with the club ever since the Kohlers split."

"Was it what happened on their honeymoon?"

Wendy shakes her head. "No one knows what happened on that cruise, but when they came back Al and Annabelle were through and Philo was very upset."

"Upset about the divorce or something else?"

"I don't know, he was just angry," says Wendy. "But the atmosphere with the Havens was never quite right after that—that is what I wanted to talk to you about, Eric. The Havens are in trouble, and Ed thinks there could be as many as five more divorces."

"Really?"

"Already almost a dozen more have left, trying to get out before their wives catch on, I imagine." Wendy laughs, "It's funny that Eddy and Herb could be the last two standing and Louise and I know all about the other side!"

"So does Marie," I say, "and look at Philo now."

"Ed and I are good, Eric," assures Wendy, unamused. "But it's been tough on him," she continues. "I think he feels guilty that his divorce has been easy while his friends' lives are unravelling, especially John's."

"Helen filed for divorce, too?"

"Sadly, the Mattinglys didn't surprise me. You saw how John was—he flaunted his mistresses like he wanted to be caught," she mutters. "The point is the Havens are falling apart, and I don't think Philo can hide behind them anymore."

"That's interesting"

"That's a lot of potential ammo there, Eric," winks Wendy. "Anyway, Martha said you were working with Philo's wife and I thought this might help her case."

"It does, thank you, but—" I pause, "why are you trying to help us?"

Wendy simpers. "Because it's the right thing to do, and I don't want Ed to wake up one day feeling guilty that he let loyalty to his father's friends hurt an innocent woman's life."

I understand what Ed is grappling with, and how easily loyalty can trump your conscious, but remain frustrated that the Havens' culture continues to hinder me. Even though the club may be toppling, I think Wendy is underestimating their loyalty and the lack of incentive to turn on each other.

"This is great information, Wendy, it's just … it's too bad Ed won't say it."

"I know," she concedes. "Even if I could testify without Ed finding out, I'm not sure the word of a former mistress carries much weight."

Wendy's right, and I can hear Hees saying the same. Philo's lawyers would destroy Wendy's character. Even if there are five more divorces filed, as long as the Havens keep their mouths shut about the code and the mistress parties, no one will be found guilty of adultery by benefit of circular reasoning. We still need Annabelle.

"Maybe you can help me with this," I say. "Do either you or Ed know where I can find Annabelle these days?"

Wendy shakes her head, "And I doubt Ed would tell you if he did. This is the best I can do, Eric, I'm sorry."

In the days that follow I am so embittered that I can't bear to show my face at the next meeting at Hees' office. Not only am I no closer to finding Annabelle than I was when we started, but now I have a basketful of damning information about the Havens and no means to exploit it.

Over the next few weeks I retrace my steps, starting with the day I met Annabelle. I visit dozens of hotels where the founders' circle had partied, restaurants where we'd dined, and streets we'd gallivanted late at night. I know the chances of bumping into Annabelle at these places are slim, but legwork is my only option, and I've gone beyond desperation.

"I feel like I've already done this," I growl to myself, trying to shake my déjà vu. I must be thinking too hard, too, for my memory is getting foggy in places.

Late on a Friday night, resting on an icy bench in Grant Park after another unrewarding evening of wandering the city, a filthy young man stumbles across the street. He bumps into a pile of trash that had been forgotten on the corner, and barely catches himself before toppling into oncoming traffic. A black car slams on its breaks, and the group of socialites riding inside laugh at the young man as he stumbles to his next drink.

Don't laugh at him.

Even out of sight, the strong smell of booze on the vagabond wafts beneath my nose, and I can feel the sense of disappointment he'll feel once he sobers up. Does he have a bed tonight? Is he eating dinner out of a used can of beans? Is anyone helping him … and is that worse?

After some time, I head back to my apartment. When I make it to the top of the stoop I see my neighbor's newspaper, forgotten this morning. I pick it up. Next, I fix myself a warm dinner—beef, vegetables, and a tall glass of milk—and sit down to thumb through the paper while my food gets cold.

"My God!" I gasp at a story of a mother of four who was electrocuted for the insurance murder of her own brother.

"Oh, please," I grumble at an article about a man who was ordered to pay a $5,000 settlement for being "cruel to his wife" after she "accidentally disturbed the arrangement of his daily soaps and perfumes."

"Interesting," I muse at a woman in Jacksonville who came up with the idea of installing tracks in her garage to make it easier for her and potentially other women to guide their cars in and out.

I flip the page and take another bite. A slender woman in a large hat and a knee-length fur draws me in, and directs my eyes to the headline: *The Most For You! Decisive Clearance.*

"A sale at Rothschild's is still too expensive," I mumble. "Rothschild's!"

Hand-held walking, gaily talking—leads to a noiseless night.

I'm wandering through racks of women's clothes …

I will display once he's away, suggests the noiseless night.

...hiding behind well-dressed mannequins ...

A stalking fox while she shops until I find my chosen sight—a Rothschild's sale, here I'll unveil, and end my noiseless nights.

...staring at Annabelle as she pilfers through dozens of expensive winter jackets.

"I've found her before," I realize aloud; maybe I can find her again—at Rothschild's Department Store.

The next day, I head to Rothschild's at State and Jackson, just four blocks south of the Marshall Field's that started it all. Inside I pass rows of counters pitching the overstock of Christmas colognes and perfumes. The sales girls are insistent on spraying me with their wares, reeking of desperation to make a sale. I don't recall perfume in my vision, though, and put my head down until I'm on Floor Five: "Women's Overcoats."

I swivel my head around the crowded floor of weekend bargain shoppers, searching for the top of Annabelle's strawberry blond head. I wander a few aisles when a short, balding man with a bushy mustache and a name tag stops me.

"You are barred!" shouts the guard.

"Excuse me?" I say.

"You are bored," repeats the man—his voice sounds familiar, "that's why you're wandering around this section, right, pally? What happened, your wife dragged you here and now you can't wait to get home?"

"Yes, that's it," I say quickly, continuing to scan the floor.

"Well, men's overcoats are on Floor Six," he says. "Might be more interesting to you."

"Right, thanks. I'm just going to look around here a bit longer."

I start to walk away, but the man puts his hand in my face.

Poisoning my sight.

"I'm sorry, sir, but we've had complaints in the past of men bothering our women shoppers. Unless you're here for your wife, I must kindly ask you to go to Floor Six."

My eyes start to burn.

I get uneasy.

"Listen," I say, unable to control my piercing tone, "I'm looking for somebody. As soon as I see she's not here, I'll leave, but until then I'm going to stay."

The diminutive mall guard examines me closely.

"Have we met before?" he asks skeptically.

I don't say anything—for too long.

"Alright, time to go, buddy," and he grabs me by my shoulders and starts to push me toward the elevator—

But then she sees me ...

"Erikas?"

"Annabelle!"

And she ends my noiseless nights.

"Do you know him, ma'am?" the guard asks, still clutching me by my jacket.

"Yes, he's a friend," Annabelle replies.

The guard looks at me again, then lets me go. Annabelle flattens out the temporary creases in my jacket.

"What are you doing here?" she asks.

"Looking for you," I say. "You don't know how hard you were to track down."

Annabelle stops patting. "I didn't know you were looking," she says with a warm smile.

I fight hard to stay focused.

"First off, I know about the arrangement between you and Philo … and Al … and me … everything."

"You do?" she says, unfazed. "Tell me."

"It's more than that," I say. "I'm looking for answers."

"Oh?"

"Like what exactly you're getting from Philo," I barrel forward, knowing I can't afford to lose momentum. "I know he's been taking care of you, and I know he kept Al and I around to make him look innocent. But I also know you and Al got divorced, so I'm not sure where that leaves things."

"Have you been talking to Martha?" Annabelle inquires with a foreign gravity in her voice. "Because I told her I won't speak of it."

"It's not about your divorce," I assure. "It's Philo's. I'm working with Marie—she's filed for divorce and we have a good case built up."

"You do?"

"It'd be even stronger with you."

Annabelle doesn't react right away.

"We can offer compensation," I add.

Annabelle's eyebrows arch. "How much?"

"How much would you want?"

Annabelle ponders some more. "He's giving me fifty a month now," she says.

"How about a hundred?"

"How much are you getting?" she says bluntly—I hesitate. "I'm joking, Eric! I don't want money for this. Of course, I'll help."

"You will?" I say, relieved.

"Yes. Philo and Marie haven't really been husband and wife for years," Annabelle explains assuredly. "It's time to end this sham so they can both move on."

"That's great!" I exclaim. "We'll have Marie's lawyer get in touch with you and we can schedule your deposition."

"Sounds lovely," she says, pulling a small piece of paper from her purse and scribbling her address on it. "Have her lawyer contact me at the Drake."

EXHIBIT 11

22

EXHIBIT 11

Annabelle gets in touch with Rudolph Hees and, after a few conversations to go over her take on Philo's scheme, in early February 1938 we amend Marie's bill to assert Philo's adultery with "Misses J & A."

"And no one will know I am Miss A?" asks Annabelle as she's about to sign her statement to appear for a deposition the following week.

"There will never be public record with your name of your involvement with Mr. Olin," says Hees. "You'll have your deposition next week and you won't even have to appear in court. No one will know it was you except those in this room and Mr. Olin's lawyer."

Annabelle glances around Hees' office, absorbing the rest of our team's eager smiles.

"Good," she says simply, finally signing the document.

On the deposition date, the four of us meet at Philo's lawyer's office. When we arrive, the secretary asks us to wait in the lobby until he comes out to greet us. He's an average-sized man with slicked black hair that overcompensates for his receding hairline.

"I appreciate you all for coming in today," says the lawyer, sporting an excessive grin as he shakes hands with Hees. "I'm Daniel Capelli and will be leading the questioning for today's depositions."

"Good to see you, Daniel," says Hees curtly, patting Coppock on the shoulder, instructing him to follow them into Capelli's chambers. "We thought we'd start with Mr. Coppock."

"Actually, Rudy," says Capelli carefully, "we thought we'd start with the young lady."

Hees grumbles, but Capelli doesn't waver. With a skeptical nod, Hees urging Coppock to sit back down and Annabelle to rise. Capelli flashes an unnerving smile at me then follows Hees and Annabelle into his office.

"What's that about?" I hiss to Coppock once we are alone. "Why does he care which order we go?"

"Relax," Coppock replies, folding his hands behind his head as if settling in for a nap. "He probably wants to look at her while her makeup's fresh."

"Maybe ..." I say, convincing myself there's nothing to worry about. We already got the key witness on our side— all we need to do is tell the truth and Philo is through. I remember that Coppock wants this at least as bad as I do, so if he's calm then I should be, too.

Suddenly, the door to Capelli's office bursts open and Annabelle storms out, clutching her purse and cursing in short, pointed bursts.

EXHIBIT 11

"Annabelle," I gasp. "What's wrong?"

Annabelle swings around and points back at Capelli.

"They ambushed me!" she shouts, her voice trembling. "That man is with the papers. He was going to take my picture and print my name!"

A third man, younger than the two lawyers and wearing a brown fedora, emerges from the office. Everyone but Capelli is frozen as Annabelle continues to wave an angry finger toward the office.

"You said nobody would know I was involved," continues Annabelle erratically, "but you invite this newspaper man. How dare you!"

"We'll ask him to leave," says Hees, not doing a good job of calming Annabelle, "but we need to get your statement."

"I'll give no statement," Annabelle affirms. "How can I trust anything you say?"

"Annabelle, please," I say.

"I'm sorry, Eric, but I cannot help you."

Annabelle spits at the feet of the lawyers and reporter, and tromps out.

"Alright, who's next?" snarks Capelli.

"We'll be back," grunts Hees, ushering Coppock, Marie, and I to the door.

"What's happening?" blubbers Marie.

"We need to go," says Hees, preventing her from looking back.

"Rudy, I'll see you in court!" crows Capelli.

Without Annabelle's cooperation corroborating my story, the divorce goes to trial, set for April 28th. Further complicating things, we are to appear in front of Judge Peter J. Fitzpatrick, who Hees says detests divorce cases.

"Peter hates drama," explains Hees. "For divorces that go to trial, that's all they are. I wholly believe Peter will rule in favor of the side that bores him the least."

"That's a good thing, right?" Marie supposes.

"Hard to say," ponders Hees. "He definitely isn't a misogynist, that's good for us. But we must be careful to stick to the facts—Peter doesn't take to speculation."

"Well, shit," cries Coppock, "half our case is speculation!"

"But so is Mr. Olin's," states Hees. "He's arguing Marie committed misconduct with Schuyler Hendriks, motivated by a terminated employment that occurred several years prior, and that they carried out a cross-country relationship in the presence of his newlywed wife. Can you see how speculative that is?"

"But he has witnesses that put Schuyler in the Olins' house for six weeks after Philo left," I say. "Including me."

"Eric, I've told you," asserts Marie, "Schuyler was an old family friend, and his wife stayed with us for most of his visit."

EXHIBIT 11

"But we don't have any witnesses who will speak to that."

"Then lie, Eric, and say you saw her there," says Coppock.

"Eric's not lying, and I'm working on getting Mr. and Mrs. Hendriks to speak to that," assures Hees. "The point is our claims are no less substantiated than Mr. Olin's. Without Annabelle, this truly could go either way."

With roughly two months until the trial, and our testimonies as good as they'll be, most of Hees' attention is on regaining Annabelle's cooperation. While his first two attempts to talk to her end in similarly disastrous fashion as the deposition in Capelli's office, she starts to wear down by the third.

"She'll consider testifying if all press is barred," reports Hees.

"So, have them barred," says Coppock. "I don't see the problem."

"I do, though," says Hees. "Open trials are the norm, except for juvenile cases. I will try to explain to the judge that our key witness' testimony is dependent on full privacy, but the case has been all over the *Tribune* for weeks. I'm not optimistic he'll find that relevant anymore."

"Of course, you're not," grumbles Coppock.

While I, too, am getting frustrated with Hees' cynicism, he's probably right. Hees appears before the court with a motion to ban all media and press from attending any of the depositions or divorce hearings ...

"Motion denied."

...but we don't get it—Annabelle is out.

Hearing Annabelle's side of the story (and knowing that it fully supports Coppock's and mine) had given our team a false confidence that we could beat Philo. Not having her means that, with only a month until the trial, we are no better off than we were six months ago when Coppock and I first swapped stories over cake in Marie's kitchen.

At last, after four more weeks of rehearsing our stories for the stand, April 28th arrives—it's time to go to trial. Coppock and I meet Marie and Hees in the expansive, marble-floored lobby of the Cook County Circuit Courthouse, just a few blocks from Philo's office.

"And what is our goal?" quickly quizzes Hees.

"No drama—don't be boring," we recite in unison.

Coppock and I are to sit and wait in the witness holding room until we are called to testify. Here we are joined by three others: Mack, Miss Beulah (who harrumphs at my entrance), and a familiar-looking brown-haired man in a cheap blue suit whom I assume to be Schuyler Hendriks.

"Hey, kid!" whispers Mack before Capelli glares at him for fraternizing. Mack lowers his head but sneaks a smirk.

"Make sure none of them talk," says Capelli to the bailiff, "especially Mr. Sunshine in the cap."

"You got it, bossman!" says Mack as Capelli exits.

EXHIBIT 11

After waiting an hour, Coppock is the first witness called to the stand. "Wish me luck!" he mouths on his way out.

After what doesn't seem like more than a few minutes, though, Coppock plops back down next to me in the waiting room. His posture is slanted and he lets out a humbled groan. I look at him to gather unspoken feedback, but he just throws his head back to nap. Then they call my name.

"Hees was right about the judge," Coppock sighs, his eyes still closed. "Good luck."

I am led down a hall and into a modest courtroom—in size. The two rows of the gallery are bursting with reporters and photographers eager to snap my photo and grab a quick statement. The bailiff walks me toward the bench, where I take a seat on the witness stand and get sworn in.

Judge Peter J. Fitzpatrick is an imposing figure on the bench, with a strong jaw and a critical stare. He is every bit the hardened judge of Hees' description and Coppock's parting words.

"Mr. Mihlfried," starts Hees, "can you describe, in your own words, your association with Philo Olin?"

Philo is slumped forward at the defendant's table, working his jaw back and forth as he glowers at me. With his neatly-coiffed, wavy white hair and designer suit, he looks like a movie villain contrary to Marie's matronly, flower-print dress and jolly disposition perked up at the plaintiff's table.

"Mr. Olin was an old friend of my father's," I state slowly. "But we didn't meet until a few days before Christmas in 1932 ..."

Prompted by Hees' carefully-planned questions, I tell the judge about my arrangement with Philo—living with him, first at his house and later at the Stevens Hotel, attending Havens events, and escorting Annabelle and her Shiner friends around Chicago, all while he was using me as a front for his affair.

"Mr. Mihlfried, put plainly, do you mean this to believe that Mr. Olin was unfaithful in his marriage to Mrs. Olin?"

"I do."

"Thank you," says Hees, sitting back down.

On the cross-examination, Capelli questions my motives for associating with Philo. As Hees warned, he is focused on making me sound like I was desperate for money—specifically, Philo's—when we began our association ...

"Is it true that you lived rent-free at my client's upscale Hyde Park residence from January until October 1933?" proposes Capelli, making a large swooping motion with one of his hands to emphasize the length of my stay.

"Yes."

"And that upon seeing Mr. S's luggage in Mrs. Olin's bedroom that you followed Philo into his new residence at the Stevens Hotel, where he let you stay, again rent-free, until the following November?"

EXHIBIT 11

"That is correct," I say, prompting Capelli to throw his arms in the air like he's received a divine revelation. Judge Fitzpatrick glazes right over this.

Daniel Capelli is similarly demonstrative for each of his questions. If he's not twirling his hands he's swinging his head to underscore his words, a stark contrast to Hees' style of standing still with his hands in his pockets.

"Given as much, would you say your association with Mr. Olin has always been financially motivated?"

"Objection, Your Honor, Irrelevant," states Hees.

"Your Honor, may I respond?" says Capelli.

Judge Fitzpatrick nods.

"I'm trying to establish the witness' motives for testifying against my client," Capelli explains. "It is valuable to evaluate the witness' credibility in his testimony, and his past motives may affect the credibility of his present testimony."

"Your Honor, may I respond?" Hees interjects.

Judge Fitzpatrick lets out the slightest of yawns, then nods again. Hees recognizes that I also notice this, and flashes a wink.

He's turning Judge Fitzpatrick against Capelli.

This back and forth between Capelli's questions about my character and Hees' objections takes an increasing toll on the judge's patience, as his boredom become progressively perceptible. After some time, though, Capelli catches on and switches his strategy.

"Your Honor, the Defense moves to introduce Exhibit 11 into evidence," says Capelli wryly, holding up a stack of hand-written letters.

"Objection, Your Honor," growls Hees. "Withholding of Evidence. Mr. Capelli never submitted an Exhibit 11, and we have not had a chance to examine it."

"Your Honor, may I?" says Capelli, defensively pulling his hands back to his shoulders.

Judge Fitzpatrick nods.

"The Defense is submitting written letters between Eric Mihlfried and the alleged adulteress, Miss A, which establishes their close relationship during her time at school. Mr. Hees' witness had equal access to such letters, and there was no reason for Mr. Mihlfried to withhold this evidence other than to cover up his ongoing relationship with Miss A."

"Objection, Your Honor," says Hees. "Counsel is Testifying."

"I apologize for that, Your Honor," says Capelli.

"I'll allow the evidence," Judge Fitzpatrick drones. "Please proceed, Mr. Capelli."

Rudolph Hees looks daggers at me, and I don't blame him. How could I forget about the letters? Philo was always so insistent that I write to Annabelle while she was at school—how did I not see that he was using them to set me up? My paper trail ...

EXHIBIT 11

"Mr. Mihlfried, do you recognize these documents in my hand?" asks Capelli, waving the letters, then placing several—one-by-one—before me.

I look at Judge Fitzpatrick; he isn't yawning anymore.

"Yes," I say. "They are letters I wrote to Miss A while she was at school."

I stare at the top letter of the stack. It was the first one I wrote where I asked her about her classes and talked about getting settled in Marie's mother's old bedroom. I flip through a few more and see the one where I talked about the incredible St. Patrick's Day party Ed threw—I can't believe that was over five years ago ... And here's the one about Herb's party that got rained out where John started calling himself "The Mattress"—of course, I didn't mention that part in the letter, but just the sight of them brings back so many memories—

"And in several of these letters, Mr. Mihlfried," says Capelli, "did you tell Miss A how you wished she could come to the city more often, and how you missed seeing her?"

I wish Martha was here right now.

"Yes, but she was always just a friend."

"A friend you drove over four hours to see at school, and with whom you attended several lavish date parties going back to December 1932?" says Capelli, throwing his arms up trying to find a logical explanation. "Come on, Mr. Mihlfried, we're all adults here ..."

"Yes, but it wasn't romantic."

"Your Honor," says Capelli, rearranging the letters in front of me, "I'd like to draw the Court's attention to Exhibit 11-P—Mr. Mihlfried, would you please read the highlighted portion aloud?"

I clear my throat.

"*I miss the feeling of your soft hands against my cheeks*," I read, glancing quickly at Hees, who's turned pale. "*Life is too short to be kept apart.*"

Capelli looks to Philo, then Hees, then Judge Fitzpatrick and nods proudly.

"*I saw two cars get into an accident today*," I continue, "*while at lunch with Charlie and Sid—*"

"That'll do, Mr. Mihlfried," cuts in Capelli, snatching the letters from me. "As you can see, Your Honor, the claims of the Witness, Eric Mihlfried, that my client was in an ongoing romantic relationship with Miss A were, in fact, a projection of his own intimacy with the same.

"The paternal and often-financial relationship between my client and Mr. Mihlfried explains the occasional associations and monetary support in the form of school tuition between my client and Miss A, as implied in the plaintiff's examination. No further questions."

I step down from the stand and am led from the courtroom. I pass by Hees as he frantically whispers into Marie's ear, probably about how I just blew the case by not revealing my Annabelle letters beforehand. Perhaps if we spent some time with them we could have come up with a foolproof explanation, but in this context, they just look bad. Philo got me—he had me from the beginning.

EXHIBIT 11

As I'm led back into the waiting room, Coppock looks for my reaction. When I avoid eye contact, his head drops, his mouth curses, and his knuckles crack.

I let everyone down.

As Miss Beulah steps out of the waiting room to give her testimony—probably about how not only was I Annabelle's beau while she was in school (another string Philo pulled), but that I also showed poor character by disrespecting that relationship with Annabelle's friend, Louise—I start to panic. Not only did I just lose us the case and all that money for Marie, but I might be held in contempt for "lying" about it.

I finally get my life together and now I could be going to jail.

I can't believe I forgot about those letters. I haven't thought about them in ages. But now they're at the crux of this case and quickly coming back into focus. I definitely wrote about her coming into the city, and wanting to see her. I remember writing it then signing my name to it, like a legal admission. It's exactly the kind of evidence Philo needed from me to tie my name to a fake relationship with Annabelle.

The paper trail to Julia had been Coppock's leverage over Philo, and we even had Philo's Shiner payments for his paper trail to Annabelle. But my letters are much more compelling proof of a relationship, making Shiner that much easier to explain away: "I did it for Eric."

He looks like a hero.

Maybe if our relationship wasn't fake—if the timing was right—this wouldn't sting so badly? When the case was over, at least I would be able to go home to Annabelle:

My face warms as I recall the first time Annabelle kissed me, then every other time—even if they weren't romantic, I still recall them electrifyingly. And that first day we met, I remember the feeling of her grabbing my hand and pulling me toward the dance floor. These moments have never left me, and are as clear and present as they were when they happened.

Her skin is beautiful, her lips are perfect, and her hands feel so soft against my cheeks.

Actually, I don't remember that last one.

23

JAGGED HANDWRITING

I can't summon of a single instance of Annabelle touching my face. With further certainty, I don't remember seeing a car accident while at lunch with Charlie and Sid— or ever meeting Sid Reid, for that matter.

I don't remember anything in that letter.

"Mr. Hees!" I shout down the hall, running after the lawyer after we are let out for lunch. "Mr. Hees, we need to talk!"

"What is it, Mr. Mihlfried?" grumbles Hees. "I only have an hour, and Capelli just destroyed my direct examination."

"It's about those letters. The one I read wasn't from me."

"What are you talking about? I thumbed through them, and each one had your signature."

357

"But I can remember what I wrote. If you just give me an hour with the letters, I can show you which are mine and which are not."

"You should have told me about them in the first place," Hees scolds. "I'm not sure what good it'd do to scrutinize them after what just happened in there."

"But we need to try," I assert, fed up with Hees' pessimism. We lock eyes and I won't let him look away. He wipes his forehead, and I nod assuredly.

"Yes, of course we can try," agrees Hees. "Let's grab Marie and get started—we haven't much time."

The three of us head to a nearby café to pour over the Exhibit 11 letters. We begin by separating the ones I specifically remember from the those I don't.

"Are you sure you didn't write any of these?" says Hees.

"No, but I don't remember writing them," I explain. "But now we can look for any patterns in this stack."

We divvy up the potential imposters so each of us can look for any striking commonalities. Fanning through my pile, I compare the signatures ... the ink color ... the word choice ... the penmanship—

"I've got something!" exclaims Marie. "These letters are much more romantic than Eric's."

"That's not very—" starts Hees. "Thank you, Marie," he concludes.

She smiles proudly.

"I have something too," I add. "Look at the handwriting in these, it's different than mine."

"It all looks sloppy to me," Hees observes.

"But in these letters I'm sure I wrote," I say, running my finger along one of the lines, "my penmanship is fairly curvy. Look back at these others—the marks are almost jagged."

"That looks like Philo's handwriting," Marie adds.

I smile proudly at Marie.

"Philo wrote these letters," I say. "He wrote them and signed them from me to cover-up his affair's paper trail."

Hees gestures to slow down. "This proves that someone other than you wrote these letters, but there's nothing tying Mr. Olin to them."

"But his handwriting," I remind, "Marie just identified it."

"Marie's biased," Hees retorts.

"Then what if we found another piece of Philo's handwriting and compared it to these letters?"

"He could just as easily claim someone else wrote it just as you're doing with these letters."

"That's preposterous!" says Marie. "Who would think of such complicated nonsense?"

"Philo would. That's exactly what he did to me," I admit, then think for a second. "We could have him write his name in court. He couldn't deny what he wrote right in front of the judge. Then we compare that handwriting to these letters and there's our proof!"

"This isn't Hollywood, Eric," says Hees bluntly, checking his watch. "I appreciate the enthusiasm, but we have to be back in court in ten minutes and I still need to figure out how to salvage this mess."

Hees digs into his leather case folder and examines a few documents while Marie munches on biscuits. I look over the fake letters again, and wish that there was some definitive proof that Philo wrote them, but Hees is right about the holes in my suggestions. It's such a pity because the penmanship, writing style, and subject matters are all so different between Philo's letters and mine. Then there's the signature—I concluded every letter with: *"Always, Erikas."*

In Philo's: *"Always, Eric."*

In my letters, whenever I wrote about the Havens it was very general—like about the decorations at the St. Patrick's Day party—because Philo said it was against the rules to talk about parties in public, and I assumed that extended to letters. As I flip through Philo's, on the other hand, they speak at length about other Havens members. Even stranger, he often wrote about Havens he hardly ever interacted with, like Sid Reid and Francis Papp—he seemed to write about them more than anyone else, even John and Ed. Now I wonder if Philo even wrote the fakes …

Who else is connected to both Annabelle and the Havens? Andrew Coppock took an early interest in her at that first Christmas party, but I don't think he is clever enough to be playing both sides … Felix double-crossed me once with Louise, but he always seemed too admiring of the Havens to be so involved … *Danielius* Kruger seemed pretty taken by Annabelle at that first party, too, but I have a hard time tying him closely to Philo—has he ever said anything to believe there's more?

"You don't happen to work on Michigan Avenue, do you?"

Sid Reid works on Michigan Avenue.

"It's a code," I gasp.

"What was that?" grunts Hees.

"Philo's letters are a code," I realize aloud. "They all mention two Havens—that's how the club communicates the locations of their parties so none of the wives or mistresses find out and show up uninvited."

I shuffle through pile again, quickly scanning for names of Havens.

"Their names correspond to the streets they work on, and the two names together are the venue's intersection," I explain. "The one I read in court had Sid Reid and Charlie Lords, which is Michigan and Oak—the Drake ... This letter has Ed Carmen and Daniel Kruger, or LaSalle and Madison—the LaSalle Hotel ... And here is Sid Reid, again, with Francis Papp, or Michigan and Congress—the Congress Hotel."

"You're saying this is how he tells Annabelle where to meet him," reasons Hees.

"Yes!" I exclaim, still digesting the contents of Philo's letters. "It's all here. There's even a number near the names, that'd be the number of days from the date of the letter. *'Two* cars' ... *'Four* drinks' ... 'Every Night at *Eight'* ..."

"I'm not following, Eric," moans Marie.

361

"That's the point," I say. "The Havens speak in code so no one can figure out where their parties are because sometimes they're for the wives, and sometimes they're for the mistresses. This code is how they communicate right in front of the women without them knowing. Or in this case, right in front of the judge."

"Intriguing," ponders Hees. "Is there anything else?"

"Sid Reid."

"Oh, I remember Sid," says Marie. "I was always very fond of him."

"Philo kicked him out of the Havens before he started bringing me around," I continue. "But he was the only one who worked on Michigan Avenue, which is where a lot of the hotels are, so he still came up in toasts for years after he was out of the club. Someone even asked me at my first party if I worked on Michigan because they wanted to replace Sid Reid in the code, but they never got anybody."

"This is good, Eric," says Hees. "We can use this. However—"

"We can't have me take the stand again after what happened in court today," I say, accustomed to Hees' tendencies by now.

"You're right," he agrees.

"That's fine, because I know somebody who can."

For the first time since this case began, Marie and Hees beam at me with confidence.

"I'll talk to the judge and get us more time," says Hees.

"And I'll get ahold of our new witness."

"We're going to beat my husband, aren't we, Eric?" says Marie.

"I think we are," I say. "He covered up a bit too much."

Really, Sid Reid?

Hees convinced Judge Fitzpatrick to give us an extra day. We spend the evening making phone calls and hypothesize scenarios deep into the night before turning in close to three in the morning. When we reconvene the next day, the courtroom's press presence has doubled from yesterday. Apparently, the unexpected twist of my letters has invoked further interest in a case that was already lauded a "Money Bags Cash Grab." If the press likes that, they'll love what we have for them today ...

"Please state your name for the court," says Hees at the start of the second day.

"Ed Carmen."

Philo slams his hand against the table top, drawing Judge Fitzpatrick's displeasure. Ed keeps his eyes fixed at the back of the peanut gallery, where his mother and Wendy are sitting, until Capelli gets Philo to calm down.

"Mr. Carmen, can you state your association with the defendant, Philo Olin?"

"Philo and I are both members of the Havens Club of Chicago, an exclusive gentleman's club that he, my father, and another friend founded in 1908."

Philo adjusts his glasses and is working his jaw so hard that I wouldn't be surprised if it fell off its hinge.

"And can you expand upon this club and its purpose?"

"Well, officially, it is a place for successful businessmen to socialize," explains Ed, avoiding Philo's death stare. "My father invited me to join when I was twenty-eight after I started having some marital problems."

"And why then, Mr. Carmen?" Hees carries on, "Can you tell the court why your father invited you to join the Havens Club once there was trouble in your marriage?"

"Because he wanted to help me be happy again, and this was the only way he knew how," says Ed, adding his mother to his optical evasions.

"Why did he think the Havens would make you happy?"

"Because the Havens are really about hiding members' affairs," says Ed. Mrs. Carmen swallows hard as tears well in her eyes. Wendy grabs her mother-in-law's hand as she fights back tears of her own.

"Can you clarify that, Mr. Carmen?"

Ed adjusts his seat and clears his throat. "Well, before this case, every man knew the Havens as the best, safest gentlemen's club in Chicago because of their rules and codes."

"What would those be?"

"The ones Philo developed to keep us safe. At each party, the host of the next one gives a toast thanking that night's host. This is when he reveals the date and location of the next party through a series of codes."

He pauses, and Philo straightens up, making himself look as dignified as possible. After making brief eye contact with his mother, Ed is starting to sweat. I can see a glimmer of concern in Hees, but Ed pushes forward.

"Saying the names of different members corresponds to the location, the mention of a number tells us the date, and whether the speaker was wearing his jacket or not indicates if the next party is for our wives or mistresses."

"And this code was used at every party?"

"For as long as I've been a member, yes," nods Ed, breathing heavily.

"Your Honor," says Hees quickly, "I'd like to bring back Exhibit 11-P—the letter Eric Mihlfried read as his own during yesterday's cross-examination."

Judge Fitzpatrick nods.

"Mr. Carmen, can you please read the same highlighted portion that Mr. Mihlfried read yesterday?"

"*I miss the feeling of your soft hands against my cheeks*," Ed reads shakily. "*Life is*—

Ed stumbles. He looks up from the letter, finding Wendy again, who nods encouragingly.

"*Life is too short to be kept apart.*"

Capelli looks at Philo curiously, then at Hees, then at Judge Fitzpatrick, who is listening as intently as he has during this case.

"I saw two cars get into an accident today," Ed continues, *"while at lunch with Charlie and Sid."*

"Mr. Carmen, considering your testimony on this system of codes, which you stated Philo Olin developed for use by the Havens Club of Chicago, what does this letter mean to you?"

"Be at the Drake Hotel in two days," says Ed immediately. "Charlie and Sid stand for Oak and Michigan Avenue. They were a common mention—the Drake is a gorgeous hotel."

"Mr. Carmen, couldn't any of the Havens have used this code in the letter you hold, including Eric Mihlfried?"

Judge Fitzpatrick leans further forward, while Philo and Capelli exchange comforted glances.

"Any Haven could have used the code that way."

Philo and Capelli nod at each other.

"What about this one?" says Hees, handing Ed another letter. "Exhibit 11-R."

Ed scans the letter, muttering, "Sid Reid … Francis Papp …" then looks up and says, "No."

Philo's eyes narrow.

Hees hands Ed a few more letters. "And what about this one? And this? And the other sixteen letters dated 1934 alone?"

"No—no other Haven would have written these."

"Why is that, Mr. Carmen?"

Ed holds up one of the letters and points to two names. "Sid and Francis," he says. "These two names mean the intersection of Michigan Avenue and Congress, which is the Congress Hotel—Philo is the only Haven who would willingly do anything at the Congress"

"Why, Mr. Carmen?"

"Because everyone knows it's haunted," says Ed.

"Objection, Your Honor," says Capelli, "this is highly speculative."

"Overruled," says Judge Fitzpatrick.

"The Congress was built for the first World's Fair in 1893," continues Ed. "Its history is full of murders, suicides, and ghost stories, and its only gotten worse since the recent Fair. The ballrooms are nice, sure, but even the mayor couldn't get a hooker in a room at the Congress—with all due respect."

The Shiner girls always did make a fuss about staying there—they even stayed at a different hotel when Philo hosted Annabelle's wedding at the Congress.

"Objection," interjects Capelli again. "Your Honor, how is this relevant?"

"Get to the defendant, Mr. Carmen."

"Mr. Carmen," says Hees, "would Philo Olin stay at the Congress?"

"Absolutely," says Ed bluntly. "The only people who stay at the Congress are tourists and cheapskates."

Philo is glowering.

"Philo was so paranoid about getting caught, even by the other Havens, he knew he'd never run into anybody from our world at the Congress," explains Ed. "And it's no secret his company took a bigger hit from the depression than some of us—in his shoes, if he wanted to maintain his lifestyle and see this 'Miss A' on the side, the Congress would be an affordable option. That would be the only reason to go there, though."

"Going back to Exhibit 11 then, do you think Philo Olin wrote these letters to Miss A?" asks Hees.

"Without a doubt," says Ed coldly. "That's the Havens code, and only Philo would take a girl to the Congress."

"Thank you, Mr. Carmen. No further questions, Your Honor."

Judge Fitzpatrick quiets down the press in the gallery as Ed Carmen steps down from the stand. As he walks out of the courtroom, he kisses his mother on the cheek then throws his arms around Wendy, who rubs the back of his head.

It's nearly forgotten due to the energy in the room, but there is still plenty of additional testimony to hear, mostly from Philo's accusations of Marie's own alleged misconduct. And though Capelli tries his best to spin a compelling narrative with vivid scenes …

"And did you think it proper to invite a married man to sip cocktails in your parlor while your husband was away?" asks Capelli.

"No."

"Then why did you do it?"

"Because I didn't," says Marie firmly. "What an improper implication, Daniel."

…but Marie handles herself with admirable poise, even as Capelli's questions get more personal.

"And weren't you devastated after your mother passed away?" asks Capelli.

"Of course, she was my mother," replies Marie. "She'd lived with us her last few years—we'd grown close."

"And didn't you go on record saying you were disappointed in the lack of sympathy from your husband while you were grieving?"

"Yes."

"And didn't you respond to this by going on vacations by yourself and sleeping with other men, including Mr. S?"

"Certainly not."

"But you did go on vacations without your husband?"

"I did," admits Marie coolly, "but only because Philo was out every night, so we rarely had time to schedule one together."

Hees doesn't object a single time during Capelli's questioning of Marie. Every difficult question thrown her way is deflected by bubbly charm, and Judge Fitzpatrick eats it up.

"And that was before he moved out," Marie adds after a short pause, "nearly five years ago, on October 13, 1933."

"Thank you for reminding us, Mrs. Olin. But what about Mr. X?" presses Capelli, his words growing increasingly pointed. "You were seen kissing him in the public lobby of his place of employment. Are you denying this affair, as well?"

"That's enough, counselor," says Judge Fitzpatrick.

"It's alright, Your Honor, I can answer," chuckles Marie. "Yes, I kissed him, but there's nothing to it. Why, he's only a kid of forty. I'm a wrinkled old grandmother— do you really suppose a vital young man would want anything to do with me?"

"He'd want your money, wouldn't he?"

"Perhaps," hums Marie, "if I had any—isn't that why we're here, Daniel?"

Judge Fitzpatrick snorts, but quickly composes himself.

"Okay, Marie, just tell me this," snaps Capelli, clasping his hands together. "If you haven't been stepping out on your husband, what do you do all day? For years you've employed a driver, a maid, a cleaning lady, a laundress, and with no employment of your own. What did you do with yourself all day?"

"Oh, I just sat around and twirled my thumbs," says Marie lightly. "No, seriously, I baked cakes my family liked."

"Cakes," repeats Capelli. "All day?"

Philo laughs to himself, and Marie smiles at him.

"Yes, my husband loves this special layer cake that I bake him," explains Marie. "It's a four-layered cake with frosting on the top, and the sides exposed. I just love baking Mr. Olin's cakes."

"That does sound good," remarks Judge Fitzpatrick, leaning on his chin and openly smiling for the first time this trial.

"Oh, it really is," says Marie to the judge. "I could make you one after this trial is over. What kind of filling do you like? Mr. Olin was always partial to strawberry—"

"Can we proceed, Your Honor?" says Capelli tartly.

"I think we're done here, counselor," says Judge Fitzpatrick. "You may step down, ma'am."

Marie squeaks excitedly to the judge as she scurries down from the stand and takes her seat next to Hees.

In Judge Fitzpatrick's ruling, he first dismisses Philo's charges of misconduct against Marie, describing her alleged affair with Mr. S (Schuyler Hendriks) as "speculation."

Philo, on the other hand, does not fair nearly as well. Judge Fitzpatrick describes his take on Philo's affairs with Miss J and, especially, Miss A as scandalous, deliberate, and manipulative, sternly stating that "even if nothing consummated with these young women, the thought of you taking advantage of money-strapped young men to front your extramarital affairs conjures imagery of a spider weaving his web."

The judge grants Marie her divorce on the grounds of Philo's misconduct, and awards the full $700 a month in alimony.

"We won!" crows Coppock, violently shaking my shoulders.

Capelli hastens Philo out of the courtroom just as the gallery erupts in photographs and statement requests.

In the courthouse lobby, I walk up to Rudolph Hees just before the press gets to him.

"Great job, Mr. Hees," I say, shaking his hand.

"Thank you, Eric," says Hees stiffly. "Same to you."

As soon as Hees walks away, I am bombarded with a suffocating bear hug.

"Oh, thank you for helping me, Eric!" squeals Marie, pinning my arms down.

"Sure thing," I gasp, and Marie loosens her grip. "Really, Ed deserves the praise, though. The letters meant nothing without him."

"But you figured it out, Eric!" says Marie. "Oh, look— there's our hero now!"

I turn around and Wendy is supporting Ed's weight as they saunter over.

"You stayed," I say.

"You sound surprised," says Ed. "I wanted to see what happened."

"What do you think of the ruling?"

"Honestly? I was sick to my stomach my entire testimony," admits Ed. "It was obviously too late once they swore me in, but most of the time I felt like a traitor—to my father and mother."

"Oh, Eddy—" coos Wendy.

"But thinking about what would happen if I didn't testify," Ed continues, "that helped. I never would have forgiven myself if Philo had won and left you destitute, Marie—but now you'll be taken care."

"Well aren't you the sweetest," gushes Marie, pinching Ed's cheeks. "You've made this old grandmother very happy, Ed Carmen—Patsy must be so proud."

"Hard to tell …"

"Marie," interrupts Hees, "I'm sorry to steal you, but the *Tribune* is asking for a statement."

Marie's smile widens. "Thank you again," she says, then departs with her lawyer.

"You were very brave, Eddy," says Wendy, putting her arm around his waist. "Your mother will come around."

Ed frowns at me and shrugs. "We better get going. Goodbye, Eric."

"Ed, before you go," I say, "what made you change your mind?"

Ed and Wendy turn to each other. "I'll wait for you outside," she says, giving us privacy.

"It's like I told Marie," says Ed, "I never would have forgiven myself if Philo won and she was left penniless."

"But what about the others?"

"You mean the other Haven marriages I just ruined?" Ed clarifies. "This won't help—you heard about John, right?"

I nod.

"They'll hate me. They'll say I killed the Havens, and they'll be right. But what kind of club discourages love? They guilt you into thinking loyalty to the Havens is what's most important, but what about loyalty to your partner?

"Philo tried to deny Wendy even after she was my wife because of when we met. It didn't matter that we loved each other, or that Winnie and I made the joint decision to end our marriage, or that I continue to take care of Winnie, Little Ed, and Wendy—all that mattered to him was that I got divorced, and that's against the rules. Really, Eric, think about that—*my divorce is going to get them caught*. Not their affairs. *My divorce.*

"After Wendy told me about your meeting I was at a loss why she would go behind my back like that. But I'm glad she did, because I did want to help Marie, and I didn't want to see the Havens' culture prevail. When you came to me yesterday afternoon I was ready to fight, because I believe in loyalty to your spouse, your children, and the ones who deserve your love. I'll have to live the rest of my life knowing I ruined my friends' marriages, but I'll be able to sleep knowing I stopped Philo from hurting his wife."

Down the hall, I see Marie with Andrew Coppock, Schuyler Hendriks, and another older gray-haired woman. Marie hugs Coppock, hugs Schuyler a little longer, and then Schuyler hugs the other woman longer still.

"I think we did good, Ed."

"I haven't taken the best path with my relationships," he sighs, "but I think I found the best path from here. I don't believe we can say the same for Philo."

"Agreed."

A few reporters wander into the lobby, and I get the feeling they are looking to grab a quote from me or Ed

"We better get going," says Ed, spotting them, as well.

"One last thing," I say as we slip past the reporters. "Is that true about the Congress being haunted?"

"That's what they say."

"It's interesting. The girls always complained about staying there, but I never understood why."

"Did they? I suppose a good story never dies," he says as his car pulls up to the curb. "I made up the part about him being a cheapskate, though," he winks. "I knew it'd rile him."

We shake hands, then Ed staggers down the courthouse steps where Wendy's waiting for him. They kiss then get into a black car and drive off.

It's time for me to go home, too. I almost walk—it's a beautiful day—but then decide to take a cab.

24

BREAKFAST OF PATRICIANS

Pearl holds up the book for all to see. "Look what I have!" she sings, shaking it at us like a dog treat before passing it around the table.

"That's Philo Jr.'s, isn't it?" says Wendy, prodding the slouching man next to her. "Eddy, we were just talking about it the other day!"

Ed smiles dully, "That sure is something."

"One of Charlie's clients got him a copy and he gave it to me," gushes Pearl, squeezing her husband's stubby arm.

"And they say he wrote this with his wife, huh?" says Herb when the book lands with him.

After the Havens' fall during the Olins' divorce trial, a few of us started meeting on Sunday mornings for a sort of group therapy session over breakfast. Originally Wendy's idea to help Ed forgive himself for his testimony's role in the club's demise, these meetups provided a safe space for the Carmens, Martha, and I to process our roles in the scandal.

"What makes me any better than them?" said Ed at our first breakfast. "John and Philo were my father's best friends—those three men built the Havens, and I was one of them. How could I turn on them like I wasn't?"

"You mustn't blame yourself for their behavior, Eddy," said Wendy.

"They were already caught before you said a word," I added. "The divorces were inevitable."

"What are you even upset about losing with that club?" asserted Martha. "Your relationship with Wendy—your son and Winnie, too—is so much better without the Havens. Think about what's important, Ed!"

After a few weeks in the comfort of this logically supportive company, Ed started letting go of his guilt. His recovery was undoubtedly aided, however, by Pearl Lords' forgiveness of Charlie's involvement in the Havens. Despite the cousins' previous squabbling, Ed was clearly anxious over whether Charlie would become the next Haven divorcé. Fortunately, Pearl decided to stay with Charlie because, according to Wendy, he "only went on dates" and "never fully cheated." As such, the reaffirmed Lords became our first breakfast club expansion which, because of their peripheral role in the Olins' divorce, also injected gossip into the dialogue.

"I just can't accept that Philo felt like a victim when his mother-in-law died," said Pearl a few weeks back. "That man was looking for any reason to step out on Marie."

"Clearly their love wasn't strong enough for the tough times," added Charlie with a peck on Pearl's cheek.

The anti-Philo sentiments were more indulgent than what I had initially signed up for. It was cathartic to vent my frustrations, however, at least enough to keep me coming each week, even after the additions of Herb and Louise further intensified the subsequent breakfasts.

"Is it really that difficult to have a happy marriage?" said Louise one Sunday. "I can't imagine Herb and I ever getting to the point of cheating."

The Carmens and Lords are noticeably tight-lipped.

"We're so fortunate to have found each other, sweetheart," crooned Herb.

"I wish everyone could have something as special as we have," continued Louise, flashing an omniscient grin at Martha and me.

"Maybe after law school," said Martha in stride.

"You're so focused," admired Wendy. "It's impressive, really. I can't wait to see what you do after you graduate."

"Everyone—" Louise interjects, "except for Philo. He deserves to rot in hell!"

"That's right, honey," encouraged Herb.

Which brings us to today. While being a good sport the past few weeks in recounting every reason Philo burns me up, lately I have grown unsatisfied with the repetitiveness of these meetings. Unfortunately, I may be alone in that sentiment …

"It's funny," comments Ed as he fans through the book before passing it to Wendy, "for months we heard about his son writing this, but never on what it actually was about."

"It's obvious why Philo stopped talking about it," says Wendy, "no matter how strongly Philo Jr. claims it wasn't about his parents."

Wendy passes it next to me. I hold it up to clearly see the cover's bold blue letters: *Lovers Never Marry*. I had seen the title before, but running my hands over it still gives it an ambiguous power, and me a compulsory curiosity. Then, Pearl rips it away, clutching it like a carnival prize won by her beau.

"Has anyone actually read it?" asks Herb. "Other than what the papers have been saying, of course."

Everyone shakes their head.

Before the *Tribune* ran the advertisement a few days after Philo and Marie's divorce trial, the last I had heard either gush about their son and daughter-in-law's book was after they cancelled their trip to New York for the launch party. From a sales perspective, it is not surprising that it has reemerged after nearly five years of obscurity on the heels of the Olins' very public divorce.

The book's newfound interest lead to the paper running a follow-up article where Philo Jr. was quoted saying "the title is merely a coincidence." Of course, I am no longer able to take an Olin man at his word, so after the article ran I bought a copy to find out for myself. But every time I opened it up—

"What are you doing?" I would say aloud.

—I stopped short of reading a word. Do I need to study this book to find out that Philo is awful? No. The trial may have left lingering questions with what really happened between Philo and Annabelle and me, but I had stood up to Philo, and Anabelle wasn't there for him, either. Though it wasn't perfect, it was enough. It had to be enough. But it wasn't enough as long as the book kept staring at me, so I threw it in the trash.

"I can't feel enough for Marie," says Wendy. "I wanted to believe at some point Philo truly loved her, but between the years of scheming and this book—kids see everything—it doesn't appear so."

"But what I find interesting is why his grown son was compelled to write this," says Pearl. "He clearly has no respect for his father, and I don't blame him—Philo was a monster."

"It makes me even more thankful that I got one of the good ones," adds Louise, grabbing Herb's hand.

"We all did," says Wendy, also taking Ed's.

Martha peers at me. I peer back, then whisper, "Are we still talking about the book?"

Over the next few weeks, the denigration of Philo Olin continues …

"Thank goodness he never corrupted my Herbie," boasts Louise.

"I don't think Philo ever had the capacity to love," says Wendy.

… until the husbands start buying into it …

"At least John was friendly," says Charlie. "Philo never even tried."

"And he was so selfish," exclaims Ed. "The way he handled Andrew Coppock was inexcusable. He could have assaulted a hundred girls and he would have kept him around if he thought it'd keep him quiet."

... and in the moment, I savor the opportunity to freely express my frustrations ...

"Ed's right," I assert. "Philo would do anything to get his way. It didn't matter who it hurt, or how, just as long as he was in control."

"Yes, Eric, let it out," encourages Wendy.

... but then afterwards I feel terrible.

"Then stop coming," says Martha as we walk to the train station. "This was supposed to help us feel better, and it's clearly not for you."

"It did when it was just the four of us," I say, barely staving off hyperventilation, "but we keep talking about him, and I feel like I'm caught in a cycle, and I can't calm down."

I have to pause to take a deep breath, then hunch over when I can't. I was weak when I bought Philo Jr.'s book, but strong when I threw it away. Then when Pearl brought it up again, everything I feared was inside it had come out, and no one's even read it. This is not what these breakfasts were for.

"What do you want to do?" says Martha, patting my back.

I stand halfway up, resting my hands on my knees. "I want to feel better," I say. "I want to move on."

And by the time I get back to my apartment, I do feel better. Then a week passes, another Sunday arrives, and I'm left deciding if I want to do this all over again.

"You came," says Martha. We are the first to arrive at the restaurant.

I hold the door open for her. "It's better than wandering the streets by myself," I simper. She frowns.

As the others trickle in after us, it is quickly evident that this morning will be different.

"You sure look happy, Louise," grins Pearl. "Is there something the rest of us should know?"

Louise and Herb exchange glances, and then she casually brushes back her copper hair to reveal a large, flawless pearl dangling from her ear.

"Louise, it's beautiful," gasps Wendy. "Did Herb—"

"No," says Louise proudly, "Annabelle."

My heart jerks. I have done so well not thinking about her since we last spoke, surrounded by lawyers as she stranded us against Philo. I suppose that's why the negative focus on Philo of late has been sufficient—it wasn't about Annabelle. Now, here's a sign of her activity, and I am left wondering, how has she been? Where is she staying? What is she doing?

Annabelle.

"She came to our house on Friday to give Louise these wonderful earrings," says Herb.

"She asked me to be her maid of honor," Louise preens.

"Maid of honor?" I blurt.

What is she doing?

"She and Philo are eloping in Colorado, and she wants me to be there with her," explains Louise brightly. "These earrings are her way of thanking me."

"Already?" exclaims Ed. "But he hasn't been divorced two months!"

Some of Louise's cheerfulness wanes.

"I hope you told her no," says Pearl. "You can't seriously support this marriage?"

Louise looks like she just swallowed a fly—this was clearly not the reaction she had expected.

"Well, I-I don't think Louise meant—" sputters Herb.

"Annabelle offered me the same deal," says Martha distantly, visibly shaken. All eyes move to her, beckoning for details. "At first, I didn't know what to say, I was confused. I hadn't heard from her in months, but she's still my best friend, and I didn't understand why she was—at least, it seemed like she was bribing me ..."

"Oh, Martha, I'm sorry," says Wendy. "I know you want to support her. It must have been hard turning her down."

As everyone sympathizes for Martha, Louise's face has turned purple.

"I'll always stick up for her, but I don't have to encourage every decision," explains Martha, "especially when I do disagree."

The frowns get longer.

"Of course, I said no," snaps Louise, before quickly re-composing herself.

"Really?" remarks Ed. "And she let you keep the earrings?

"That's because I told her I'd have to think about it," she explains, "but in my head, I had already turned her down."

The table remains quiet as Herb nods affirmatively.

"It's like she knew we'd reject her, Martha," continues Louise. "She must be the loneliest girl in the world if she can't even bribe people to go to her wedding. It's sad, really."

"Louise, we don't know that it's like that," reminds Martha. "I just wasn't comfortable with the offer." The others seem to be with her on this, while Louise is starting to sweat.

"Same here," claims Herb, wrapping his arm around his wife. "At first, I was glad Louise turned her down so we wouldn't have to get involved in that mess," he says to the skeptical table, "but the more I think about it, as a happily married man, I feel disrespected by their wedding."

Before anyone else reacts, Louise turns to Herb and mouths, "Thank you!"

Martha and I look to each other again to roll our eyes. *Louise looks like such a fool.* But then we're disrupted by some light murmuring—among every one of the couples.

"Well, we know it's not about love," concedes Wendy.

More murmuring.

"I think we all know why Philo's doing it," mutters Charlie.

Then some nodding.

"Annabelle, too," adds Pearl wryly.

The three couples are aligned. There's a different energy now, and it's rather surreal. Then, Martha lets out an audible "Ha!"

Wendy's eyes narrow.

"It's not funny, Martha," says Louise. Martha is about to rebut, but disapproving looks from Ed and Wendy intervene. "It's different when you're married," Louise continues, "you wouldn't understand."

Martha leans back in her seat, miffed, but given Louise's particular brand of hubris, not exactly shocked.

"Well, I'm not the least bit surprised," says Pearl. "The girl is shameless. I'd been hearing ever since the divorce of Annabelle travelling all over the country with him ... New York ... Florida ... even California. Did she even wait for Marie's ink to dry?"

"We know that answer, too," says Herb.

"We also know where she got the money for these pearls," says Louise, flashing the earrings again. "She'll run Philo dry before he even has the chance to pay Marie."

Martha tuts. She burns to say more, but it's too late—

"Yeah, well it wouldn't be the first-time Annabelle's hurt Marie," adds Ed. "Philo could have owed her even more if she just cooperated during the trial. Philo screws Annabelle, and Annabelle screws Marie—Eric knows."

Frustratingly, I don't know. Yes, Annabelle backing out of her testimony probably cost Marie a little money. However, she did come for the deposition—she was going to cooperate—but then she left when she saw the reporter. I never got the opportunity to ask her why she was so opposed to speaking in front of the press; there could have been a perfectly reasonable explanation, I just don't know— but now I'd like to. I do know that Marie still won, and Annabelle didn't help Philo, either. In fact, the letters she kept from him is what sealed his fate. I suppose on this matter, with what we know she's neither innocent nor guilty. Of course, I can't say all of that so instead I shrug, "It wasn't all about the money."

Ed's shoulders slump. "Well, that's real supportive, Eric," he snaps. "I went through hell because of her and you shrug?"

The marriage brigade turns on me. For years, I hardly speak a word and no one but Annabelle seemed to care. Today, six pairs of burning eyes are bearing down on me because I'm not saying enough?

"I think what Eric means is there's a lot more to the story than we know," says Martha. "Remember, Annabelle was Philo's victim, too."

"That's right," I say. "I don't agree with everything Annabelle did, but she's not the enemy."

This doesn't resonate.

"Well, now we know Eric's still in love with her," mocks Louise.

"Eric, how can you still support her? Annabelle's the only reason Ed had to get involved at all," says Wendy. "Have some respect for why we're here."

I scoff. I struggle to believe I'm really under attack, yet Martha's still the only one not glaring at me.

"I agree with Wendy, let's all remember why we're here," stresses Martha, "and it's not because of Eric."

Wendy ponders this.

"Right, it's because of Annabelle," says Louise bluntly.

Four heads nod.

"What happened to Philo?" says Martha. "Have we really forgotten everything we've gone over these past few weeks? The trial, our stories, the book ..."

Oh, if I only had that book now.

Ed and Wendy look at each other soberly.

"He's the schemer and the manipulator, and like Pearl said, the monster," Martha continues, "yet, we're blaming

Annabelle. She was supporting herself working at a department store when she met Philo—do you know what they put those girls through? Does any of us have any idea of her struggles?"

Almost.

"I'm glad I don't. But I can't crucify her because she found a way to a better life."

Martha takes a deep breath, and I can tell even she's processing her words. Our waiter comes by to check on us, but I shake him away. The table is completely somber as everyone has hung their head, except for one—

"Exactly, no matter who it affected," concludes Louise.

Slowly, heads start popping back up. Herb, Pearl, and Charlie, then Ed and Wendy ...

"We saw what she did to Eric."

Look who's talking.

"Louise," scolds Martha. I see her covertly gesture toward me.

"Alright, fine," Louise relents. "Then what about Al Kohler? I feel sorry for him, I really do. Even though their wedding was a sham, after things ended the man was a wreck. Isn't that right, honey?"

"That's right, dear," says Herb. "Part of me regrets firing him now, but when they returned from their honeymoon, poor Al could barely function. He'd show up to work drunk, if at all—Annabelle sure did a number on him."

"He meant squat to her," says Louise. "Marrying Al was just a step to Philo—this wedding proves it."

"Then what was I Louise?" I say. She doesn't respond.

"You know what I think?" says Pearl, also ignoring me.

"Well?" I press Louise.

"Martha doesn't want me to say," she finally replies.

"Annabelle was part of Philo's scheme from the beginning, right?" Pearl continues, her voice growing louder to draw everyone's attention.

"What was John?" I say, several eyes bouncing back to me. "And Felix?"

"But she's taking it a step further by playing him, too—"

Martha beckons me to stop as the optical pendulum increases momentum.

"Philo may have cheated …" Pearl practically bellows.

"Knock it off, Eric," says Herb, acting as tough as a beanpole with a babyface can.

"… but Annabelle's the real monster." Pearl concludes.

Louise firmly nods.

As the dust settles, so emerges everyone's judgment. They've already formed their opinion of me, and Annabelle, and themselves before that. But like Martha said, they don't really understand, and probably never will as long as they stay on this path. But they're not the enemy, either, and I'm not here to change their minds. A blanket of numbness wraps around me, but I still need to address them. "Sorry," I say.

Then, everyone stops, and there's an echo of rattling forks on plates.

Wendy gasps.

We look up at the comely figure standing behind Louise, who must crane her neck unnaturally backward for a partial glimpse at the strawberry blond visitor in matching mink coat. A white-haired, bespectacled man with slumped shoulders tries to slip by unnoticed, but halts when it's apparent his companion isn't straggling.

"Annabelle!" exclaims Martha.

There is no immediate response—Annabelle stares serenely across the table, soaking in everyone's shock. Beyond the coat, she's dressed as showy as I've ever seen her, sporting a sequined gold dress and a menagerie of jewelry. Bolstering her delight, other tables are starting to take notice, too, and it's no wonder—she looks like a star.

What a contrast this is to Louise, facing forward again, eyes fixed on her plate and fidgeting with her remaining food scraps. Prince Herb has also started to sweat, nervously looking to his wife, then everywhere except our two guests. Philo, meanwhile, is like a sodden tabby, shaking and sneering, while compulsively fiddling with his glasses.

"Fancy seeing the two of you here," says Ed, earnestly trying to lighten the mood.

"You picked a great spot," adds Wendy quickly. "The eggs ...

Utterly unmoved by Wendy's words, Annabelle puckers her crimson lips.

"... are wonderful."

Still focused on no one in particular, Annabelle reaches over Louise's shoulder to her plate, and picks up the last half-eaten piece of sausage. Then, as if no one was staring at her, she takes a bite, unapologetically chewing so that everyone can hear the juices sloshing between her teeth. With a faint moan, she slides the rest into her mouth, licks her fingers, and dries them on the tablecloth.

"Good Lord, Annabelle," winces Philo.

Louise keeps staring at where her half-sausage had just been. Then, Annabelle reaches over Louise's shoulder again, this time grabbing her hair, and pulls it back to expose one of the pearl earrings. She flashes a half-smile at Martha, then turns to me and says, "You shouldn't be sorry, Erikas," and leaves. Philo is delighted to follow as Annabelle glides away.

Everyone exhales, except for Louise, still staring at her plate as she fixes her hair.

"I didn't even see them come in," says Martha. "She must have heard us talking about her."

"No, she didn't, Martha," hisses Louise shakily, yet to look up.

On the opposite side of the dining room, Philo and Annabelle take their seats. He keeps glancing back at us, while she carries on as if the only patron in the restaurant. Intentional or not, her manner—a deft arrogance—makes her difficult to pity. At the same time, if she did hear us, would she even entertain vulnerability?

"I agree with Martha," I say. "She was right there—who knows for how long—and we'd been talking about her for a while."

But the table is fixated on Martha staring down Louise, who still won't look up.

"Is everything alright, darling?" says Herb gently, rubbing the middle of his wife's back.

"Louise?" says Martha carefully.

Suddenly, Louise's eyes squint, she clears her throat, and sits up with her best, most perfect Shiner girl posture. "Was that not the most classless display you have ever seen?" she states sharply. "Even from her."

"Without a doubt," grimaces Pearl. "Disgusting."

"She's still just a crude farm girl," continues Louise, "like when she first came to Shiner—Martha remembers, even if she won't admit it."

Martha doesn't indulge.

Back across the restaurant, Annabelle and Philo face each other like perfect strangers—nothing is engaged about them. When Philo appears to offer Annabelle sugar for her coffee and she ignores him, he's not bothered, or even surprised. Then, a few amnesiac seconds later, Annabelle utilizes the sugar bowl on her own. Still, there's no anger or resentment from either party, or any emotion at all—it's just an arrangement, devoid of all expectation.

"Did you see Philo standing there helpless?" says Charlie.

"It was like he was under a spell," says Ed, "and she didn't care how uncomfortable it made him."

"And after he spent all that money on finishing school, too," adds Pearl. "She's unbelievable."

It's because she doesn't love him.

"I always knew she didn't belong," confirms Wendy.

And on, and on, and on …

This breakfast convinces me to never come to another. It once served a purpose, but that's been overshadowed by the group's increasing willingness to accept whatever truth buoys their self-esteem. Wouldn't it be nice to look at Annabelle with that same pretension? Maybe then I would feel better, but I cannot—not when I got out and she's still stuck marrying another man she doesn't love. My hands are empty, but I can still feel Philo Jr.'s book, along with the sensation of being sucked back in; maybe if it's under my own cognizance, I can better control the outcome …

After we pay our bill, the Galloways and Lords are the first to leave, while Ed heads outside to call for his car. I'm ready to walk away from this breakfast forever, but decide that Martha, at the very least, deserves a formal farewell. While I wait inside with her, I endure Wendy's wobbly apology for letting the conversation get out of hand …

"I never meant to get carried away," explains Wendy. "You know I'm sympathetic toward Annabelle, but I get so frustrated when I think about if she had just followed through with her deposition Ed never would have gone through what he did after the trial."

"It's okay, Wendy," says Martha with veiled aloofness. "You're just protective of Ed, like a good wife should, that's nothing to be ashamed of."

Wendy likes this. "Louise was way out of line, though, right?"

Martha grins, "A touch."

"Well, it's just gossip anyway," rationalizes Wendy. "Anyway, I'm impressed at how centered you've remained throughout this—you make Ed and I proud, you know."

"Oh, thank you," blushes Martha.

A car pulls up in front of the restaurant, and Ed waves for Wendy. The two women hug and close their reconciliation with the same brand of warmth found in Philo and Annabelle's date. Then, Wendy says to the both of us, "See you next week," and walks out. Wendy gets into the car, and Martha continues to look after her, smiling and waving at she and Ed until they drive out of sight.

"Regretting taking Ed's money now?" I say.

Martha furrows her eyebrows. "No," she huffs. "Thanks for waiting, though. Shall we walk to the train?"

I nod, and start to follow, pausing for a quick glance back inside the restaurant to where Annabelle is sitting. She is being friendly with her handsome young waiter, laughing, touching his arm, and being completely familiar, all right in front of Philo. The poor fool refuses to see it.

Maybe that's why he's always adjusting his glasses.

"You're not coming back next week, are you?" says Martha, catching my stare.

"No," I say, looking away just as Annabelle playfully pushes the waiter's chest. "Let's go."

We walk to the end of the block, where we must wait for a parade of honking cars to pass before crossing the street. Once on the other side, however, Martha opens up:

"Eric, what am I going to do?" she groans. "I don't want to hate Annabelle, but if I keep going to these breakfasts and this is how it's going to be, I know it's only a matter of time."

"Then don't go," I say.

She scoffs.

"I'm serious. Take your own advice, and leave with me. We can break out of this cycle and actually find some answers."

Martha plants her big round eyes on me for a second, then shakes her head. "I'm not where you're at, Eric," she says. "I was fine until she offered me those earrings ... I was her best friend!"

With little warning, twenty-some years of armor falls off Martha. For the countless times I've witnessed her biting passion, I finally see Martha's raw, unfiltered soul pour out. This is a genuine personal relationship that has broken, and it's hurting her.

"She doesn't need to bribe me to be there for her," she says, "even if I don't see why she's marrying him."

Louise may be right about Annabelle using Al to get to Philo, but what would she gain from using Martha? There is something bigger going on with Annabelle.

"Maybe it is for the money," I relent. "She doesn't love him, I know that."

"I know that, too …"

Hearing Martha say that feels good.

"… but I don't think it's ever been about love for her."

That doesn't.

"When Louise was talking about Annabelle when she first started at Shiner, it wasn't the crudeness that stood out to me, it was her defiance."

I think back to that first drive up to Mount Cary when she mocked Philo for trying to choose her classes for her. She hated that he was trying to control her.

"I admired that," explains Martha. "I was never comfortable with *Uncle Philo*, but I understood—he was her way of climbing the social ladder. She was a lowly sales girl, but she could use him to get to the lifestyle of her clientele. I wouldn't have done it, but I understand."

"But she could have had that life if she had stayed with Al," I reason. "Why would she give that up? She must be looking for something else."

"I know what you're thinking, Eric," says Martha slowly. "Don't do this to yourself again."

"You think I'm wrong. But you told me before the trial that Annabelle cared for me once," I remind her. "Maybe that's what she's looking for. She was going to help me testify against Philo—"

"But she didn't," states Martha.

"But she did save the letters that incriminated him—"

"Freeing him up to marry her."

"Did you see them in there? She doesn't want him."

"I don't know what she wants, Eric!"

"You seem to have all the other answers!"

Suddenly, the ground starts shaking madly as the train arrives at the station above. We don't budge, though, as we'll never make it up the flight of stairs before it departs. Then, a few seconds later, there's a second rumble as we miss it, which we both use to project our frustration.

"I don't have all the answers, Eric," says Martha, "that's why I go to breakfast every Sunday. And I know they're just going to make her sound awful, but maybe that's a perspective we need to consider."

I can picture Louise's smug smile if she heard this ... *The new queen on her throne.*

"I can't believe you're saying this, Martha. Of all people, you're turning on her, too."

Martha looks like she's about to hit me. "I'm really not, Eric," she says sternly. "I know you were in this deeper than any of us, but you're not the only one affected by it now. I just want to consider everything before accepting that this wedding could pull her out of my life for good." She swallows hard. "And if Annabelle really thinks I need jewelry to be there for her, then she doesn't know me at all—maybe I never knew her, either."

A string of people marches up the stairs toward the platform. A faint thunder sounds in the distance signaling the next train is nearing.

"We should go up," says Martha blandly.

"Sure," I say, and we head up the stairs to the track level, but then I stop again halfway. It takes her a second, but Martha notices the growing distance between us, and pauses.

"Do you really believe that?" I say, prompting Martha to turn around. "You were never with the real Annabelle?"

Another pair of passengers runs past us.

"No," she shakes her head, "not always."

I inhale until my lungs won't let me. Then, the stairs start shaking wildly, and we both grab for the railing to keep our balance. Martha says something, but I can't hear her as the next train pulls up to the station. She takes a lingering step up, but I don't budge. Though also drowned out by the train, I still shout, "I need to go!" then dart down the stairs until my feet land hard on the concrete, and I continue down the street.

Did I ever know her?

As I blow past empty storefronts, I play back the conversations we had when Philo was sulking in a corner— were those fake? She wrote me letters that Philo would never read—those, too? What about the kisses we shared

398

when Philo wasn't around? He never had to know about them.

Who's deceiving who?

As I round the corner, suddenly, the full weight of their ruse comes into view. Did either of them ever consider what their actions would do to me? Annabelle knew that Philo was using me all along and never gave me a clue. He's the monster, but she allowed him to be!

But what is the point?

Back on the busy Michigan Avenue sidewalk, I am forced to weave between the crowd of Sunday shoppers.

"Eric!" I hear Martha screaming.

If Annabelle wants Philo for his money, and I never had any, then why did she want me once and it just never happened? Something changed with her, but I never got any answers. I thought defeating Philo would give me all the closure I needed, but he's not what this is about. He used me until she didn't want me, and then they both threw it in my face. But if I can't have her then I deserve to know why. I don't want to be like this anymore, I want answers ...

I stop. I'm in front of the Congress Hotel. I can still hear Martha running down the block after me, yelling my name. I want to go in, but my feet hesitate. I've stood in front of this hotel (along with a half dozen others) too many times over the past five and a half years, but the Congress is where my shoes have taken me today. It keeps coming up, and there must be a reason—something is here, and I need it.

"Eric," pants Martha, "what are you doing?"

SOCIETY GIRL

"So many terrible things happened at this hotel," I say, my eyes fixed on its marquee as I both recall and try to ignore memories of the Shiner graduation party and Annabelle's wedding. "You and the girls hated it, too. Why?"

"Eric, it's—it's just a drafty old hotel."

"Ed said it was haunted," I remind her. "Did something happen here?"

My mind is fraught with possibilities. *Noises ... Energies ... Sensations ...*

"Like with ghosts?" she replies, shaking her head, and almost breathing normal again. "No, those are just stories that give people an excuse to hate it."

Since I've been planted in front of the Congress, dozens of people have gone in and out. Some have looked tired, but some have been smiling, and it's been hard to generalize their impressions. I want to ask them—are the stories true? Do they even care about what people say? Do they even know?

What happened here?

"I want to go in," I say, "but I'm afraid..."

"Eric, what is this about? There are no ghosts in the Congress—"

"No!"

Martha has that hitting face again.

400

"I'm afraid if I go in I'll never let what happened with Philo and Annabelle go," I admit. "I keep revisiting these moments, and it's killing me."

I wait for Martha to interject, but she just listens. Doesn't she know I need answers? Haven't I said that enough? Where is that opinionated girl who argued with Ed at the World's Fair? The one who never found a man she wasn't afraid to tell off—*tell me off!* But she just listens. *Tell me I have no claim on Annabelle. Tell me I need to let her go!*

"Why do I think obsessing over her will bring her back to me?" I seethe, as she still just listens. "She saw me today, too, but she isn't running around downtown Chicago like a lunatic. What do I even expect to find here?"

My hands are sweaty and my chest is heaving.

"I don't know," says Martha finally, "but let's find out."

She grabs my arm.

"What?"

"Let's go inside," she says, pulling me toward the door. "If you think the answers to your problems are inside the Congress, then let's look for them. Where should we begin?"

I lean back and get a good look at Martha. She's not joking.

"Where are we starting? The lobby? The ballroom?"

"I-I don't know," I sputter, procuring my arm from her.

"Well, then let's start with why you think rumors about a creepy old hotel will help you move on from an awful time of your life," she says firmly. "I think it's great that you want to understand everything that happened between you, and Philo, and Annabelle, but you need to accept that this was just something that happened. It doesn't have to define you."

My shoes are wet. I look down and see that my shoes are not at all wet, but they still feel soggy and cold. Then, Martha wraps her arms around me.

"I will go inside this hotel and search every floor with you if that's what you want," she says, "or we can stand out here like this all day if that's better—but I want you to get through this, Eric."

My shirt is wet. But it actually is, and it's coming from Martha. Her tears softly land on my shoulder, and I can feel even more of her strength shaking away as quickly as she lost her friend. This scares me—I no longer have Philo's money to fall back on, nor Annabelle's affection ... I can't lose Martha's sensibility, too.

I am alone.

My knees grow weak, and then I stumble. Martha stumbles with me, but she catches herself. Then, with a docile snicker, she wipes away her tears and smiles a broken smile.

I squeeze her tight.

"It's over, isn't it?" I say.

Martha laughs a little freer this time. "For us," she nods, "but not for them."

25

ALPHABET SOUP

As Louise said they would, Philo and Annabelle were married in a small ceremony in Colorado in the Summer of 1938. Whatever privacy they were trying to maintain with the out-of-town wedding was quickly squashed upon their return to Chicago, however, when they were spotted moving from Philo's Stevens Hotel bachelor pad of the past five years into a bigger three-bedroom apartment on nearby Chestnut Street.

Though I did my best to avoid the gossip, I couldn't ignore the general lack of surprise regarding Philo and Annabelle's matrimony. Even my mother, all the way in Cincinnati, caught wind of their wedding, and threw in her two cents— "Philo already sacrificed his marriage and dignity for her, he might as well marry her, too."

But a short blurb in the *Tribune*, another small advertising push for *Lovers Never Marry*, and a few days later, the new Mr. and Mrs. Olin were old news. That was well enough, as even high society finally believed it time to pay attention to the concerning happenings in Europe. Four months later, though, the rumblings started up again as, a few days before Thanksgiving, Philo filed for his second divorce in less than a year.

What a magical four months it must have been, too … up until Philo's secret recordings of his new wife's phone conversations revealed what he believed to be proof of an affair with a wealthy New Yorker named Lou Ross. Annabelle, on the other hand, insisted her calls with Ross were friendly in nature, which made sense since both Olins had met him in Florida during their honeymoon. Indeed, there was a trace of Schuyler Hendriks in the relationship, which likely contributed to Philo dropping his suit less than a week later to reconcile outside of court.

Surprising to some, the next three years were generally uneventful for Philo and Annabelle. While not exactly hermits, the Olins did keep an unquestionably lower profile than before. At one point, they even had some convinced there's was a real marriage— "I haven't heard anything of either cheating since the honeymoon," said my mother in May 1941. "Seems to be working out after all."

In September, Philo filed for divorce again on the grounds of misconduct. Whether Philo had increased his trust in Annabelle or she had become more careful in what she said over the telephone, there were no secret recordings implicating her this time … but there were letters.

In a shocking display of hubris, Annabelle had regularly communicated via mail with the same Lou Ross from their honeymoon. My initial reaction was that someone should check the handwriting, but there was no tampering on Philo's part—she really left another paper trail.

Later that month, after Philo's lawyer, still Daniel Capelli, filed for divorce with the courts, a deputy sheriff served Annabelle her divorce papers while she was dining at a popular rumba café on State Street. As Annabelle read over the petition, the deputy sheriff turned to her companion, a rugged, voracious man with a bald top and traces of white fuzz on the sides, and presented him a similar set of papers.

"What? Me, too!?" croaked Lou Ross.

Philo looked on, an unnoticed peering pussy, from behind a pillar of the adjacent storefront. I can only imagine the contorted satisfaction on his face at the horror on Ross', while knowing that at that same moment his locksmith was busy Annabelle-proofing their apartment.

"Come on," said Ross, grabbing Annabelle's hand and leading her to the café's dance floor, "we have the rest of the day to be frustrated."

The next Monday, after Philo had left for work, Annabelle was able to convince the apartment doorman to let her into the residence after she "can't get the key to work." She only stayed long enough to retrieve a few pieces of jewelry and other small trinkets that she could fit into her handbag, including the Lou Ross letters.

After bidding farewell to the obliviously-helpful doorman, Annabelle took the letters to Ross. She then asked him for money, or else she'd return the letters to Philo and let Ross, who was also married, crumble in the public arena with them.

Lou Ross, who made his money in manufacturing, had amassed a considerably greater fortune than Philo. Despite his boisterousness and impulsivity, he was also impeccably shrewd, and quickly realized he had been drawn into an extortion play. A divorce for Ross meant a great deal more than paying off a pretty blackmailer. At the same time, for

Philo, as a repeat offender, misconduct allegations could prove even more lucrative for Annabelle than shaking down Ross. Thus, an agreement was born—Ross would help Annabelle win the divorce against Philo. However, should Philo manage to win, in exchange for hiding the incriminating letters, Ross would financially support Annabelle.

Now backed by two millionaires, Annabelle hired one of Chicago's most respected (and expensive) attorneys. The mousy, near-sighted Gus Sabath was equally renowned for his sterling reputation with both his clients and the courts as he was for his devotion to his champion race horse ... and 1941 was a busy year for his colt, Gustav.

In the case briefing, Sabath noted their fortunate judicial draw in Thomas J. Stern, who was known to be fair and intolerant of "circus lawyers" like Daniel Capelli. Still, he was wary of Capelli's extensive and growing Chicago network. Utilizing a tip from Annabelle, Sabath devised an attack on Philo's own infidelities—in particular, his proclivity for prostitution.

Frustratingly, Sabath didn't find anything in his initial discovery attempts. When he wasn't away for one of Gustav's races, Sabath spent most of his time interviewing Philo's co-workers and other associates for any clues of misconduct. Annabelle reminded herself that Sabath was the best and would eventually find something, but just in case she went back to Lou Ross for a little more help.

While Ross paid for a private investigator to dig up Philo's dirt, Sabath and Capelli met to discuss evidence Disclosure. Even without the "missing" Ross letters, which Capelli made a point for no one to forget, Philo's camp revealed several witnesses willing to testify on his behalf, as well as a few more recent incriminating phone recordings between Annabelle and Ross. Suffice to say, Disclosure was a disaster.

Sabath encouraged Annabelle to settle, suggesting Philo would likely agree to pay a nominal $100 a month for her cooperation. Annabelle was adamantly against settling; however, that didn't stop her from relaying her attorney's recommendation to Lou Ross. That and a reminder that she could give the letters to Capelli at a moment's notice.

Unfortunately for both Annabelle and Ross, either Philo really had gone faithful, or else he'd learned from his mistakes with her and Julia, because the private investigator couldn't uncover a shred of evidence against him. Emptyhanded, their plan of attack was muted, and Sabath didn't seem to have anything in his back pocket.

Suddenly, Annabelle's deposition was only a day away, and she had no leverage against Philo, and waning confidence in her lawyer. She asked Sabath if she could delay the deposition until they found something, but he told her no—he'd read the case records of Philo and Marie's divorce, and knew that "Miss A" had left that deposition without answering a question. In Sabath's opinion, that constituted "improper behavior," and to do it again would kill Annabelle's credibility with Judge Stern, even off the record.

What else could Annabelle do? Firing Sabath this far into the process would likely rile the judge as much as a missed deposition, so she went to Ross again. The next day, they enlisted a ghost lawyer named Harvey Keele to help Annabelle where Sabath was unwilling. Like Ross, the former New Yorker Keele was loud and aggressive, and with an appetite to match. While Sabath was a firm and proper lawyer, Keele was every bit as greasy as his hair, which was even bigger and wetter than Capelli's.

On October 9th, while Judge Stern, Capelli, and Sabath were set up and awaiting Annabelle's arrival for her deposition, they were instead joined by a dewy-eyed junior associate from Sabath's office who had been tasked with escorting Annabelle from her room at the Drake to the deposition. But when the young lawyer got to the hotel, Annabelle handed him a note from Doctor Ferdinand Seitzer, excusing her from the deposition for "health concerns." Capelli laughed, Sabath steamed, and Judge Stern sent Philo's doctor, William Anderson, to check on Annabelle.

Having been delayed almost three hours, Doctor Anderson finally returned with a report that Annabelle was well. "She opened the door for me, and seemed fine," he said. "She couldn't tell me what was wrong with her, but she wouldn't come with me, either."

Judge Stern promptly denied Sabath's request to delay the deposition, then sent two deputy sheriffs to the Drake. "Bring her in on a stretcher, if necessary," ordered the judge. "Get me Doctor Seitzer, too!"

The next morning, Ferdinand Seitzer sat on Judge Stern's stand and answered numerous questions on his note excusing Annabelle from court. The newspapers were starting to cover the divorce by this point, too, jumping on the narrative of another missed Olin divorce deposition (even if they still weren't overtly connecting "Miss A" then with "Annabelle" today). Like Annabelle, the presence of the papers didn't sit well with Seitzer. As a result, each subsequent question posed by Judge Stern was accompanied by another stream of sweat falling down his forehead.

"Why did you say Mrs. Olin was too ill to appear yesterday," said Judge Stern, "when Doctor Anderson examined her no more than two hours later and said she was fine?"

"W-well, you see … at the time …" sputtered Seitzer.

"Would you describe her quick recovery as an act of God?" quipped the judge.

"No, but—"

"What *was* wrong with her, Doctor?"

Seitzer opened his mouth, but nothing came out. He looked as though he was about to break down in the middle of court, but was saved when then the doors burst open. Everyone turned to see two deputy sheriffs flanking Annabelle, who was dressed in a flattering beige dress with matching hat over her curled reddish locks.

"Your Honor," interrupted the male deputy, "we have the defendant."

"*Voilà*," said Annabelle aloofly, carelessly waving her hands to present herself.

"Please approach the bench, Mrs. Olin," instructed Judge Stern.

Annabelle strolled toward the judge with the deputy sheriffs still attached to her sides right up until her final step to the bench.

"Do you feel alright?" he asked.

"Yes," said Annabelle, almost indignantly. Judge Stern cast a nasty glare at Ferdinand Seitzer, who then threw his face into his hands.

With a sigh, the judge asked, "Will you be present at your next deposition appointment?"

"Yes."

"Good, it will be one week from today. I look forward to it," said Judge Stern, dismissing Annabelle.

With a curt smile, she rejoins her uniformed escorts and the three of them walked back out of the courtroom. Then, the judge turned his attention back on Seitzer, "You were saying what was wrong with her, Doctor."

Seitzer lifted his head up enough to confirm Judge Stern's seriousness. With a deep breath, he droned, "When I examined her yesterday morning, I discovered she had been suffering from spastic colitis."

The judge and the lawyers stared blankly.

"Diarrhea," clarified Seitzer.

Capelli cringed and Sabath rubbed his temples.

"It's a common response to stress—"

"That's enough, Doctor," snapped the judge.

Judge Stern ultimately decided against perjury charges for Doctor Seitzer, but dismissed him from the stand at ten that morning with a biting, "Thanks for turning my courtroom into a circus."

At five after ten, Daniel Capelli was the next to leave the courtroom, with a spring in his step and twinkle in his eye. At twenty after ten, Gus Sabath emerged, looking like he'd just pulled up lame on the second furlong, and just in time to see Lou Ross and Harvey Keele castigating Ferdinand

Seitzer on the courthouse steps. At ten-thirty, Sabath had withdrawn himself from the case.

"I'd like to spend more time with Gustav," claimed Sabath. "He has a big year ahead of him."

Annabelle was not without representation long, as Harvey Keele was more than ready to step in as her primary counsel. This new arrangement seemed to please Lou Ross, too … until Capelli hit hard again.

The change from Sabath to Keele didn't sit well with Judge Stern, which some speculated as why Philo's team got their wish in ordering a court-assigned nurse—a pretty, young brunette named Joan Wootten—to stay alongside Annabelle for the duration of the divorce trial. "We want to ensure she remains in good health," claimed Capelli.

While Keele continued his balancing act of building rapport with Judge Stern and strategizing a potential crossbill against Philo, Capelli kept throwing knives. This time, it was a court-ordered stipulation banning any communication from Annabelle to Philo:

"Mrs. Olin has been annoying my client about court dates, while his work is building cranes for the United States Navy," wrote Capelli.

The word from Annabelle's camp was that Lou Ross was furious about how Capelli was gaining leverage against them, and how even Keele was about it. On the other hand, Keele felt Capelli played the patriotism card too close to the representation change and nurse assignment to have much incremental impact. Indeed, he may have been right, as the newspapers focused their coverage of the divorce at this point on "the beautiful Nurse Joan."

One week after Sabath's departure, Annabelle— escorted by Keele and Nurse Joan—finally showed up for a deposition.

"Harvey, you actually got her here," said Capelli upon their arrival. "At least you'll always have that over Gus Sabath."

Keele just snorted.

"Of course, there's still time for your client to run out," continued Capelli, gesturing toward the newspaper reporter scribbling away in the corner. "Unless Joan's cured her phobia!"

The nurse blushed, Annabelle smiled politely, and Keele urged Capelli to move on and get started. But while Annabelle listened to the first question about her association with Mr. R, her reply was not what Capelli expected:

"I refuse to answer," she said simply.

So Capelli rephrased.

"I refuse to answer," repeated Annabelle.

After a few goes at Annabelle, Capelli started to understand what he was working with.

"I refuse—"

"You refuse to answer," barked Capelli. "We get where this is going. Your Honor, I can't work with this."

"I understand your frustration, Counselor," said Judge Stern, "but it is Mrs. Olin's right to refuse to answer any questions that may incriminate her."

Capelli uttered an Annabelleian oath, which the reporter was buzzed to note.

"Mr. Capelli, it was my understanding that you had, in your own words, 'several other witnesses' willing to testify."

"That's right, I do," relented Capelli, waving Annabelle and Keele away.

Judge Stern excused Annabelle and Keele, who flashed an instigating smile at his counterpart as he gathered his notes to leave. With a dismissive snarl, Capelli folded his arms and leaned back in his chair, but not so smoothly as to avoid several thick strands of his slicked hair violently rocking out of place.

"We have so many witnesses to get through today," continued Capelli.

Annabelle turned around to stare at Capelli, but Keele ushered her away. "He's got nothing," he murmured.

Capelli's threats didn't scare Harvey Keele. The two had sparred several times over the years, and were well aware of each other's tricks—for Capelli, that was threatening (and occasionally paying for) additional witnesses. That was because Daniel Capelli was a prolific seeker of settlements. Many of his clients were high-profile, or involved in high-profile affairs, and didn't want their names leaked to the press. And while many lawyers preferred settlements to trials (less work and fewer hours to collect their fee) Capelli took it to another level.

Haplessly, Daniel Capelli was on the wrong side of the Olin divorce. While Annabelle would have gladly taken a healthy alimony settlement at this stage, Philo was willing to risk so much more, as he'd done in his divorce from Marie, to preserve whatever of his dignity remained.

While Capelli continued boasting about his numerous witnesses, Keele called him out on his strategy, and broached a settlement. Typically, that would have been the final bell for Capelli, and he would have raised his fist in triumph, but Philo wanted a knockout ...

In addition to Mr. R, Philo's team also alleged Annabelle's misconduct with Misters F and P, along with several Mr. X's, whose names were yet-unknown—it had turned into "*a true case of alphabet soup*," as the papers were delighted to report.

While the press took care of Annabelle's character, Capelli continued to work the legal system. Less than a week after the deposition, Capelli asked the judge for an order on Annabelle to answer his questions. "Your Honor, this isn't a criminal trial," explained Capelli, "and the defendant has a history of obstructing civil cases."

While Judge Stern said he'd consider the motion, Keele hit back with a change of venue request. "I don't believe Thomas Stern can be a fair and impartial judge in this case," he alleged. Keele claimed that Judge Stern was allowing Annabelle's illness-induced first missed deposition to cloud his judgment in a motion that would force a defendant to answer "potentially-incriminating" questions.

The Cook County Chief Judge agreed. Stern was out, Harrison was in, and Philo was fuming.

Newly-appointed Conan Harrison was a relative unknown in Chicago's judicial system, even to Keele. But as he reminded the press: "Any judge is better than Stern."

Capelli's first move after Harrison's assignment was to ask the new judge for the same motion Stern had been considering.

"Young lady," said Harrison suavely as Annabelle winked at the judge, "do you believe that answering the counselor's questions would either incriminate or intend to incriminate you?"

"I do so believe," answered Annabelle sweetly; Harrison winked back.

"She doesn't have to answer the questions, Daniel," ruled Harrison. "You may proceed."

"Alright," said Capelli, unfettered as he drew a large stack of papers from his case folder. "Ninety pages, and I intend to ask every question written here."

Keele rolled his eyes and the reporters all groaned. Harrison, however, seemed perfectly happy to let Capelli's circus commence.

"You may answer any question you feel comfortable with," said Capelli wryly, "and refuse any that you don't. But if that's your choice, you're going to be listening to my voice for a very long time."

He cleared his throat.

"And apologies if my cadence slows," Capelli continued, winking at Keele through a sip of water, "I've been feeling rather peaked today."

For two and a half hours, Daniel Capelli laboriously walked Annabelle through a repetitive series of questions on her alleged affairs with Misters A to Z. While Harrison seem rather beguiled by the display, the real victims were in the gallery as she responded to each with a pause, then a subdued "I refuse to answer." By the ninetieth page, it was unclear who had dragged this Battle of Wills on longer.

On the way out of court, with his notebook almost as blank as it was the start of the day, a *Tribune* reporter asked Annabelle if there was anything she did want to say.

"It's a nice day, isn't it?" she smiled.

With Annabelle's persistent lack of cooperation, the divorce was going to trial. And though Philo and Capelli lacked an admission of misconduct, Annabelle, Keele, and Ross had even less dirt on Philo. It seemed as though the case was headed for a crossbill, but there was one thing Keele had over Capelli: Annabelle. They had four weeks left to prepare.

The first day of trial—which the papers referred to as *"The Start of the Alphabet Parade"*—commenced with Philo taking the stand and outlining his simple, yet scandalous allegations. He claimed knowledge of Annabelle's "indiscretions" with Mr. R starting in Havana and Key West while they had been vacationing together, then continuing in Chicago upon their return. Philo also recounted subsequent trysts in Detroit, New York, Niagara Falls, and other cities along the Atlantic seaboard. He also alleged encounters with a Mr. F in Chicago, a Mr. P in New York, and with the several other Mr. X's in or around those same towns.

When it came time for Capelli's direct examination with Annabelle, he acknowledged the unlikelihood she would answer any of his questions anyway. "To maintain the sanity of Your Honor and the jury, I'll spare the pointless testimony, or lack thereof, of the defendant," he declared heroically.

In Keele's cross-examination of Annabelle, however, she would finally make her true court debut, as the two slowly brewed their defense.

"Mrs. Olin," said Keele, "are the allegations put forth today by your husband, Philo Olin, true?"

"Regrettably so," she said, bowing her head.

Whispers fluttered from the jurors.

"I see," muttered Keel. "Can you explain to us why?"

"As has been stated, one of my suitors, Mr. R, is a highly successful manufacturer," said Annabelle. "In fact, quite a bit more successful than my husband. As we know, the recession had been quite difficult on even the most successful manufacturers, but still, some were able to thrive better than others. It is with much frankness that I recognize Mr. R as more fortunate than my husband, who has seen his own lifestyle dwindled by a previous divorce just three years ago from his first wife."

Philo worked his jaw back and forth, as Keele paused to give Capelli ample time to object, but he didn't. Instead, he leaned back in his chair, appearing as relaxed as he had attempted to do after his first failed deposition attempt in Judge Stern's office. Keele shrugged, then urged Annabelle to proceed.

"We met Mr. R while vacationing in Cuba," she continued. "My husband was immediately taken by his immense prosperity, and a potential business opportunity between their companies. I have no doubt such a relationship would have been a greater benefit to my husband, but Mr. R was in an unhappy marriage, and it was clear he found me attractive."

"Mrs. Olin, can you please summarize for the jury what this story implies?" asked Keele.

"It is difficult to say ... but my husband encouraged me to have relations with Mr. R to solidify a business deal," Annabelle solemnly confessed. "He even facilitated our early assignations."

More murmuring wafted from the jury box.

"And did these indiscretions with Mr. R result in a business deal?"

"No, the negotiations broke down."

"Do you know why?"

"I don't," admitted Annabelle. "I was not someone my husband confided in. He often brought leaders of industry to our apartment and encouraged me to entertain them to 'strengthen their relationship,' as he put it."

Philo's face was an overinflated balloon as he growled into his lawyer's ear, who calmly dismissed his protests.

"You also admit to dalliances with several other men?"

"I do."

"And can you name these other men for the jury?"

"I cannot."

"Why not?"

The jurors leaned in with great intent ...

"Because doing so would most certainly destroy at least three other marriages, and their children deserve better."

... then leaned back contemplatively.

"I'm sure they all thank you for your civility, Mrs. Olin," said Keele. "No further questions."

As it was Thanksgiving eve and the court was only working a half day, Harrison put the trial into recess. As the jurors were being ushered out and the gallery cleared—save for Nurse Joan, who was waiting patiently behind the defendant's table for Annabelle to leave the stand—Harrison complimented the redheaded witness.

"That had to have been difficult," acknowledged the judge, clasping Annabelle's white-gloved hands. "I'm sure those other families appreciate your sticking up for them."

"Why, thank you, Your Honor," said Annabelle warmly.

"We're not in session," grinned Harrison. "Call me Conan."

"Conan?" giggled Annabelle. "Okay, I will!"

"Is my name funny?" Harrison laughed back.

"It's just that your name sounds very similar to the Lithuanian name, *Ona*," explained Annabelle, "which is a name for girls!"

"Oh, no! Really?"

"Yes! It is actually Lithuanian for my name—it means *Anna*."

"No kidding!"

As the pair continued their shameless flirting on the bench, Keele and Capelli exchanged pompous glares. Neither seemed phased, nor concerned why the other was not ...

Before the start of day two, Harrison granted Daniel Capelli's request to make a pre-trial statement:

"In light of yesterday evening's events, my client and I would like to amend our charges from misconduct to cruelty," stated Capelli, as Philo bowed forward to reveal a large purple mark upon the side of his face. "While at a private Thanksgiving Eve dinner among friends at Mr. Olin's residence, the defendant, Annabelle Olin, broke her court order to stay away from my client during their trial to, as she claimed, 'collect some vases and perfume.'"

Keele turned toward Annabelle, who remained about-face as Capelli continued his speech.

"Unfortunately, her recklessness did not end there. When Mr. Olin kindly asked the defendant to leave so that he could resume his friendly evening, she insisted on discussing how they were to distribute their household effects. At that point, my client and the defendant moved to the bedroom so as not to disturb Mr. Olin's dinner guests.

"It was there that Mrs. Olin requested all three beds, which my client reasonably declined."

"I thought two were enough," added Philo, wincing and clasping his bruised face as he spoke.

"That's when Mrs. Olin slapped my client," said Capelli. "Not once, but four times, repeatedly, causing Mr. Olin a great pain and suffering. For that, we are asking the court to grant this divorce solely on the grounds of cruelty."

Annabelle turned around to face Lou Ross. He was sitting stiff as a board directly behind her and Keele in the gallery, with anguished tears swelling in her eyes.

"That said," added Capelli, "we are still prepared to proceed on the original charges. But given the recent events, and in respecting Mrs. Olin's wishes to protect the families of the other men involved in this case, on top of preserving her own dignity, we wish to waive the remaining scandalous details of this divorce."

"Mrs. Olin," said Harrison sternly, no hue of flirtation in his voice, "is what Mr. Capelli says true? Did you intrude upon Mr. Olin's private dinner last night, then proceed to slap him four times?"

"It is," said Annabelle with downcast eyes.

"Mr. Keele, do you or your client have anything else to add to these new allegations?" asked Harrison.

Harvey Keele, who was breathing heavily, placed his hands on his desk and started to rise, but Annabelle placed a hand on his shoulder and shook her head. Keele's eyes widened for a second, while Annabelle's narrowed. She shook him off again, then he sighed and sat back down.

"No, Your Honor," he finally said.

"Then I hereby grant the plaintiff, Mr. Philo Olin, his divorce from Mrs. Annabelle Olin on the grounds of cruelty," declared Harrison. "As both sides have insinuated, there need not be any more names or families dragged into this courtroom's drama."

Annabelle turned around to grasp Lou Ross' hands, and his chin rose a few inches knowing his name was safe; she turned back around to hear the rest of the judge's verdict ...

"With this ruling, Mr. Olin is free of any and all alimony requirements."

... just in time for a weighty realization to hit the wealthy New Yorker.

"Thank you, Jury, for your service the past two days. This court is adjourned."

Upon Harrison's gavel strike, Nurse Joan, free of her assignment to Annabelle, darted out of the court room revealing the flock of reporters on the other side of the door, waiting to grab a picture or a quote from the ruling's aftermath. Alone for the moment, Lou Ross wiped his hand across his baldness.

Just a few feet away, Philo and Daniel Capelli exchanged a firm, emotional handshake, while Harvey Keele rubbed his eyes in disbelief. On their way out, as Keele and Annabelle moved past Ross she offered him her outstretched palm. He simpered, squeezed her hand for a second, nodded, then let her go to face the reporters with her lawyer ...

"Mr. Keele! Is there anything you were surprised by in this trial?"

"There wasn't much that didn't surprise me in this case," said Keele, with Annabelle by his side. "The entire trial was outrageous from the get; it is no secret that I am not a fan of Daniel Capelli's cheap antics."

"Mrs. Olin! Who was that bald man sitting behind you in court?"

"Who?" peeped Annabelle. "It must have been an admirer, I suppose."

Several other reporters blurted out follow-up questions all at once, but Keele led Annabelle to a car waiting for them at the curb, ignoring their pleas.

"Mrs. Wootten!" screeched a reporter near street level, directed at Nurse Joan as she walked out.

"Miss Wootten," she corrected brightly.

"Miss Wootten, you were at Mrs. Olin's side throughout the trial," continued the reporter. *"Since we didn't get to hear your testimony, can you confirm the slaps?"*

"Yes, I was there when they happened," she confirmed. "It was horrible for Philo—she got what she deserved."

"Mr. Olin!" barked a different reporter at Philo, who was just a few steps behind the nurse. *"How does it feel to come out victorious after the loss of your first divorce?"*

"I learned a lot from that," said Philo.

"Do you ever think you'll marry again?"

Philo snorted. "Right now, I'm only concerned with recovering from this," said the former football player, rubbing his bruised face.

"Counselor!"

Daniel Capelli stood at the top step of the courthouse, unable to proceed further as he was mobbed by the media, who were shouting over each other for his attention.

423

"Counselor!" repeated an unseen reporter from the back of the mass. *"What do you make of Harvey Keele's comments about using 'cheap antics' to win this case?"*

"Cheap antics, eh?" scoffed Capelli. "I could ask him the same question—if he had won, that is. I will say this: Don't talk good or bad about what doesn't concern you anymore."

The reporters started shouting for Capelli's attention again.

"Daniel!"

"Ah, my old friend from the *Tribune*," beamed Capelli. "Bring it on."

"Why did you and your client drop the charges of misconduct against Mrs. Olin?" asked the familiar reporter. *"Did it have anything to do with your evidence against the claims?"*

"Everything that my client testified to was true," said Capelli. "We wanted to do everything in our power to protect the families of the men Mrs. Olin was unfaithful with."

Another round of shouting erupted.

"Since we never got to hear the details of Mrs. Olin's indiscretions," said another reporter, who stood directly before Capelli, *"can you share anything of that with the eager readers?"*

"I don't think that's my place," laughed Capelli to a smattering of groans, then relenting, "however, I will commend Mrs. Olin for her ladylike approach to the

424

affairs—she always locked the doors after her husband left for work!"

The reporters scrambled to get their next questions heard, but Capelli cut them off. "I think that's enough for me today, boys," he grinned. "But I see two attractive women down there who I'm sure are a lot more fun to talk to."

26

THE MONEY MAN

After finishing her last year of law school, Martha returned to Chicago full-time. Three months into fruitlessly applying for associate positions, and too proud to accept any further allowance from Ed, she took a secretary post with a large private firm in the Loop. But a year of waiting for her "opportunity" to arise pushed Martha into a more proactive approach of getting noticed by the partners. She started stretching her work days deep into the night, long after her paid hours ended, to help the associates with their cases in any way she could. I initially took this as her reason for not joining me at Annabelle's trial ...

"Do we need to go back to the Congress, Eric?"

... but she was quick to show me otherwise.

Indeed, I still struggled to keep a distance from Annabelle's life, which was exasperated by the increasing frequency her name appeared in the papers. I tried to be more like Martha, throwing all my energy into my career that was finally gaining traction again, but it didn't fill my days and I still had sleepless nights. I absorbed every article Annabelle was in and, regrettably, attended the trial—alone.

In the end—and I doubt Martha would have understood this—seeing Annabelle lose to Philo was good for me. Unlike Philo and Marie's divorce, I was an outsider in this trial. Everything the lawyers presented was new to me, from the parade of Mr. X's to "The Slaps," and it demonstrated how non-existent I had become in her life.

Though I never told Martha of my attendance, we did talk about the trial the day after it ended. Building from our breakfast club days, Martha posited that Annabelle had let the survivor in her take over, which led her to collecting men like stocks:

"To put it in your terms, she was hedging her bets," said Martha. "She invested a small amount of her equity into several men, hoping one would hit it big."

"If that's true, there's her mistake," I replied. "She wasn't investing, she was speculating on a big payoff. A better strategy would have been pursuing consistent dividends."

"Which was Philo—are you really suggesting she should have stayed with him?"

I shrugged. "Strategically ..."

"Okay," said Martha, rolling her eyes. "Then strategically, why couldn't she have both? She goes for her big payoff with Mr. R, but keeps Philo and the others on the side for a smaller, but safer return."

"But the problem with that is stocks don't care who else you're invested in."

"Unless," countered Martha, breaking into a smile, "you're preferred."

"Sure," I laughed.

That conversation would be the last time Martha and I would speak face-to-face. We did keep in touch for a few more years via the occasional phone call or letter, but ultimately the war, and then life set us on diverging paths.

Before then I learned her extra hours at work led to a promotion (along with a few other women), filling the vacated spots from enlisting male associates. When the men came back, however, the other women were let go, but Martha was retained—she was simply too good for the firm to lose. I always figured she'd make partner before long, but the last I heard she was still fighting ...

Six days after the trial, Pearl Harbor was attacked, and I found myself on a train to see my mother; not long after that I joined some of Martha's colleagues in Europe. When I returned, it was to Cincinnati, where it was time for me to be a son again. I took a job with a large regional bank, and after a few months I felt settled in my new old home, on a steady path at work, and rekindling my relationship with my mother.

Cincinnati was a fine town at the time, albeit one still recovering from a terrible flood a few years earlier. While many weekends were spent listening to the likes of Benny Goodman and Eddie Condon on the radio, broadcasting live from the same ballrooms in Chicago I used to visit with the Havens, this comparatively slower lifestyle was what I needed.

When I first moved back home, my mother was keen to learn as much as she could about my thirteen years away. It was difficult to be open about everything, so initially I focused on the trivial details of parties and restaurants, and big events like the World's Fair. This assuaged her for some time, though not likely as long as I believed …

In May 1946, I accompanied my mother to the funeral of her close friend, Clara Magee, the wife of another one of my father's football teammates. Unlike Philo, I remembered Mrs. Magee and her surviving husband, Frank, quite well. They had both offered tremendous support after my father died, and were always there for my mother in the years following when I wasn't. They were just good people.

Upon our arrival, my mother gave Mr. Magee a tight hug, and the two shed a few tears. Frank Magee was unapologetically an ogre, with a mountainous build and arms like a rug. He also wore heavy bags under his reddened eyes. It was beautiful to see his mournful embrace of the love he held for his late wife.

"That was a lovely service, Frank," sniffled my mother. "Clara is smiling down on you, I'm sure."

Mr. Magee nodded. "I know, I can feel her."

After the funeral, Mr. Magee invited me for a beer with him and a few more of my father's teammates. I didn't hesitate to join.

"Attaboy!" exclaimed a squat man with wide shoulders, who looked like he could still lay out a wayward quarterback. "Frank, get Mihlfried's boy here a drink!"

After a few rounds, by design the previously-somber mood had mutated into full-blown merriment. The beer was flowing faster, the stories growing raunchier, and I learned that no one believed Mr. Magee when he told his teammates that Clara had asked him out when they were in college.

"You're off your trolley, Frank," said the squat man. "Clara was a sweetheart and you had a face that'd stop a clock!"

"Don't listen to Clyde," said Mr. Magee, assuredly waving a thick finger as the others roared, "she at least walked up to me first."

But then Clyde gave me a reason to listen ...

"Not to discount the miracle Frank pulled off back then, but even that doesn't top what Olin's doing now."

My hair straightened up like a soldier. While the old teammates grinned stupidly at each other, I leaned forward and asked Clyde to clarify.

"You must have just missed him," said Mr. Magee. "He only stayed a short while, but he had this pretty woman with him—"

"Pretty?" interjected Clyde, nearly spraying a mouthful of beer. "She was a brown-haired masterpiece!"

I felt bad for Mr. Magee, squirming in his seat as he clearly agreed with Clyde's assessment, but felt guilty about doing so after his wife's funeral.

"Philo was a good-looking kid when we were young," continued Clyde, "but that wrinkled bag of bones must be worth some kind of penny to end up with a hot nurse!"

Nurse?

"That's fine, Clyde," shakily laughed Mr. Magee. "Maybe she can take care of him when he gets older."

"When's that, yesterday?" said Clyde—the others laughed again, slapping their knees and slamming their mugs against the bar top. Then, Clyde faked an injured elbow. "Say, where can I get me a Nurse Joan?"

I was speechless.

When I returned to my house later that night, I had trouble falling asleep. I kept thinking about how Philo had won his divorce, then still ended up with another beautiful, even younger woman—and Annabelle's former nurse, to boot. But that wasn't mentioned at the bar, nor anything about Annabelle. She wasn't the only one ignored ...

The next day, I was late arriving at my mother's house for dinner, which she was happy to point out.

"Sorry, but it took longer than I remembered," I said, holding up the pan for her to see.

"You bake, Eric?"

"I hope you like strawberry."

My mother started to get sick over the next year. By then, a few more Clara Magees had passed away, but she did reconnect with Marie. After Ed and I helped Marie win her divorce from Philo nearly a decade earlier, she sold the Hyde Park house and moved to Florida year-round. She never remarried, stayed out of the papers, and enjoyed her new life lounging by the pool and spoiling her grandchildren, all on Philo's court-ordered dime. Though I never took the receiver when my mother was on the phone with her, I still enjoyed hearing them rekindle their friendship, even when they were gushing over having my company.

Shortly after my mother passed, an opportunity arose to join the financing division of a successful automaker in Detroit. With no one tying me to Cincinnati anymore, I accepted, and joined big city life once again. It was an exciting time to be in Detroit, and I put in long, hard hours to keep up. I continued to do well professionally, living in a comfortably large house surrounded by more grass than I could properly tend to, while putting away more money than I ever would have imagined.

I never married. Part of me thought that moving to Detroit would give me the kind of fresh start that would re-open my heart to love. I figured that I was still relatively young, had a great job, and "interesting" experiences to talk about—what woman wouldn't be interested? Then, a newspaper landed on my front porch, and I turned to page five:

Six years after Annabelle's divorce from Philo, she was back in the papers. After waiting nearly two years for Lou Ross to leave his first wife, Annabelle and the wealthy New Yorker eventually tied the knot. Although outlasting her Annabelle Olin stage by a year, it became clear that still-comely redhead simply wasn't meant to be married. But while her abilities as a wife hadn't improved, that wasn't the case for her as a defendant.

As it turned out, Philo must have truly loved Annabelle, for he gave her an incredible gift at the end of their trial. By being identified as "Miss A" during the Marie Olin divorce, Philo's past infidelities with her were never brought into question during the Annabelle Olin divorce. Likewise, Lou Ross' identity ("Mr. R") during the Annabelle Olin divorce was also kept off the record, along with every other Mr. X that could have been purported. Ultimately, every charge of misconduct was stricken from the record, and replaced with cruelty. As a result, Annabelle had no legal history of any form of infidelity. To her credit, she used this gift expertly.

There was more.

Lou Ross had leveraged his wallet to get his primary witness against Annabelle—a moderately wealthy, middle-aged ex-Naval sailor—to testify on their continued "relaxations." But following Annabelle's teary testimony, it was readily apparent that the veteran wasn't at all comfortable turning against his lover.

"I'm sorry, Lou," sniveled the man in court, "but I can't speak ill of your wife—I love her! You can keep your money."

And with that, Lou Ross was done. The sailor was the perfect lovesick puppet for Annabelle to exploit for a reasonable amount of doting, while providing the emotional testimony critical to painting her as the victim and Lou Ross the bribing bully. The judge awarded Annabelle $900 a month in alimony—$200 more than Marie's award from Philo.

Outside the courthouse, the reporter caught Annabelle as she was walking away from the sobbing sailor, ignoring his please to take him back.

"What will I do now?" said Annabelle, straightening her fur coat. "Why, I hear Florida is nice this time of year. Wouldn't you say?"

That would be the last time her name was in the papers.

By the time I turned fifty, my laboring lifestyle had caught up to my health, and my doctor advised me to relax. Because of my saving tendencies and a few wise investments, I was able to semi-retire early. I sold my house in Detroit and, with a tip from a former client, bought a lakefront cottage in Golden Township, a one-road beach town in West Michigan.

I also bought the small, local financial planning firm—a single-room brick building with "Golden's Money Man" painted in large, white cursive letters on the side. According to my client, the original "Money Man" had passed away, and his cash-strapped son was eager to sell his father's firm. I loved the idea of keeping somewhat busy, but still having as much time as I wanted for reading and fishing—a small firm sounded perfect.

Shortly after moving into my new cottage, the elderly couple next door urged me to introduce myself to the local priest, Father Claude Papineau, the de facto mayor of the unincorporated township.

"Fr. Papineau is just wonderful," gushed the wife. "He's so charming and handsome—everyone loves him!"

"Claude's a great guy," added the husband. "He'll probably want to grab a beer with you. If he does, let me know!"

I walked down the windy, tree-lined dirt road to a small, wooden Catholic church; inside, I was met by a dozen rows of empty pews.

"Hello!" I announced, my voice bouncing throughout the expansive white interior.

There was no answer. I did hear voices and laughter coming from somewhere, so I followed them until I arrived at a back room. The door was partially ajar, but I still softly knocked to grab its occupants' attention.

"Hello," I repeated, slowly pushing the door. "Father Papineau?"

A handsome middle-aged man with black, feathered hair was leaning casually against the window at the back of the office. He was playing with a pair of tiny metal objects, which he placed on the desk when he looked up and spotted me. With a warm smile, he walked forward to shake my hand.

"Yes! You must be Eric," said the priest. "Our new money man—I've heard so much about you. We're all very excited to have you in Golden, isn't that right?"

As I squeezed Father Papineau's hand, I noticed the objects on his desk were a pair of old, silver cufflinks. Then I realized the person whom I had heard him laughing with was sitting in the leather desk chair between us, and they were still facing the window he was leaning on.

A breeze wafts through the window …

Smoky, spicy vanilla.

… then, suddenly, the chair swings around.

"Hello, Erikas."

ABOUT THE AUTHOR

Robert **Gomez** is originally from Troy, MI, and currently resides in Los Angeles, CA. When he isn't writing, he enjoys watching the Michigan Wolverines, exploring Southern California's independent coffee scene, and making Christmas songs with his band, the Submarine Racers.

Society Girl is Robert Gomez's second novel, following 2012's *Keeping Atlantis.*

Author Photo by Camila Gomez